The Emergence

Book One

By J.B. Myron

The following story is a work of fiction. All characters, names, locations and events are fictitious and any resemblance to reality is unintended.

Digital ISBN: 979-8-9911976-0-1

Hardcover ISBN: 979-8-9911976-1-8

Paperback ISBN: 979-8-9911976-2-5

Cover Design by Dumitru-Adrian Păsărin

News and more stories by J.B Myron can be found at: *https://sites.google.com/view/jbmyronbooks*

or by contacting: *Myronbooks@proton.me*

Dedicated to my elder brother, Ronnie.

For always letting me be the hero.

Also dedicated to my friend, Michael.

For inspiring the creation of Sophia.

Final dedication to all the family and friends along the way.

The Continent of Jerrovia

The Greatest Sea
or
The Final Waters

Chapter 1
Under the Old Elm Tree

George was dreaming. He knew he was because it was the sort of dream he couldn't escape by waking up. His fingers were blurry and his face was barely his own, but he could feel every ounce of weight the atmosphere pushed onto his chest.

"George."

The word bounced off the walls of an empty stone hallway. It was a soft voice, motherly, and yet filled George with dread. A dim glow cast a myriad of shadows, leaving the young boy standing in the middle of a colorless dance of dark and light. His hands were trembling, folding over themselves anxiously as he walked the hall. Even a dream held the horror of reality, and in response his voice came out like a squeak.

"Who's there?"

The ethereal voice came again. "Come here, George."

This wasn't the first time the voice said this, George had heard it before. What he never heard, though, was why and just as always, before he could ask, her voice once again cut through the scene.

"George!"

George jumped. The voice was now much closer than he expected. With his heart in his throat and blood rushing cold through him, he turned to the direction the voice came from. As his eyes laid upon an old red door, he felt his face go white. It was real. Even in a dream, it was real. A gentle laugh came from behind the structure, and he could see shadows play underneath the threshold.

"My child?" This time the woman's voice was softer. "Can you open the door for me?"

The boy felt his hands raise against his will towards the doorknob. Words spilled through his lips, though he wasn't sure he was saying it. "Why?"

"Please?" He could hear the woman place her hands against the other side of the door, her palms scratching against the wood. "Just open the door for me."

A thick shadow fell over George, and in his periphery he could see a light at the end of the hallway. Wrenching his eyes from the door, he saw what he always saw, a silhouette. It was massive, larger than a man though shaped like one, with two horns. George was frozen, fingertips on a doorknob and eyes on a horned stranger. He croaked. "I—I have to go."

"No!" The woman slammed her hands against the other side of the door. Her anger bubbled away as quickly as it came. "You have to stay. Open the door."

George let his hand fall to his side. A chill ran up his spine and he knew he was in danger.

"Please!?" The woman's words broke into a sob behind the door as George stood split between the two directions. He felt his heart rattling against his chest and an intense fear was rising inside of him. Black smoke started billowing from under the door and the overpowering stench of fire filled his nostrils. "Open the door! Stay with me!"

Again, the shadow stole George's attention. It took a heavy step forward, forcing George to shrink away from the door. Adrenaline shook his boyish frame and a plume of black smoke engulfed the scene. George closed his smoke-stung eyes and only when he took his first true step back did the door start to rattle violently. The woman was banging against the other side, causing the door to jump and pillars of black smoke to bloom wildly. Each bang sent a wave of terror into George's chest.

"Open the door!" The woman shrieked, "George!"

"—George?"

George's grey eyes shot open. His mind was yanked from the nightmare and thrust back to the sun-soaked book that laid open in front of him. A string of drool hung down his cheek and onto one of the pages. The young prince stammered. The smell of fire was replaced with the gentle waft of the imperial gardens and his vision was captured by his grimacing teacher, Reginald. George shot up straight, nearly smacking the back of his head against his chair.

The teacher stood under an elm tree that dominated the flower freckled scene. Shafts of light threaded through the leaves and collected over his bald head like a spotlight. Reginald folded his arms behind his back and wrinkled, old eyes flickered down to the book on George's lap. "You're supposed to be reading."

Letting out a shaking breath, George looked down at the book but his vision couldn't adjust to the words. His heart was still pounding and all he could think about was the voice and shadow from his dream. They weren't new to him, with that dream having haunted him for the past few months and not just when his eyes were closed.

George looked around the garden before glancing back at one of his shaking hands. He wasn't safe, he knew that much, but he would change that tonight. His heart hiccuped and he closed his eyes. Voids... the lingering chill of his nightmare still gripped him.

"Prince George, really!" Reginald's frown deepened and knocked George out of his thoughts.

Clearly frazzled, George blinked his focus back to the pages in front of him. The words '*Emperor Frederick's Imperial Memoir on the Financial Crisis of Southern Barcena*' were boringly transcribed across the top of the page. This reminded George all too well which mind-numbing history book he was subjected to for the day and nearly released him from the snare of his nightmare. In the hopes of replacing the echo of his dream with his innate displeasure for academics, George gave a flinching scowl before looking back up at Reginald. "Don't suppose we could pick a different subject?"

The wrinkles around Reginald's mouth crinkled with thought. "It is imperative that you learn your history."

"But why?" George protested, now actually feeling the resentment. "I'm never going to use it."

Reginald squinted at the boy and fell into a lecture, "As an Imperial prince, knowing your history is paramount alongside manners, economics and knowledge of politics."

"I'm not even the heir!" George slowly started to close his book, thinking Reginald was distracted. The old man tilted his head and shot out a glare that ripped the book right back open.

"Maybe not." Reginald crossed his arms. "But you will most definitely find yourself in a position of administration."

George groaned and Reginald sighed, his eyes hardening. George knew that look a little too well. The old master pinched the bridge of his nose and spoke slowly, "There will be time for your adventures in between your duties, but for now, read."

Swallowing his next rebuttal, George flicked his eyes back down to the pages of the history book. The words inked on the yellowed paper seemed to blend together, his vision blurring around them. George's lids closed halfway; words sounded in his head but his mind refused to take any substance from them. In short, he was restless. How could he not be?

The hum of dragonflies overtook the scene as George mechanically scanned the pages with not a drop of information relaying to his mind. He saw the red door in between the letters, the horrible shadow at the head of every sentence and the endless hallway spanning across the pages. He saw himself sneaking away, to find the answers to his dream.

While the fore of his mind coped with the danger of his dream, the back was devising a way out of his lessons. He coughed deep in his throat, catching Reginald's attention.

"Something, my prince?"

George idly flicked the page he was reading and shook his head. He knew he would have to ease into this, he shouldn't be too obvious. Reginald gave an approving nod which only soured once George made his move. "Although this chapter did remind me of something that Uncle Caleb had told me."

Reginald looked down at the chapter labeled 'Emergency Liquor Tax' and furrowed his brow. "Oh?"

"He was telling me that you used to be a knight for my grandfather." George tilted his head, a shard of hope twirling in his chest when he saw a thought flicker behind Reginald's dark eyes. The look was similar to the one that George's uncle would get right before telling a story from his military days, but unlike the look his uncle gets, Reginald's ended with a quizzical and unamused expression.

"How in the entire Mortal Empire did a tax on alcohol remind you of that?"

Quickly, George attempted to salvage the situation with a sympathetic look. "The Graces work in mysterious ways." He nodded slowly. Reginald's hard stare put a frown back on George's face and he dipped his head back to the book. A tiny sparkle teased his thoughts and with one last attempt, he looked back up at the old master. "Do you want to play some chess?"

"Are you really this motivated to skip out on today's lessons?" Reginald crossed his arms.

"More than you think you know, Reggie." George gave a snake's grin and Reginald sighed. There was a long pause, long enough to make George regret calling him 'Reggie', but just when he was about to apologize, Reginald waved a dismissive hand.

"Fine, go."

Excitement bounced in George's chest. "Really?" He was already about to pounce to his feet, book teetering out of his lap.

"Yes."

Unbarred, George leapt up and his book jumped into the air along with him. With quick reflexes he snatched it before it could get too far and gave a sheepish grin. Reginald watched the prince with his elbows folded square behind his back and a blank, slightly judging look on his face. The two stood in silence for a moment, George breaking it with a polite nod, covering a tinge of guilt that was growing in his chest. "I'll be ready for tomorrow's lessons, I promise."

"I'll hold you to that," Reginald answered.

George smiled, but the guilt hung in his chest; would he really be here tomorrow? Regardless, he nodded his thanks and with a twist of his heel, faced the freedom of the gardens. The tall alabaster-colored walls of the palace that surrounded the central gardens guided his vision to a cobblestone path. The path itself cut through flower beds and winded its way out to unseen courtyards. Even though George walked this path every morning, taking it out of the gardens always felt like the start of a new adventure. Although lately it felt like a prison walk. In rebellion, he tried to savor the first step anyway, his mind only wrenched from his imagination by the intervening voice of Reginald.

"Oh, but there is one last thing."

George felt the slap of reality wash away his 'great quest' and he turned. "Yes?"

Reginald stood under the old elm tree, hands folded and a stoic smile buzzing on his face. George had missed something, he knew it, or perhaps Reginald knew something he didn't. The old master kept George in suspense long enough for the boy to run through every possibility he could think of, his own personal payback perhaps, until finally he said, "You still owe me a game of chess."

"After dinner?" George offered quickly, eager to leave the gardens. Reginald took a minute to think, on purpose, George figured, before nodding.

"That will be acceptable."

The rush of freedom gripped George and with as much restraint as he could muster, he kept himself from sprinting out of the gardens lest something else make him stay, opting for a more controlled fast walk down the path. He could feel Reginald's gaze in his back but he didn't care. The flowers that surrounded him seemed brighter now that lessons were over and a crisp smell goaded alongside the breeze. It was a scent that reminded him of old fairy tales and great escapes into the world of the unknown.

Anxiety still tainted the moment, though. George hated lying, and on top of that, he could still feel the squirming uncertainty of his nightmare deep in his gut. In an attempt to find some serenity, George closed his eyes as he walked. The late autumn sun that heated his face guided him down the path as did the telltale clap of his boots against the stone walkway. He let himself sink into the sound of the rustling trees and the distant bird calls. All was slowing to a peace, even as he felt the walkway disappear underfoot in favor of solid brick. The cooling shade of the garden trees left his back and he knew he had walked right into the rear courtyard.

With a terrible heartbeat, the red door from his dream flashed across George's mind's eye and cut his peace in half. He wrenched his eyes open to a blinding light only to flinch when his sight adjusted to the blue-eyed stare of his older sister, the Imperial heir, Josephine.

Even though she was older by three years, George still stood at the same height as her, but that's where their similarities stopped. George had the black hair of his mother and broad frame of his father while Josephine had the golden blonde hair of their father, and a thinner frame that, while toned and muscular from her training, was drained by sleepless nights. By all means she was considered beautiful by the courts, but being her brother, George could see past the superficiality of it and notice the bags under her eyes and the pale in her cheeks. Behind her, two imperial guards stood. Both were armed with menacing spears and wore opulent cloaks with one half dyed purple and one half red—the colors of the Empire. On their breastplates was the Imperial seal, a falcon in full flight.

Despite being only eighteen, Josephine had taken advanced duties around the palace. This included greeting high profile visitors, and by the stern look on her face and the escort behind her, George knew it could only be one thing: the ambassadors from the northern province of Gavaria had arrived. He straightened his posture as Josephine attempted to go past him unbothered.

"Gavaria?" he asked, forcing her to stop.

"The Duchess," Josephine said quickly.

"Requesting more troops for the war?" George's face brightened; this could be an easier way out than his current plan. Josephine caught his excitement and sneered.

"Unfortunately," she said.

"Can I come?"

The shift in Josephine's face told George all he needed, but Josephine spelled it out for him anyway. "George, this is a very sensitive and important meeting discussing the release of imperial troops," she emphasized, "*imperial lives*, to aid in a brutal and ruthless war up in the north, and against the Vagrants, no less."

"That's not exactly a no," George did his best to nudge in but an unamused exhale cut him back down.

"You should be practicing with Reginald."

"You're not my mother," George scoffed. "Come on."

Josephine narrowed her eyes. "No, I guess I'm not, am I?" George paled under the stare and before he could apologize, Josephine broke into a rant. "This isn't a game where soldiers are just tiny wooden things and war is an afternoon jaunt in the woods with stick swords and giggling friends, this is a matter of death and serious logistics. Go do whatever you do, but leave this sort of thing alone."

With little else, Josephine turned sharply to the right and marched on, leaving George alone to watch the capes of her escorts sway.

"I don't even do any of that stuff!" George slapped his sides with his arms, his shout bouncing off the courtyard walls without any replies. The prince shook his head and looked to his left, where a lone guard stood stalwart in front of a door, face blank and focused. "You know, I bet you three faces that she is going to apologize later and then do it again the next day. If it's not a stupid prank or feeling sorry for herself, it's patronizing me."

The guard flicked his eyes over to George. "Yes, my prince."

George folded his arms, and grinned. "Wait, yes to the bet?"

"No, my prince."

George sighed. "Ah well, thanks for the chat... Keep up the good work." The guard tipped his head and George tucked a frown into his cheek. Josephine's patronizing was wearing him thin, and it certainly didn't brighten his already bleak day. Even still, he supposed this might be one of the last few times he felt this way. He looked up from his feet, only to catch the stares of onlookers along the edge of the courtyard. George shivered and went to move on only to freeze. Two orb-like eyes were staring at him from between an allee of trees. The nearby walls cast the whole area in a shadow, a shadow not unlike that of a dim hallway. In a blink, they were gone. George shivered again, and this time he hurried away. He couldn't stay.

Chapter 2
The Plan

The day droned on into the afternoon, blunting the fear of the morning and giving George the feeling that he didn't quite make the most of his freedom. After his conversation with Josephine and the fright of the allee, he had helped himself into the palace pantries to cool his nerves. Once inside, he, admittedly, angrily devoured just enough flaky pastries that the cooks wouldn't notice any missing and yet still fill his stomach. There was something comforting about breakfast food, until it started to make his full belly ache. As far as George was aware, the only cure for such a predicament was a lazy nap at the edge of the western courtyard, far from any shadows.

He always enjoyed the western courtyard. It was wedged between the Imperial Palace and some of the external guest houses that dignitaries and various visiting nobles often housed in. His visit wasn't one of pure habit though, as he was hoping that 'by chance' he would run into one of the visitors from Gavaria, or perhaps even the Duchess herself.

The thought put a smug if not slightly sticky smile on the boy's face, hands comfy on his belly. Wouldn't that just bite for Josephine, by chance getting a word with the Duchess? Maybe he would even be invited back to Gavaria. George let out a sigh at his own imagination and closed his eyes to the sun above, taking in the feeling of the coarse stone under his rump, the gentle breeze, and the swaying of the leaves in the distance. It was as if the morning never happened.

A wooden clatter drummed at his feet, forcing him to peek with a single eye. Standing over him was one of the gardener's sons, Williams. Williams was every bit different from George, with long scraggly blond hair to contrast the prince's short haircut, a lanky body and calculating eyes (with one hiding behind a bruise). Between the two boys was a wooden training sword, matching the one in Williams' left hand. He jutted a chin at George. "Busy?"

"Extremely." George had opened both of his eyes now, waving at the scene.

"Oh, shut up."

George cracked a smile and scooped up the sword on the ground. Shaking the nap from his limbs, George found his footing. Bending his knees and positioning his hands accordingly he nodded at Williams, signifying he was ready.

With a solid thwack, the two training swords collided. Despite George's weight advantage and the force behind his swing, Williams seemed to take it with stride. The two boys let out a series of simple yet powerful blows, having done this countless times before. Fat with pastries and dreams, the muscle memory seemed to lull George back into his imagination until a well-placed strike nearly buckled his knee.

"Oooo!" Two other boys by the side lines jeered. George turned to get a look at them, only to greet them with an eye roll. One was a rather tall boy named Gregory-Hector Von Imperia, though everyone just called him Hector. He stood at the edge of the impromptu sparring ring, wooden sword in his own hand and his entire head shaved to a curly coal-black stubble. Despite being only a few months older than the others, his height overshadowed both George and Williams, as well as Franklin Davids, the short, cheery faced boy to his right who was known for his bright eyes and sharp tongue.

"You won't last a second against a rebel if you're going to be fighting like that, let alone a giant." Franklin pointed his own sparring blade at George. George pointed his right back with a mocking grin.

"You wanna show me how to fight then?"

"The prince himself wants lessons from the likes of me, I'm touched." Franklin wiped away a fake tear before stepping forward with a mighty grin. George shook away a laugh and stretched his limbs, getting back into position. He kept his eyes firmly on Franklin, knowing well enough that his short friend was full of unexpected tricks that he picked up from his father, the captain of the palace guard.

Franklin seemed to stall, so with a small rash of impatience, George swung overhead. Franklin easily sidestepped the swing and went for a chop across the back, but George was expecting this and used the momentum from his own swing to fall out of range. The two spun to meet each other again, the battle reset.

This time as soon as they faced each other, George kept his energy and threw out an onslaught of swipes. At first, Franklin managed to deflect most of them, but as George pushed harder and harder, the shorter boy opted to use the bounce of the most recent parry to riposte, striking George in the shoulder.

"Hah!" Franklin managed taunt before George suddenly shoved Franklin backwards, his sword clattering to the floor.

"Williams! Now!" George laughed. The skinny boy obediently appeared behind Franklin, sticking out his foot and tripping him. Franklin landed with a wide-eyed thud and growled past a friendly grin. George picked up his blade and pointed it at Franklin's face. "Do you yield—?"

Hector came barreling in from the side, tackling George to the ground. The prince felt Hector's weight press him into the stones of the courtyard, nearly smothering him as he scrambled for a way to get out of the pin. In the corner of his eye, he could see Franklin scuffling with Williams. Refocusing on Hector, George saw an opening.

Slipping a knee under Hector's gut, George pushed up with all his force and pried the older boy off of him. George rolled to his knees to find his fighting stance again, but Hector wasn't done and came rushing back at him. The two collided with a lung-crushing clap but neither of them lost their footing. Stuck in a heated grapple, the two tried their best to bend the other to the ground.

Sweat began to dampen George's forehead, his muscles straining as he tried to get a chokehold on Hector. Without warning Hector's arms began to glow a honey-gold, causing the other boy's eyes to widen with surprise. George gulped as he felt the battle suddenly slipping from him. "Hey no magic—"

It was too late. Hector had lifted George off his feet with unimaginable strength, and tossed him to the ground. "Bah!" Air escaped George's lungs as he collided with the courtyard stones. A raw pain was already throbbing in his side. He croaked, trying to recapture his breath. "No... fair..."

"Oh, get up." Hector gave George that goofy smile he always wore when he won something. The magic faded from Hector's arms as he lent a hand to George, who took it easily. Franklin clapped the prince on the back while Williams handed him his dropped sword. George nodded his thanks, admittedly still out of breath from the beating. He put a hand on his stomach, the contents of his sugary breakfast all stirred up. His face twisted for a moment then he let out a belch.

"Awh, come on man." Franklin waved a hand in front of his face.

"Don't blame the messenger," George defended, not a speck of shame in his soul, "Hector is the one who beat it out of me." The prince shot a look at Hector, "With some unfair tricks."

"Isn't your uncle teaching you Stromism?" Hector argued back. It was true, but it was also true, much to George's chagrin, that he was terrible at it. The prince twisted a frown.

"Yeah well... good fight."

The four plopped by the edge of the courtyard to catch their breaths. Franklin let out a long exhale, mumbling at the end. "Golden-spanked Graces, I need some water."

George felt a laugh coming but stifled it when he saw Hector's unamused face. Only one thing passed through George's mind: *here it comes.*

"You shouldn't abuse the name of the gods so freely," Hector suggested, his voice as calm and collected as a saint's. Even with all his practice with the other Stromist monks, Hector never quite lost his faith in the Graces, even if the Tagists weren't too fond of the monks.

Franklin got a stubborn gleam in his eye, and it wasn't just George who noticed it. Williams interjected, "Got any plans for the rest of the day?"

The gleam seemed to stay just long enough for everyone to notice Franklin struggling between a hotheaded debate and just giving in and answering Williams. Finally, Franklin spouted, "I just don't see why supreme gods would care about how I address their names, like, that's the least of their worries."

"Ugh, not this again," George threw out his opinion, gathering a chorus of agreement from Williams and Hector.

Franklin shrugged. "I'm just saying! It's not like any one of us here are really devout Tagists anyway. Except maybe you, George."

"I don't even know what the name represents," George dismissed the claim, but it was true. As an imperial prince, it was his public duty to endorse the two major religions of Tagism and Stromism, both having eased their way into politics. His friend Hector wasn't amused though and crossed his arms.

"Stubborn bastard, you're a Dweller's advocate in every debate, you know that?"

George pointed to himself, surprised. "Me?"

"No, Franklin." Hector nudged the shorter boy, who shoved him back.

Williams rolled his eyes. "Well, *I'm* picking up my father's new shears from the blacksmith down on the bay street later on." A long pause followed and George could only imagine that Williams was waiting for the topic to change. The scrawny friend was always avidly against debates and arguments.

Franklin took the bait. "Doesn't the palace barrack's man usually do your father's tools?"

"Yeah, but he and his apprentices are all busy with the new order being shipped out, most of the city's smiths are. It took my father an entire day to find an open slot," Williams answered.

"Oh right, the reinforcements that are being sent up north," Franklin laid back to rest his head on his hands. "You hear about that, George?"

George gave him a squinting look and leaned back himself. "No idea what you're talking about, is there some sort of war going on?" His voice dripped with sarcasm.

Franklin propped himself up just as the other boys decided to lean back. He went wide eyed. "Yeah!" He matched the sarcasm. "You know... giants, chieftains and vagrants with enough potential room for a runaway prince and their handsome friends."

"Oh, shut up." George tossed one of the discarded wooden swords at him, a smirk on his face, a smirk that was hiding a growing anxiety in his gut. Franklin laughed. Slowly though, they all fell silent. George knew why, they all knew why, it was just a matter of one of them saying it. The prince gulped and cleared his throat. "Is everyone still on board with the plan?"

There was another silence, brought on by a doubt that George felt himself. It may have not been entirely his plan, but he would be a liar if he didn't admit to himself that he was one of the major proponents of it. It was a sort of responsibility he wasn't sure he wanted if anything went wrong.

Finally, Williams broke the silence. "I still don't know if this is a good idea." He rolled onto his side to face the others. "You have to admit that this is a bit drastic, especially just for a dream."

"It's not just a dream," George argued back, "I wanted to leave before then. This is my way out, and if I can also figure out what everything means while doing it." George chewed his cheek, besides, he couldn't help shake the feeling that he truly wasn't safe at the palace anymore.

"How again, does running away help you figure out a nightmare?" Williams pushed, not with malice.

George winced. "I don't see the nightmare whenever we leave the city. I can't stay here, Williams. It's not..." He trailed.

"It's not what?" Williams pushed.

"Safe."

A buzzing silence overtook the scene. Williams was eyeing George, as if stuck between judging him and believing him. "We could tell you uncle."

"You barely believe me," George countered. "If I tell anyone other than you guys, I'm sure they'd lock me in a room and let whatever thing I keep seeing find me stuck."

"Um," Franklin interrupted, "It was my idea to use the reinforcements to smuggle ourselves north anyway," Franklin said. "I don't know much about dark omens and stuff, but I want an adventure too, and I'm not going to find it here. Are you flaking out on us, Williams?"

Hector simply looked at Williams with a grin and shrugged, summoning a reluctant sigh from the Gardener's son. "Well, if you are all going no matter what I say, then of course I'm going with you." He scanned his friends. "Someone has to keep you all out of trouble and be the even-mind."

"Oh, you're the even-mind?" Franklin curled his lips, eyes full of jest.

"Well, it's not you," Hector murmured, getting an elbow to the rib.

George nodded, his friend's casual quips putting him at ease. "Okay, grab what you can. We can slip in with the reinforcements as they march out of the city."

"And don't tell anyone," Franklin quickly added, eyes bouncing between all of them, "Imagine the trouble we would get into if we got caught."

"Do they even have rules against such a thing? It's like... reverse desertion," Williams scoffed before sneaking a peak at Hector, the resident know-it-all.

George felt his anxiety creeping back. "Let's just not get caught," he said, "the last thing we need is to make complete fools out of ourselves."

"Hey, speak of the Dweller!" Franklin almost spat, forcing all eyes to follow his line of sight. George felt his stomach twitch from sudden paranoia, only to settle into plain annoyance when he saw who Franklin was talking about.

Walking across the courtyard was Fenric, a provincial prince from Gavaria itself. He was a year older than George and wore a sword on his hip and a smug grin on his face. The grin turned into a lip-splitting smile, the kind that was begging to be stamped out. George rolled back to his feet.

"I see you are still spending more time on your lazy ass than your narcoleptic sister." Fenric placed a hand on the pommel of his blade, his almost-jumping northern accent hissing through his smile. Even the way he spoke just made George's fingers curl into a fist.

"That's cold." Franklin rose to his feet with a puffed-up chest.

"And untrue," Williams added with a growl of his own. He and Hector got back to their feet, shoulders square.

"Oh, so it's Josephine who is spending more time, then? Maybe the stories of her curse are true." Fenric stepped up to Williams, bright eyes sizing the poor boy up. Williams didn't seem to recede but instead held a protective stare that could only lead to trouble, though George couldn't imagine any of this *not* leading to trouble.

George felt anger rising past his previous anxiety until it culminated into words. "Do you have a problem?" He took two steps behind Fenric, forcing the older boy to turn from his friends.

Fenric sneered. "I was just stopping by. Father has requested an Imperial garrison for the war on our borders and he sent me to march it up north." The braggart smirked. "You understand I'm a soldier now, commander by birthright even."

George crossed his arms and tilted his chin up. "Is that why the duke also sent your mother down?"

"Can't handle giving his dimwit son all that authority all at once, so they gotta have momma chaperone." Franklin put a hand on George's shoulder. A collective chuckle escaped Hector and Williams.

Fenric visibly reddened and his smirk twisted into a frown. The Gavarian's fist whitened over the pommel of his blade and he spat back, "say the ticks latched to the bastard prince."

"Bastard?" George raised his brow and took a step forward. In truth anything Fenric could have said would have provoked him, a large part of him burning to silence Fenric.

"Ticks?" Franklin looked at Hector, who shrugged.

"I have my father." George narrowed his eyes.

"What's left of him," Fenric scoffed.

"He is grasping at straws," Williams said, "Leave him to it."

"No." George took a final step closer to Fenric, putting them chest to chest, "Fenric has something to say."

"Wilhelm is a lunatic," Fenric said slowly, "A useless lunatic who is driving this empire into the ground quicker than he did his wife—"

With a resounding whack, George's fist slammed into Fenric's jaw. The older boy rocked backwards and swiped out with his left. The fist weakly slapped against George's shoulder, but a second suddenly came as Fenric found his footing and he stuffed a fist into George's stomach. The prince let out a hoarse cough and took a step back.

The other boys ringed around them as the fighters took their stances. Franklin bared his teeth. "Teach the baby duke a lesson!"

George swung angrily, but Fenric ducked under only to rise with a punch of his own. His knuckles connected under George's chin, summoning a wincing "ooo" from Franklin and Hector. The force of the blow pushed George onto his backside.

"Stay down." Fenric hissed between his teeth, hand slithering down to the handle of his blade.

George spat and kicked to his feet, but before he could get up, Fenric had already planted his knee into George's face. Pain rocked through George's body and back as a ringing shock sent his mind reeling. A spurt of blood dribbled down to his chin, sending George's friends into an uproar.

Williams was the first in, the scrawny boy wrenching Fenric away from George with a kick to the ribs. Franklin was next with a kick of his own, followed by Hector with a shimmering hand that grabbed the back of Fenric's collar and tossed him aside.

Fenric bounced back to his feet quickly, his ribs audibly popping and projecting a pain that could be seen in his face. He narrowed his eyes at George, who was wobbling between his friends with a cocky, blood-smeared grin and dizzy fighting stance. Feeling outnumbered, Fenric's hand gripped his blade.

Just as Fenric's blade was about to scream from its scabbard, a scarred and calloused hand gripped his wrist from behind. George felt a weight drop from him that he didn't know he was carrying only to be replaced with the fear of being caught red handed.

"Let's not do anything we will regret," warned George's uncle, Caleb. He stood behind Fenric, his approach unseen and his tone as calm as the summer sea. A rasp of experience carried in his voice that otherwise held a youthful energy unfit for his age. Uncle Caleb's fierce chestnut eyes stared down. Fenric opened his mouth in protest but before he could utter a sound, his own mother, Hilda, came storming down from the palace doors.

Wry smiles collected on the faces of the other boys, while Fenric began to sulk in place. Fenric's mother was fair, short, and her son looked very much like her which made it all the funnier to the others when she began to lord over the situation. "What's going on here?" Her voice was stronger than her size let on. Before anyone could answer she began to roughly check Fenric for wounds. Hilda turned to the bleeding George, eyes widening. *"Fenric!"*

"You assume it was me?" Fenric backed out of his mother's closing grip, only to catch sight of Caleb's squinting look. "And what are you looking at?"

"I'm not too sure, myself," Caleb said without missing a beat. Fenric's eyes widened. George let out a small laugh, each chuckle putting a sharp sting in his broken nose.

"Say that again!" Fenric barked at the veteran.

"Come!" Hilda hissed at her son. "The emperor is expecting us." The duchess grabbed Fenric's arm and with a force unexpected of her smaller stature, she began to drag the young warrior away. She turned back to briefly apologize to Caleb with her eyes, getting a nod in return.

George's uncle stood next to the boys as they watched the two disappear into the alabaster palace. Caleb snickered, "What a little shit." Before George could laugh again, Caleb gave the back of his head a steady whack which sent a drop or two from his nose. "What sort of trouble were you getting yourself into?" He pointed a finger at all the other boys, some of which were sneaking away. "And what about you?"

"We were just practicing, sir." Franklin jutted his chin at the wooden swords. "Then Fenric came in and started the fight."

Caleb looked over at Williams and cocked a brow. "Williams?"

Everyone looked over at the boy, his face turning a bright red. George widened his eyes and Williams gulped. Caleb cleared his throat and the blond boy sighed, "We threw the first hit, *but!*"

"I don't care for the rest." Caleb waved a hand, admirably calm yet clearly disappointed. "I can only imagine a certain boy's anger fueled the strike."

"Fenric insulted the emperor," George defended, knowing damn well it was in vain.

"And the heir," Williams added quickly.

"Wilhelm and Josephine are easy targets for slander," Caleb dismissed the defense as easily as George expected. "A figure in your position can't be seen acting violently to mere words, save that for actions." Caleb paused before looking up at the sky and squinted his eyes. "Almost dinner-time."

The boys took the hint and began to file away with groans. Williams patted George on the shoulder, wishing him luck as he walked away. George gave him a no-worries nod in return, but didn't quite know what to expect. Franklin dragged his feet the most but soon the courtyard was empty save for Caleb and his nephew.

"Lecture time?" George asked, bouncing his eyebrows in hopes for a laugh. Caleb broke a grin, which was close enough.

"I think Fenric already gave you one." Caleb produced a handkerchief from his pocket and tossed it to the boy. George dabbed it over his bloody nose. The older prince waved for George to follow as he began a slow trek away from the battlefield. Looking down, Caleb furrowed his brow. "I'm just going to assume that my lessons went unused in the altercation?"

"I can't do magic," George defended, "so I just went with what I know."

"Getting your ass kicked?"

George gave a fake "ha!" and shook his head. "Very encouraging."

"I'm just saying." Caleb folded his hands behind his back. "People in our position are quite lucky in the ways of resources." He stopped and turned to George. "After dinner, come visit me in my study."

"Are you not joining us, again?" George inspected the now bloodied rag he held.

"I just got my hands on some books that I want to give a proper look," Caleb explained.

George wiggled his nose and looked up at his uncle. "You know you won't escape rumors and speculation with that story."

Caleb pinched his chin and a humoring gleam sparkled in his eye. "What do you suggest?"

"I'll tell them you've answered the Countess Von Hetsbin's call to courtship and took her out for a stroll."

"And now who is making rumors and speculation?" Caleb guffawed.

"Hey." George held up his hands. "Better people spreading rumors that you're finally looking for a wife rather than flipping through occult and possibly..." George whispered almost mockingly, "*illegal* Nachtist writings."

Caleb rolled his eyes. "Slander."

"We get a lot of that, huh?" George gave a pitiful tone.

"If only we could just knock 'em in the face and be done with it, hm?" Caleb winked back. "See me after dinner."

"I have a match with Reginald," George said as the two began parting ways.

"After you lose, then!" Caleb shouted behind him.

"That might take too long!" George called back.

"Ha!" Caleb laughed from the other side of the courtyard. "Give my best to the old master."

Chapter 3
A Deranged Dinner

The massive hall that George, along with the rest of the imperial family, simply referred to as the dining room was hot with fragrances from the kitchen. Despite the modest name, George couldn't say he ever felt like it was truly just a dining room, not since he had spent dinner at Franklin's home so long ago. The long wooden table that was centered in the massive room was a deep reddish brown, a gift from one of the powerful dukes in the deep south. If that wasn't impressive enough, the table was *then* sent to the far north to be carved and decorated by one of the empire's finest craftsmen just to be sent back down to the capital and *then* dressed with the largest silk tablecloth ever sewn.

One would think—and for the first half of George's life, he did—that the opulence of the table was simply for the enjoyment of the imperial family, but in truth it was more for the crowd who watched them eat. The crowd, that was the first thing George had noticed was missing at Franklin's and to be honest ever since, he couldn't help but notice them at his own dinners. Even now, a group of roughly twenty people sat in a depressed alcove by the common entrance of the grand hall. They seemed almost like gutter-bound squirrels as they waited there hoping to take any leftovers home. It was an old tradition, but one that gave George a creep down his back whenever eye contact was made.

Even now, George sat thinking about it. He held a silver spoon in one hand, the utensil hovering over a gold leafed bowl of squash bisque, but his eyes were warily placed on a bearded man staring hungrily at his bread roll. The irony of the spoon wasn't lost on George, but in such a situation he didn't have time to enjoy it or to even poke fun at his perceived misfortune of being wealthy. Blinking a few times, George craned his neck to look deeper into the crowd. Sometimes he could find Williams in there or one of the others doing something stupid for a laugh or two.

George froze. An uncanny shadow lingered behind the bearded man, unbeknownst to the commoner. It didn't match the man's body, it was taller than it should be. It blinked. George's heart jumped and his fingers gripped the table. It couldn't be, again, could it? Horns. It had horns. George shut his eyes, but all he could see was the hallway. "Tonight," he hissed through his clenched teeth. "It'll all go away tonight."

A cane rapped against the floor. George's eyes shot open, blood pumping in his ears. The shadow was gone.

The cane rapped again, forcing everyone's attention to a loudly dressed man by the noble entrance of the hall. "Duchess Hilda of Gavaria! Ducal prince Fenric of Gavaria!" He announced with practiced volume. Shortly after, the Duchess and her son walked in and took their seats across from George, their backs to the crowd. They each gave George a funny look, likely since he had already taken a bite of his dinner. George simply turned just far enough away to roll his eyes without them seeing. His blood settled, all was normal once again, or as normal as it could be.

Murmurs began to overtake the crowd, and George knew what was coming next.

"His Imperial Majesty, Emperor Wilhelm the Second of Jerrovia!"

"As if any of us forgot where we were," George mumbled before turning to watch his father enter. Wilhelm, as much as George would hesitate to admit it, often looked like a man who shrunk just as the tailor finished stitching him in. It wasn't entirely false, the emperor was once a large and imposing man before the death of George's mother but now as he was walking into the hall, his bright purple robe was wearing him more than he was wearing it. A floor length cape only added to the apparent weight of the wardrobe. The emperor himself had the flimsy smile of a man not all there, wild blue eyes, and an explosive nest of wiry golden hair stuffed under a bejeweled crown. Still, seeing his father, especially with a smile, made George smile back, only to frown shortly after as he noticed Wilhelm's escort.

Instead of Reginald, a servant woman dressed in a nice but simple dress walked behind the emperor, her eyes on the floor. The woman's hair was fitted with baubles, some which George alone recognized as his late mother's. He had to tear his eyes away from Sophia before it completely ruined his mood. George wasn't the only one to be disturbed by the sight, his ears perking to the murmurs in the crowd and the myriad of rumors that followed.

The emperor took a seat in the massive throne that was fixed in the center back of the table. Sophia stood behind him out of servile respect which was a tradition that saved the emperor from even more lascivious rumors that often hung around his entanglement with her.

George himself was sitting just to the left of the throne, which put him in perfect range for when Wilhelm's hand came down on his shoulder. What could have once been a thunderous clap was reduced to a wispy brush as the emperor smiled at his son. "My boy." He shook George's shoulder, a gentle hiccup in his voice, "My boy!"

"Yes, Dad." George tapped his father's hand, returning the smile, albeit much softer than it was given. The two shared a look but before they could say anything further, the herald called out again.

"Heir Apparent, Princess Josephine of Jerrovia!"

Josephine came walking in, her political attire still on and looking very much the image of her office in spite of her youth. She was being escorted by Reginald, who wore high quality clothes but still in a simple solid style to denote his servile nature in the palace. George was always curious why Reginald opted for such a position, surely the veteran could wear his medals or whatever other trinkets of war he had won. The prince stopped staring. There was nothing too special about the event, seeing how they used this dining room most of the week.

George's sister sat to the right of Wilhelm, putting their father between them. It was at this moment that Wilhelm began to spoon small doses of his soup to his shaking lips while the others took the initiative and followed suit. That was it, the fun was over and yet the crowd never really disappeared, and no engaging conversation ever popped up. George frowned and dunked his roll into his soup just to watch it slowly soak through, eyes half closed. A nudge from Reginald forced him to sit up straight and just in time to watch the guests from Gavaria do that one thing every visiting noble did when eating in front of his father. George sneered, the Duchess and Fenric were eating so incredibly slow so as to not make a single slurp or even a munch of the crusty roll.

Looking past his father, he eyed Josephine who seemed to notice as well and the two shared a rare but welcomed mutual look of amusement. Wilhelm sputtered after a hefty slurp and looked around wildly at no one in particular. "This is good soup!"

Josephine seemed to cringe.

"Yes, your majesty!" The Duchess nearly shouted her response, as if she had built up pressure from waiting for the emperor to break the silence. Quickly, Hilda capitalized. "Um, your Majesty, what of prince Regent Caleb?"

Wilhelm blinked at the Duchess, a slow smile winding up as he thought. "He is pretty good in his own right, as well!"

"I beg your pardon, your majesty, but I mean where is he?" The Duchess meekly tried to correct the conversation. Wilhelm went blank again, his brow knitting.

"What?"

"The Regent is entertaining a guest," George quickly covered. Josephine looked up from her food and studied the exchange quietly.

"Oh?" The Duchess put down her spoon, "And who might that be?"

"Countess Von Hetsbin," George blurted.

"She's in the capital!?" Duchess Hilda went wide-eyed.

"Um." George looked at Reginald who gave him nothing but a look. He looked back at the duchess, but Josephine had already started to speak. She managed to do it in such a way that looked disinterested, politely folding her napkin into her lap as she talked with absolute certainty.

"Her head servant Timothy is. Uncle Caleb happens to be screening potential suitors, I hear, but that is hardly news for such a table, yes?"

"Unlikely," Fenric hissed under his breath, only to be jabbed by his mother. George rolled his eyes but before he could snap something back, the kitchen staff came swirling out from behind two purple doors with plates of roasted duck, onion, and potatoes in hand, alongside a few healthy bowls of cranberry jams. The crowd suddenly seemed even more interested, the gossip about Caleb not getting nearly as much attention as the food. Bejeweled goblets in front of the diners were quickly filled with a plum-colored wine, poured without a bubble to be noted.

George looked down at his own cup, the only one to have been filled with crystal clear water. Fenric made a face that George could only define as stupid, knowing that Fenric himself knew damn well that alcohol was restricted from Stromists in training. The two boys shared the look, George counting the seconds, waiting for-

"Still too young for wine, George?" Fenric sneered.

"And there it is," The prince said under his breath. Fenric let out a loud hum as if asking George to speak up. George obliged and began to slowly and loudly announce to Fenric, *"My Uncle's re-gi-me-nt."*

"Oh—"

"Be-cause I am." George prodded a thumb into his chest. *"Learn-ing Stro-mist ma-gic."*

"Alright I get it—"

"Do you re-mem-ber that?"

"Grace's balls, yes!" Fenric shouted and his mother's hand slapped the back of his head. George slunk into his chair with a goofy smile on his face while Hilda chastised her son for blasphemy. Sneaking a look over to the side, George saw Josephine roll her eyes at him, but a small smile of her own and a slight nod was all the proof George needed of her own enjoyment.

A small pause in the conversation was filled with a grainy laugh as Wilhelm began a red-faced chuckle. George looked over with a grin of his own, thinking it was his own antics that caused it, but frowning when seeing his father simply staring at a piece of duck and laughing.

"Something, your Majesty?" The Duchess furrowed her brow.

Wilhelm looked up and muttered something so quickly and quietly, that no one at the table quite caught it. Duchess Hilda leaned forward, her expression deepening. "I'm sorry?"

The emperor gave her a suspicious look. "For what?"

Before Hilda could do more than stare blankly at the emperor, the sound of metal clanging filled the dining room. George jumped at the sound of steel rings scraping as red velvet curtains were being pulled to block the view of the commoners. His head spun to look for a reason only to fall on Reginald who was ordering the guards to do it. Silently George asked Reginald a question with his eyes, the old servant quickly looking towards Josephine then back at the guards.

Peering over, George saw Josephine leaning against the high back of her chair with eyes closed and her breathing shallow and short. George flicked his gaze over to his father and saw that Wilhelm had not noticed yet. George all but jumped from his seat to put himself in between his sleeping sister and the emperor but Hilda suddenly gasped.

"Is the princess alright?"

George felt a stone fall in his stomach. The groans of the now-blinded commoners were radiating from behind the curtains, but all George could hear was his heartbeat as his father silently stared at Josephine.

"Your Majesty?" Hilda went to stand up, a face full of concern.

"She's fine!" Wilhelm hissed, almost violently, and caused everyone to jump. The emperor continued to stare. The whole scene was surreal but all too familiar.

"Should we see her to—"

"I said she's fine!" Wilhelm slammed his fist onto the table, causing the plates to clatter and a cup to spill over. The pale face of the emperor was replaced with a deep red.

"Go!" He stood up, barking at the Duchess and Fenric. "Stop looking at her!"

They forced their vision to the floor.

"Get out of here!" The emperor slammed the table again, saliva dripping down his chin. The pair began to shuffle away, both visibly shaking. George couldn't blame them, even he was.

Wilhelm was fawning over Josephine as they left, his fingers threading through her hair. The emperor's eyes were wet and shimmering with emotion as he muttered to himself obsessively. George stood helpless.

"My poor girl." Wilhelm closed his eyes. "My poor girl."

The ever-silent Sophia reached out gingerly, but the emperor swatted it away, only to immediately go wide-eyed and spin. He sputtered at the servant and George felt the stone in his stomach burn a little.

"Sophia!" Tears were forming in Wilhelm's eyes as he embraced the servant.

"George!" Reginald's cutting voice pulled him away from the sight of his father. The old servant had Josephine standing, supported by one of his shoulders. Knowing exactly what to do, George swooped in to support her other side. He was always surprised by how light his sister was. Her sleepless nights and tired days clearly drained her.

Together, George and Reginald walked Josephine out of the dining room and into the cavernous gilded halls of the palace corridors. The guards posted between legendary works of art and priceless crafts stood sentry, as silent and still as stones even as the trio shuffled past. No one wanted to admit it, but this particular march was common enough that the soldiers were used to it, not that either Reginald or George would allow them to carry the princess on their behalf, be it for care or pride.

The fortunate piece that came with the high frequency of Josephine's bouts was Reginald's foresight to move a few palace doctors to rooms closer to the dining room and other busy areas, a relief George was beginning to feel in his right shoulder. Taking a sharp left, they entered one such room.

Inside, the duo placed Josephine gently onto a feather bed and pulled plush blankets over her. A lone doctor watched, her wrinkled eyes were devoid of worry but instead filled with routine. Reginald turned to the woman and gave her a brief nod with the only words passed between them being customary thanks and greetings.

George ignored them for the most part, his eyes on his sister's face. She was sleeping soundly, but now and again her nose would twitch, or the corner of her lip would droop into a sharp frown. Reaching out he gave her shoulder an affirming tap, as if dispelling away whatever dreams could be causing her expressions. Her face softened, and George felt a sense of relief in himself, though he couldn't help but wonder if her nightmares were anything like his own.

The door behind him swung open again and two men in flowing blue robes came hurrying in. They were supposed to give off an air of humility and modesty, but George immediately felt the pride they carried in their walk. Tagist Sages, that's what they were, the holy elders of the Tagist religion and keepers of the mist. It didn't take long for one of the Sages to get to Josephine's bed and begin a low chant. Their voice hummed and dipped with the words, a ball of icy blue mist forming in their mouth. The tiny ball grew and grew until it spilled out into a wispy waterfall, the gentle magic pooling around the princess.

It was a healing magic, as if Josephine's affliction could be healed. Certainly, eighteen years of mist-talking had yet to produce any results, though George couldn't deny the usefulness it had in healing his arm a few years back when he broke it during a stupid bet with Franklin.

Looking away from the Sage elder, George's eyes snapped to the gaze of the younger Tagist. He was staring daggers at George. The prince leered back. He had no idea why, but a good many of the Sages never seemed to like him. Usually, George dismissed the strange rivalry as a side effect of his close relationship with his uncle, a man the Sages truly despised, but lately, George wasn't sure. The feeling of suddenly being unsafe found George's heart again, if but for a moment.

"George," Reginald's voice called out to him.

The boy turned to his teacher, the old man's eyes soft and full of a certain care. He nodded. "You should run along and let her sleep."

Looking back at his sister, George slowly agreed, "I know."

The prince slipped out the door and closed it behind him. Fenric's face greeted him. The older boy was standing next to an Imperial guard who was keeping him from getting too close to the door. George furrowed his brow and let irritation overtake any sorrow. "What do you want?"

Fenric made a face, "I was just checking."

"Checking?"

Fenric frowned. He was an ass, but something told George that in this rare case he wasn't trying to be. "Older siblings can be scary," Fenric said cryptically, "if you lose them."

"Do you really care?" George couldn't help the venom.

Fenric's face twitched and his usual demeanor came surging back. "Why not? Can't I?" It was a hiss.

"You were poking fun in the courtyard not a few hours ago."

"You were too sensitive," Fenric lifted his face upward. "Swaddled and spoiled. I should have expected that."

George squinted through the insults, he was done with this farce. "My Uncle is waiting for me." With little else, the Prince pushed past Fenric.

Chapter 4
Ascending the Tower

Uncle Caleb's tower was situated in the southwestern corner of the palace complex, attached to the main body and overlooking the western courtyard as well as the southern walls. The walls sat atop a sheer cliff face that skyrocketed downwards into the city below. In total, the top of the tower gave a great view of the rocky hilltop the palace was built onto, as well as the winding roadway down to the surrounding city, the sight only ending past the docks and into the mists of the Great Jerrovian Sea to the far south.

Despite this legendary view, Caleb often kept the windows closed and shades drawn, a fact George suffered as he climbed the nigh endless stairs to the top. Closed air kept the dust in, making a dull and bitter smell that was similar to that of a cellar. The walls of the stone tower weren't even decorated with the art of the rest of the palace with the only hint of nobility being the crimson and purple dyed curtains that were tied shut with golden tassels.

This high, the only sounds were the occasional bird chattering outside the tower and George's own footsteps on the stone. He always found that he made heavy footfalls on these steps, the play of the echo reminding him of when he was a kid and when such things endlessly fascinated him, and as he supposed, some things just don't change. With a particularly loud clap of his foot, he landed in front of the thick and imposing iron studded door of his uncle's study. A large shackle was fitted on the edge of the door and aligned with a metal hoop screwed into the stone wall, fit for a large lock that was always missing. Caleb used the study far too frequently to bother locking it.

George opened the door to be greeted with the wafting smell of sun-soaked wood, musky stones and the sharp scent of old paper. Large round top windows fed in colored light, creating a shattered rainbow over the study, with blue and red freckles dotting Uncle Caleb's back. The man was leaning so far over his desk, his nose was nearly pressing into the large book splayed open before him not unlike a wolf before a kill. A stray hand was already lifting the page to turn it. Before George could say anything, Caleb's voice reached out to him.

"IAO, father of Stromism, the first of the Imperial Stromist Marshals, and legendary conqueror who supposedly carved the Mortal Empire of Jerrovia alongside the first of our ancestors..." The page flipped. George knew the story, but what he didn't know was why Caleb was acting so skeptical.

"Supposedly?"

Without looking up, Caleb tapped the book he was reading. "This book says otherwise."

"Who cares what one book says?"

"I do." Caleb finally glanced up. He blinked and George watched his uncle's eyes adjusted to something that wasn't a spattering of letters. "This book is incredibly old in itself, old enough to have a kernel of truth." He paused. "According to its author, IAO was most of what we believed him to be, but he was fighting a civil war alongside Emperor Victor Heinrich, not carving an empire for him." Another pause. Caleb tilted his head as if expecting something from George. The prince furrowed his brow and shrugged.

"You know I'm bad at history."

Caleb shook his head and tapped the book twice. "If this book is right, the Empire is a lot older than our current historians think... meaning once again we may be unaware of how our dynasty, let alone the Empire, really began. Void! On top of that, it may mean that the Vagrants really *are* an old splinter of a long-lost civil war."

George let out a confused, "Oh." He was sure there were consequences to this, even if they were a little vague in his own mind. Silence grew between the two as Caleb's eyes snapped back to the text.

"I thought you had a chess match to attend?" The Imperial Regent finally said. He stuffed a bookmark into the crease of the book's pages before gingerly closing it. George shrugged and walked over to a stiff looking couch that sat in front of a low table. He put his hands on the arm of the sofa before settling down on it.

"Josephine had... an episode."

"Her narcolepsy?"

"Yeah, she fell asleep right at the table. Reginald is watching over her in one of the infirmary rooms." George slipped off the arm of the couch and into its cushions below. Caleb shook his head slowly.

"Good old Reggie," Caleb announced as he stood up, "He was there for me and your father, there for you guys, and since time and death seem to shy away from him, I wager he will be there until the Graces give up and swallow Jerrovia whole."

"The unbeatable man!" George laughed, putting his feet up on the low table. Caleb nudged them back to the floor with a boot before taking an almost heroic pose.

"You should have seen us, George, back in the old days." Caleb adopted a sly grin. "Your father was a cunning warrior, Reginald, our great teacher, and your mother... Well she had the sharpest tongue in the courts. If it wasn't for her, we'd all be frozen corpses in the far north." Caleb scoffed, "Your Grandfather couldn't keep us down. No matter what challenges he threw at us, we overcame them."

He gave George a sideways glance. "We never could have done it all without Reginald... but your father was the real hero. The things he did, the battles he fought. He was the sort of champion you read about."

George's boyish smile faded along with Caleb's enthusiasm. "Was."

Caleb slowly nodded, looking down at the floor. "We are all doing what we can to help him."

"Even up in a tower, away from the world?" George said slowly, trying his best not to offend. He almost expected Caleb to get mad at him, but the Regent's eyes were calm. Caleb tilted his head as if weighing a decision before shaking it.

"Something on your mind, George?" The change in topic was abrupt, but even George had to admit it was accurate. He hadn't even noticed it, but a stone of unease was still sitting on his stomach. There was something that was on his mind, something that had been on his mind since he had made his secret plans with his friends.

"I know we are supposed to be doing everything we can for my father, but..."

"But?"

George sucked in a breath and met his uncle's gaze, "When does our need to help end and our need to live our own life begin?" He immediately felt regret web across his face and his stomach churned with anxiety.

"Hm..." Caleb pinched his chin and fell into the cushions beside George. The man kicked his boots up onto the low table, summoning a frown from George while Caleb fell into thought. Finally, Uncle Caleb tucked his hands behind his head and gave George a sideways glance as he so often seemed to, "That's a question as old as altruism."

"Altruism?"

"Compassion," Caleb sighed, "and I'm afraid it has a very fuzzy answer that no one can quite agree on."

George turned in his seat to face his uncle, "Well, what do you think?"

Another pause as Caleb thought it over. A small whine formed in his throat as he looked for the right words. Finally, he turned to face his nephew. "It's contextual George, it really is... but." Caleb swallowed. "You're a young man with a life worth living ahead. I'm getting old and my brother is getting older..."

George squinted, not quite following. Caleb clapped his hands onto his knees and cleared his throat. "What you do and everything you've done for your father is noble and you should be proud of it, George. That said, I can't, nor could anyone else, blame you if you indeed want more to your life than helping your aging father. You're young. It would be a shame to see your youth whittled away so soon. If there is a direction or a path or something you want to do, then do it. Wilhelm has a crowd of those who are here for him, myself included, and I know he wouldn't want you to waste away in that crowd without taking a few steps outside to enjoy the Empire we all protect, and to find a life of your own."

George slowly rose to his feet, the stone in his stomach melting in the heat of validation. The prince knitted his brow, just a small pebble of guilt left. He gave Caleb an intense stare. "I love my father."

"I know you do."

"I'd do anything for him."

Caleb nodded. "I know you would."

"But I need to... I need to work on my own things."

"I wouldn't stop you even if I could." Caleb stood up and held out a hand. George clasped it and his uncle's rough fingers tightened around his own in a handshake. The regent smiled at George. "I think that will do it for lessons today. A Stromist needs a balanced mind."

George winced behind a smile, that tiny pebble of guilt knowing he wasn't going to be here tomorrow. Maybe Williams was right, maybe his Uncle would understand if George told him about his dreams and visions. Maybe he would understand the danger George was in, or maybe he wouldn't, and George would be sealed into this fate forever. Even that chance scared George more than not telling his Uncle. Caleb tilted his head, seeming to have caught the grimace growing on the boy's face, but George did his best to force a big smile and his uncle smiled back.

"I'm going to check on Josephine," George made the excuse, eager to leave on a good note and before he slipped up and told his Uncle everything.

Caleb slinked back into the chair by his desk. "Good thinking... I'm hardly close to finishing this chapter."

George was by the exit now, hand on the knob. "You'll have to tell me how that goes."

"You won't have much of a choice." Caleb's eyes were already glued back onto his book. "We'll make a scholar out of you yet."

"Until then." George was slowly closing the door behind him, an absent wave of his uncle's hand dismissing him entirely. The loud clunk of a metal latch sealed the door, the sound matching George's heartbeat. He was one step closer to being gone.

***

George was one of the worst liars he knew, and he knew Williams. With that in mind, he actually did have the intention to check up on Josephine, and not entirely as an excuse. He spent a good ten minutes by her door watching her sleep before he felt uncomfortable. His mind couldn't help but wonder what dreams could possibly cause her to twitch and grumble so much or even why she was afflicted with this strange disease to begin with. He paused, or if even he himself was coming down with it. George had often tried to discuss the topic, but wouldn't ever get too much from Josephine, the princess finding it a sensitive topic. Reginald on the other hand would go into a speech or two, but never quite answer the original question posed. It was times like these that George would try to finagle an answer for himself with a thoughtful walk through the palace halls.

So, that's where he found himself, his feet marching through the halls with half his mind on his great escape, and the other half on his family he would be leaving behind. As his thoughts raced, so did time and before long he had no idea how many minutes or hours flew by. George was sure he was doing a big loop, but after a while he had to stop and wonder exactly where he was.

Scratching the back of his head, George spun in place, trying to make a landmark out of some of the paintings and vases, the suits of armor, and even the very real, very still palace guards. George mused, eyes caught on one of the armored men, the things they must see and hear. The prince shook his head, tipped a polite nod, and continued on. Figuring he had done enough thinking for one day, George simply let his feet lead him further into the palace.

Slowly the prince pieced together where he was, and slowly his feet led him to a part of the palace he often avoided save for the random nights when he couldn't sleep and emotion swam in his head. As George walked, he crept by the usual sights this hall had to offer: the painting of Emperor Frederick, the vase with the naked lady disproportionately etched on, the suit of armor gifted to his great Grandfather, and finally, the red door.

Scuffling to a stop, George faced it, suddenly able to feel his heart in his throat. The door was made out of thick planks of wood, a deep and vibrant red painted onto it and a black handle keeping it closed, just like in his dream. He was told the other side was painted purple, completing the colors of the Jerrovian standard, the old plum-and-wine. Why the prince had to be told was simple: he never had the courage to go beyond the door itself, even before the nightmares started. He took a daring step forward.

George held out a palm, as if he was going to touch the door, but instead, he kept it hovering a few inches away. Gulping, his anxiety swam. If there was a time to finally see the other side, it should be now. He froze and the reality of his escape dawned on him. An ethereal whisper passed under the door and George stood frozen. He was awake, right? Of course he was. Her voice was hissing through the wood, George knew what she wanted. Curling his fingers, he went to turn away, only to nearly bump into his sister.

Josephine's presence made him jump but her fingers tightened around his shoulders to hold him still. "Woah there."

"Josephine!" George backed out of her grasp, a shiver running up his spine, his back pressing against the 'forbidden' door. A silence fell between the two, the door just as quiet, for a while before Josephine opened her mouth to speak, but so did George.

"I—"

"Sorry—"

"You go—"

"George!"

George bit his lips shut and Josephine eyed him carefully before clearing her throat. "What are you doing here?"

"Well, what are *you* doing here?" George retaliated.

"Looking for you." Josephine put her hands on her hips.

"Why would you look here?"

"You always end up here on days you get starry eyed and thoughtful," Josephine said matter-of-factly. "Especially after my... episodes."

George pointed his nose up. "I do not."

"George."

The prince shrugged. "Alright so you got me on that one." Doing his best to ignore the fact he was standing next to one of the most untouchable and gut-wrenching parts of his home, he put on a broken smile. "What do you need?"

"I wanted to talk to you about something Williams told me before dinner." Her voice softened. George grit his teeth.

"*Williams!*"

"Have you—" Josephine pointed at the red door, one eyebrow arched. "Have you ever been in this room?"

Knowing this was likely more to disarm him than change the topic, George craned his neck in thought. "Perhaps."

"You haven't." Josephine folded her finger back, answering for him.

"Yeah, so?" George immediately closed his eyes in regret for giving up that easily. There was a soft clank and the creak of hinges. George stiffened. Josephine was standing with the door wide open, her eyes digging into him.

"Well come on then."

Just like that, the immovable barrier was peeled away. Fear kept George outside the threshold, the whispers of his nightmare grating in his ear. He stood there until his curiosity finally pushed him past the door and onto a set of stone steps after his sister. The ascension was quicker than the one to his uncle's tower, but the shock of actually being past the red door made it slow and his mind soaked it in. The stairwell was bland, plain, all decoration removed, leaving the bare walls to be conquered by dust. George didn't even have the mind to enjoy the bouncing echo present in this place. His body was in a form of shock as he surmounted the final step and took a weak stride into the room above.

The room itself seemed unremarkable if not abandoned. Dust covered everything, creating a grey film over what once was a polished hardwood floor that dominated the center of the room. George knew it used to be a sparring room where his father would practice with his uncle and it definitely looked as such. Weapons lined the walls, all wooden and blunt save for a single sword. It mesmerized George for a moment. Its edge was sharp and sleek, with a white handkerchief tied to the end of its pommel, but before he could take a step closer to examine it, his eyes were forced by his subconscious to dart elsewhere.

On the far side from where he stood, a great window let in copious amounts of light, and a thin wooden door stood between the room and a small balcony that overlooked the gardens. George could see the top of the old elm tree from where he stood. In fact he could smell the gardens as clearly as if he was standing in them down below. In spite of the calm smell of the flowers and sound of the boughs swaying, George felt sick. He could have sworn he saw shadows flicker in his periphery, but his vision was stuck.

"That's it?" George heard himself ask. His finger pointed at the balcony. He didn't remember lifting his hand.

"That's it." Josephine said, a hue of sadness in her voice.

"You saw it?" The prince continued.

"Everything, from below." Josephine's voice grew absent.

"I'm sorry." A teary choke was caught in George's throat, the somber atmosphere of the room growing around him.

"It wasn't your fault." Josephine admitted, though that wasn't what she used to say. Still, hearing it gave George something to cling to in his vortex of thoughts and anxiety. He got caught on his next words, closing his mouth a few times before finally speaking clearly.

"Maybe if Reginald didn't cut me—"

"She was already dead." Josephine turned to her brother and her face contorted as she forced away a sheen in her eyes. She was gritting her teeth. "Reginald did what he had to do." She flourished a hand as if presenting George. "You're here because of him."

Even if she didn't intend it, George felt guilt pressing in his chest. He hung his head in defeat. Josephine seemed to notice, her tone changing to that of a hurt child. "You're all we have left of mom."

Something dawned on George and the realization steeled his gaze and gave him the strength to meet his sister's eye. "Why are you telling me all of this?"

"Because I don't want to lose you, too." A tear dripped out of Josephine's eyes, her composure starting to collapse. George stood in shock. His mind had frozen over at the never-before-seen sight in front of him. He opened and closed his mouth, making tiny babbles as Josephine stared in silence.

"You're not going to lose me," George said slowly.

"Don't lie to me," Josephine wiped a sleeve over her face, "Williams told me you were going away and by the way he was talking about it, it didn't sound like you were just going to the woods for a day or two."

"Williams is dramatic." George took a step back, still in shock at the sight of his sister crying. "He was probably trying to get your attention, it's no secret he has feelings for you."

That got a weak chuckle out of Josephine before she shook her head, "Don't leave me alone with father. Don't leave me alone in this palace."

"I'll be back?" George asked more than he said.

"So, you *are* leaving!?"

"Well, who cares if I am, anyway!" George felt his quick anger swoop in to save himself from further sadness. "It's not like you even interact with dad, that was my job! It always was. I've been his caretaker and overseer since I was barely old enough to not crap in my own pants."

Josephine flinched but George kept barking, years of pent-up frustration releasing. "This is the first time we've talked about this, for real, and only because you think I'm leaving. Not until right now did I see the damned spot, despite living under it my entire life." Josephine went to speak but George cut her off, "do you know what it is like to live a life where you're almost always paired with the crime? I hear the rumors and feel the blame every time a new noble visits or a servant doesn't see me listening."

Josephine was crying freely now, but George pressed on, his growing regret overshadowed by rage. "Now that wouldn't be so damn bad if you at least pulled your weight and endured father's madness, or at least pretended to like the bastard. Do you know how heartbreaking it is to see him cry because he thinks his daughter hates him? He is always telling me you're visiting him, but you never come. It's the same smile broken every damned time. And now, just because I want to leave and catch my breath, just now, you want to talk to me, cry to me, tell me to stay?"

As his anger drained and his sister's face turned more and more red, George felt the growth of regret and guilt return to his belly. Josephine was stuck on her words, gasping, "I—I—"

A final lick of rage pushed George away from her. "Yeah, I'm sure," was all he said before walking over to the wall of weapons. He ripped the blade with the white cloth from its place on the rack, swiped a scabbard and slammed it in. He closed his eyes, forcing away the desire to break down in his own tears. Not being able to turn and look at his sister, he stomped back down the stairs and slammed the red door shut behind him.

Chapter 5
Sleeping on a Guilty Stomach

George couldn't sleep. He was laying on his bed staring up at the vaulted ceiling with a lump of guilt in his stomach and anxiety in his limbs. Of course he was antsy, the great escape was only a few hours away, if that, and he hadn't slept a wink. But it was more than anticipation, he felt bad. He shouldn't have blown up on Josephine like he did. She deserved better for their last conversation in who knows how long. Tear stains were on George's cheeks and his new sword was laying across his chest.

The room was dark, with a pale beam of moonlight keeping it from being utterly black. Even if George could sleep, he wasn't sure he would find rest with the dreams he had been having. This level of exhaustion and worry was perfect ground for his mind to sow doubts. Would leaving the palace really get rid of his visions, would he be safer out there than he was in here? Is he even in danger, or is he going insane like his father? Maybe he should have told his Uncle the truth, or maybe Reginald.

Before he could think on it further, George was scooting closer to the edge of his oversized bed. His friends would hate him for it, save Williams, but maybe he should just tell Uncle Caleb, while he can. His feet tapped the ground and he swiped the shirt he had thrown over the back of a chair. Shrugging it on, he slipped on some simple shoes.

A scraping sound. The light of the moon brightened in the room.

George spun around, his sheathed blade tight in both his hands. The curtains of his window were nearly fully spread now and before his eyes he watched as they continued their journey, slowly scraping against the metal rod. Fear entered George's chest and a shadow formed in front of him. It was tall, very tall, and crowned with horns. Golden eyes as dangerous as the uncovered sun glared from the shadow and George felt his body twitch back to life, his instinct kicking in.

The shadow moved first, a heavy hoof slamming into the ground. George panicked and before he could think on it, he blasted into a sprint and burst through his bedroom door into the hallway. He went to scream, but his eyes locked on the figure of the hallway guards. They were all slumped over, as if asleep. The hallway stretched out in front of him, it was his dream. George felt horror drip down his throat. Voids, it was his dream.

Mighty hooves pounded through the door and George broke into a run. The wall decorations whipped by him as he sprinted and the beast charged behind him. Why were the guards asleep, where was everyone? George ran, feet throbbing with pain and the hallway running out of twists and turns. His mind was going blank and before long he slammed through a set of unguarded doors and stumbled outside into a pocket of flowers tucked by one of the minor courtyards. His eyes widened with recognition.

Two hands came shooting out from the bushes and with a splash of golden light, yanked George behind the shrubs. In the leafy prison, Hector's eyes glittered against the shadow of the night. "You're early," Hector whispered. Franklin squirmed awake from the ground. He was cradling a pair of axes and a bill for pruning trees.

"George?" He yawned.

The prince's eyes were still wide with worry and bounced between the two. Was this luck or coincidence? The heat in his chest couldn't decide, but his fear didn't care. "We have to move! Now!" George commanded.

Franklin blinked. "Wha?" But George kicked up instead of answering and scrambled out of the bush, sword tight to his chest. The other two scurried after him, questions silenced by the anxious atmosphere. George whipped his head around to look behind him as he pumped his legs into a sprint. The dark of the night mingled with the moon, making everything seem like a chasing shadow. He couldn't tell if the horned monster was still there, but he knew he couldn't turn back. Franklin caught up to him and huffed with each bonding breath. He peered at George almost pleadingly, stunned by the fear in George's eyes.

"Williams should be ready to let us in," Franklin managed in harsh whispers between puffs. "The plan is still on?" George could see the worry in his friend's eyes. Instead of answering him, George simply nodded and ran faster.

Together the three cut through the side garden and a manicured grotto until they run up on a wall shrouded by the night. It was clear by the large blocks that it was a part of the defensive wall that spanned the palace hilltop, but what wasn't so obvious was the portcullis gate behind a row of bushes. Adrenaline was still in George as he scrambled to the thick iron bars of the gate.

A set of eyes flashed from behind the bars and sent cold down George's spine. It took him a second for him to realize it was only Williams. The boy pushed the gate open and the other spilled in. George immediately yanked the gate from Williams' hands and closed it firmly before setting the latch and clicking it closed with a metallic thunk.

"No turning back now…" Williams muttered. George flashed a wild look at his friend.

"We are being followed, do you know the path?"

They all peered past Williams and into the dark pit that was the portcullis tunnel. It was an ancient design choice, put in the wall in case the inhabitants of the palace ever needed an expedient and silent escape from besiegers. Of course the Imperial guards control the keys that open it but that was easily solved by Franklin swiping it from his father and returning it before anyone noticed it was missing.

"I explored a little, as asked," Williams responded. Frantic steps echoed from the grotto beyond the bushes and before Williams could explain further, George rushed in. Darkness stole his vision and his feet slapped against stone. He didn't know where he was going, but he had a feeling there was only one way to go. He reached out with his hands and found the wall to follow.

Cold air cut into his lungs and when a bang rattled the iron bars, he hiccuped and sprinted faster. His friends were sprinting loudly next to him, their breath hoarse and their steps quick. Together they made quick work of the winding tunnels and burst out the side of the Imperial hill.

It was a small hole, covered in grass. There was no way anyone would know it was there. It was high up on the mighty hill that dominated the city, putting the boys between the walls behind and the top of the city below.

George stood frozen, eyes looking behind him. The moon hung over the palace, putting it against the night sky as a silhouette. A certain melancholy found George through his earlier panic. He was looking at his home, or maybe what was his home. It wasn't his anymore, that much was clearer tonight than ever. The prince's eyes widened and refocused.

Atop the wall, a single figure stood staring down at them. It was tall and horned. George took a step back, only for Franklin to nudge him. Hector and Williams were already making their way down the hill and into the city.

"Come on," Franklin said. "We can't stay here."

George looked at his friend. Franklin couldn't know how right he was.

***

The creature never caught them, the guards were never called, and no one from the palace was alerted to the plan. As far as George could tell, everyone remained ignorant. All that happened between George storming out of the palace and his rendezvous with the marching army was a nervous approach, shallow smiles as he and his friends assimilated into the rank and file and a near-breakdown as the group passed through the city gates.

Since plate armor needed to be tailored to the wearer, the four friends were stuck with old mail hauberks Franklin had swiped from his father's trunks and stashed in the city below. Hector had smuggled some tabards bearing the plum-and-wine to pull over them, and the group already had various tools that could pass as a weapon in a pinch. George had the sword he took from the room the previous night, Franklin held his bill meant for pruning trees, while Hector and Williams both had old axes.

The group managed to slip into the ranks of the other newly conscripted soldiers easily, with no one batting an eye as they walked into the column of men and women making their way through the city. Of course, most of the marching soldiers had already received their imperial kit (including a breastplate and an open-faced helmet) and as such looked much more the part of soldiers than the four boys and their mismatched outfits. Still, no one seemed to think it was that out of the ordinary. The captain of their particular section simply gave them a deep frown and nothing more.

Marching out of the city was an experience enough for George. He watched the hills of the palace fade away and then give way to the wealthy manors that sat past the palace gates. Complete with smooth bricks and tall columns, clay tiles and spots often seen with bustling servants. That in turn gave way to the various cobble and wood structures that made up the merchant's square and burgher's quarters. Eventually George saw the less than fortunate areas of the city, where houses and outhouses weren't always easy to pick apart and multiple families were crammed into constricting hovels. He wasn't proud of it, especially with the luxury he lived in, or had lived in. Maybe he felt a little guilty that he couldn't spare it more than a single thought, with the rest of his mind focused on escaping whatever had accosted him in the palace halls.

His stomach was already churning again, he had no idea what to expect. Between the unknown assailant and ending his interaction with Josephine still on such a low note, George felt nauseous. He was starting to get sick of that feeling. Closing his eyes, he attempted to fight it and avoided looking back at the city as it fell behind him. The buildings and busy morning roads slowly turned into a cobble paved highway with rich farmlands flanking it.

As if reading George's discomfort, Franklin suddenly smacked him on the shoulder to get his attention. The prince craned his neck and Franklin held out a small ball of crumpled leaves, a ball of the same leaves poking out of his mouth. George raised a brow.

"Chewing leaves from the South," Franklin managed to muffle past the large dose he was currently gnawing on. Making a face, George hesitated, his hand unsure and not quite grabbing it.

"Don't those leaves rot your cheeks?"

Franklin's eyes widened. "Do they?"

Without looking up from his marching feet, Hector answered, "they do, yeah."

Williams slapped the back of Franklin's head, the wad of leaves spitting out with a small, breathy pop. George grimaced as the dampened clump nearly hit a marching soldier and Franklin's sudden shout only deepening the grimace.

"Grace's name, Williams!?" Franklin swatted Williams back, who held up his hands. George lurched to stop them, but a powerful voice came cutting through the scene and froze the friends in their spots.

They weren't sure where the voice originated, but the authority it commanded brought the marching columns to a halt. The more experienced soldiers around them planted themselves still, while the fresh recruits and other vagabonds similar to the friends spun in place, confused.

A great silence overtook the scene. It felt strange, having all these soldiers dressed in links and plates of steel, and yet not much sound coming from them. In fact, the birds that zipped through the late Autumn tree line along the sides of the roads made more sound than the army. George himself was spinning in place. Snapping to look behind him, he was met with the sight of the road stretching backwards into farmland, the spires of the city distant and hazed in blue. He had been marching longer than he thought.

As the silence continued, George continued to watch his surroundings. He flicked his eyes above the northern ridge of the surrounding woods. The mighty Achian mountains peeked high above them. Their immense size made it seem like they were close, but George knew that they were quite a long way away. The Achian mountains was the tallest range in the Empire, rivaled only by the infamous Arctic mountains to the far north.

George's imagination wandered into the mountains as he stared. He remembered the stories Reginald told him about the strange people that lived in its peaks, the aptly named Achians. They were a race of strange men and women with slate grey skin, and coarse, surly bodies. If the rumors were true, they were some of the most formidable people in the empire, capable of withstanding the barren, wind-scarred peaks of the Achians.

He let his eyes trickle back down from the mountains, remembering the stories of the Kafshe, the Achian babies who were abducted by the elusive Paleskins for their strange shamanistic rituals and raised to be wild and powerful masters of natural magics. The empire didn't hold a lot of love for the Kafshe or the Paleskins, the two collectively ignoring or going against Imperial settlements and regulations.

His eyes trickled lower, to the dark spaces below the boughs of the trees. There in that magical void between the plants, his imagination took liberties. Was he really safe now that he was out of the palace, or was he in even more danger? At the very least, his life was finally in his own hands. Fading from his thoughts, George blinked and the area he was staring into blinked back.

A cold froze his chest. Two yellowed eyes stared at George from under the naked branches of a sapling. Blindly swatting behind him, George got Franklin's attention, this time George wasn't going to face the unknown alone. The boy leaned to the side of George, a speck of chewing leaf still clinging to his lip. His face grew wide with surprise.

"Yellow eyes," George whispered, not daring to point.

"I see them." Franklin added, taking a step past George. The eyes seemed to narrow momentarily before disappearing back into the trees. The prince bit his lip in thought, if his life was in his hands, he might as well defend it. Finally, he slapped Franklin in the chest, his other hand smacking Williams'.

"Come on."

With nothing else, George quietly left the still silent column of soldiers. It took all his will to keep himself from running. Strange eyes in the woods, could the answers to his dreams really be this close already? No, that seemed too easy, but then again, who knew? He grit his teeth, he already ran away once.

George was so trapped in his thoughts that as he was pushing through the branches of the undergrowth, he didn't realize he was letting them snap right back into Franklin's face. Eventually, the other boy gave him a swift kick to the ass, extorting a hissing apology. Williams seemed the least excited of the friends, gripping his weapon tightly, while Hector lazily trailed behind.

With another push, George spilled into a tiny glade. Spears of sunlight seeped through the canopy and tiny critters scattered from the scene and into the brush. Standing there with his sword glistening, he felt like a hero in a fairytale, a short reprise from feeling like a victim of fate... until his immersion was soiled by Williams.

"We should be getting back, what if the others begin to march without us?"

"Says the one who didn't even want to be a soldier," Franklin retorted.

"Well, I'm here now, and I'd rather be there than dead in the woods," Williams snapped back

"Shh!" George had his eyes fixed on subtle movements behind a dense shrub that hugged the base of an ancient tree. He tightened his fingers around the grip of his sword, taking precise and careful steps forward. Williams matched his awareness, taking to the left, while Franklin took to George's right and Hector kept the rear flank.

The rustling continued. George's worry began to chip away at his courage. If it was the creature from the palace, could he really contend with it? He chewed his lip as he rounded the shrub—

"Yabbadai!" A gibberish screech oinked from a small, three-foot-tall pig man with rows of bone-crunching, flesh-tearing teeth. George immediately paled and fell backwards as the grotesque creature lunged at him with a crude shard of metal.

"P-Piggut!" He heard Franklin yelp and Williams' boot shot into view. Williams' kick knocked the beast away from George long enough for the boy to get back to his feet. The gardener's son came back in with another kick, this time George saw it connect with the piggut's head. The small beast was launched off its cloven feet and slammed into the tree before crumpling to the ground, whimpering.

"Kill it!" Franklin shouted over to George, but as George held up his blade, he felt a sudden hesitation. His blade stilled, his heart in his throat as he looked down at the now helpless beast. He never took a life before. A numbness went over his fingers, only to be refilled with adrenaline as the gurgled oinks of other pigguts began to sound across the glade.

Turning from the defeated piggut, George found himself and his friends surrounded. Twisted snouts known to eat children as well as each other drooled while small three-fingered hands excitedly gripped tools best for carving flesh. Their crusty, misworn clothes of uneven buttons and stained children's pants only added to the implication of their crimes. Franklin rested his shoulder next to George's, Williams taking the other side, and still Hector at their back.

"There are at least nine," Williams announced. His voice was serious and without the usual nervousness.

"The only way out is through," Hector added.

Hand shaking, George leveled his blade so it was pointing at the piggut in front of him. The piggut jerked and juked, making confusing footwork as it charged him. He heard the other pigguts come crashing down from the glade edge, and doing his best to pretend the sword he held was the comfortable wooden one of the training ring, he thrust his blade where he pictured the Piggut would be next. There was a tug on the edge of his blade as it struck true. Rich red blood came spilling out across the surface of the sword. The animalistic eyes of the piggut filled with panic as they stared directly into George's. He felt a clench in his jaw as he yanked the blade out of the piggut's chest. His arm was fuzzy, like it wasn't his anymore.

George didn't have much time to think about what he did before more pigguts came swarming out of the treeline. In his peripherals he could see Franklin's billhook and William's axe keeping some of the Piggut's at bay and only the Graces knew how Hector was doing. At this rate they were going to be overrun.

Readying his blade, George let his instincts overtake his consciousness as he prepared to chop at the approaching horde.

"On your left!" A deep voice cut through the woods, the sound of metal following. Crashing through the undergrowth of the forests and kicking up droves of fallen leaves came a small squadron of plate and mail encased soldiers, their legs glimmering with magic. They moved with unnatural speed. Two cleared a leap over the entire fight with a single bound. George recognized the purple and red capes as well as the golden falcon pins on their chests. They were the Stromist Vanguard.

In a matter of moments, the pigguts who had surrounded the friends were in turn surrounded. The veteran soldiers and masters of Stromist magic made quick work of the pigguts. Their weapons struck cleanly and precisely against the now clumsily retreating beasts. The horror of the cannibal creatures was reduced to a grisly comedy as George watched them fall like wheat to a scythe.

George was pulled from his frozen thoughts when one of the soldiers approached him. The prince noticed the golden elm leaf badge hammered to his breastplate and immediately knew he was looking at a commander. The other badges riddled alongside the leaf only further explained his decoration. The man himself looked much older despite likely being only a decade or two older than George. His aged face could be explained by the deep cynicism etched deep in his frown. Beyond that, the Commander was oddly clean shaven for a soldier and had the complexion of a man born from both the lighter skinned north and the darker skinned south, causing his dark brown eyes to almost pop as they studied George angrily.

"What are you all doing here? Why aren't you with the column?" The words came out quick, stuffed in a second, with the energy of battle still in the Commander's voice. Before George or the others could answer, the Commander waved his sword at them. "You *are* soldiers?"

The friends look among each other, not realizing the gravity of the question or the threshold this query opened. George was the first to answer, realizing that for once he wasn't called a prince. "I am."

"As am I," Franklin said shortly after, a puff in his chest. Hector nodded along and Williams sighed.

"We are."

The captain flickered his eyes among the misfits, his frown deepening. "Then get the void back into line!"

George and his friends deflated as the man continued to bark at them, all sense of achievement quickly evaporating. "The column stops, you stop! The column marches, you march! All the way to Fort Torskyla, got it!?"

"Y-yes." George felt meeker than he'd like to admit, but the Commander didn't seem to stop there.

"And get yourself a kit as soon as possible. You all look like something a blacksmith would shit after mistaking scrap for dinner." The Commander slammed his sword back into its scabbard. "And for the Glory of our Emperor say 'Yes, Commander Darius.' You sound like fools blubbering out your weak affirmations. Got it?"

"Yes, Commander Darius." The friends all pounded a fist to their chest. Williams pushed a step forward with an apologetic look on his face.

"We're s—"

"I don't give a rat's ass who you are." Commander Darius nudged his chin in the direction of the road. "You're in the army now, let's move."

George skipped over a branch, the curling feeling of getting caught red handed still squirming inside him. "Commander Darius, Sir?" There was no answer. "Isn't Fort Torskyla deep in the North?"

"Yep." The Commander let loose a springing branch, George just managing to duck underneath it in time. He emerged with another question.

"Will there be any stops before that?"

"You ask a lot of questions, boy." Darius didn't even bother to look in George's direction, "You a spy?"

"What?" George yelped, "no!"

In complete honesty, George knew the Commander was messing with him, but he couldn't help but feel patronized enough to react. Williams gave George a headshake, as if advising him to drop whatever comes next.

Giving George a sideways glance, the Commander didn't stop his trek back to the road. "Right... I know." Darius turned briefly to take a long look at the group of boys, "I already know who you are."

They all flinched, eyes wide with a sudden dawn of fear. Hector spoke first, his quiet skepticism breaking the tension, "You do?"

"I thought you said you didn't give a rat—" Franklin's muttering was cut off by the Commander. Darius pushed his face right into Franklin's.

"I'd wager you're one of two things. Either vagabond orphans hoping for free food and a place to sleep in exchange for a quick desertion." Darius looked away from Franklin and stared directly at the prince. "Or runaways."

George felt a pang in his chest and he had hoped it didn't reflect on his face but the twisting smile of the Commander told him otherwise. Darius slowly nodded, confident. "Oh yeah, I've met your kind. Most of you break, really quick." His boot snapped a twig, "notice I didn't ask for your names, or who you were before you walked into this wood? It's because that person is dead."

Reality began to dawn on George as the Commander continued his speech. "...And either this person." Darius shoved a finger into Franklin's puffed-up chest, pushing him back down, "...will be dead before I learn their new name, or you'll live long enough to be able to actually call yourself soldiers."

Standing with their mouths gaping, the friends were unsure of what to say. Darius' hard stare was broken as he snorted, "that or you'll apparently turn into a bunch of overgrown trout." He slapped George's back with the flat of his sheathed blade. "Get your asses back in line."

It was only a small step over some underbrush and the friends were back on the road, walking towards the still silent column of soldiers. They found their spots without issue, eyes glued to the ground. George found himself chewing over Darius' words over and over, each time making his final argument with his sister seem all the more final. He could only begin to wonder exactly when the rest of his life would seem as distant as that conversation, and if that was what he truly wanted. He knew he had to leave the capital, though, to go far away until he could make sense of everything, or at least grow strong enough to face his shadowy enemies, and he knew this was how he was going to do it.

George's fingers gripped the hilt of his sword and he looked over at Williams, the gardener's boy giving him a firm nod, the kind he always gave before giving in to one of George's stupid ideas. The prince gave him a smile, then turned to Hector who seemed to be reading the situation, answering it with a grin of his own. The trio turned to Franklin, who was biting his lip.

"Regrets?" Williams asked.

"Yeah, that I didn't knock his ass out." Franklin threw a fist into his palm before cracking a grin.

"Your ego is ever taller than your own height," George slapped his friends back, knocking him forward a step just in time for the other soldiers to start marching again.

"No turning back, now." Williams looked at his friends before joining the march.

"Only way out is through," Hector added, receiving a chorus of agreeing grunts.

Chapter 6
A Chill in the Air

Despite the action-packed start to their journey, the following days fell to a dull monotony. They were spent on increasingly less and less sophisticated roads, and the nights were spent in hastily built camps that were never quite good enough for Commander Darius. The orange burn of Autumn had deteriorated to a dull brown, and the mornings brought coatings of frost. The experienced soldiers escorting the recruits would constantly remind them that this was the second worst time of the year to march, the first worst being when winter truly reared its head.

The convoy had skirted to the west of the Achian mountains in an attempt to stay on relatively flat ground, and as such George found himself in the hilly grasslands that populated the valleys. To get here he had to march through the dense forest which stretched directly west of the Imperial capital. He had always heard stories of dark practitioners and bizarre monsters that dwelled near its heart, but during his brief stay with the army there, he didn't see much other than trees, but then again, he did stick to the Imperial roads and checkpoints.

A small, childish part of him was disappointed when the sunny hills overtook the deep woods, especially since no real stories came from his encounter with the legendary Imperial forest. Williams in his good intent reminded him that they were likely to get more stories than they bargained for anyway and to simply enjoy the quiet for now. It was at the tail end of that conversation where

George found himself. He had a bowl of hot stew in his hands and up above the sun was disappearing from a pink evening sky.

All around him soldiers were resting from setting up the short wooden palisade and endless tents, George included. The tips of his fingers were bright red from the chill of the air and from the strain of pounding stakes with a poorly-wrapped hammer. A small pain pricked his fingers while they warmed up on the sides of the wooden bowl. He grimaced at what could only be old meat or perhaps fibrous vegetables as he sipped at his meal. Looking up, he caught Williams looking at him and waiting for a response.

Shifting on the log he was sitting on, George made a face. "I won't get stronger in silence. I ran away once, but I'm not going to stay the victim. " The warnings of his nightmare were fresh on his mind. The sudden absence of the dreams since he had fled the capital was not lost on him, nor on his anxiety. "I think I'm safe," George rolled his jaw in thought. "But I don't know how long that'll last." His eyes wandered over to his blade.

"You also won't get stronger by throwing your life away," Williams reminded.

George frowned, knowing Williams was right. Opting for an agreeing nod, George put his empty bowl down into the dirt beside him and picked up a stray stick. He began to push the soil around, flakes of quartz catching the glow of the evening campfires up until his stick snagged on the grooves of old, buried stonework. He would have jumped with curiosity if he wasn't half expecting it. Ruins were quite common in the Imperial Province, even this close to its northern border with the province of Caldora. Often, rumors would rise up about Dweller-worshiping Nachtists taking refuge in old excavated areas, but George wasn't sure how true it was. He always had a hard time believing practicing Nachtists could be so close to the Imperial City.

"You." Darius' voice came flooding over the scene. He showed no signs of work or strain despite the long day. His finger stabbed towards George, the prince sticking a thumb in his own chest.

"Me?"

"Yes, you." Darius didn't move from his spot. "Take your scrawny friend and head into the field with the Quartermaster's crew and fetch some rabbits."

George opened his mouth but closed it, opting for a soldier's nod, or at least the best one he could muster from mimicry. It didn't matter much, since Darius had already turned his attention to a bowl of food. Frowning, George plucked at Williams' collar. "Let's get going, then."

***

Williams and George made their way through the camp and down to the telltale black tent of the quartermaster. Outside, a boy maybe a few years older was standing, his chin fuzzed with the beginnings of beards. Next to him was a girl maybe an inch taller with almost white blonde hair and the remains of a laugh on her face. They both wore the black tunics that were iconic for the members of the support auxiliary, a massive branch of the military that kept things running smoothly.

"Hey," the girl called out as George and Williams approached, "are you the Commander's boys?"

George bit his tongue on the word boy, hoping for a little more recognition as a real soldier but nodded. "Yeah. I'm George and that's Williams."

"Williams?" The boy frowned, "isn't that a surname?"

"It is." Williams flinched. A small grin formed on George's face, knowing where this was going.

"Well, what's your first name?"

"Doesn't matter much. Don't we have a task?" Williams changed the subject.

"Right," the girl took a step forward, "I'm Baldra, that's Lawrence. So, um, let's catch some food, yeah?"

With little else, Baldra plucked a pair of small hunting bows that were leaning against the tent and handed them to George and Williams. George plucked the string between his fingers before taking a small quiver from Lawrence.

"Ever hunted before?" Baldra asked.

"With my uncle." George nodded before looking at Williams.

"No, but I can use a bow," Williams answered.

"Good enough." Lawrence nudged his chin towards where the rolling hills met the ever-stretching forest. "I thought I saw a few rabbits running about when we first came up through, figure that's a good place to start."

Through the camp and down the hill they went in utter silence. George wished he had given the pair a fake name but at the same time he knew his name was common enough, especially since people tended to name their babies after royal ones, himself included. He looked over at Williams who looked back and for a second George thought they were thinking the same exact thing.

"You know I once caught ten rabbits in one day." Baldra broke the silence.

"Is that a lot?" Williams asked.

The silence came back. After a second Baldra cleared her throat. "Ye-yeah!" She looked over at Lawrence, who shrugged.

"It was my only time out and my brother helped," Baldra admitted after a moment, "but everyone seemed impressed, and ten seems like a big number. Well, George you hunt, what do you think?"

"I—" George pinched his chin. "I mean yeah, that's a lot."

"You don't sound very confident." Baldra frowned.

All eyes dug into George, the prince shrugging with an unearned confidence. "Well, I never hunted rabbits."

There was a pause.

"Shit." Lawrence swore.

"What?" Williams looked up from his feet, the hill growing steep and the shadows of the forest stretching their way.

"That means none of us have." Lawrence sighed with frustration.

"Well, I have—" Baldra began.

"Once! With your brother doing most of the work," Lawrence reminded her.

"See a rabbit, shoot it... it can't be that hard," George suggested. He was met with a round of grunts. George rolled his eyes and stopped, making a show out of his point. "They *are* just rabbits."

"You shouldn't underestimate things." Lawrence wagged a finger.

"That is true." Williams nodded.

"BUT they are just rabbits," Baldra backed George.

"And Ai was just a horse." Lawrence tilted his head, letting the old proverb speak for itself. George slapped his sides at the mention of the proverb and continued his walk.

"Ai was IAO's horse, not *just* a horse."

"Yeah, he had all that magic." Baldra pushed Lawrence's shoulder. "Ya thinking, we gonna bump into a magic bunny?"

"Imbued with Stromism?" George added, getting a small laugh out of Williams.

"Maybe!" Lawrence snapped desperately, a grin curling the side of his mouth. "First sight of a rabbit marked red like Ai and I'm out of here."

"And I'll be right behind you," George snickered.

"Hey! Psh, sh!" Williams sputtered, forcing the group to a halt. Without the sound of the grass swishing against their boots, the hill turned into a stunning quiet. The only noise was the ambient clatter of the camp in the distance and the quiet chirp of evening crickets.

"What is it?" Lawrence ducked close to Williams.

"Is it the magic rabbit?" George poked his head over Williams' shoulder, a stupid smile on his face.

"I think so," Williams said but quickly corrected himself, "I mean, a regular rabbit." His eyes narrowed in on a thicket of vegetation by the forest's edge. Baldra followed the line of sight and nodded.

"I'll get em." She trudged a few steps before Lawrence grabbed her shoulder.

"Not walking like that you aren't," Lawrence hissed, "We gotta go in slow and quiet-like."

"Just follow me and fan out," George cut in. Lawrence wrinkled his nose but ultimately the group decided to just follow the advice. Crouching down so that the grass brushed against the hems of their shirts, the group strung arrows to their bows, but anticipation kept their grips shaking.

There was a tiny sound coming from the woods, as if something had rubbed up against a branch until it snapped. The group turned their attention that way, peering into the gaps between the leaves. George made a face as he thought about the situation, how could a rabbit snap a branch—

All at once the group saw two brilliant eyes staring at them from the darkness, curving horns adorning the massive beast's head. The group didn't get any more details before a horrible, shaking adrenaline spun their bodies around in fear, sending their legs into a full sprint. Only George stood his ground. His hand fell to his sword but before he could tug at it, a freezing fear washed over him and the shadow of the creature darkened his view. He wasn't ready. Swearing, George turned and ran.

George's lungs burned from the sudden intake of chilled air as he pumped his legs back up the hill. The hair on the back of his neck was on end and he could feel his heart pounding in his chest along with shame. He pushed his stride further and caught up to Williams, the boy unaware that George was ever missing.

Williams' foot slipped under a root and he jerked forward. George's hand caught his collar and pulled him up as the two stumbled back into a run. A chilling wind breathed over the back of their necks and George senses refused to look behind him, be it fright or frustration. Finally, the first of the camp's watchmen called out to the running boys. It was more of a grunt than a word, less of a shout and more of a yelp of surprise.

"Beast!" Lawrence shouted back.

"Beast!" Baldra echoed.

"*Failure,*" was all George could think.

It didn't take long for the shouts to multiply. Soldiers began to form around the perimeter of the camp with various accusations flying around as to why. Ambushes, raids, and sometimes beasts were all tossed around as the recruits armed themselves and the seasoned escorts frowned. By the time George and his friends were crossing the perimeter of the makeshift palisade, Commander Darius was waiting with the true soldiers of the empire standing at his flanks. A sour look dominated his face.

"B—" Baldra started.

"There's nothing behind you." Darius nudged his chin to point behind the group.

George whipped around to see the empty hills, the twilight catching on its otherwise green grass. He furrowed his brow, desperately searching for the glinting eyes of the monster, some sign that he made the right choice to run once again.

"You four, my tent," Darius commanded before signing an unknown gesture at the soldiers beside him, the closest nodding before they all fanned out past George.

***

Darius' tent was exactly what George expected. The white sheets were immaculate, with not a speck of dirt on them, which in itself was a wonder considering the dirty work all the soldiers had just gone through digging the defenses for the night. The rest of the tent was spacious, with little personal effects and a severe lack of any decoration. There was just a cot in the corner, a plain leather-bound trunk, a currently bare armor-stand and one rickety table with a set of three chairs.

"Sit." The command came without it being clear who of the group was supposed to be sitting. The Commander himself took a lone seat facing the others, his gaze impatient. The group hesitated but eventually Baldra awkwardly plopped into one of the chairs. Williams hesitated before taking the other chair, giving George a look. The prince shook his head so slightly he wasn't sure if Williams would even register it.

Darius clasped his hands over the table. "Report."

"Are we in trouble?" Lawrence blurted.

"No. Report." Darius frowned.

"It feels like we *are* in trouble," George insisted. Darius gave the prince a hard stare, forcing the boy to avert his eyes.

"We saw a beast, sir," Williams answered the captain.

"Explain."

"Well, it's hard to put it into words," Lawrence started, "We, or at least *I*, didn't see much of it."

"All I saw was horns and sinister eyes," George reported. He couldn't meet the Commander's gaze. It felt weird admitting the horned beast was real.

"How many?"

"Just the one," Baldra answered for the group, "Well two eyes and two horns but just one—"

"I get it." Darius waved a hand before falling into a silent thought.

"It was the wild prophet," Baldra spoke up. All eyes fell on her, the Commander's in particular narrowing. Williams chewed his lip and looked over at George, who did his best to keep a straight face.

Darius folded his hands and leaned forward. "The wild prophet?"

"I saw his face." Baldra shivered, "the face of a bull, but with the emotions and structure of a man."

Kicking his chair out from under him, Darius stood up, "Is that your final report, or do you wish to revise your story?"

Baldra gulped, "It matched the descriptions of the stories."

"It's not like we all don't know the Wild Prophet is real," Lawrence defended Baldra, "the entire royal court saw him the day of the princess' birth."

"And we all know what happened to her," Baldra continued, a cringe forming in George's gut. Of course it occurred to him that his shadowy hunter could be the horned prophet, but to hear someone else claim it was surreal, as if his entire situation was becoming more of a reality than it ever was.

"Oh, I'm very aware of the stories and attributes given to the wild prophet," Darius finally spoke up, "the bad omen... responsible for the princess' disease, the unfortunate birth of the prince, and an assortment of other unlucky events. Not to mention the dispenser of wonderful riddles to baffle the simple minded."

Darius put his palms flat on the table and leaned in towards the group, "It's all horse shit, and the last thing a detachment of new recruits needs is the idea that a bad omen is lingering over our heads on their way to war. Sure, maybe you saw the one and the same creature from the stories, but even if you did, we don't need to send superstition across this camp. Is that understood?"

"Understood," George was the first to agree, there was no reason to agitate the situation, and next time, George swore, he would be ready. His brow furrowed, it had to be true if he swore it. Off to the side, Williams offered a silent nod, with Lawrence shortly after. The last holdout was Baldra, who remained in a tense look of contemplation. Her and Darius shared a long look before the auxiliary finally nodded.

"Good." Darius stood straight up and folded his elbows square behind him, "return to your posts." The four saluted before backing out of the tent.

Immediately an evening breeze washed over them. There was a chill in the air that the thick cover of the tent had muffled, but now that they were out in the open, it came biting back. George tugged at his tunic, wishing he brought his cloak with him and scrunched his nose at his own absentmindedness, but was quickly pulled from his shame and to Baldra's whispered rambling.

"We're screwed," the girl muttered.

Not wanting to engage her in conversation, George tilted his eyes upwards to the dusky purple sky. Content with the distraction, he went in search of some of the early night stars Reginald had often schooled him on, but his mind wandered to his oath, an oath to be ready and to be stronger. He was shamed twice now, a runaway doubled. A palm slapped his shoulder.

"Screwed!" Baldra shook George's arm.

"Yes, I get it!" George hissed back, his frustration easily released at the girl.

Baldra made a face. "No need to bite the messenger."

Tension swirled between the two before George relaxed his shoulders and blew a sigh. "I'm sorry," George started.

"No time to be sorry," Baldra interrupted, ignorant of the mood, "the omen works quick, what—" she paused to count in her head "—within weeks of the wild prophet showing up both the princess and the empress were sick with scarlet fever, set to die. I'd say we have about a month before things go sour."

"Enough of that." Williams said. "You know that's how these things work, if you focus on it so much it becomes true, rather than the other way around."

"I don't know." Lawrence was wide eyed in thought. "What about the strange sayings of the prophet? He did predict the empress' death."

"What?" George felt a pang in his chest. "How?"

"Well, he said that weird stuff at princess Josephine's birth," Baldra pointed out.

"Yea, er..." Lawrence thought for a moment, "The first will open the door and the second will push them through. Next thing you know, the Empress was falling from a balcony to her untimely death."

"Three years later you mean!" George felt his stomach tighten. "Also, I'm pretty sure the saying was 'the second will lead them through.'"

"Well yeah," Baldra pushed back, "the first, like they mean Princess Josephine, will open the door, the door to the balcony, and the second will push them through, Prince George. He was born after the fall."

"Josephine was nowhere near the balcony." George was more irritated than he expected, as if he was defending himself.

Without thinking, his voice turned to a growl. "And it's 'lead them through.'" He could hear the woman from his dream's voice in his head now, the shriek playing over and over.

Baldra flinched. "Geez alright, no need to get so worked up."

"Still weird they both survived scarlet fever." Lawrence stirred the pot, hinting at the many rumors surrounding Wilhelm and how he could have possibly saved his bride and baby.

Baldra grew contemplative. "Do you really think he signed a deal with the Dweller?"

"Guys!" Williams cut in before George could even register what Baldra had said.

George's eyes snapped to Williams' finger, which was pointing into the distance. The orange glow of torches cut through the growing dusk, illuminating a morbid sight. A sad procession of wounded men, children, women and soldiers was making their way south towards the camp. The prince felt the worries of his past fade away as the stark present made itself known.

Even at this distance he could make out the mutilation of the victims. Limbs missing, eyes gouged, dark bruises ringing people's heads. Clothes were in tatters and faces were blank. The reality was in front of him, and he could feel a justice fester within him.

"Damn the rebel bastards," Baldra said for the group.

"They'll get theirs," George agreed softly. A spark of guilt was in his gut now, guilt over using the life of a soldier to solve his problems, to get stronger. He chewed his cheek, eyes intent on the wounded, but what if he used that strength to save more than himself, could he be guilty then?

A new voice cut in. "Not even sure why they thought they could hold a light to the power of the Empire, eh?" George turned to the face of Franklin, Hector right behind. George smiled at his friends, the distraction welcome, only to find it fading as Lawrence spoke next.

"Some say they didn't have much of a choice, what with Gavaria eating up their farmland."

"Nah, that was Gavaria's land first," Franklin dismissed the concern, "besides, you can hardly expect a peaceful resolution when they are in coalition with giants and warlords. If one Vagrant king or queen had an issue with Gavaria, why bring in the giants at all unless you're looking for a bloody fight?"

"I don't know." Lawrence rubbed his chin. "Seems to me like they were pushed to it."

Baldra put on a proud face, "I heard that the giants worship some even bigger giant hidden in the mountains called the titan and that the titan picks giants to speak for them and that this 'Titanspoke' convinced the giants to help the Vagrants before they even asked!"

George pinched his chin and looked at Williams, "What do you think?"

Williams wiggled his nose in thought. "I don't know."

"Hm." George looked down at his feet, brow laid heavy in thought. If he was going to do this and enter this war, he was going to do it right, and not blind, just like his Uncle would. After a moment of silence, George looked back up at his friends, eager to say something helpful. "Well, we still have a duty to do, no?" He waved a hand at the macabre parade in front of the camp, "for these people, for the Empire, for the emperor." He indeed sounded like his Uncle.

Baldra nodded, "For the plum-and-wine."

Chapter 7

Prince in a Haystack

There were no more talks about wild prophets or old royal rumors. The stories that haunted George began to fade into a certain grey tucked in the back of his mind as the recruits marched ever closer to the frontlines. In fact, as the rolling hills gave way to arboreal forests and dense conifers, talk became rare altogether. Each recruit seemed to fall into a contemplative silence while the veterans kept a stern professionalism that seemed to include an unspoken rule against discussing stories of war and battle, not that George didn't attempt to pry at first.

Even with the winter approaching quickly and the mornings dusted with early-day frost and snow, George felt a hot fire in his chest. Every step put him closer to gaining the strength he needed. His days marching were spent alongside his friends from home with the occasional visit from Lawrence and Baldra, although they were mostly cloistered along with the other auxiliary support staff. George's nights were spent on his back, with his arms and legs sorely overworked by Darius' endless tasks. As exhausted as he was, his mind remained overtaken by anticipation for what was to come, sleep coming hard through his anxious excitement in spite of his aching body. The more he picked people's minds about the cause of the war, the more he realized he needed to be there to understand it. He needed to understand it.

"George," Williams piped up one night. "I was thinking, if it is the horned prophet, why not tell your uncle? We don't have to go to war."

"Even if he believed me, the horned shadow is only one half of what's haunting me," George answered quickly, his mind made up. "If I let him fight my battles for me, I'll never be safe, I'll always be in the dark. Besides, I still don't know what to do about the lady at the door." Williams seemed to accept that answer, as that was the last night he brought it up.

The final day of marching arrived quicker than George had expected and as the march drew to a close, he found himself wrapped in the colorless grey cloaks of the common soldier. Matching his cloak, he wore wrappings for gloves, a healthy powder of white snow on top of his dark-haired head, and a contemplative look on his face.

The trees of the north spread thin, giving way to a snow ridden field. An unremarkable stone fortress sat at the center atop a great mound of earth, the whole thing blasted white by snow. A whipping wind was picking up as the column of recruits made their way to the mighty gates of Fort Torskyla. George could only assume a blizzard was rolling in from the distant arctic mountains that even now painted the horizon blue past the fort, peaking above the tree line.

Fort Torskyla's gates screamed and groaned as they were forced open by a group of ten soldiers, pulling George from a reverie. His own icy eyes flickered around as if to soak up all the sights as he took his first few steps into the fortress. The soldiers inside contrasted the veterans who escorted him and his fellow recruits. They were loud, less formal, and laughing. Most of them seemed to have altered their issued kits of armor, be it with local iconography painted on the metal plates, or even fur linings and simple bits of graffiti. Most stopped whatever they were doing, be it drinking or working, to sneer and ogle at the procession of recruits.

Past the onlookers, George's vision sank through the many open doors and windows of the various wood and stone buildings that clustered the fort haphazardly. As he blinked falling snowflakes away from his eyes, he accidentally made direct contact with a desperate looking man laid out on his back in one of the buildings. A white-cloaked doctor stood above him with both hands wrapped around an arrow sticking out of the patient's side, a bloody plate of cruel barb-headed arrows on a table nearby.

It didn't take long for George's attention to be yanked once again as the column of recruits came to a sudden stop. They had marched right into the center courtyard of the fortress, where a massive keep that was just one big bastion stood. On the steps leading up to the weather battered doors was a man just as squat as the structure.

He was in full Imperial regalia, minus any sort of headgear, giving George a clear view of his bald head and twirling mustache. Even though his mustache was as white as the snow falling from the sky, George could tell it used to be a brilliant blond and the rest of the man's complexion matched that of a Gavarian. Next to him stood a woman of equal importance, a black tunic tied tight over her armor, and scowl lines tattooed on her face. Her hair was wavy and grey, and her eyes a sharp hazel.

Darius stood at the fore of the column of recruits, his veterans filing behind him as he saluted. "General Jonsberg. Dame Honora."

Darius' salute was met by the clanking sound of the soldiers behind him mimicking the act. The recruits clumsily followed suit. George included.

"What is this mess?" The General blubbered, waving a hand over the recruits, "Is this really the best they could send me?" Before Darius could answer, the General continued his rambling, brows jumping and mustache wiggling with each accusation. "The war has barely begun, I highly doubt we need to resort to the bottom barrel just yet."

"Sir..." Darius began, the usual brick-wall in his tone broken down much to George's amusement.

"Ack, damn it all anyway. Quick war ahead of us." Jonsberg blew air through his mustache. "Whatever that entails."

There was a pause before Darius tilted his head in submission. Jonsberg cleared his throat. "Well let's get this over with. Present."

Darius pivoted on his heel to face the recruits. "Present weapons!"

Clumsily, the recruits fumbled their mismatching weapons out from belt loops, sheaths, scabbards, or simply just held up the thing they were currently holding. Immediately the General alongside Dame Honora and some other trusted personnel dove into the column. Inspecting each weapon, the General and his soldiers carried out an age-old tradition where new recruits offered their weapon in oath to the Empire. Normally what was offered was never taken and instead replaced with an Imperial forged weapon that fit the standardization of the army kits, but with the current iron shortage in the North, the more suitable weapons were never replaced.

Amid a sea of farm tools and the weapons of tradesmen, George unsheathed his fine blade from its scabbard and held it horizontal in both palms. The white handkerchief tied to the pommel draped over his wrist and its silver embroidery sparkled against the white sky more than the prince had wished. Before George could alleviate the situation, his desire to quickly rip the cloth off was interrupted by the sound of scuffling boots.

Looking up from his blade, a snowflake caught George's eye, putting him into a wince. Through his blurred vision he caught the gaze of the General, who happened to be the same height as the boy. The two stared at each other for what felt like an uncomfortable amount of time, the courtyard deathly silent or at least that's how George was perceiving it. The prince's ears were tuned in and waiting for the General to speak, to say anything.

Jonsberg's eyes flickered from George's face and down to his blade. George slowly went to move his fingers over the cloth, but Jonsberg's hand shot up to wipe George's away. Jonsberg pinched the cloth and looked back up at George, tugging on the ornament just hard enough for George to know that the General was still holding it.

"Where did you get this weapon?"

"My father." George was never much for lying, but it was close enough to the truth.

"Anybody I'd know?" The General let go of the cloth.

George pursed his lips, mind racing with all the possible ways this conversation could go. Before he could formulate an answer to fit his morals as well as his undercover plans, Jonsberg seemed to offer him a way out.

"Did he fight in Emperor Frederick's Northern Campaign?"

"How'd you know?" George winced, wishing he had asked a different question.

Jonsberg stood up straight and flicked the cloth one more time before sucking in a deep breath. "If the prince could please step out of formation."

George shrunk in his spot, his friends' eyes widening as they looked over at him. Sputtering George went to protest but the General cut him off.

"I will send correspondence to the Regent."

Stomach tight, George stepped out of formation. The eyes of his fellow recruits dug into his back as he stood off to the side. Almost immediately two soldiers winged him as if they were his escort all along, and at that moment George swore he could hear the whispers starting and his face turning red. In an attempt to look away, he accidentally caught the gaze of Darius, the Commander's stare harder than usual. Out of options, George hung his head to look down at his muddied boots, white snow sticking up to his shins.

***

After that, George was subjected to a long wait while everyone's weapons were checked. His friends were too far away for him to listen in on how they fared, the prince himself only daring to look up at them now and again, embarrassment plastered on his face. By time the recruits were checked and sent off to different areas of the fortress, the blizzard had settled in on a howling wind and George was quickly cloistered away into the main keep.

The thick wooden door to Jonsberg's office slammed closed and the next thing George knew, he was standing alone. Stone walls paneled over with dark wooden planks surrounded him, the oily finish reflecting the light of a roaring fire that was nestled deep in a blackened hearth. George's fingers immediately trembled and the heat of the room awakened his numbed digits and turned the snow clinging to his body into little droplets that puddled on the floor. Soaked, sad, and defeated, George let out a large sigh. The door swung open in the middle of his exhale, causing the prince to jump as he cut his sigh short into an accidental hiccup of surprise.

"Prince George." Jonsberg walked through the doorway, waddling over to a desk that seemed a tad too tall for the General.

"General Jonsberg." George tilted his head out of respect.

Slapping two palms on the surface of his desk, Jonsberg gave a wide smile. "You chose a strange time to make your way this far north, my prince."

"I want to fight." George stood up straight. He was finally in the North, there was no way he was going to back down now.

"I can't in good conscience let you do that." Jonsberg's smile faded.

"Why?" George narrowed his eyes, putting forth that stubborn stare he often found himself wearing during long debates with Reginald.

"Besides your age?" Jonsberg stroked his mustache, "Well let's just say I knew your mother." He pointed at George. "You look an awful lot like her, you know." There was a pause as the General contemplated his next words, "I also know your father, or at least I did, very well." He nudged his chin at George's sword. "Do you know the name of that sword?"

George frowned and looked down at the blade, completely unaware it even had a name. "No?"

"Oathkith." Jonsberg nodded, "I was there when your father tied your mother's token to the pommel and swore to come home, naming it his way to keep his oath." Jonsberg continued to play with his mustache. "I remember the hate your father held for the war, for war in general. He was good at it but he despised it, only doing it to keep himself alive long enough to see your mother once again. I know from his own words that he never wanted any of his children to experience the pains of battle and the scars it leaves long after."

Jonsberg hopped out of his chair and stood as tall as he could. "Consider you holding Oathkith a sign, as I keep a silent oath of friendship to your father and say that I am denying your deployment to the frontlines."

George opened his mouth but closed it, his fists clenching and unclenching. He wanted to yell, he wanted to explain he had just walked for weeks while the sky turned a bitter cold and his feet froze through. He wanted to mention the pains and will it had taken just to leave home, to sneak away. How being so close to what he wanted and being denied felt like a terrible blow... but he didn't, he couldn't. Jonsberg studied the boy's face, as if reading these thoughts.

"It will take a month or more for correspondence with your uncle to make its way to him and back, especially with Winter starting to bite into our hides," The General mentioned idly, "Until then, I am placing you in the support auxiliary here in the fortress. Maybe seeing the soldiers come and go will settle your spirit."

A spark of hope relit itself in George, his face clearing and fists relaxing. "Thank you, sir!"

"I don't think you should thank me at all, Prince George." Jonsberg slanted a face. "I hope by time your uncle's response comes that you'll be ready to return home." With nothing more, the

General waved a dismissing hand. "Follow the black tunics until you find Dame Honora. Auxiliary dismissed."

George slipped out of the office, nearly running. The fear of the General changing his mind mingled with the excitement of his first task as an official member of the army. Closing the door behind him, George leaned against it and took in a breath to calm his pounding heart. This was it, the true start of his journey and the beginning of the end of being the second born victim. A determined look spread across his face and the warnings and stories of the General fell into the back of his mind. He glanced down at the hilt of Oathkith and silently made his own oath, he would return to the Imperial Palace as a soldier, one who would never need to run away again.

Chapter 8
Happy Birthday

Caleb's letter came alongside one of the fiercest winter storms the North had endured in decades. It was so harsh that the lone messenger was forced to stay at the fort until nearly the spring. The snow even snuffed out most of the hostilities of the war, but none of this mattered much to George at the time. The letter was the regent's permission for the prince to remain at the fort as a member of the auxiliary.

George's excitement was quickly tempered by the monotony of life at the fort. Dame Honora was a tough and noble lady, but one who wanted as little to do with George as possible as she apparently harbored an old grudge (or perhaps cautionary fear) towards his powerful Cousin Isabella. As such, the task of mentoring the prince fell to a ragged old blacksmith known simply as Rick.

The man had George up with the sun to count inventory, even on days George simply knew it hadn't changed since the previous night, then he would run down to the quartermaster to check for orders and any incoming shipments of iron or other materials. Next came the usual sprinting about the fortress like a madman trying to do all the inane tasks Rick always seemed to conjure, regardless of how many George managed to complete. At some point George realized trying to do them all so quickly only gave him more to do, and as such he succumbed to the grey life of the fortress, taking only one at a time and shoving any frustration garnered just below the surface.

One shred of relief was that George wasn't alone in this life, with Williams being the only one of his friends not to be sent directly to the front lines. George learned later that this was Williams' own doing, having delivered a secret plea to Jonsberg to personally remain in service of the prince. So, in the later of the day, George always tried his best to meet up with Williams (who had been taken under the wing of the local chefs) and even made friends with other members of the culinary branch of the auxiliary.

It all fell so quietly into place that George didn't even notice that an entire year had nearly gone by, along with his sixteenth birthday. In fact, George didn't even notice his birthday had passed until the summer had long ended. It hit him as he stood with one hand raised to strike the hot iron on the anvil he was working with.

His nostrils flared as they sucked up the fumes, a dark shade of peach fuzz on his upper lip and his toned arms speckled with burns. Hammer still in the air, a quizzical look overtook him and a pair of milky eyes squinted at him from across the heat smothered cove that overlooked the courtyard.

"I missed my birthday." George croaked.

"WHAT!?" The owner of the eyes, Rick, shouted from the bellows.

"I missed my birthday!" George shouted over his shoulder.

"HUH?"

"I MISSED MY BIRTHDAY!"

"Oh." Rick made a disgusted face. "Who gives a piggut's ass."

"Oh, shove it." George slammed the hammer down onto the iron, manifesting a plume of sparks. "It can't be helped if you haven't remembered much of anything in the last few centuries."

"I remember that you're a little priss," Rick gurgled a laugh as he pumped the bellows.

George grinned and shook his head, "Not today, Rick, not today." Another blow of the hammer, and then another. "I'm of age now, Rick, I'm of age!"

George laughed and slammed a finishing blow onto the small sword he was working on. He quickly dipped the glowing steel into a bucket of now hissing oil before tossing his gloves onto the empty anvil. "I'll grind it later, Rick. I have an appointment with a certain General." With a hiccupping giggle, the young man began to jog out of the blacksmith's workspace and into the courtyard, Rick's voice following him.

"You better hope he reassigns your ass if you aren't going to fin—"

But George was already out of earshot of the old fool, his eyes dead set on a stone building that sunk into the walls. A large wooden board hung above the building's door with the faded word "Mess" painted across it. As he walked towards the building, spring in step, the passerby would occasionally nod his way with a simple "prince." George wasn't sure if it was intentional or not, but every time it happened it definitely reminded him of his place in this new world he had forced himself into.

The excitement of remembering his birthday seemed to fade a little as his mind wandered to these sorts of thoughts. Feelings of being an outsider, or shunned, clouded his recent bliss. He shook his head, attempting to push this emerging mental spiral away. Putting his hand on the familiar handle of the mess building, he found his smile again and pushed it open.

The late summer air wafted around him, attempting to fill the chilled dining area. Deep stones formed the building's skeleton, keeping it a gentle cool that often reminded George of Autumn in the Imperial Garden. The mess was littered with long sturdy tables that had stools stacked along them. At the far end of the dining room was a long counter with towers of simple wooden trays, tin cups and utensils. Behind that counter was the open kitchen that kept the people of the fort fed, where Williams was currently standing, up to his elbows in dough with one other working alongside him.

"Breakfast please!" George grinned. "Pastries if you could."

"George." Williams looked over at the young man. "It's the damned afternoon."

"There's never a bad time for breakfast, Williams." George put his hands on his sides, his smile still wide. Williams squinted.

"What happened?"

"I'll tell you over breakfast."

"George—"

"Oh, give the prince a little breakfast," a Gavarian woman, maybe a year or two older than the pair piped up.

"Thank you, Anne." George looked over at Williams, "Eggs then?"

"Yes, your highness." Williams slapped flour off of his palms.

"Oh, come on I didn't mean it like that." George threw his hands up, "You know I never mean it like that!"

"I don't see why not," Anne hummed to herself, turning to work on the dough Williams left. "I know I would."

"Drunk with power, eh?" George crossed his arms.

"Just drunk, usually." Williams cracked an egg over a pan.

"Ha!" George laughed as Anne swatted at Williams, leaving a floury handprint flat on his back. A second slipped by before George slapped his palms on the counter and vaulted over. Anne gave him a face.

"What do you think you're doing?"

George ignored her and took the pan from Williams, running it over the stove's open flame. Williams cocked a brow and George shrugged. "It feels kinda weird making you do this for me."

Williams shrugged in return but before he could answer, the mess doors swung open again. A group of three soldiers came stumbling in, laughing over each other for whatever reason. George could only assume it was an inside joke. He felt a sudden ping of nervousness with the soldiers there, and as if they could smell it, one shouted out to him.

"Oh hey, the prince is here!"

"And he is making his own dinner!"

"Anne, what did you do to the noble boy?" The last one called out cackling.

"I didn't do anything." Anne looked over her shoulder, "The prince decided to make his own meal."

George forced a grin. "A little afternoon breakfast, even."

"Oi, you managed to sleep in that late?" One of the soldiers huffed, scrambling something about nobles under his breath.

"Well, no-" George started, "Well anyway." The prince slipped his eggs onto a tray. "Did you guys want to join me?" He offered a friendly smile, hoping that perhaps this interaction may prove a little different.

"No," one of the soldiers said plainly, "I still have a few things left on my roster of things to do, methinks. You know the life of a soldier." He stared at George, who shrunk a little under the unsaid accusation.

"Yeah, we will come back. Let the prince eat in peace," another said before jutting his chin forward. "See you later, Anne."

"Bye!" Anne whistled absentmindedly, working on the dough. George slanted a face and looked over at Williams, who offered him a frown.

"Your news?" Williams changed the subject.

"Right." George slapped his tray onto the counter and picked up a fork. He took a steaming bite, wincing with regret at the heat of the morsel.

"I missed my birthday." He muffled through the pain.

Williams made a face and pulled out his fingers to count. "Grace's blessings, you're right."

"Aw," Anne added, "Well, we can have a little party for you anyway, you know."

"No no." George shook his head, "This is a good thing." He hunched over as if conspiring, "I'm sixteen now, I can push for my deployment."

Williams frowned. "I don't know, George, we have it pretty good here at the fort *and* you still get to experience the—"

"Bullshit." George waved his hands as if dispelling Williams' defense. "You and I both know we are ostracized and the only thing we are experiencing is the same thing we would be experiencing in the Imperial City if we got menial jobs and it was cold as balls every few months."

Anne coughed on a laugh she was holding in. George shot her a look before turning back to Williams. "I'm going to the General today, and I'm putting my foot down."

"Oh, so the prince *is* going to be using his power for once?" Anne looked over.

"Well no." George stuffed his face with more eggs and chewed quickly. Swallowing, he finished his thought, "It's just this is what I'm owed, I'm of age. Prince or not, he has to let me."

"'Has' to let you, eh?" Anne cocked a brow, "Very noble sentence if you ask me."

George frowned and Williams sighed.

"George," Williams started, "I don't think the General will go back on his oath to your father. Besides..." Williams leaned in. "We are already in the north, we're soldiers, there is no reason to go any further." Williams leaned in. "And we've been safe, with no surprise visitors."

"This isn't where I need to be." George said after some hesitation. While he hadn't talked much about his dream in a long while, and in truth it was less frequent than it used to be, the nightmare was nowhere close to being gone from his mind. "I'm in the north, yeah, but what am I doing here? I'm just sitting and waiting, I'm not improving. I'm not any more ready than I was a year ago." George huffed. "and we can't just leave the others alone on the front."

"You don't think you're improving?" Williams shook his head. "You're an adult now, you're always improving. Besides, you're worried about a shadow, so you'll rush into a war? We are safe here."

The prince's previous excitement was now a dull hum of contemplation. He wore a defeated face, brow knitted with thought. He knew Williams was speaking correctly, but something deep inside him urged him to disregard his friend's advice. It was almost scary how adamant the feeling was, but nowhere near as frightful as his nightmare. He had to do something.

George made up his mind. "I need to go."

Williams closed his eyes. "It sounds like you're confident in this."

"I am." George said.

"Then it's worth a shot." Anne finished the dough and threw it into a bowl. "But after Williams finishes his own work."

"Don't encourage him." Williams retreated to the bowl and began to partition it.

"As if he needs any more encouragement than his own damned imagination gives him." Anne snuck a glance at George, who shot a look back which broke the tension that was growing.

Feeling relieved, George tucked his plate into a wash basin and folded his arms. "If I didn't know any better, I'd say you're making fun of me, Anne."

"Never!" Anne gasped. George grinned back, knocking a stray tray into the wash basin. A splash spat out of the barrel, speckling the legs of Anne's trousers. The chef plucked the cloth she was using to clean her hands of flour and threw it square into George's smiling face.

"Ass!" she hissed.

George peeled the wet flour-soaked cloth from his face, laughing, his face now a stark floury white. Anne let out a chuckle of her own while Williams studied the scene with a pensive look on his face.

"Say George," Williams began.

"Hm?"

"Starting to think you should deliver your case to the general looking like that."

George scratched the pasty mess on his cheek and nodded. "Huh, you may be onto something."

"Maybe." Williams tossed a fresh towel at George, "Just don't be upset when you get denied."

Wiping his face clean, George gave a small huff, "And you don't be upset when I'm on my way to the front." Putting the towel next to the basin, George stood up straight and nodded. "Either way, wish me luck."

"Luck," Anne hummed, already turning back to her work. With little more than another nod at Williams, George smoothed out his soot-covered tunic and set on his way to Jonsberg. He only managed to just get out the front door of the mess before absentmindedly slamming into someone.

The prince bounced off his unsuspecting victim and by the time George realized who he had run right into, two daring eyes were stabbing glares at him.

"D-Dame Honora!" George stuttered. The older soldier was standing firm despite the force of the blow, an unamused look smattered over her seasoned face. Dame Honora was tall, about the same height as George, and had silvering hair that betrayed the color of a once vibrant brown. Her face was almost always frowning, jaded by a long life, or perhaps as George believed, she really was perpetually disappointed. It did seem that if she was not disappointed with George, then she was disappointed with everything around her. Some day, George figured he might ask his cousin about her.

"Prince George." Honora's tone matched her displeasure. "Where are you running so thoughtlessly? Hasn't Rick given you enough to do?"

"That's not it," George scrambled a defense, "I'm on my way to see the General."

"The General?" For some reason, the way Honora said this caused doubt to bubble inside of George, but before he could answer, Honora continued.

"Is this about the messenger from the capital?"

George twitched. He hadn't heard anything of the sort. "Messenger?"

Honora's face hardened, apparently George had missed something. "Disregard it, then. I simply heard that a messenger was on their way with updates and reports. Far be it from me to think you'd be interested in such logistics."

"Oh," George managed, his usual curiosity tempered by his general fear of the Dame. A silence fell between the two long enough for Honora's frown to deepen, and just about when the silence became unbearably uncomfortable, George made his move.

"I best be going, then."

"Very well."

The prince offered a polite nod and a salute before walking off. Only a few steps away and his walk turned into a jog, which then turned back into a run but this time his eyes peeled ahead and the uncomfortable feeling in his chest turned back to shaking anticipation.

***

"General Jonsberg!" George busted into the General's study. The man was sitting at his desk, quill in hand and a perplexed look shocked on his face. He stuttered a little, his jowls puffing and making his mustache wiggle.

"Prince George, I'm sure you know there are rules and processes in which to get an audience with me." He put his quill down.

George immediately felt embarrassed standing there, looking as he did. The study was the exact same as it was over a year ago, and so was Jonsberg, if not somehow shorter. Either way, George stood in this timeless room with this seemingly timeless man, to pose a question he had brooded on for a year, dressed in the marred clothes of a blacksmith's apprentice and with the remnants of both smudged oil from the forge and flour on his cheeks. Sucking in a breath and steadying his nerves, George clenched his fists.

"Sir," he began, voice tall and authoritative, "it's my birthday."

"Uhm, well." The General seemed even more confused. "Happy Birthday, my prince."

"No." George shook his head. "You know what this means, yeah?"

Jonsberg arched a wispy white brow. "What are you getting at, prince?"

"I want to be deployed."

"Absolutely not."

George frowned deep but a piece of him knew this would be the answer... at least initially. Rallying himself, George stood tall. "I'm of age, you can't stop me."

"Oh, but I can." Jonsberg sat back in his chair. "You know very well that I can. You're a soldier of the army, *my* army. I can do with you whatever I please, and that includes keeping you away from the front and denying requests such as these." The General stared deep into George's eyes. "Unless of course you want to go over my head."

Standing up from his seat, Jonsberg tucked his hands behind his back and studied George. "But something tells me you didn't come all the way out here just to throw your title's weight around and force your advancement like all those other bratty nobles, no?"

"Of course not." George furrowed his brow.

Jonsberg nodded, stepping close. "So, what you're telling me, is that you're an honest soldier and not an entitled prince?"

George nodded, wary.

"Then do as you're told." Jonsberg turned from George. "And settle in, there is plenty to do at the fort, never mind the frontlines."

A sink in his stomach, George weakly saluted before turning to exit the study. He could feel the General's gaze digging into his back the whole way out, a deep red flushing his face. He was embarrassed, ashamed even.

Not wanting to confront Williams with the news, or anyone for that matter, George took it upon himself to hide away as soon as he escaped the keep. He had a spot he liked to think at, a small cranny squeezed in between the armory, the outer wall, and some small building George assumed was one of the higher officers' personal chambers. This trinity formed a small triangle of stone that surrounded a plush bed of grass, only a narrow squeeze behind the chambers being the way in and out.

Finding himself there, George fell face first into the grass. He let out a grunt as his chest smacked the ground, promptly sucking in the comforting smell of the earthy plants. The prince grinned and sank deeper into the natural bed. Thoughts of the Imperial Garden slipped into his mind for a brief moment. Quickly his thoughts turned sour, and his grin twisted into a frown.

"What's up, grumpy?" Anne's voice caused George to scramble. He rolled onto his back and tilted his head to look over at the entrance to his little hideaway. Anne was standing there with her usual tilted smile. George let his head fall back down onto the grass.

"I don't want to talk about it," George groaned.

"Very well." Anne went to leave.

"Jonsberg turned me down," George started, ignoring his own request.

Anne rolled her eyes and walked over to sit next to the prince. "I had a feeling."

"Is that how you knew where to look?" George turned to look at her, she nodded back. The prince sighed and sat up. "Well, it's dumb."

"Is it?" Anne tilted her head.

"Yes." George slanted a face. "The only reason I'm being held back is because of the General's old relations with my father."

"Are you sure that's all?" Anne offered.

George wriggled his nose. "Pretty sure, yeah."

"George."

"They don't need to worry about my safety, I've been practicing."

Anne rolled her eyes. "I know, Williams has been lamenting. Even still, there isn't much you can do about it. Maybe it would be best to just flow with the will of the Graces on this one... you know, accept your lot in the Fort and be happy that you are able to experience this much without the scars that come with the frontlines."

George threaded his fingers through the grass between his legs, feeling the small heather flowers under his palms. An idea began to form in the back of his mind as he focused on the feeling. Finally, he plucked one of the flowers and held it to Anne. "Maybe."

Anne grinned and tucked the flower behind her ear. "Maybe?"

A mocking expression came over George's face. "Or maybe not."

"What are you thinking?" Anne furrowed her brow.

George grinned wide.

"Nothing good," Anne answered for him. "Stop that."

George tilted his head, his smile widening.

"George!"

"I think I know how to get what I want." The prince nodded to himself. Anne frowned deeply.

"You're going to do something stupid," Anne predicted.

George nodded.

"You're not going to tell me?"

George nodded again.

"And I can't talk you out of it?"

George nodded once more.

Anne crossed her arms. "You better hope whatever dumb idea you have brewing kills you before I do."

George prodded her side. "I'll do my very best."

Anne responded with a solid punch to his arm. The chef shook her head. "You're an idiot, you know that?"

"At least I don't spend my time sitting with an idiot in some random nook." George raised his brows. Anne closed her eyes in defeat, a small laugh coming from the prince.

"That wasn't even clever," Anne lamented, a curl on her lips.

"And yet." George tilted his head as he held up another flower. Anne plucked it from his fingers.

"And yet?" she questioned.

"And yet..." George opened again, leading to another topic that in turn led to another.

Slowly, bit by bit, the conversation seemed to devolve more and more as the two chatted and soon the subject of George's dumb idea and the war faded behind pleasant laughs and stupid hypotheticals. The afternoon droned on into the evening and the evening into dusk. It wasn't until the first star found its way into the sky that the two realized that they had been sitting for so long. A sudden dread sank into George's stomach. Rick was going to be pissed.

Chapter 9
An Idiot's Errand

Rick was, in fact, pissed. The blacksmith was fuming by the time George came sneaking in through the back and as punishment, the old man quickly jotted down extra tasks for George to work in the morning. He was keen on keeping George busy straight through the day in an attempt to make up for missed time. Much to Rick's surprise, however, George took the punishment with stride, nodding and smiling the entire time the sentence was being dished out. The whole ordeal left the old man tired and flustered, and as such he quickly retreated back to his room, leaving George to journey to his cot in the attic. Except George never went to his cot.

George's mind was still swollen with his grand plan, his final push to get to the frontlines. A determined grin was plastered on his face and his eyes were fierce with ambition. The energy and excitement of his great idea made his fingers shake, making sneaking around the shop that much more difficult. Despite this, he managed to collect a helmet alongside a short heater shield, opting to leave any sense of body armor in case the noise woke Rick up. He looped a coil of rope around his shoulders and after procuring a proper sword belt, he secured Oathkith to his hip. Giddy, George slipped out of the smithy, geared and ready for his adventure.

A new moon kept the night black, covering the prince's covert activities as he made his way to the Northwest tower. His heartbeat was stuck in his throat, bounding with anticipation. He knew there was a small blind spot where the tower met the top of the wall. It was the perfect location to scale down unnoticed and if luck were on his side, as it already seemed to be, he could quickly make his way into the overgrown field to be hidden from any sentries looking outwards. If all went according to how George had mapped it in his head, he would be deep in the northern woods before the middle of the night and hopefully by morning, triumphantly dragging back a rebel prisoner or two as proof of his ability. George smiled. Jonsberg couldn't deny him then.

Walking down the pathways that spiderwebbed throughout the fortress, George kept on his toes. He skirted around everything from muddy puddles to large rocks, as if the slightest sound would call upon the General himself. It was a miracle George could even see these obstacles, the night consuming most of his vision even against the torchlight that filtered down some of the streets. The walls themselves gave off no light with the sentries likely standing in complete darkness to better adjust their eyes to see anyone sneaking towards or, in George's case, away from the fortress. Wiping any inclination of being caught from his mind, George entered the northwest tower.

His eyes were relieved by the soft orange glow of dying candles. Their sorry state also relieved a tension in his gut, realizing any waking person would have replaced them by now. Putting a palm flat on the cold stone wall, George let out a sigh he didn't know he was holding in. Quickly after, he sucked in a new breath, knowing he was far from all clear—a footstep!

George froze. Feeling his entire body sink with dread, he watched with wide eyes while the sleepiest looking soldier walked clean by him, a powerful yawn stuck on their face. As soon as the random stranger exited the room George was in, the prince flashed an adrenaline-tinged smile of fear and excitement. It took several doses of willpower to hold back a relieved laugh and he made his way to the spiraling staircase leading to the top of the walls. Carefully, George peeled the final door to the battlements open just wide enough to slip through.

A gush of chilly night air blasted over George's face. The empty night sky left him and the walls shrouded in darkness. Far below, the fields were barely visible. The prince's stomach jumped. His fingers were almost too shaky to tie his rope to the parapet. Wrapping the rope around his knuckles and giving it a few good full body tugs, George gulped, uncertain but ready.

Dipping his first leg over the parapet, George felt like he was stepping into the unknown, the end of his rope lost in the darkness below. He hunched his shoulders and wrapped his ankles around the rope. Letting go of a pensive breath, the prince slowly made his way down. Halfway down, or at least what he assumed was halfway, an anxious jitter formed in his chest, as if he was going to be caught at any moment. If he was confident in his uncle's teachings, he figured at this height he could probably just have used Stromist magic to strengthen his legs and simply jump for the bottom.

George gritted his teeth and fought the urge to try, knowing all too well it would likely lead to something more dangerous. The distracting thought lasted only up until he felt the grass under his boots and as soon as solid ground found the prince, he felt his willpower fade. Without a second thought, George's legs begin to pump into a scurry. He sprinted through the fields, not even bothering to look back at the walls for confirmation of his secrecy.

His heart pumped into his throat all the way through the fields. Excitement shot through him until he felt the first branches of the tree line slap him across the face. He winced at the sharp strike, his eyes dimming as he found the growing forest somehow darker than the absolute black of the fields.

"Double edged sword," George swore at the new moon, keeping his curse to a low growl. Putting his hands forward, he began to blindly make his way forward, suddenly not quite sure exactly where he was going. Sucking in a frustrated breath, George realized he never thought about exactly where he was going to find the Vagrant for his grand capture.

A snap sounded behind him, causing George to freeze in place, hair on end. Peeking over his shoulder, his eyes adjusted just enough to make out the trunks of the closest trees but nothing else.

"Hello?" George uttered a harsh whisper, as if someone would answer him. A few drops of silence went by before George turned forward again, this time proceeding with an ear out, one hand settled around the grip of Oathkith.

Looking down at his feet, he used what vision he could to maneuver in between branches and other noisy debris, failing about a third of the time regardless. Each sound he caused sent an anxious cringe down his spine. George was sure the sound was in reality much quieter than he was perceiving, but in the dead of the night, any sound at all seemed to be a violent crash.

Around the time his left foot began to cramp, a faint glimmer caught George's eye. His mind was immediately yanked from the wrinkling feeling in his beat up and soaked through boot and back to the front of his vision. George's grip on Oathkith tightened and he narrowed his eyes, keen on the glittering orange that was peeking through black silhouetted trees.

Doing his best to remove Oathkith from its scabbard without a rasp, the prince fell into a hunter's crouch and proceeded slowly. Hunching his small shield up and above any catching ferns and bushes, George slipped behind a large tree. He pressed his shoulder against the bark, peeking around it.

Using the tip of his blade, George moved a leafy twig out of his line of sight, getting a full view of a mostly dead campfire. Squinting around the light, George could make a guess it was never a big fire to begin with and the small tent nearby had him assuming it was either a lonely hunter or—his heart skipped a beat—an enemy scout.

Sucking in a shaky breath, George moved forward, jitters in his arms and fingers. With each step he took towards the tiny clearing, he could feel his heart rap against its cage, energy flustered fear threatening to overtake him, or was he already in its grip, he couldn't tell. His first footfall on the tamped down ferns and grasses of the campground set his hair on end and his skin crawled at the faint sound of breathing coming from the tent. He knew it wasn't his own, because he had forgotten to exhale a while back. Recognizing that, he slowly breathed out, the tip of his blade on the fold of the tent. He knew he couldn't just barge in and start swinging at a sleeping man, especially since he had no idea if it was an innocent hunter or not.

George gulped, weighing his options as he stood frozen at the entrance of the tent. One option was to announce his allegiance to the Empire and ask the occupant to state their business. The prince shook his head, as much as he'd admittedly like to just ask and the person turned out to be a friendly hunter, his caution won that debate. Another option was to—a branch snapped behind him.

Spinning, George ducked just in time for an axe to whizz over his head. Raising Oathkith, he felt a follow-up blow bounce off of it, a final hit rebounding off the edge of his shield. The blow nearly sent the prince tumbling. Putting his shoulder under the shield and pushing forward, George collected a fourth blow perfectly, sending the attacker back with an audible grunt. Finding his footing, George stared down at a livid rebel, the night-cloaked Vagrant dressed in thick cottons, with a face like a Gavarian's. In each hand the enemy held gruesome looking axes and from his growling face he spat Vagrant swears.

When George had fought the piggut a year ago, he felt hesitation and guilt, now he just felt fear. Instinctively George held out Oathkith's point between them, his shield covering his right side. Time seemed to slow down as the rebel lunged, and George's arm punched out with his sword in an attempt to intercept. Oathkith missed the warrior, but George managed to wrench his shield in the gap caused by his own attack, a resounding clash booming as the broad head of the enemy's axe slapped across it.

George was on pure instinct and the will to survive, his heart in his ears and blood rushing into his arms and legs. He was reacting before his eyes could even tell him what he was seeing and soon, he felt the edge of his blade tug, and a howl roared from his opponent. Oathkith had dragged a grizzly wound along the enemy's rib. In a panic, George followed the cut up with a blow from his shield, but before it could hit, an intense burning pain shot through his arm.

Looking to his right, George saw another rebel holding a blood covered knife. George felt a dizziness overtake him as he realized where all the blood came from, a wet trickle dripping off his elbow. Before either enemy could take advantage of George's surprise, a devastating rip sounded, and the metal point of a sword punched through the back of the axe-bearing Vagrant's neck. The sword slinked back as the body hit the forest floor to reveal Williams standing, blade in hand.

Gasping with a dry mouth, George attempted to speak, but Williams was already on the second enemy. Whipping around, the rebel turned to meet Williams, and as soon as his eyes peeled off of George, the prince's arm instinctively shot out. George felt his stomach drop and reality flood in as the point of Oathkith easily stabbed into the man. The enemy's flesh offered little resistance and yet George felt it all translate into his fingers. A disgusting gurgle came from the man, his lung severed and half the blade in his torso. Yanking it out with a bloody squelch, George's arm was speckled with a stray string of blood from the wound. Turning to his killer, the man stared at George with wide pale eyes, the light behind them only there for a brief second before turning dim. The body fell with a lifeless thud. With wide eyes of his own, George looked at Williams.

"L-let's..." Williams started.

"Yeah," George interrupted, his voice cracking, "Let's go back."

Chapter 10
A Wish Well Deserved

George sat completely soaked through, with his head bent over his lap. A deep rain poured outside and the earliest rays of a cloudy morning peeked through a small window. He sat outside General Jonsberg's office, Oathkith dangling between his weak knees, and his bloodied arm wrapped tight with stained bandages. His usually perky eyes were a dull grey, the vision of a dead man stuck behind them and no feeling in his gut. He had taken a life and he wasn't sure why. George was lost in his mind, his ambitions and quest for strength struck in the knee with the pain of murder and guilt of the blade. Only when the General's door swung open and Williams was marched out, a grim look on his silent face, did George look up from his lap. With still-shaking fingers, he gripped Oathkith and stood up. He hadn't noticed but his sword hand had yet to loosen on the handle of the blade since he had killed the rebel. Gulping down a dry throat, the prince walked through the threshold.

Jonsberg sat behind his desk with steepled fingers and an unamused, tired look. "Do you know how many hours a general sleeps?" he asked, the croak of a deep rest still in his voice. George simply shook his head and Jonsberg frowned. "No, I suppose you wouldn't."

George opened his mouth to speak but Jonsberg held up a hand. "Congratulations, prince." He leaned forward. "You've been approved for deployment at the front alongside your little friend."

George's eyes opened wide, mouth sputtering. "What?"

"You're getting what you want!" Jonsberg slapped a ledger closed and stood up. "But don't go thinking it is because of your little stunt."

George cringed and his voice dipped low. "I—I don't think I'm ready."

Jonsberg scoffed, "Now you aren't ready?" He shook his head, eyes stuck on the bloodied blade in George's hand. The General's face seemed to soften for a moment before he sucked in a breath. "Sheath your blade, George."

The prince seemed frozen in place for a moment before sliding the blade back into its home. His fingers creaked off the grip, having held it for so long. Jonsberg stood up straight, as if trying to gather an inch or two in height.

"The thing is, this has nothing to do with your repeated requests." The General turned back to his desk. "It's politics. Gavaria doesn't think the emperor is taking the threat to the north seriously, and the Vagrants and giants are starting to dig in for a long war. We need every man on the front, and furthermore the Duchies need a sign from the Imperial Province that the emperor gives a damn." He looked over his shoulder. "Am I to presume this is your first time being a pawn of politics, prince?"

"No, but," George started, "...I don't know if I can."

"You'll have to start knowing." Jonsberg looked George over. "Your training is no longer just that, it's time to apply it to the real world. You wanted it and this is the best you're going to get." The words hit George hard, his chest tightening. Jonsberg exhaled, eyes on the defeated prince. "It won't get easier, but it'll get..."

The boy's eyes stared helplessly into the General's, who suddenly paused, a slant on his face.

"This is war, George, and you're a soldier."

***

General Jonsberg's words rang in George's head all the way out of the General's office and over to his special spot wedged between the buildings. After squeezing into the small triangular sanctuary, he let out a long sigh and promptly left as quickly as he arrived. There was nothing for him there right now. With the images of the dying Vagrants fresh under his lids, George kept a pensive stare forward as he made his way to the smithy that he had called home this past year. It was weird to think about it now that he was leaving, but he had gotten quite attached to some of the aspects of this bizarre home in between homes.

The dust, the noise, the smells, A pensive look came over him, Anne and Williams, even Rick. His fingers twitched over the cold pommel of Oathkith, but now everything was different. It was like someone threw a mess of paint over these memories, even as he walked past them. Red paint. His eyes pictured the blood pouring out of the rebel and he cringed, teeth clenched. It was no mystery who tossed the paint, though, his vision falling to his sword hand.

"Is it possible to cherish old memories when there is a new membrane of guilt and sadness in between you and them?" George asked out loud, thinking he sounded a lot like Reginald.

"Why not?" Anne answered.

George snapped to reality, his eyes perking open from their thoughtful daze. Anne stood in between him and the door to the smithy, a worried smile on her face. Forgetting the pain in his heart, the prince furrowed a brow, eyes analyzing her expression.

"What's wrong?"

"Williams told me about the deployment." Anne bit her lip anxiously.

Silently, George nodded. "I'm supposed to leave with him in the morning."

"So, you got what you wanted?" Anne took a step forward.

"I got what I thought I wanted." George felt a burn in his eyes. He looked down at his feet and a sudden shadow blocked his vision while two gentle arms squeezed around him. Anne's scent filled his nostrils and he let himself melt into her embrace, wrapping his own arms around her.

Her voice was close. "What do you want now?"

Letting his face bury into her shoulder, George released a long sob he had been holding in since he first felt his blade tug. "I don't know anymore."

The two stood there for a while, in complete silence, until a gruff and familiar voice cursed out from the house. "How the fuck am I suppose' to get outta my own home with you two mushy bastards in my way." Rick fumed.

Anne burst into laughter, George hiccupping right behind her with a sobby laugh of his own.

"I'll miss you too, you old goat."

"I never said that," Rick huffed, but patted George roughly on the shoulder as he walked by. George rubbed a sleeve against his eyes and sneered at the old blacksmith as he left. Turning back to Anne, George cleared his throat and motioned indoors.

The two walked in with George rubbing his hands together as if they were cold, or he was just anxious. He sniffed, even though he didn't need to, another tick of nervousness. "So, I'm just going to have to assume that you told Williams I had a stupid plan brewing and that's why he ended up following me last night."

"You know what they say about assumptions and assuming." Anne plopped into a chair as George walked over to the trunk where he kept his belongings. Looking over his shoulder, George blinked twice.

"That I'm right and you're easy to see through?" He grinned and looked back at his worldly goods. He oddly enough felt upset that he had so little things. The small variety meant that he didn't really have any reason to pack as everything was already in his trunk. Normally it was a blessing, but not so much when there was reason to keep busy.

Anne shrugged. "I suppose so. Glad I did though."

"Me too." George nodded and looked back at Anne, suddenly feeling a strange sadness at her image. It must have been clear on his face because Anne mimicked the sorrow.

"What's wrong?" She asked.

"I think I'm just going to miss you."

"You *think*?" Anne raised a brow.

"No, no." George waved his hands. "I definitely will."

"Better."

"Thanks."

"I'll miss you too, though." Anne nodded and sighed. "You're a wonderful person."

"You think so?" George tilted his head, "I think the same about you."

"I do." Anne smiled, "But I'm sure our paths will cross again, probably when you need to be bailed out of something stupid. That seems to be my usual job, hm?"

"I do get myself into a lot of trouble," George admitted with a sly grin.

"Graces know it." Anne agreed before standing up, "Shall I leave you to your thoughts?"

"Void be damned, no." George laughed, "Please keep me company."

"As the prince wills it." Anne winked.

"Please don't." George frowned with sarcastic exaggeration.

"Yeah, whatever." Anne rolled her eyes

Chapter 11
Reunion

The march to the front was surprisingly short, though George was so lost in his own thoughts the entire time that it could have been longer than he perceived. His mind was a complicated soup of emotions, thoughts and memories. Between the gut-wrenching guilt of taking a life, the warm calm and comfort of Anne, and the sharp pain of his values suddenly shifting, his journey was morphing into something new and unknown. In short, George was lost. A thought-stricken look took over his usual eager grin, only to hide when spoken to or yanked back to the reality at hand.

Reality, as it were, had arrived in the form of an encampment simply named 'The Nest' by the local soldiers. It was a deeply dug fort of wooden palisades and battle-hardened warriors, run entirely by none other than Commander Darius and the Stromist Vanguard that served under him. Even though it was only the fall, the frost of winter had already begun to dust the tips of the grass this far north, much in the same way that a sudden anxiety frosted George's anticipation as he arrived.

He was selected for this unit simply because of his title and the assumption that he was a practiced Stromist, which he was if only in the technical sense as he had never managed a spell. Williams, while not being a Stromist or even pretending to be one, was beside George all the same. Jonsberg had pulled some strings as a final mercy to the boys so that they wouldn't be separated.

The escorts who came up north with them slowly bled into the encampment past two angry looking watchmen armed with spears and crossbows. Beyond that point, the camp looked a lot like the one George had helped build in the hills and valleys of the Caldoran Achians a year or so ago. In other words, it was a mess of tents and activity. The only difference was that this time the myriad of soldiers and support auxiliaries were mixed with Gavarian civilians, probably from the nearby town of Wretchett.

"Grace's be damned." A familiar voice caught the pair's attention. Spinning, George was met with the now bearded grin of Franklin. Immediately a wide smile formed on George and Williams' faces, all three of the young men slapping each other on the backs and giving rough hugs. George pinched Franklin's rusty red beard and gave it a tug.

"What's all this?" He laughed, jutting his chin towards Franklin's wild and uncut hair.

Franklin gave a coy roll of the eyes. "Every soldier knows it's bad luck to cut your hair before a war is done." George pushed a hand through his own short-cut and nodded.

"Good to know." He grinned before slapping Franklin's shoulder. "So, what's been happening?" George's face dimmed, "And where is Hector?"

"Hector?" Franklin frowned and then beamed a wide smile, "Oh he is just fine. There is no better Stromist in the camp, not even Darius. OH!" Franklin slapped his own forehead. "Speaking of the Commander, I'm supposed to bring you to him, let's go."

The trio began their walk through the camp in an excited silence. Various activities filled in the void around them, with tent-born smithies pounding steel and grizzled soldiers growling at fresh faces. Similar to the grass, a coating of frost covered the peaks of every tent, and a mist of cold plumed with each breath. The ground itself was cold, and crackled a rebuke with every booted step.

Williams was the first to speak. "So, what's all this I've been hearing about the tensions between the Gavarians and the Imperials?"

Franklin tugged his beard. "Ah you know, just politics. The duke accused the regent of not caring enough about the war, being locked in his study and all that. I guess old Duke Ozzy—" He leaned in, "that's Duke Osbert to the layman—got the idea from some of the sages, but at the same time both armies seem to be getting along just fine. Well..."

"Well?" George tilted his head.

"Despite the duke's criticisms, he is a man of his word," Franklin explained, "And he works with Jonsberg and the others in an attempt to end this conflict as soon as possible, but Fenric..."

George's blood boiled at the mention of the name. "But Fenric?"

"Well, Fenric has been getting more and more power ever since the duke has been falling in and out of his coughing fits and the little rat bastard is more interested in looting and looking like a hero than pragmatism." Franklin shook his head, "You know, I was in the battle of Bvak and the little shit didn't even show up until near the very end. Too busy lighting a camp of Vagrant women and children on fire for whatever reason, I don't know, but he was more than eager to leap in at the end and claim the credit of the long and hard-earned victory. We lost a lot more soldiers than we ever needed to, just for one kid's glory." There was a long pause. "I didn't know how to tell you any of this when I saw you next." Franklin looked at George. "But actually, being out here in the fight, you sort of realize that glory isn't much of a thing."

"I—I know," George admitted, "I almost didn't come." He looked down at his shaking fingers. Williams sucked in a breath and hung his head along with George. Franklin stopped and turned to the pair and despite being the same age as them and having the same childhood, he stood looking like a person of a different world, the camp blending around him.

"Well, I'm glad you did," Franklin offered, "I'm sorry I have a year on you two, but uh, just know that I get it. Nothing to be ashamed of." He squeezed both their shoulders with each of his hands and jutted a chin at a large tent nearby. "But this is where I leave you, I'll see you two after you get assigned." He gave them each a clap on the back and George's vision tunneled on the tent that held his fate.

***

Pushing their way through the flap, George and Williams found the interior of the tent to be identical to the one they were in over a year ago with Lawrence and Baldra. Darius' tent was as immaculate and empty as ever, with only his bare essentials tightly organized in a single corner and a table with chairs clustered in the center. Walking in, George nearly bounced off the fur-laden chest of an exiting Kafshe, the alien looking Achian woman staring angrily at the prince. She was tall, even for an Achian, standing at the same height as George and was riddled with scars and twisting spiritual tattoos wherever her limited pelt wardrobe ceased. She looked every bit a Kafshe, from her stone-colored skin to her wavy black hair. Her fiery amber eyes lingered on George for a moment before sweeping by him and Williams, leaving a strange musky scent in her wake that George could only place as some sort of incense.

"The Paleskins sent a Kafshe to do their talking," Darius explained from further inside the tent, his eyes on a set of papers. He shuffled them idly. "The strange beasties refuse to speak the Imperial tongue, so they decided one of their cult wizards would be better suited, I suppose, as if they weren't asking for our help." The Commander looked up. "But I also suppose we are asking for theirs, too." He shook his head, assumedly at the cyclical argument. "But that's none of your business, yet."

Darius stood up. "Welcome to the 11th vanguard." His eyes narrowed with recognition. "As if I almost forgot you and the prince were one and the same." A smile cracked on the soldier's face. "So, you finally slithered your way into a soldier's life."

There was a pause and George opened his mouth to explain the truth, but Darius barked first. "Damned if I care, you know Stromism, right?"

"Right." George nodded.

"And you?" Darius looked at Williams.

"No."

"Grand!" Darius hissed sarcasm. "You." He pointed at Williams. "Report to the Support Auxiliary until I think of a better use for a regular." He turned his finger to George. "And you, report to the sparring ring, I need to see what exactly you do know."

"W—" George went to protest the separation, but Darius growled.

"Now!"

The two looked at each other for a moment before nodding and heading out of the tent. There was a slight pause as the two turned to go to their different tasks. The black tent of the Auxiliaries were clearly in view, as was the open space and wooden ring that marked the training arena, both in opposite directions. George nodded at Williams, who nodded back.

"Good luck." Williams gave a grin.

"Thanks, you too." George smiled back, although unsure.

Turning around, George snuck one last look at his friend before sucking in a breath of confidence and marching towards the training ring. As he walked, he tried his best to pretend he couldn't hear any comments about himself spouting from passing soldiers, comments regarding his pedigree, his inexperience, and every other thing he already heard plenty of back at Torskyla. With a fiery bubble in his chest, he nodded to himself. He would prove them all wrong.

With that same fire, he found himself leaping over the low wooden beams of the ring, chest puffed proudly in spite of the growing sneers. The ring itself was rather empty, save for a few soldiers batting at each other with wooden weapons and shields, their arms glowing with dull streams of magic.

A familiar smile caught George's eye and before he knew it, he was being pulled into a meaty hug with Hector squeezing him tight. The older boy was now also a taller man, with arms twice the size of George's, even after all the blacksmithing the prince went through. Unlike George, though, not a scar or flaw was on Hector's body, at least none George could see.

"Stromism is treating you well," George commented. There was a hint of envy in his voice, but it was clouded by actual appreciation for his friend. Hector pursed his lips and gave George's arm an analyzing squeeze.

With a nod, Hector grinned again. "It's treating you well, too!"

"That's just hard labor." George frowned.

"Nah, not just, " Hector said, "well either way, friend, what's up?"

"The prince will be sparring against you in an exhibition of ability," Commander Darius answered for George, having snuck up on the pair. The sudden announcement threw George into a double-take, not even noticing Darius had been sitting right by the ring for Grace's knew how long. The Commander was settled on a wide stool made of wood, arms crossed and a disappointed look already on his face.

Hector eyed George from the side of his vision before turning to the captain and tipping his head. Looking back at George, he offered the same respectful tip and George returned it. Slowly Hector backed away from George, making space for the oncoming battle.

"Don't go easy on the prince," Darius ordered.

Hector nodded, but under his breath, he shot a comment at George, "I never have." With little else and a patch of dusty ground between the two, Hector squared himself into a fighting stance.

"That's true." George cracked a grin before mimicking Hector.

As soon as George dropped into a stable fighting posture with hands open and ready for anything. Hector's ankles shimmered a magical gold. In a flash, Hector already closed the distance and his left fist flew towards George. The golden aura of Stromist magic sputtered around George's arms but never quite caught aflame. Adrenaline pumped through George as his magic sputtered out, but luckily instinct overtook the failed attempt at magic and he managed to dodge the lightning-fast blow, narrowly avoiding a strong clip to the ear.

Caleb's mantras repeated in George's mind as he ducked and dipped, avoiding the crushing jabs and hooks of Hector, but he couldn't quite believe them. They spoke of a calm mind, a secure mind, the secret to unleashing the uniformity required to stabilize Stromist magic, but all George could feel was the chaotic energy of the fight he was in, or worse still, the memories of the *last* fight he was in. His breath was shaking with adrenaline and a growing sense of fear. The feelings spiked when he noticed an opening and landed a punch on Hector's ribs with a hesitation in his arm.

It was like he had barely touched Hector, the experienced Stromist absorbing the blow with ease. George found another opening and landed a few more punches, himself being too dodgy for Hector to quite get a hold of until with a thunk, a shimmering punch landed square into George's belly, folding him forward. Of all the blows George managed to land, Hector just needed one. The prince could feel tears in his eyes as his breath popped out of his lungs, leaving him with shallow gasps. Gripping his stomach, George fell to his knees, begging for breath. Onlooking soldiers began to hoot and cheer at the amazing blow, turning George's pained stomach inside out all over again, this time with embarrassment.

"I've seen enough," Darius announced over the hoarse gasping. Hector was already helping George to his feet by the time the Commander made the short few steps to the pair. He stood stoic and ever unimpressed.

"You're hard to hit, I'll give you that," Darius admitted, "but you lack the stability to use your magic, and you definitely lack a clear and calm mind needed for prolonged battle as a Stromist in the frontlines." The Commander frowned. "I'd send you to the auxiliaries but I think I may have a use for you as a scout in an upcoming event."

"Event?" George finally found his breath again, a throbbing pain in his gut.

"We can talk about it in my tent." Darius looked at Hector and gave a dismissing nod.

The soldier gave the Commander a salute, then flashed an apologetic look at George, who simply nodded back in recognition. Hector lingered for a moment longer before walking off, leaving George and the Commander alone. A silence fell between the two, and instead of breaking it, Darius began walking back towards his tent, George in tow.

While the way to the sparring ring was ripe with cynical comments and questions, the way back was littered with smiling faces and amused laughs. Any embarrassment George found in the ring was here to stay it seemed. Instinctively he put his eyes to the ground as he walked.

"Do you know why you can't use your magic?" Darius suddenly asked.

"Why?" George looked up, hopeful.

"I don't know, I was asking you."

George frowned. "Well, my uncle says I'm too emotional, with far too many thoughts at once. I can't ground and balance myself." Darius just let out a long and thoughtful hum, as if further disappointed. George slanted a face. "At least that's what he says."

The pair skidded to a stop, the Commander's tent right before them. Darius simply looked at George with a blank stare and opened the flap of his tent as if offering the opening to the prince. Before he could enter, though, Darius replied.

"Maybe that's it. That's the usual problem with most beginners." He paused again. "But everyone is different."

Darius pinched his chin and ducked into his own tent before George could. The prince stood alone outside the tent for a brief moment, a sudden thought in his head: was he different? Possibilities began to flood into his head, but he waved them away for now, he had a task to do.

Chapter 12
Heart of Iron

The iron mines of Kerring's mountain held some of the richest deposits of ore in the Empire. Despite its impressive age, it never seemed to run thin on iron, the rock basically handing it to whoever was in control of the vast system of tunnels. If you owned it, you had the fuel for industry, and if you had the fuel for industry, you had the tools to properly run a war. That's how Darius put it, at least, and up until a year ago, the Empire owned it. Its loss was partially responsible for the iron shortage but the Empire wasn't the only party to feel its absence. When the Vagrants and the giants ripped it from the Imperials, the elusive Paleskins and Kafshe also lamented.

According to the Kafshe that George had bumped into the previous day, the Paleskins believed that a spirit of nature resided on the top of the mountain. When the Imperials owned it, the Paleskins and their Kafshe had no issue utilizing this sacred ground, but ever since the Vagrants took it over, they found themselves even more persecuted than usual, to the point that ritual meetings were impossible. The Paleskins sent Opane, the Kafshe George had already met, to negotiate with Commander Darius. It seems a deal was struck, because now George was assigned to a scouting party that was looking into the defenses of the mines.

The whole thing was uncomfortable. George's group only had three other Imperial soldiers, while the rest of the party included Opane herself and two Paleskins. Never having seen one before, George couldn't help but stare. They were short, but not very broad. In fact, they were more wiry than anything, with thin yet strong looking muscles corded under tight pale skin. They had long sharp ears, absolutely no hair on top of their heads, be it shaven or otherwise, and two slits where a nose should be. What put George off the most was their eyes, the large black orbs better suited for the deep night than the broad daylight.

Content with the distance offered by put-off Imperials, the Paleskins chattered among themselves in a strange toothy language and barely paid George or the other Imperials any mind. Deadly looking knives with serrated edges adorned their belts and despite the chill in the air, they only wore baggy fur pants and shoes, showcasing bare chests and backs littered with scars and religious markings.

George himself was tucked in thick wools and furs that covered his entire body, the sting of Winter a little early this Autumn morning. He wore no metal, to keep his movements quiet, but he had Oathkith tied tight to his hip, one hand hugging it. A piece of him wondered if foregoing the armor was even necessary with all the noise one of the other Imperials was making. In the soldiers' defense, the small scouting party found themselves in the thick of an ancient conifer forest that had opened up just enough for young trees and shrubs to spread low hanging boughs between the old trunks of their predecessors. Either way, George quickly grew to admire how silently the others were moving, and as the Paleskin chatter suddenly ended, the prince knew they were closing in on their mark.

Feeling a little nervous, George had to remind himself that Darius and the Vanguard weren't far away, quietly awaiting the report and ready to pounce if able or needed. That was at least one safety net, not that George wanted to use it. Shaking his head, George pulled himself out of his thoughts and to the scene in front of him.

George's group got a good look at the main clearing through the needles and leaves of the surrounding trees. The mountain side was littered with cave mouths and false alcoves but the one in front of them happened to be the original mine entrance, and the largest. At just a quick glance, George could see that the Vagrants had already dug their heels into the new territory.

Presumably migrant workers from other villages had moved in close by, eager to make some trade through the mines. They worked alongside militant looking individuals that George could only assume were direct representatives of the rebel horde. The warriors were dressed in quilted cotton and thick mail pads if not directly wearing a hauberk, and almost every one of them had both a spear in their hands and a sword on their hip. George turned his eyes to these armed sentinels, ignoring the workers. With a squint he started to count, but before he could get close to finishing, he heard Opane whisper, "sixty."

"Easy, we can take 'em." George nodded.

"And that's only this entrance," Opane reminded, making the prince frown. Looking at the Paleskins, Opane said something in that same language George didn't really understand. The Paleskins themselves didn't have that issue and responded with curt nods before slinking off silently.

"They'll move up the mountain while we try another known entrance near here," explained Opane as she looked at her now entirely Imperial party. A look of defeat seemed to flash in the Kafshe's eyes as she did, and George noticed it especially when it fell on a soldier by the name of Jacob, a man from the East and the noisy Imperial from earlier. Jacob was still looking out from the bushes towards the enemy, but the problem wasn't so much his vigilance as much as the way he stood. His slight angle and clumsy bracing made it look as if he was about to fall over at any second. George nudged an elbow into the man's ribs and he straightened up, turning to look at Opane. The Kafshe offered a pitiful grin before motioning with her head in the next direction.

"We'll have to get a little closer, this entrance is dug into an alcove that rubs by the woods we are in, so no talking, just follow." Opane looked at every scout, deadly serious. She was met with nods. George went to speak affirmatively but was shut up by Opane's raising hand. Closing his mouth, George simply nodded along.

Snapping a nod of his own, Opane turned from the tiny group and began to sneak forward. George did his best to mimic the well-placed footsteps of the Kafshe, but found the whole experience akin to trying to copy the sneaking crouch of a hunting cat. Making the connection, George sort of saw why the Kafshe were often referred to as bestial, or at the very least he hoped this was the reason. Opane raised a hand again, snapping George to attention.

"They have dogs." Opane had whispered so softly, the prince figured it was his own thoughts.

George flicked his eyes about and tried to snag a view of any clearing through the dense boughs but he couldn't see anything other than more foliage and the occasional glimpse of stone. The scouts stood in the thick of the woods, too far in to see any entrance let alone any guard dog by it, begging the question of—

"I can smell them." The Kafshe frowned as a breeze trickled in through the leaves. The statement just raised even more questions in George's mind. Whatever the questions were, they were put on hold while Opane explained further, "Which means the dogs can smell *us*."

The quizzical looks of the Imperials seemed to coax even more whispers from Opane. "They wouldn't think much of our scents this far away, besides I bet you all smell like Vagrants to the mutts, no I'd be more worried if..." Her eyes cast to Jacob. "If their ears heard us in the woods."

Finally catching on, Jacob whispered sharply, "I resent that!"

Jacob's hiss made everyone flinch, ears twitching and eyes scanning. The fear of being found pounding in everyone's chests. A few thumps later and Opane turned her attention back to Jacob.

"You." The soft whisper was back. "Stay here. Myself and the other three will move on... you watch our flanks." The final order was dripping with sarcasm and everyone knew it. Amber, Kafshe eyes bounced over to George. "By me."

George gave a last look at Jacob and then the other two Imperials before nodding, maybe a bit too eagerly.

Moving even slower than before, the Imperials followed Opane obediently. As the group snuck ever closer to the rocky walls of the mountain, the boughs began to thin. To George, the waning foliage felt something similar to finding yourself suddenly naked, with thick branches being the only thing between himself and an unchecked enemy. His heart rose into his throat, which then skipped a beat when he caught sight of a man ahead. A dangerous looking Vagrant was standing by a large crack in the mountain.

Opane stopped, and George moved to her side to see what she was looking at. From this new angle, there were at least five more Vagrants in and around the alcove, with mean looking war dogs sniffing about. They were big and deadly, with grey hairs bristled like a boar and square jaws dense enough to snap bone. George watched Opane's eyes, the reflection of the dark cave bouncing off them.

George couldn't help but wonder if she could see into the darkness itself.

A loud bark brought the group to a panicked freeze. George could have sworn he was about to throw up his own heart when his adrenaline smacked the roof of his mouth. Opane's eyes seemed panicked as well, flickering in every direction until at last it dawned on the group that the bark came from behind. Then it really sunk in—Jacob!

The bark turned into a chorus of noise as the dogs both behind and in front of the group all joined in, their owners none too quiet either. Shouts rose among the Vagrants while they funneled towards the woods. Opane shook George's shoulder, who in turn grabbed his closest companion's. The Kafshe started to trudge away swiftly, yet quietly. This discrete shuffle turned into a run as the noise grew and then the next thing George knew, he was sprinting through the woods behind Opane, with the shouts of Vagrants and barking dogs right at his heels.

Dense branches slapped George as he ran through the woods. Needles bit into his thick clothes and Oathkith rattled against sapling trunks that hugged too close to his escape route. The heavy breaths of his fellow escapees were drowned out by his own deep heaving. It dominated George's hearing so much that even the shouts of the enemy seemed dull under the chorus of his own terrified heart. Before long, the group came to a sudden scene. Jacob was flailing on the forest floor with a monstrous dog about the same size as the soldier right on top. The drooling maw of the beast snapped hungrily at the man's face, his arms pushing back on its throat just enough to keep the teeth at bay.

Without slowing down, Opane ran full force into the struggle, using the momentum to rip the dog clean off of Jacob. Once free, Jacob scrambled to his feet and began to sprint away, straight into the direction of the hidden vanguard. George and the other two came to an abrupt stop, stuck between Opane wrestling with a dog, a fleeing Jacob, and now a cluster of Vagrants bursting onto the scene.

Looking amongst themselves, the two Imperials standing by George summoned a golden shimmer around their legs before bounding away with a burst of explosive speed. The boughs of the woods creaked angrily as they whipped by. George now stood alone with a decision. As if answering for him, the Kafshe sent out a boot, knocking the dog away before running by the prince. Passing him, she gave George a push.

"Run, dammit!"

Not having to be told twice, George once again scurried behind Opane, only this time George seemed to be gaining on the Kafshe. As he passed the Achian, he noticed a large puncture by Opane's knee. The dog must have gotten her. Something in George told him to slow down, matching the weakened gait of Opane as they followed in the waking mess of broken branches and squalls of dried leaves and needles the other two scouts had left behind.

Every second seemed like a whole minute, the enemy barely a stone's throw away and growing ever closer. George knew they were on borrowed time and that the dogs from the second entrance could catch up with them any moment now. Their only hope was to reach Darius and the Vanguard before that happened. The prince sped up, not willingly, but his fear drove adrenaline through his veins and knowing that Darius, and his rescue, were so close just pumped it even more. A sharp yelp from behind caught him off guard, forcing him to spin mid sprint.

Loose forest soil and needles kicked up as he spun to see Opane back on the ground with another dog on her George looked at the direction of salvation briefly before drawing Oathkith and charging back towards Opane and the enemy. George pushed by the Kafshe, Oathkith shimmering as it swung to catch the falling axe of a rebel. The prince didn't have time to think or worry or feel guilt or shame, his right-hand balling into a fist and slamming into the rebel's exposed gut. The enemy bent forward under the blow, George's pommel coming crashing down onto the back of his head. The Vagrant toppled over, but three more took his place.

A flash of blue pulsed from the fight between the dog and Opane, a burst of frozen air erupting from the Kafshe and freezing the dog solid. Opane scrambled to her feet and jumped beside George just in time to throw a sharpened shard of ice into an enemy's gurgling throat, stopping a charge at George's flank. The prince himself was busy with a man who stood a head taller, Oathkith and the enemy's own deadly blade stuck in a battle of parries and heavy shoves. Finally, George saw an opening and ran the edge of his blade under the man's unprotected armpit, a hideous tug as it cut through tendons. The man screamed and fell backwards, George not having enough time to deliver mercy as he dodged the stab of an enemy spear.

Eyes wide, George could see more and more Vagrants running in. The spear came back around, but this time Opane's hand came shooting forward, grabbing the shaft. The Vagrant who had thrusted the weapon looked surprised, but only for a moment. Opane's free hand slammed palm-first into the Vagrant's chest, and an explosion of frozen air and icy shards blasted from the slap, sending the opponent flying backwards in a mess of frozen gore.

The display seemed to slow the advance, but then, an arrow came whizzing in. With a thunk, it dug into Opane, sending the Kafshe spinning back to the forest floor. George felt fear leak into his body, but he forced his hands to move regardless. On instinct, George slapped an enemy blade away with Oathkith stabbing blindly in riposte. The prince stood over the Kafshe, pulling his blade free from the stomach of a dying enemy. He barely had time to refocus before another enemy came barreling in, and just like that, he was surrounded.

George could only hear his heart, the clouded words of his uncle, and the gurgle of Opane. His mind shut off, this was not the way of the Stromist, yet the world seemed to slow down. Inside, he felt a swirling smoke of emotion, its black tendrils whipping a calm blue reservoir of power into action and sending a flood of magic through him.

Shimmering gold tickled George's skin, wrapping around his arms. A Vagrant charged him, but with a shove of his forearm, George sent the Vagrant clean into the air. Another swung their axe but George's arm moved in a blur and Oathkith cut through the haft like straw and continued clean through the arm, before cutting back to thrust at another opponent. The stab punched into the enemy's chest, but the force of the blow was so strong that George's fist nearly went through with it.

George's body started to feel fuzzy as the magic pulsed through him quicker and quicker, his vision sharp and tinged brutally red. He started to lose count of how many were falling around him, but no matter how many he cut down, there always seemed to be more. It was only a matter of time before the Vagrants tried a different approach, if he could even last that long. The heat in George's chest began to turn into a burning exhaustion with the natural limits of his body bleeding through whatever magic was sustaining him.

A roar sounded behind George. His body tensed. They've flanked him, or so he thought. The plum-and-wine colors of the vanguard troops flooded past George, fresh faces fierce and ready. The imperial soldiers shook the ground as they pushed the line away from George, leaving the prince in a sudden pocket of calm.

George's breathing was ragged and stunned. Adrenaline was still raging through his body and his eyes were stuck in confusion while he stared at the backs of his saviors, embroiled in the same battle he was just in. Small stars and pocks began to fizzle over his vision and he could feel his magic fading away alongside his body. He wobbled, legs shaking. Falling to his knees, his head spun, fatigue and pain slowly emerging from whatever numbness he was feeling during the fight. The pain started in his fingers and slowly cracked and splintered up his arms and into his chest, and finally down to his stomach, where a gross glob of nausea churned. His eyes rolled into the back of his head. Everything seemed to catch up with him as he fell face first into the soggy forest floor.

Chapter 13
Celebration

Every time George's heart beat, he felt a painful pulse in the fore of his head. The prince's body felt like it had been trampled by horses and then mauled by bears. Even just twitching his fingers caused a sharp pain to shoot up his arm. Groaning, he rolled to his side (pained all the way through) only for a bit of straw to stick into his rib, the little poke feeling like a stab. He groaned again and, fighting back the pain, sluggishly sat up only for the blurry world to spin into focus.

George was lounging upright on a mattress stuffed with straw and set off the ground by a wooden frame. Observing the white canvas that made up the walls around him, paired with the musky smell of camp, he knew he was in a tent. People dressed in black tunics were running amuck through the tent, tending to other beds with other pained looking soldiers. *Auxiliary.* A cold sensation brought George's attention to his chest. He was shirtless and wrapped in heavy bandages, the center of which was soaking through with some unknown dampness. Taking a sniff, the dense smell of poultices burned at his nose hairs and forced a dramatic gag.

"Awake, then?" Opane's winter voice brought George's attention to a chair near his bed. The Kafshe sat with an arm in a sling and heavy bandages around her shoulder, but otherwise the Achian seemed lively. George, on the other hand, was the opposite. All he could muster was a blink at his scouting partner.

"I never saw Imperial magic exhaust someone so heavily," Opane continued. "But to be fair... I never quite saw Imperial magic like that before."

George managed a hoarse, "Oh yeah?" It was more of a cough than a sentence, causing George to scan around for something to wet his throat.

"Here." Opane lifted a cup of water, as she knew. Snatching it, George took a long sip, feeling the cool water trickle down his rough throat.

"Thank... you..." George said in between gulps, "I... really appreciate it."

Opane waved a dismissive hand. "Think nothing of it... Although I admit I'm here for more than a friendly visit."

"What?" The prince looked confused and let the cup fall from his lips.

"I know you don't owe me any favors, and in fact it's quite the reverse, but..."

Slowly, George placed the empty cup down, eyes narrowing on the Achian. He cleared his throat and sat up as straight as possible. "What do you mean?"

"You're really the prince, yes?" Opane's eyes seemed desperate.

"I... uh... I am."

"It feels strange asking this of an imperial, but I saw the way you defended me. You did it as a comrade." Opane shook her head. "But enough prose. We won the battle, and the mine is yours." She raised a finger. "However, the Imperials are refusing us access to the holy site on the peak. It was promised in our deal."

"Why are you telling me this?" George asked, a sudden shame clinging to his conscience, as if he himself denied the Paleskins their rights.

Opane pursed her lips into a thin line. "You're the prince."

"So?" George scoffed at the suggestion brewing, "I'm the second-born and a runaway."

"I saw you lead once already." Opane stabbed a finger right into George's chest, their eyes meeting. The Kafshe's voice shook with authority, "Your people's decisions are your decisions, and so are their deals. What will you do?"

"The Commander—"

"The Commander won't see me. What will you do?" Opane stood up tall, eyes stern and expecting. Reading her face, George knew she was at her limit regarding imperial slights.

George frowned and slowly rose from the bed he was in, his pain washing away into burdensome emotion. There was suddenly a lot of weight on his shoulders, weight he wasn't expecting. He never thought he'd be negotiating deals for the Kafshe, but then again, he also never expected to be fighting Vagrants over an iron mine. He was starting to wonder what sort of a fool he was to let a dream lead him to his current position.

He perched a brow. Then again, it was a little more than a dream and besides, that dream was leading him to other things, new things he didn't know he wanted or needed. A chance at his own name, his own strength, maybe even a life free from the deep stories of the palace, free from the shadows. His frown deepened as Opane's serious face reminded him of one important detail. He still was the prince, he still had the responsibility of one, and this decision would define what kind of person he was going to be.

"I'll talk to him."

***

"Welcome back to the Nest." Darius called over to George. Letting the cloth panel flap behind him, George stepped into the Commander's barebones tent. Almost immediately, George noticed that Darius was looking at him differently, the condescension normally present in his eyes was overtaken by a brighter look. Even the Commander's lips were almost free from its perpetual frown of disappointment. Sucking in a breath of confidence, the prince closed the distance of the barren tent before speaking.

"It's good to be back." George let out a small smile of relief, hoping the rest of the talk would be this smooth. The Commander didn't get up from his seat, opting instead to slide whatever paper he was studying off to the side and look at George pointedly. Such a look reminded the young man of how Jonsberg often looked at his subordinates.

"What do you need, soldier?"

"Soldier..." George mimicked under his breath, feeling the word on his tongue. Darius on the other hand met the mimicry with his usual frown. George gave a panicked cough, in an attempt to clear his throat and thoughts.

Full of hesitation and confliction, George started, "Commander, I'm here on behalf of Opane, actually."

Darius' frown grew deeper. "Oh?"

"She relayed to me that we are stalling our part of the bargain struck with her and the Paleskin scouts." George let his words linger, soft and almost questions rather than statements.

"No," the Commander said. "The paperwork is being done, it will simply take some time." Punctuating his point, Darius tapped a quill in its ink jet and began scribbling something unrelated on a new piece of paper.

George looked down at the ground, ready to leave when an urge pushed him to look back up at his superior. He deepened his voice, "I don't think that's true."

The scratches of the quill pen stopped and the tent fell silent. Muffled noises coming from the camp outside were all that stood between the two as they met stares. George hardened his under Darius' glare, squeezing a sigh out of the Commander.

"Opane is just using you, George," Darius began, "maybe even to just get her deal processed quicker."

"I know," George didn't back down, "but I don't care about that. Opane has a point. You and I both know the history we share with the Paleskins and how many times we burned them on deals *we* wrote out. I'd be skeptical too, and I just want to make sure that this deal... Well maybe it can be the first of many where neither side feels neglected." George slammed a fist into his palm. "You know I'm right."

Darius rubbed his forehead and closed his eyes. "George, you can either be an idealist or a soldier, but you can't be both."

"My mistake." George remained adamant, his sarcastic words punctuated by a hardened stare.

The Commander rolled his jaw and opened his eyes to meet George's. They both held firm for a long pause before Darius gave a deep exhale. "I'll give you this one, *prince*," the word stung, "But all I can do is write a recommendation to Jonsberg."

"That'll have to do." George said.

"Very well," Darius stood from his seat. "You are dismissed."

"Thank you, Commander." George tipped his head, but was met with a lazy wave. Knowing not to push it, the prince took his victory and slipped out of the tent. A fire started in his chest that made him numb to the bitter Autumn chill that was waiting for him on the other side. First magic, now this. A smile started on his face, only to be extinguished by a sudden punch to the arm. George spun to meet Franklin, the short man holding both a beaming smile and a folded white letter.

George blinked through a gust of wind and frowned. "Oh no, what have you done?"

"More like what have *you* done?" Franklin hooked an arm around George's shoulders and pushed him into a stroll. "First, I hear you managed to fend off an entire horde of Vagrants using magic that would put Hector to shame, and then..." He slapped the letter into George's chest. "A saucy little letter arrives for you from some lady named Anne."

"Anne!" George perked up and snatched the letter. He twisted out of Franklin's embrace and held the letter barely an inch from his nose. The prince paused and looked over at Franklin, the other young man putting his palms up.

"I didn't read it. I just saw the name signed all big and flowery."

George gave him a skeptical look before unfolding the letter and scanning its contents. Anne's handwriting was awful, and her grasp on letters was loose at best, but George knew exactly what each word said and what each sentence meant. A big dumb grin snuck onto his face and he could hear her voice in the words. She talked about her day, asked about his own, and complained about this or that, but tagged on the end was how much she missed him. Underneath that, was Anne's name signed really big and next to it was, as Franklin said, a tiny doodle of a flower similar to the ones from George's secret place.

Folding the letter back up, the prince safely tucked it into his pocket. Franklin was staring at George's huge lingering grin and finally poked him in the rib. "Georgie boy, do you have a girlfriend?"

"What? No!" George turned red. "She's just a good friend is all."

"Well, we're good friends and you never doodle *me* flowers." Franklin frowned.

"No, but I do for Hector."

The two broke out into laughter, only to end with Franklin jabbing George in the rib again.

"Speaking of good friends, you should come with me and Hector to Wretchett tonight. A lot of the soldiers are going to the tavern there to celebrate our victory at the mines. Bring Williams too."

"Oh yeah?!" George agreed with a questioning face. "How did the battle go anyway?"

"Crushing victory." Franklin stood tall. "They didn't stand a dream's chance in the void." The young man swapped the conversation back, "So I'll see you there?"

"Yeah, of course!" George nodded. "I just need to talk to Opane first and then I'll prepare—oh! Would it be okay if I invited Opane, as well?"

Franklin seemed hesitant for a moment before nodding. "You know what? Yeah, I think you should. She and her people were a big help in all this and I think it might be nice to remind ourselves of that."

George grinned. "Perfect then, I'll meet you there tonight."

"It's the only one, can't miss it." Franklin beamed a bright smile. "And glad to have you back, George."

"Good to be back." George clasped Franklin's shoulder and gave him a stiff pat on the back, the gesture happily repeated by Franklin.

From there George split off from Franklin, nearly leaping with each energetic step. A large smile stretched across his face as the events of the day unfolded in his mind. George stuffed a hand into his pocket to feel the paper of the letter and his smile grew even tighter to the point that his cheeks started to hurt.

George made a small detour to meet Opane and tell her of his success with the Commander. The Kafshe was extremely thankful, but when George offered her an invitation to the tavern, Opane politely declined. Respecting her decision, George left the Achian alone and with nothing else to do, he made a quick beeline back to his own abode.

***

Bursting into his tent, George immediately headed for the only other bed besides his own to reside in the small fabric cell.

"Williams!" George shouted loud enough to cause the sleeping man to wince and cough on a long string of drool. The gardener's son was still wearing his black tunic and tabard from the day's orders. He turned onto his back and lazily looked up at George. His eyes were puffy and pink, blinking slowly to fend off the dryness of exhaustion.

"What?" the tired man croaked.

"We are going to a tavern tonight."

Williams blinked again before rolling face down, drowning in his pillow. After a few silent seconds, a muffled voice pushed through the bedding. "Okay."

With that task complete, George slipped into his own bed and shoved the letter back in front of his face. He reread it, eyes scanning to the bottom and then slipping back to the top and to the bottom again. Tucking his tongue into his cheek, he gently placed the paper on a simple stand he kept by his bed.

Underneath the stand was a small pile of paper and a slim stick of charcoal. Collecting the stationary, George got to work scratching a letter of his own. Remembering Williams, the prince slowed down his eager strokes in an attempt to make as little noise as possible. And so, the pair's afternoon whittled away between gentle snores and several crumpled bits of paper.

It wasn't until the sun was bruising the sky pink that George found himself standing with his arms outstretched, the perfect letter pinched in his grasp. Williams was lazing on his side, eyes half open and examining the victorious prince.

"What's that?" Williams said through a yawn.

"A letter." George wouldn't meet Williams' eye.

Williams blinked and sat up. "Defensive?"

George rolled his eyes. "It's for Anne, I'm just replying to a letter she sent."

A smile curled on Williams' lips but before he could get a word in, George interrupted, "You're one to talk."

"I didn't even say anything, yet!" Williams started a tired laugh. "You madman!"

"Ah, you don't need to." George couldn't help but laugh back before pausing. "You know Williams, you could always use my paper if you ever wanted to write a letter yourself."

"You know my parents don't care for letters." Williams frowned but George caught him in a strong stare. The prince shrugged before looking away.

"I didn't really mean for your parents," George suggested. Williams' frown softened.

"Really?"

"Why not?"

"Thanks," Williams smiled. "I appreciate that."

"And I'd appreciate it if you got out of bed," George added as he knelt by a trunk, fiddling with the latch. He popped the lid open to reveal some folded clothes. "We got a tavern to attend and a Franklin to meet."

***

Wretchett would have been an unremarkable town if not for the influx of soldiers from the nearby encampments. The Nest wasn't the only tent city to spring up near the once quiet farming community. Gavarian forces occupied the opposite side and an additional yet smaller Imperial camp sat to its south. The layout of the town was simple, with vast fields for farming all surrounding a single nexus of buildings.

While the local noblewoman who owned the land had a squat yet strong keep in the center of the town, no other walls or defenses were available. This sense of lacking may have been one of the reasons Wretchett's locals didn't seem to mind soldiers lingering around their sole tavern too much, or perhaps it was the money. George could only speculate as he and Williams pushed through the crowd that had accumulated outside the old stone building of the tavern.

The stars were already up, not that George could make them out through the haze emerging from the doors and windows. Wisps of smoke slithered into the prince's nose and brought with them the smell of pine and campfires, which were common enough scents for George to assume it was Gavarian tobacco. With each breath, he could feel the thick smoke pushing in and out of his lungs.

"Williams, George! This way!" Franklin shouted at his mesmerized friends. The pair followed Franklin's voice while looking like lost dogs. Squeezing through some red-faced soldiers and bouncing off some spatially unaware drunkards, the duo finally made it to the front door, if only a little roughed up. George had put on a dark blue shirt whose belly had already collected the spill of an outside drinker. Williams didn't fare much better with loose embers spotting his right sleeve.

Hector stood by Franklin, the two much more casually dressed in their soldier's cotton-quilted whites. Franklin gave the others a quick once over before cracking a grin.

George frowned. "What?"

"He can tell it's your first time at the tavern," Hector said.

"Considering this is our first time to Wretchet, I fucking hope so." Williams shook his head and pushed through into the tavern.

"What's his problem?" Franklin scoffed.

"He's sleepy," George answered and both Franklin and Hector nodded simultaneously.

"Ooooh," they chorused.

"Sleepy Williams is quite the monster," Hector said sagely.

"More like a snapping turtle," Franklin rebounded. George rolled his eyes over a smile and walked past them.

Slipping by an exiting soldier, George found his way in. The inside was masked in a sea of smoke (much more than the outside was) that split the orange glow of the fires and candles. Boisterous laughter competed with ever-growing voices as friends struggled to hear each other and idle nemesis' barked threats. Heavy iron darts slammed into a wooden board painted with a game target, and mugs of both wood and metal thudded and clanked on a sticky bar. There was hardly anywhere to stand, let alone sit, and moving through the crowd had George bouncing off of every stiff shoulder and protruding belly.

By a miracle, George managed to find an empty stool by the bar. He raised a hand toward the exhausted bartender and the old man hobbled over to him. Before George could order, a strong voice came from behind him. "An ale for the young prince." A coin slapped onto the bar.

George turned to the voice, his eyes immediately catching the inebriated stare of Commander Darius. The prince went to stand up but a gloved hand fell on his shoulder, keeping him seated. Darius looked at the seat next to George, and the soldier who was occupying it slipped off with a grumble. Sitting down, the Commander let out a long groan of relief.

"Something on your mind, Commander?" George studied the thoughtful lines on Darius' forehead. Two mugs landed in front of the pair and the Commander nudged one towards the prince. George took it in both hands, and stared down at the foamy head.

"Sir." George watched the bubbles break. "I don't drink alcohol."

"Because of your Stromist training?" Darius gulped at his own. "Mine works best with a little beer, what does that say about those theories?"

Reluctantly, George took a sip of the beer. It held a bitter taste that turned nutty over time. He frowned. "What exactly do you mean it works best?"

"Exactly what it sounds like." Darius sipped at his beer and stared blankly ahead. "For most of my career I couldn't even use the damn magic. I tried everything the masters would teach, played as pure as possible, but it wasn't until I needed it the most that I got it, and after that it came better than most times with something relaxing my thoughts."

"Needed it the most?" George parroted.

"Prisoner of war," Darius stated. "Stale bread, naked, old beer. My body was at its worst when I found my Stromism."

"I'm sorry, sir, but why are you telling me this?" George took another sip.

"Because I'm drunk," the man said simply, "and I admit, you remind me a little of how I was. I saw how your magic ignited, it only came to you when you needed it. Something in you told you that it was needed. Some sort of trigger." Darius pushed his empty cup away. "What did you feel before it ignited?"

George took another hesitant sip of his drink, too focused on the question to really enjoy the beverage. Pushing his memory, he found that he couldn't quite place what exactly he was feeling, just the sensation. "My emotions. I felt them all. They appeared like a black smoke, clouding everything else."

Darius furrowed his brow and gave George a long and hard stare. "Smoke?"

"Yeah," George continued, "black smoke, wild black smoke."

"I... wouldn't tell anyone else this," Darius said, the concern on his face overtaking his drunken stupor.

"Why?"

The Commander rolled his jaw in thought, as if carefully picking his words. "Black smoke is the tool of the Dweller herself. Her Nachtist followers use it, summon it even. It's a bad metaphor to use for your emotions, people might mistake your intention and think you're in communion with the Dweller. The Imperial Family has enough of those rumors already, I hear."

George could think of a few, with most of them accusing his father or uncle of being entwined with the void-dwelling devil. It made him uncomfortable now, and he squirmed in his stool. He didn't like the thought that something iconic to the Dweller was the first thing he reached for to describe the power inside of him. It must have showed on his face, because while in his thoughts, Darius changed his expression to one more teasing than strict.

"Don't let an old veteran's drunken stories ruin your night." The Commander stood, kicking his stool back in place. "And try to stay out of bars. Only the stupid or broken souls find their way to places like this."

Wrenched from his mind and to the irony of the statement, George went to protest. "But you—"

"I know what I said," Darius cracked a grin, "don't forget to sleep tonight, the war isn't over yet."

With little else, the Commander turned on a heel and started his journey away. His very presence seemed to summon an invisible barrier that parted the soldiers and fools in his way, allowing Darius an easy and casual exit into the mass. From the opening caused by Darius, Williams managed to slip through the crowd and steal the open seat next to George.

"Still grumpy?" George pushed his beer to the side and looked square at his friend.

"Only a little," Williams admitted.

"I'll cut his balls off!" Franklin's voice hissed over the noise of the crowd. George and Williams perked up to see their friend jabbing a finger towards a trio of red-faced soldiers, with only Hector between the two.

Scurrying off their stools, the pair approached the scene. Hector was speaking in a calm voice. "You're not going to cut his balls off."

"Whose balls are we cutting off?" George inquired, crossing his arms as he analyzed the other soldiers. They were perhaps a few years older and definitely looked the part of gruff and drunk. The one at the fore, a man with glossy drunken eyes, was staring daggers at Franklin.

"No one's, the balls are safe," Hector replied. "We're actually just going to leave this gentleman and his friends alone, they've clearly had too much to drink."

"Oh, piss off." One with a gruesome scar across her nose groaned.

"They were telling lies about the Imperial family, calling them a bunch of crooked cultists. Saying Wilhelm is possessed and pushed Empress Sophia." Franklin didn't remove his eyes from the soldiers.

George gritted his teeth, hating how frequent this topic seemed to appear tonight. Williams put a hand on his shoulder, though his own eyes betrayed his exhaustion with the theme. "Not worth it."

"You're right," George admitted, but kept his fist closed.

One of the soldiers scoffed, "If you think that's bad, then don't even get me started on the 'miraculous' recovery of that witch, Josephine—"

A loud crack sounded as Williams' fist rocked the soldier to the floor. The grumpy auxiliary spat on his fallen foe.

"Go Williams!" Franklin grinned wide, only for his smile to be smashed closed by the scarred soldier's fist. The rusty-haired man shook away the blow before diving in on his new foe. Another second passed and Hector had another one of the soldiers in a single-armed headlock, glittering magic covering over his flexing bicep.

A fist hit George in the back of the ribs, forcing him to turn with a punch of his own. The flat of his knuckle cleanly railed his assailant in the stomach. Before long, the entire bar was a mess of drunken brawls and tossed mugs. Hands flew and so did the occasional splatter of spit and blood. Stools were knocked over and the ground became sticky with spilled beer and wine.

George rolled away from the weight of a fallen man three times his size, his shirt picking up every stain on the floor as he did. His shoulder bumped into Franklin's. The young man was also prone under the fighting.

"Fancy seeing you here at this hour." Franklin smiled. "Come here often?"

George blinked. "Are you missing a tooth?"

Franklin dodged a stray foot before rolling back to George and poked his own mouth with his forefinger. "Fuck. That's going to hurt later."

"Why isn't it hurting now?"

"Liquor?"

"Fair."

The two began to crawl towards the exit, avoiding falling fighters and misplaced stomps. Debris and splatter were flung overhead, the occasional shrapnel bouncing off their backs or their hand-covered heads. With the clean air of freedom seeping in through the door right in front of them, they kicked with their heels and sprung through and into the cool night air outside. George launched his head right into Hector's knee, and Franklin landed at Williams' boots, the two waiting for them with wide grins and helping hands. They wrenched their friends to their feet.

All together the group started laughing and chaining their arms around each other's shoulders. They began their wobbling journey away from the tavern and into the blanket of night, one with a tooth missing, a black eye on Williams, and a dirty bootprint pressed across George's chest. Only Hector seemed less worse for wear, if his booze-soaked clothing didn't count.

"Hey, pshhht," Franklin caught the others' attention. He snuck a hand under his shirt and pulled a flat glass bottle from under it. Amber liquid swished inside, the eyes of the others growing wide.

"Imperial almond?" Hector grinned.

"Swiped it when no one was looking." Franklin flashed a bloodied smile.

"You thief." George smiled, a hesitant wince in his right eye.

"I—uh... screw it." Williams closed his swollen eye and peeked at Franklin with his one good one. "Let's just dive in, then."

Franklin popped the cork from the bottle and pushed it into George's hands. "You need to catch up."

George looked down at the mouth of the bottle and before he knew it, the sweet yet burning liquor was streaming down his throat, his eyes up at the night sky, and stars twinkling off the bottom of the glass. The bottle went around, and he found himself there again, and again, until he suddenly found himself somewhere completely different.

He stood alone in a mess of trees near The Nest, his vision fuzzy and his friends nowhere to be seen. In front of him was a tree that had been knocked over by an ancient storm, its roots webbing in the air. George wobbled over, his footing not exactly straight. The roots had a deep, heart-pink color to them that George could appreciate even through his unsure vision. Sliding his knife out of its pouch, he began to cut off a chunk. Slipping his prize into his pocket, he felt the world quickly spin, the ground coming rapidly towards him.

Chapter 14
The Dweller's Boy

A dark smoke swirled all around George's vision, his body feeling ethereal and weightless. He wasn't sure, but he could have sworn he was looking at the face of a woman. Her face faded in and out of view through the bursts of smoke and misty blue swirls. Her eyes were blinking in and out of sight, George's vision never quite taking in their detail. When he tried to turn away, he noticed that he couldn't move his head, or feel it. What was he? Where was he?

That familiar voice from behind the door called out to him. "George... I've missed you..."

"Who are you?" George retaliated.

Her voice was sickeningly sweet. "I've been busy, all stuck in my lonesome, but I've found you again. You won't let me stay like this forever, right, George?"

George could feel anxiety creep into his mind. "What do you want from me?"

As if answering him, a force gripped George's neck and started violently pushing him back and forth. He could feel his throat close and his bones crackle under the pressure. Back and forth, threatening to rip his head off, back and forth until all at once his eyes snapped open and the real world sprinkled into focus. Williams was shaking him by his wrinkled collar, each push nearly toppling him out of bed. The prince couldn't remember when he had crawled into his bed, and guessing by William's own wrinkled clothing and sunken eyes, he had no idea either. George pinched his brow with one hand and swatted Williams away with the other.

"Wha-whaat?" his voice cracked with both fear and sleep.

"The camp is moving out," Williams said.

George shot up out of bed, nightmare thrown to the back of his head as he nearly toppled over lunging for his boots.

"Moving? What? When?" he sputtered as he kicked the worn leathers on. Williams ran a hand through his own messy hair.

"I don't know the details but I'm sure the Commander will have answers at line up."

"Guys, hurry up," Hector's voice came from outside the tent, "the others are starting to fall into rank already."

"Coming!"

The prince burst out of the tent, only to get knocked back by the brightness of the sun, which was already high in the sky. Blinking the crust from his eyes, the image of Hector slowly registered. The young man was already dressed in his armor, from his steel greaves to his hauberk, breastplate, and cape. Hector's dark eyes sparkled as if he just had the best sleep of his life.

"Void, Hector, how are you so alive?" George looked the part of a beggar next to him.

"Good genes." Hector shoved a collection of armor and colors into George's arms. "The Commander asked me to give you these."

George's eyes widened. "This is the kit for the vanguard."

Hector tilted his head and shot a smirk. "Now we just need to get Williams in and we'll have the whole set."

"That's the plan." George held the kit tight. His eyes soaked in the equipment. Nightmares or no nightmares, he was becoming his own, a true warrior. He won't be a victim forever.

"Yeah? Whose?" Williams cut him from his thoughts as he walked out of the tent. The young man was tugging his auxiliary tunic down straight, eyes black with exhaustion.

"That's a good question," Hector laughed. "To the lineup, then?"

***

George was quick to slip into a quilted gambeson and a pair of trousers before throwing on his chainmail and strapping on his greaves and breastplate. All that was left was to toss the purple and red cape of the Empire's Stromists over his shoulders and don the iconic open-faced helmet. Slots were put by the ears, maybe giving it a slightly goofy look but greatly aiding in hearing. After tightening the metal cheek straps with a leather string under the chin, George looked every bit a soldier of the Stromist Vanguard.

However, upon actually finding the lineup, George removed the helmet after seeing no one else wearing theirs. He then quickly found a place next to Franklin and Hector while Williams was forced to rank with the other black tunics. All around them, the camp was being dismantled and wagons loaded. Commander Darius stood on a wooden platform overlooking the rank and file of his troops.

"Soldiers of the 11th Vanguard," he opened. "Our temporary stay outside Wretchett has come to an end and so soon too might this war. The Duke of Gavaria has requested a joint assault on the field of Kors in an attempt to cleave the territory of our enemy in twain. By tonight our camp will be dismantled, but you won't be there to see it. All vanguard soldiers including myself have been asked to make haste and as such we will march ahead to meet the duke's encampment. Prepare packs for march, call will be given in two hours."

The response was a loud silence. Everyone's face seemed to wear the same look, one of both anticipation and maybe even worry on the younger faces. The faces didn't last longer than a few seconds, as once the dismissal came, everyone started to break off to ready their packs.

"It was inevitable," Franklin commented, "real war, real battles." The group stood still amid the sea of movement.

"Hm." George made an agreeing hum laced with a sudden hesitancy, as if he wasn't just excited to be a warrior a minute ago.

"What's wrong?" Hector raised a brow.

"Nothing, really," George rolled his jaw. "I just never thought I'd be here." He spoke without thinking.

"Isn't being here a good thing?" Franklin quickly interjected.

"Yes... but," The pale eyes of a Vagrant flashed in George's memory, "there are some experiences I could do without." The voice of the woman echoed behind his thoughts. She said she found him, did that mean he was in danger again, could he even afford to be so traumatized? George closed his eyes, all he knew was that he needed to be strong. Something in him told him that she won't be hiding behind a dream forever, let alone her horned friend. The prince rested a hand on the pommel of Oathkith. He needed to be ready.

George paused long enough for Hector to cut in. "Are you thinking about going home?"

"What?" George looked up at his friend, his nightmares fading into the back of his mind. "No! I'm here to see these battles through. There *is* a purpose to all of this, and I'm not going to be leaving you guys hanging. Someone has to be here, and someone has to do this... besides, I've always wanted to be a soldier."

Franklin clapped a hand on George's shoulder. "Then let's go be soldiers."

"And pack up before we run out of time," Hector added.

"Yeah, that's part of what I meant." Franklin crossed his arms.

"I know, I was just—"

"Oh, I know!" Franklin interjected. He pointed a finger at his friend. "Mr Last-Word-Hector."

"We all know." George forced a hesitant smile.

***

The small group cut off there to go and quickly pack their essentials and gear for the march. Unfortunately, due to the nature of the task ahead as well as the expediency, Williams was being left behind with the other Auxiliaries, though George hoped he'd catch up before the battle.

Before long, George was thrust into a train of soldiers, dressed head to toe in his new uniform. Marching with other soldiers gave George a sense of pride, the warm feeling cutting away his lingering doubts, or at least pushing them back. Any chance for further contemplation about what he was doing up North, his dreams, the smoke, or about the war was interrupted by the scenery all around him.

Looking past the sea of metal-clad soldiers, George's vision was caught up in the beauty of the northern autumn. Reds and oranges burned the late fall trees, and deep green conifers sparkled with frost. Beyond the clank of the march, George's imagination pieced together the songs the more stubborn of the northern birds might be trilling and chirping among the wide boughs of the forest. A certain shame poked its head into the prince's chest, a shame he didn't have the mind to try and enjoy this area's natural beauty more when he had the chance.

A heavy wind carried the smell of the pines to George along with the rattling of Franklin, the other young man discussing the nature of Kors with Hector and another soldier that George didn't know the name of. She was about their age with mousy brown hair and a lazy look to her eyes.

"No, you see, it's absolutely genius," Franklin explained while holding out a flat palm. "Since the Vagrants allied with the giants, Gavaria couldn't really push them north without hitting deeper giant territory and getting swallowed, but!"

"So, the giants really allied with the Vagrants? Huh, maybe there is merit to the whole Titanspoke theory." The other soldier cut in.

"Titanspoke?" George bit.

The soldier nodded sagely, "They say the giants finally got a new Titanspoke, you know. A spiritual leader of sorts picked by a legendary titan to guide the giants as one tribe, could even get them to ally with the vagrants—"

"But!" Franklin frowned, before continuing, drawing on his palm with a finger, "If we head west and take Kors, we cut them off from each other or at the very least make it very hard for them to reconvene and reinforce." The young soldier formed a fist. "If the Vagrants try to move north to retake it, Gavaria can hit them from the south. We've isolated our enemy."

"Surely they know the risk of losing Kors," George added.

"I expect that's why this will be a joint battle," Hector responded with a nod.

George raised his brows. "Well, here's to the end of the war then."

"As if they'd give in that easily, we'll be fighting stragglers until we are grey," the other soldier puffed her cheeks in a huff.

"Let's just see about that one, then." Franklin crossed his arms and thoughtful silence followed.

"Do you think the titan will fight with them?" George asked.

Franklin bit his lip and thought hard. "I feel like a titan would show up in a scouting report, or you know, any report in the last hundreds of years."

"Hm." George looked down in contemplation. Titans, that's new.

"They say the Titanspoke was led to the titan by visions and dreams," The soldier continued. She scoffed and started rattling on about what her dream was last night, but George was staring at her with wide eyes, not hearing a drop of her story. The enemy was led to power by a dream? The implications passed behind the prince's eyes as the soldier fell into silence, no one picking at her story. George remained in his thoughts, marching alongside the others.

The rest of the day went by in a similar fashion, a silence would overtake the conversation until a new topic arose, then a soldier unknown by the others would jump in, and eventually it would end with a silence once again. On and off the conversations went, and in and out of his contemplations George went. It wasn't until a sharp elbow jutted into his rib did he pull himself free, dazed and completely lost.

"Huh!?"

Franklin was staring directly at George, the twinkling of stars breaking through a growing dusk. "You're getting really good at marching in your head, huh?"

"Are we there?" George stood on his toes to look over the soldiers in front of him. Light danced around a hill just ahead, making it look as if it was on fire by natural means. "Gavarian camp?"

"I hope so, we are in Gavaria." Hector cracked a smile.

George shook his head. "That was cheap and awful."

Franklin pointed loosely. "Just like your—"

"Okay, let's cut it off there while we are ahead." George squinted, attempting to see the silhouette of Darius at the head of the line. He couldn't catch sight of the man before a chorus of orders ricocheted down the line and soon the column was marching into the Gavarian camp.

As the picket of the active camp surrounded them, Darius was standing by the entrance with some soldiers in deep blue tabards. On their hips they wore fancy scabbards with strings of badges latching them to their belts. They seemed to be studying each Imperial soldier that walked in, thankfully with welcoming and even relieved eyes.

Before George could walk by, Darius held up a hand to instruct him out of the column. Giving Franklin and Hector a confused look, George stepped from the moving line and up to the Commander. The oldest of the men among the bunch pinched a peppery beard before speaking.

"Prince George?" His voice was akin to a warm rumble, something George imagined a grandfather would sound like.

"That would be me, sir."

The man looked at Darius with an amused smile before looking back at George. "Do you know who I am?"

George wrinkled his brow but looked the man in the eye, finding them oddly sunken and weary. "I'll be honest, it is far too often people know my name but I don't know theirs. I'm not proud of it, but—"

"Think nothing more of it," the man dismissed George's apology and upon granting the prince a polite smile, he continued, "I'm Duke Osbert of Gavaria and it is I who should be calling you sir."

The duke bowed his head low. "To think last I saw you, you were but a small baby in your father's arms. Now you're a soldier wrestling back the iron mines for my people. I thank you for your interest and arms in the plight of the North."

A gentle heat warmed George's chest, the praise settling into his ears. The prince's grey eyes were struck wide, only shrinking as George prattled for a response. "I-I'm honored, si—DUKE, Duke Osbert."

Osbert let out a hearty laugh that was quickly followed by a hoarse cough and then another. A fit of coughs and gags flinched out of the man long enough for one of the other Gavarians to offer a white cloth to cover the reddened face of the man. After a few more gags, one spit and a sniffle, the duke cleared his throat.

"My apologies, your highness," Osbert sniffled, the title feeling a bit heavy to George. "I've been feeling under the weather as of late."

"It's alright, I've heard—"

"Ah, no privacy for the noble I suppose." Osbert cleared his throat. "Speaking of, I couldn't help but notice that you're in the armor of a common man, walking in their ranks, and, though I am forever grateful, scouting their battles. You are of age, why not take a command role as is your birthright?"

George stood blinking, his mind grinding at an answer. He pursed his lips into a thoughtful line and tilted his head, as if the solution would fall from his ear. Finally, he exhaled and stalwartly replied, "Because I *am* a soldier, not yet seasoned beyond that to lead. People would likely get hurt and besides, I'd much rather prove my worth by action than birthright."

A simple grin appeared on Darius' face, matched by the duke's.

"You know," Osbert began, "You remind me of my son."

"Fenric?"

"*Commander* Fenric..." The duke seemed displeased. "No, not him, he's off securing a different location during all of this... at the very least he can *pester the enemy* while we advance. No, I meant my firstborn, well, when he was around that is."

An awkward silence brewed for a moment, broken by the duke suddenly changing subjects, "But! If you want to work your way up to your position, then I can only surmise it would help if you got to see generals and commanders in action. Come, we were just about to go over the battle once more, and having the Imperial prince along could only be a boon in many ways."

A determined look overtook George's visage. "Of course!"

"Very good!" The duke clapped his hands proudly. "The tent is just this way."

***

The meeting in the tent went about as much as George had expected it. For the most part it was a bunch of old military men and women barking over a large map with figurines, but what stuck out to George the most was how casually they would move these small indicators as if they didn't represent the lives of thousands. Perhaps Darius felt the same way, as George would occasionally catch the Commander frowning deeper than usual when the Duke or another Gavarian went on a brutally hypothetical tangent over the fate of each piece.

It wasn't until General Jonsberg himself entered that the real talks began, and of course a plan was already drafted long before this tent full meeting was even scheduled. The hypotheticals were quickly abandoned for the true plan, albeit with some alterations according to fresher information and perhaps some aftertaste from the previous tangents.

George himself didn't get to speak much, or at least he felt he couldn't, though occasionally the duke would pull him into the conversation by using his Imperial Title, but only when looking for a small amount of support for a new idea he was brewing. Though, George did give the duke credit in trying to explain each tactic and reason to him, oftentimes straight over Jonsberg's own explanation.

Eventually Jonsberg slammed a fist down onto the table, making the pieces jump. His aggressive strike cemented the plan amid a chorus of approving grunts and one confused squeak from George, which he quickly deepened into a grunt. Next thing the prince knew, he was standing in a frostbitten field on the right flank of an army of Stromists.

He was suited in the heavy armor of the vanguard, much like the rest of the large rectangular formation he was in. The rectangle was West adjacent to another which in turn was West adjacent to a third. Much like the one George was in, the farthest formation of soldiers was heavily armed, while the center army had a purposefully underwhelming looking frontline. George knew Hector was in that column, as were all the other best Stromists the 11th Vanguard had to offer.

George wasn't sure the enemy would take the bait laid out, wherein the flanking armies such as George's would close in on whoever dared strike the center, but Jonsberg had similar doubts and so the Gavarian cavalry was stacked to the far west of George, prepared to scoop up the enemy should they be so wise. On top of this alteration, the three rectangle formations were stacked in a slight diagonal, with George's being the furthest back (or South). The prince did object to being put so far away from the fight, but Jonsberg had quickly reminded him he was a political icon, not a scheduled martyr.

A banner from Jonsberg shot up in the center formation and soon the entire configuration was moving down the open fields of Kors. All George could see was a flat tundra, the bite of winter starting to dig into the browning plants. The enemy hadn't appeared on the battlefield yet. Their army was likely still filtering through the monstrously large conifer forest at the very far end. Scouts had checked for possible flanks beforehand but this field was chosen for its strategic geography situated with an impossibly rocky mountainside to the west and a sucking marsh to the east. If the enemy was going to defend their territory, they had to meet the Imperials and Gavarians headfirst.

Step by step, George kept in sync with his line. The cumulative sound of each footfall gave George a small burst of pride and security, drowning out the hesitation he felt in his gut. His fingers trembled against a spear as he marched, eyes struck forward. It was strange, but the scene of an empty battlefield right before the battle, without any enemy, reminded George of any other natural scene if only strangely quiet. The wind blew softly, as if keeping its voice down, while the birds altogether were silent save for one rebellious chickadee hidden somewhere at the field's edge.

Frozen, brittle grass swished roughly against George, the blades growing longer the deeper he went into the fields. The grassy tug, the chickadee, the gentle wind—he let it all take him away, only to be pulled back to reality. He spotted something move in the trees far ahead. Very slowly, indistinct figures began to pop out of the conifers, short like a man. George grit his teeth. They kept coming and coming, forming a long dark line of mail, helmets, and spears in front of the trees. Just as soon as it seemed the enemy was done forming, the line of warriors opened up down the middle and taller figures lumbered out of the woods behind them.

Giants, or so George assumed. They were as tall as two men and just as wide. On their bodies they wore dense mosaics of pelts and chains and in their hands were weapons the same size as George himself. Gruesome single-edged swords more fit to be called cleavers, devious spiked clubs, and axes that lived up to the folktales. The prince could feel doubt enter his mind, and he could feel it entering those next to him, though he must've not have been the only one.

Darius shouted from George's formation, "HOO-AH!"

A thunderous "HOO-AH!" roared back at Darius, the battle cry involuntarily erupting from George. The young soldier along with the others began to pick up their pace, turning their steady march into a slow jog. The rhythmic steps were replaced with the bouncing clash of metal as the Empire's forces approached the enemy.

As Jonsberg predicted, the enemy started to veer to the far East in an attempt to hit the weak side of the diagonal, but a quick horn and raised flag fixed this possible flank. The indicated order set the army to move slightly more to the East themselves, putting the marsh on their flank. The Gavarian cavalry began to rear into a shallow trot themselves, the threat of a charge or getting caught in a marsh putting the Vagrants back straight. One of the giants in the center of the enemy horde let out a chilling war cry traced with flakes of temper and annoyance. The time for tactics had ended and the enemy bolted into a charge.

The ground shook under George's feet, each quake betraying the sheer mass of the enemy army. George readied his shield and gripped his spear tight, pointing it forward alongside his shield mates. Behind the prince and the other Imperial infantry, archers let loose a volley of high arcing arrows. Bowstrings twanged and echoed across the field as arrows whistled. A black mass of projectiles showered in front of the diagonal, catching the enemy charge. Bodies flew forward with momentum, and gurgled screams protested. A sickening cacophony of arrows plunging into flesh thunked alongside the slaughter.

Any confidence gained from the volleys fell short as the enemy made it to the halfway mark, their biggest and best slowing down to throw their own projectiles. Javelins both small enough for a man and big enough for a giant came rocketing down towards the Imperials. George was far enough in the back of the fight to be safe from chance but he raised his shield along with the rest of his formation anyway.

The front-most formation wasn't as lucky, with a sapling sized javelin slamming into the front lines. Though the breach was quickly filled, most shields of the surviving were discarded after too many javelins littered their faces to be effective. Vagrants took the opening, and before long the top most formation in the diagonal was embroiled in battle, the Imperial soldiers doing their best to push the enemy west.

George himself was awkwardly stuck in the calm of the battle, his formation moving forward slowly. A loud bang sounded as a group of giants slammed into the middle formation. George cringed, hoping Hector and Franklin were alright, though the prince didn't have much time to dwell on it. The enemy was straight ahead.

Steeling his resolve, George pointed his spear at the enemy lines. Their rage-twisted faces were clearer than he would have liked. The giants had mostly taken to the center formation, leaving George and the rest of his rectangle against mostly human. Buckling his knees, George held his shield up, its surface standing between himself and the charging enemy.

Curdled war cries throttled George's ears while he forced his eyes up and ahead. His head shook with the loud sounds of war, rattling his brain. Only the prince's adrenaline was able to push him forward, just in time to catch an enemy with his spear.

The weapon tugged as it punched through the rebel, their own spear drooping just inches from George, a surprised look on both their faces. George didn't have enough time to think about who he just killed and quickly pulled his weapon free. A rebel swatted George's spear away with a round shield but before he could capitalize, another Imperial had already forced him back with a precise stab.

Soon the crisp cold air of the field turned into a muggy fog of breath and blood. George's spear arm grew tired and when the enemy broke past the spear range, he dropped it in favor of Oathkith. The line battle had turned dense, leaving George with little room to move. Using shallow stabs, George attempted to clear some space in front of him, but more and more enemy soldiers kept appearing.

George could only assume the cavalry had met the backside of the enemy, or why else would they be packing themselves so tightly against the Imperial soldiers. Feeling a pang of panic, George looked to his East, catching glimpses through whatever gaps he could find. The center formation was level with his now and bowing outwards, they were in trouble of breaking and splintering the Imperial forces in two. George's view was quickly being screened by the enemy, their line now packed much too tightly against his own.

The shoulder of a vagrant rammed into George's shield with a bang, pushing his arm against him while the bloody back of another vagrant pinned his sword arm under the weight. A soldier behind George was pushing him forward, squeezing the prince against the lines of the enemy. George felt anxiety rise in his chest. He couldn't move, what was going on?

Squirming didn't help, as each movement somehow locked him deeper and deeper into the grunting and coughing mass as the two armies were plied against each other. He felt his shield arm press deeper against his chest, shallowing his breathing. What air he did pull into his lungs was musky and filled with sweat. His eyes started to strain, heart beating in his ears.

A horn blasted.

A shimmer of gold erupted around George's allies. The order had flown: the enemy was contained, activate your magic. A blast of light from the center formation once again put the column into George's view and the illuminated figure of Hector burned the brightest.

George watched Hector scream over the chants of battle and charge out to meet the largest of the giants. The young soldier leapt all the way to the beast's face with a single earth shaking bound and used his immense strength to tear the giant back to the ground. Another blast of light splashed from the fight, signaling a brutal victory. Franklin and the other soldiers of the center were next to advance, the pulsing magic in them leading the push against the enemy.

Turning to his own fight, George found enough room to slam his shield into the rebel that previously had him pinned, freeing him once again. The prince's mind groaned and itched as it attempted to scratch open his own wealth of magic. He could feel it tingling in his fingertips and in his lungs, but George couldn't get it to erupt through him. In his body, it felt like a dense fog or mist seemed to stand between him and his well of power. No raging smoke.

Oathkith sliced an enemy open before stabbing into another. George tightened his grip, his shield mates pushing faster than him, their shimmering arms blurred with speed and strength. Desperate, George grit his teeth and even smacked the pommel of his blade against his helmet. Nothing.

Another horn, different from the last blasted from the fractured enemy horde and soon pockets of enemies not already fighting for their lives began to break away and flee. The battlefield opened up and George could see the cavalry running the scattering enemy down. Holding formation with his fellow soldiers, George could only look on as the scramble was swiftly dispatched with brutal precision by the Gavarians. Any other enemy remnants had long since retreated into the conifers. George let his shield and sword droop to his sides and what magic he had brewing fizzled away. The sky was blue, the ground was red and Kors was theirs.

Chapter 15
No Longer a Boy

George found himself sitting on a bench in the outskirts of Castle Kalvin which was a well-dug in fortification built into the hamlet of Korku. White flakes of snow were falling from the sky and collecting on his broad shoulders. The man's attention was past the light snowfall and towards an empty road that cut through the hilly farmland, not that he could see far past the falling veil of snow.

It had been two years since he managed to use his Stromism at the skirmish for the iron mine and two years of it still being beyond his ability to unlock on command. Two years since his failure to keep up at the battle of Kors, and two years since the Imperial victory. It was also two years since he first left Anne, and three months since he last saw her.

A fresh red scar that notched George's stubbled jaw spoke to the truth that the war didn't end after Kors, even if the enemy was greatly crippled by it. The boy, now a man, had hair that fell to his shoulders in long black locks, adding to the visual of time passing. Such hair now curtained him as he looked down at his hands and twiddled his thumbs, calloused and nervous. All that war, and right now all he could think about was Anne cresting the hills of Korku and coming down the road. Anticipation soured in his chest and squeezed into his heart with anxiety. Her last letter was bare, and a deep concern kept George worried.

Eager for a distraction, George plucked the small pendant of pink wood he had cut two years ago from his pocket and rolled it in his fingers. She was already late and even though George got there early, the sun was well past high noon along with George's imagination.

He tried his best to keep his growing anxiety from winning him over and shoved the pendant back into his pocket. Looking over to the empty spot on the bench, George smiled nervously at the small bundle of flowers he had scavenged for Anne.

"It's just stress," he told himself. "Stress from training, stress from the winter, stress from it all. That's all the anxiety is."

George's final words faded into the snow fall, lingering between him and the shifting sky. Time seemed to be passing slowly, but at the same time it seemed to be passing too quickly. It was just him, his thoughts, and the sound of the wind brushing the snow. Closing his eyes, George took in a nervous breath and just as he was about to exhale, a voice entered his ear.

"George."

The prince coughed in surprise, opening his eyes at the image of Anne. "H-hi!"

"Hey." Anne smiled weakly. George went to move, but noticed Anne's eyes lingering on the flowers beside him, a guilty look on her face.

George spoke. "How are you?"

Anne gave another misplaced smile, one that hardly belonged to her. "I'm okay, and you?"

George's stomach sickened, this was too much. "What's wrong?"

Anne stood surprised for a moment, face red and fingers shaking. Looking away she all but whispered, "I... I don't think I can do this anymore."

George's eyes widened and a cold pang hit his chest.

"I'm sorry I kept you waiting." Anne didn't look back at him, clearly distraught. "I just can't do this anymore."

"What do you mean?" George was more concerned about her than anything, standing up slowly to meet her.

"It's just too much for me," Anne explained, "waiting to hear from you, the battles, the fighting, being so far away and not knowing what's happening... too scared to do my own things, feeling selfish. All these letters... I just... it's wearing down on me, George. All this time, it's eroding me."

George stood paralyzed, hands out as if offering nothing. He gaped and grew pensive before resigning a sigh. Emotions swelled his thoughts, but even still, the shock he was in held it back just enough for him to reason. "I understand."

Anne's face softened and looked over to the man. "You can hate me."

"I don't hate you," George's voice was soft and defeated. "... Are you sure about all this?"

"I am..." Anne crossed her arms, hugging herself. "It's not good for me."

"Then okay," a sad croak came from George, "I can respect that."

"You can?"

George nodded with his eyes downcast. Only simple truths escaped the flurry he was feeling. "I care about you."

"I care about you too, George."

A silence overtook the pair as they both stood looking at the ground. Finally, George looked and opened his mouth but hesitated.

"What?" Anne questioned.

The prince closed his shimmering eyes and let himself speak without thinking. "Can I have a hug?"

Nodding slowly, Anne stepped into George and the man wrapped his arms around her. She returned the embrace, squeezing the sad man gently, her own eyes wet with more than snow.

***

Tear stricken weeks flew by faster than George would have liked. Grief seemed to make time move too quickly while also making it feel slow, and in the end, the prince felt that he was left with no time at all. In an attempt to at least fill his stagnant winter with more than sadness, George took to the training field.

"Hyah!" the prince grunted, his voice bouncing off the stone walls that ringed the snow-laden court. His sword arm swung wide and Oathkith took a bite out of George's wooden enemy. George stood on a sheet of white with only his exertion fending off the sharp cold of winter.

Holding a shallow hum in his throat, George swung mechanically at the dummy, a trick he picked up from Hector. He could feel his magic vibrating along with the hum, and yet it still felt past his grip, like an itch under the skin. Oathkith took another chunk out of the wood. A well of frustration hiccupped the hum. George cringed and threw an angry slash at the dummy. His blade struck deep.

"I think your uncle would likely have something to say about letting your irritation control your mindset in combat," Darius plied from the sidelines.

George yanked Oathkith free, a snarl on his face. "Yeah, I'm sure he would."

"Don't be snarky," The Commander frowned. "Unless of course you find a way to weaponize *that* against the giant Chieftain."

"If that doesn't work, we can just throw Hector at this one like we did the last one." George slipped his blade back into his scabbard and turned to the Commander. George's frustrated face mismatched Darius' own look of confusion.

Darius raised a brow. "Hector didn't tell you, yet?"

"Tell me what?"

"He's leaving the front."

A feeling of shock momentarily broke George's frustration, the man taken aback. "What? Why?"

"Commendation. These last two years haven't gone unnoticed by the Council of Stromism."

"Seems counterintuitive to pull someone capable from the front just to thank them for being on the front," George scoffed and shook his head, his agitation rearing its head again. He pinched his brow. "But what do I know about anything?"

Darius stared blankly at George for a moment. "You're sounding an awful lot like a whiny bitchy princey today. Is something on your mind, soldier?"

George offered the Commander a small smile before sighing. "No... I think it's just the calm of winter driving me insane. I have too much time to think."

"What did I tell you about thinking?" Darius stood straight and authoritative.

"Don't dwell?"

The Commander gave a single nod. "Too much thinking is bad for your health, and doubly bad for magic."

"You're right," George conceded, "and thank you again for helping me practice."

"Think nothing of it." Darius paused in thought, a grin growing at the notice of the pun.

A silent moment passed before George spoke up again, "I should go congratulate Hector."

"As a good friend would." The Commander nodded and folded his arms square behind his back. "Dismissed."

***

Hector laid on his back with his face to the sharp blue sky above and a solid stone block beneath him. From his spot he flicked through the pages of a few letters. Chairs were haphazardly pulled up to the stone block as if it were a table, but were scattered and empty like scars of a busier moment. Snow was heaped on top of them, a tiny mirror to the larger piles that layered the edges of the rear castle courtyards. Franklin himself faced one of these piles, idly whistling a chirping tune.

White conquered the lazy scene. It was in the snow, in the fat clouds above, in the banners of the castle, and dusted in every soldier's hair. A gentle trickle of water finished the portrait, though no stream could be seen. If it had been warmer and filled with flowers and the buzz of bees, George maybe could excuse it as a memory of the Imperial Gardens. The prince's approach crunched the snow.

Franklin's whistling stopped abruptly and then the sound of running water quickly faded, followed by the buckling of a belt.

George closed his eyes in shame only to open them to the wide smile of Franklin and the curious stare of Hector.

"Hey Georgie boy!" Franklin's greeting was loud and happy.

"Practicing your writing?" George folded his arms, doing his best not to smile at his own joke. Franklin looked confused for a moment, only to chuckle and shake his head.

"Speaking of writing," he began, "letters came in."

Hector fanned the thick stack of papers that he was reading and looked over at George. "Double the usual, I guess the messengers have been backed up from last week's storm."

"Ah." George waved the fuss away, the mention of letters still poking him in his recent scar. "I only wanted to come down to say congratulations to Hector."

A white smile tugged at Hector's lips. "Hey, thanks George."

George couldn't help but return it. "Of course, I'm proud of you."

"That means a lot to me." Hector sat up. He pulled a mess of envelopes out from under his surcoat. "Snagged your mail for you, by the way."

George's smile faltered a little and Franklin broke his silence. "Georgie! Are you still messed up about Anne?"

"I'm trying not to be," George admitted.

"Yeah, I know, friend." Franklin slapped a hand onto George's shoulder, "People move along when you're not around, and you have to give it to Anne, she was honest and never strung you behind her."

"I know, and I'm happy for her. She's my friend... but..."

Hector gave a sorrowful nod. "But you're sad for you?"

George hung his head. "As awful as it sounds."

"It's not awful, you're human," Hector assured.

Franklin hopped back into the conversation. "Yeah! Well anyway, me and Hector were actually talking about this earlier and we think it's high time you relax. Between Anne and your training, I don't think you've had enough time to unwind."

"And on a similar note," Hector started, "being that wound up isn't good for your mental state or as a backdrop for magic anyway. Also, I'm leaving soon."

"Also, he's leaving soon, George!" Franklin sounded exasperated. He closed his eyes and wagged his finger. "That's it young man, now it's mandatory!"

"Relaxing?" George almost giggled at the scene.

"Tut tut! Mandatory relaxing!" Franklin deepened his voice.

"To the barracks!" Hector mimicked the tone.

Franklin nodded. "To the ba— wait." He dropped his shoulders and looked over at Hector. "Why the barracks?"

"It's a bit, I meant the tavern."

"To the barracks!" Franklin resumed his role with heart.

George couldn't help but laugh. "To the barracks!"

***

"So, you see, it's hard to find security, especially in a romantic relationship, when you're always traveling around like us soldiers do," a red-faced Franklin explained. He sat at a round table amid a hazy room of quiet drinkers. Stained windows let in green tinted light, the speckled color painting old wooden floorboards and blushed faces alike. A gentle hum was all that challenged idle chatter, its owner tuning a Gavarian lute in the corner.

Across from Franklin sat a sober-yet-drinking Hector. On Franklin's arm was a woman about his age with the pale face of a Gavarian and blonde hair to match, she wore a tipsy smile. On the opposite side of her, and next to Hector, sat George, beer on his mustache and a wince in his eye. The prince cocked his head.

"Are you trying to make me feel better or are you just bragging that Johanna here was silly enough to say yes to marrying you?"

Franklin frowned and stuck up his nose. "Not everything is about you, George."

George blinked. "I didn't even ask for the lecture, we just ordered drinks and you started ranting."

"I felt you needed to hear it."

"Why?"

"Because you've been whiney."

"I'm not whiney."

"Well, you're definitely grumpy, then." A new voice with a southern trill interjected. The table turned to the owner of the voice. A woman with a dark complexion and frizzy raven black hair sat on a chair leaned towards them. Her own friends were smiling behind mugs.

Johanna let out a single laugh. "Then it's settled, George is grumpy."

"By the Graces, let it be known." Franklin clinked his mug against Johanna's.

A smile eventually cracked George's bewilderment. "Well, winter has been..." He trailed off.

"Winter, what," the woman cocked a brow, "Enjoy it while it's here. You've been blubbering behind my ears for only ten minutes at best and I can already tell you're too go-go-go for your own good. Take a lesson from a snowflake and enjoy the slow drift down."

Hector cocked his brows. "She's good."

Conceding, George nodded along. "She's right."

The woman offered a smile before letting her chair back down on all four legs, back with her own table. George in turn leaned his own chair towards *her* table, mimicking her earlier interjection.

"Blubbering is a bit harsh though, no?"

The woman blinked. "Isn't that what you're doing right now?"

A thought flickered behind George's eyes. "Do you want to take this outside?"

A scoff. "What, are you going to beat me up?"

"No!" George's face grew a shade of red. "I meant for a walk, perhaps?"

An apologetic curve bent the woman's brow. "I think I want to stay with my friends, sorry."

"I can respect that." George did his best to hide a frown before letting his chair fall back into place. Hector slapped a hand on the prince's back and the rest of the evening fell to soft laughter and simple conversations. Outside the light of the sun began to fade, dimming the colors of the windows and signaling an end to the time at the tavern.

The cold wash of a dusky winter's breeze tickled the group through their cloaks, making them savor what rare rays of the setting sun still found its way to the street. Soldier's boots thumped against cobblestone in harmony with the chatter of the young men.

"Rick was so pissed," George spewed through a fit of laughter. Franklin held onto both of his friends, eyes closed and mouth open in a silent laugh, tears forming in his eyes as he tried to inhale but instead created a wheezing croak. Hector himself couldn't seem to resist, a rolling chuckle rumbling from him.

"Oh man..."

A chorus of exhales followed the story, all their eyes wet from laughing so much. Hector cleared his throat. "I'm going to miss you guys."

"We'll miss you too," George replied.

"It's only for a while, anyway," Franklin added.

A sly grin appeared on Hector's face. "You know, George."

The prince cocked his head. "What?"

Hector's eyes started to shimmer with golden magic for a moment. A determined look spread over his visage and the magic began to hum in his arms as well.

"H-Hector?"

"Consider this a reverse parting gift." Hector said with a smile before suddenly pushing George, his magic sending the prince backwards at an incredible speed. Stumbling to maintain his footing, George pedaled desperately before falling completely backwards and sliding across the stone street. Coming to a skidding stop, the dazed George looked upward at the evening sky, only to find a familiar face looking back down at him.

It was the woman from before. She looked down at him with as much shock as he looked up at her with.

"I'm so sorry." George broke the silence as embarrassment seeped into him.

"It's alright." The woman fidgeted for a moment before offering a hand. George took it and pulled himself to his feet.

"My friends thought it would be funny to push me into this, it seems." George looked past the woman, but Franklin and Hector were nowhere to be seen. He scanned for a moment before finding his eyes stuck on hers. She had deep brown eyes with bursts of a dark red around the pupils. The two stood in silence for a moment before the woman spoke.

"I'm glad."

"Glad?"

"I actually meant to apologize to you."

George blinked. "Apologize?"

The woman motioned ahead and the two began their walk together. She nodded and crossed her arms. "Yes, I feel like I was being a little mean earlier, and definitely interjecting."

"No." George shook his head. "You were right, and insightful, really."

"Ah, only because I just got done hearing those same words myself." She snuck a false laugh through her nose. "And just got done doing my own blubbering."

"W…" George didn't know what to do with his hands. Shoving them under his armpits in an awkward stance, he continued, "Did you want to talk about it?"

Stopping, the woman turned to George. "I don't know you."

"I don't know you, either," George spurted.

A smile cracked on the woman's face and she cocked a brow. "You're really good at selling your case, huh?"

An embarrassed pink swelled on George's cheeks. "I meant to say: hi, I'm George."

"Rosaline."

"I like your name!" George cringed at his own words. Rosaline gave a pitying smile before George quickly followed up, "...you were saying?"

Rosaline winced, "I-I don't know." She faced into the evening breeze and took a long breath, the sounds of their footsteps on silent stones taking over.

"I'll go first, then," George said confidently. He pushed a hand through his hair and gave himself a resolved nod. "Honestly, I didn't have much right to be blubbering on like I was earlier. I've had quite some time to get over myself, but I've been festering on it and blaming the endless winter."

"What happened?" Rosaline was studying George's face. The prince frowned.

"Nothing even bad. It's just I got carried away writing a girl back at another camp. We had been lightly back and forth for a couple years, but this time I think I got too presumptuous and it was just too much for us."

Rosaline knitted her brows. "I'm sorry you had to go through that."

"It's not the worst that could happen," George admitted.

Rosaline shrugged a single shoulder. "No, but if something matters to you, it can feel like it is."

"You seem to know a lot about this," George said, face steeped in curiosity.

The two stopped walking and Rosaline faced George. "Do you really care enough to know this much about a stranger?"

Blinking, George answered, "I do."

"Why?" Rosaline was quick.

"Maybe I'm wrong," George started, "But you have a wisdom about you that I couldn't help but notice."

Rosaline looked away, eyes flickering above bashful cheeks. "Almost sounds selfish of you."

"Probably is," George agreed, "I can leave if you'd like?"

"No..."

"No?"

Rosaline curled a small smile. "Maybe I'm a little selfish too. But let's start with the stupid little conversations first, yeah?"

"Yeah!" George agreed as the pair turned down the long road home. The prince gave Rosaline a smile, who returned with a matching one.

"So, you're not from Korku?" George asked.

"Barcena, way down south." Rosaline nodded. "You?"

"Imperial Province," George quickly replied. "I have never been to Barcena."

"It's warm, unlike here. It's almost always summer, and not the hot stinging kind." She shook her head. "I miss the summer rains. Ugh and the ocean!"

"The ocean?" George seemed to ponder it for a while. Rosaline narrowed her eyes before pointing a finger.

"Grace's favor, you've never even seen the ocean, have you?"

"I've seen the Imperial Sea!" George defended.

"Not close enough!" Rosaline goaded. "You'll have to, it's magnificent."

"I will!" George assured, "But if you miss Barcena so much, why are you up here?"

"Auxiliary... medical," Rosaline explained, "I wanted to help the... well I don't want to say war efforts but rather the people getting hurt by it."

George chewed his cheek. "That's noble of you."

"I was wasting away on the blackberry groves and vineyards my family owns. I figured I could at least spend my time helping others."

"Not to take away from how noble that all is—" George put a hand on his stomach. "But blackberries are the best berry."

"Ever have them smothered on an oily cake? Second only to an oily cake smothered in maple."

"Oily cake?"

"Ocean, oily cake—make a list!"

George laughed. "The list will be made!"

"Good!" Rosaline smiled wide.

"Captain!" A fresh soldier came running down the road, a letter flapping in his hand.

"Captain?" Rosaline mimicked in shock.

"What is it?" George spun to meet the courier.

"A letter for you, stamped in the Imperial seal."

"Imperial seal?" Rosaline was bouncing her eyes between the two.

George took the letter from the man and snapped the wax seal before unfolding it. His eyes quickly scanned the contents. "It's from my sister."

"S-sister!?" Rosaline's eyes widened. George folded the letter back up and looked over at the soldier.

"Thank you, soldier." The prince turned to Rosaline. "I have to go."

"I... think I understand." Rosaline's eyes were still wide.

George gulped and gave the woman his full attention. "Maybe we could have another walk soon?"

Relaxing, Rosaline found her grin once more. "Of course, George."

George returned the smile. "Same auxiliary camp as the others?"

"You'll find me there."

"I'll find you there, then."

"I know, I just said—" Rosaline stopped and stared at George. Her eyes fell from his own and down to his cheeks. "Are you blushing?"

George cleared his throat and looked over at the soldier still standing there. "Report to Commander Darius and tell him I'll be there shortly with news from the Capital."

The soldier shook to attention. "At once!"

Looking back at Rosaline, George still had a soft burn on his face. The prince went to say something but closed his mouth and smiled instead. Rosaline smiled back.

Chapter 16

The Sister

"Mhm-mhm…" Darius sat on a fur covered chair, fingers steepled and a tense look on his face. "Absolutely not."

On the other side of the stone room, George stood with his arms outstretched. "Why not!? It's my sister!"

The room they were in was a stone-brick cube made cozy with a roaring fireplace and pelt rugs that hung on the walls, floor, and even ceiling. Such an arrangement gave the place a nest-like feel that easily captured the warmth of the fire. As usual, not much else decorated Darius' office save for the same chipped armor stand he lugged around during marches and some furniture that came with the room.

From the other side of a dense desk, Darius cleared his throat. "That may be, but I can't be losing one of my captains just for an escort."

"You'll still have Franklin, and you know as well as I do that a request for company from Josephine is not just any escort." George stamped his finger on the open letter that laid on Darius' desk.

Darius sat up. "Are you really playing the royalty card?"

"No." George crossed his arms. "But Josephine sure is."

Darius fell silent, annoyed. "Her Highness's request will be filled but all she is getting is you."

"And Williams?" George smiled wide.

"Fine, you and your retainer. I'm sure that's more than enough for a trip to the Gavarian capital on Imperial roads."

"She just wants to be safe."

"Which explains the mess of palace guards that will be with her. Just like a noble to—" Darius caught himself and George raised a brow.

The Commander started to laugh. "Grace's might, I'm getting too casual with you Imperial family members." He stiffened his face into its usual scowl. "Dismissed."

George slapped to attention and saluted, but held a defiant sparkle in his eye.

***

George and Williams rode hard to where one of the many backroads to Korku intersected the Imperial Road. The Great Imperial Road was a common sight no matter where in the empire you were. Built and funded by one of George's ancestors, it spanned all the way from the Gavarian capital of Jornho to the Imperial City and then all the way down to each of Barcena's three capitals, a portion of which George had used three years ago on his way through Caldora when he was a recruit.

It was obvious when they found it, as the dirty, sparsely-cobbled road buried in snow that they *were* on quickly stopped to make way for a wide, raised stone road. The way the road was raised kept the worst of the snow off of it, and the rest was taken care of by common travelers as these types of roads saw frequent use even in the dead of winter.

"It's been a while since we've been this close to civilization," George commented as he stared down the road. Its flagstones and engravings held countless engineers' signatures and reminded him of home. Williams didn't reply right away, his eyes hungrily scanning the horizon where Josephine should be arriving from. In the past two years, he had grown into a man just as George did, but kept a clean face and a nest of golden hair. He looked like a storybook knight, one who got in the habit of writing letters to a certain someone.

"Williams?"

The retainer sat up straight, his old black auxiliary tabard long since replaced with a deep purple one that bore the Imperial crest. Underneath, he wore the chainmail and breastplate of an Imperial guard. Blinking, Williams refocused on his friend. "Sorry, what?"

"Nothing important." George snorted a laugh.

Williams shook his head. "Do you think we are at the right spot?"

"Worried?"

"Humor me," Williams pleaded.

George scanned the road until he found one of the milestones sticking up a few feet. Squinting, he read the number. "That's the same number from the letter. This is where we are supposed to be."

"Early? *Late?*"

"Williams." George dropped his brow. "The letter said Graces'day, today is Graces'day."

"Maybe I should have said a prayer." Williams looked back at the horizon.

George made a face. "You never even go to mass."

"It's been three years, George."

"Williams, it's my sister, don't you think I—oh, look!" George pointed down the road and Williams whipped around so fast that he nearly fell off his horse, summoning a hearty laugh from George, but as funny as it was to the prince, he wasn't joking.

Coming into view from under a hill in the road was an Imperial carriage. It was easily identifiable not only by the gilded wood and stark white horses pulling it, but by the twelve palace guards riding alongside it on their own steeds. Plum-and-wine capes draped over their decorative yet functional armor. Four of the soldiers rode ahead of the carriage, four behind, and two on either side of the left and right.

It was George's turn to be jittery. He could feel the anticipation in his chest, down to his joints. It really had been three years. The procession came to a standstill, all eyes on the prince and Williams.

"Prince George of the Mortal Empire," George announced himself. He waved at Williams. "Retainer Knight Williams of the Imperial City."

The eyes of the guards seemed to soften. It had been three years and George is sure he had changed a lot, but he could see recognition seeping into their stares. He himself could pinpoint a few of the faces in the procession. That said, there was one face in particular that he was the most nervous to see again. George tightened his grasp on the reins and sent his horse forward toward the carriage. *What do you even say after three years?*

There was a thud and the side window to the carriage snapped open. Josephine's head popped out. "Are you getting in or are we waiting for winter to thaw first?"

George was speechless, Williams was blubbering. The two demounted their horses and made their way to the steps of the carriage. Even in the Gavarian air, the carriage held the scent of the palace in its wood. A brief melancholy put a pout on George's face as he ascended to the door of the cab. Sucking in a breath, he swung it open.

Immediately he was hit with the familiar smell of Josephine's perfume, second, he was struck by the sight of luxury he had been without since he had run away. Red velvet seemed to cushion everything except the walls and ceiling. Sturdy yet fashionable stands of glass and metal held carafes of water and other potables, and then there was the fruit. Pears, apples, berries, all cached away from the long summers of Barcena.

Pulling his vision away from the food, George quickly felt the impact of three years just by looking at his sister. She had definitely grown, and her deep blue stare seemed sharper if not slightly jaded. The bags that persisted under her eyes were still there, and a crease of stress was starting to form on her forehead. One last thing seemed apparent to George, even with her sitting and him standing.

"Oh, I'm definitely taller than you now."

Josephine gave a pitied look. "And matured way past your years."

"Perceptive as ever!" George puffed out his chest.

Josephine frowned. "George!"

"Sorry." Her little brother sank into a seat opposite of her, putting Oathkith across his lap. The princess's eyes wandered to Williams, her scowl turning into a polite smile. "You can sit as well, Sir Williams."

A red hue was on Williams' cheeks as he tipped his head and took a seat by George. The prince leaned back to get a view of them both simultaneously, a snake's grin on his face. Both Williams and

Josephine were staring back at him, narrow eyes, the fuss only causing George's smile to grow wider until Josephine herself turned a shade of red.

"What brings you this far North?" Williams saved them both.

"The duke!" Josephine immediately capitalized.

George blinked. "Osbert?"

"Or lack thereof," Josephine answered, "In fact most of our news about Osbert have fallen silent, so Uncle Caleb thought it best to send an ambassador to his court."

"Investigation? Isn't that more of an Imperial Proctor's job?"

Josephine shrugged. "Maybe, but this isn't exactly a crime scene. Osbert is old, and his heir is a dumbass. A little Imperial presence could only help straighten any wobbling pieces."

"But why send our own heir just to check up on the two?" George raised a brow, eyes glancing off Josephine and onto a stray bowl of blackberries.

"Well, in truth." Josephine ran a hand through her hair, letting loose a long sigh. "I needed to get away, I more or less assigned myself to this."

"I can understand that, my lady," Williams added.

George plopped a berry into his mouth, savoring the rush of sweet juices before replying. "So can I... but I mean you already knew that."

"Speaking of *that*." Josephine gritted her teeth and George flinched. "Ne... nevermind." Josephine relaxed her shoulders and George peeked at her from behind his defensive hunch. "It's been three years," Josephine continued, "best not start off with me chewing you out for stuff you already know, but really, you leaving put a lot of strain on me. Uncle Caleb is more and more absent by the day, holed away in his studies and then there is Father! I feel like I'm doing everything but sitting on the throne itself."

"I'm sorry." George sat up at the mention of his father.

Josephine huffed. "Don't be sorry... just come home."

George's brow dropped. "What?"

"This is too much for me, I need help," Josephine pleaded. She leaned forward and caught George in a stare. The prince made a face and slowly forced himself out of the contest. Josephine scowled. "George!"

"I can't leave—wait, so there has been *no* news out of Gavaria at all?" George quickly covered himself in a new topic.

"There has, just not *from* the duke himself—George! It's your duty!"

Williams' vision bounced between the two as they entered another long stare. George shot hot air through his nostrils.

"My duty is here," George answered, "I can't just leave in the middle of a war."

"It's the winter lull." Josephine crossed her arms.

"For now!" George crossed his own.

The carriage came to a wrenching stop. The small bowl of fruits flew off the side table and clattered all over the still creaking floor. Williams nearly toppled off his seat, and George was already reaching for Oathkith. Sounds of clanging metal erupted outside alongside shouts. On guard, George ripped his blade free of his scabbard and burst out of the carriage.

Immediately he was met with the sight of an ambush. The Imperial guards were embroiled in combat with what looked like

Vagrants. The enemy's armor was painted in strange markings and their swords appeared more masterful than what was usual for the northerners. Their blades clashed against the Imperials' and George's eyes snapped to the real mystery.

A dense blue mist enveloped the horses, the strange magic keeping them frozen in time. The stream of mist was pouring out of the lips of a shaman-like figure dressed in dark, tattered robes and bone-carved talismans. She spoke softly under the steady flow of mist, the sight causing George's chest to seize.

"Mist-talking?" Josephine's voice came from behind George. Williams' blade rasped from its scabbard.

"No time to question it." The Knight pushed past the two. Even with Williams pushing towards the Mist-talker, the enemy's eyes were stuck on George, glaring at him. Pushing the thought away, George trotted to catch up to Williams, Oathkith at the ready.

The alien chanting grew audible as the prince approached. Metal shrieked, a glint caught the morning sun, and George threw his sword arm up. A clang vibrated off of Oathkith, George's blade catching the sword of the mist-talker just in time. George didn't even see the woman draw her weapon. Close now, George's grey stare caught the Mist-talker's. A deep hatred radiated from her eyes.

Williams let out a roar, breaking the stare and sending his own weapon arcing towards the Mist-talker. In a fluid movement the chipped blade of the shaman shredded away from Oathkith and caught Williams' sword just before it connected with their knee. Bouncing his blade from the impact, Williams counterattacked with a steady stab, but the woman was ready, slapping his blade with a parry.

George came in strong from her blindside, a short stab, only for a rush of mist to pour from the talker's mouth and catch his arm. A chilling tingle pricked along George's skin as his arm was forced nearly still in time. The prince's eyes widened as he watched his arm move in an intensely slow motion. Panicked, he swung with his off hand but another chant hissed from the shaman and another cloud of blue mist captured his other arm.

The mist-talker caught Williams' blade and slammed her shoulder into the knight, sending him backwards so she could refocus on the captured prince. Williams was too quick, though, and jumped back into the fray. He threw his entire weight against the shaman and sent them both to the ground, their weapons clattering away.

Helpless, George watched. He could hear the other fights behind him, grunts of the palace guards and even Josephine, but couldn't do a thing about it. Struggling with the mist, George's arms moved as if they were weighed down by bricks and drowned in sap, he knew he wouldn't break out in time. The mist-talker rolled onto her back and wedged her boot between herself and Williams. With a strong kick she knocked the knight off of her. She ripped a hidden dagger from her robes and dove for Williams.

Dread stabbed George's stomach, adrenaline pumped into his chest, and he could feel a dark smoke rise inside of him. It was strong, chaotic and angry, whipping energy and power throughout him. The prince's body flexed with a rush of magic and suddenly he was free. The magic shimmered gold and red ribbons along his arms, pushing the mist from his limbs. The powerful energy surged through George's body, causing him to grit his teeth in sheer primal emotion, eyes finding the mist-talker. Locked onto his enemy, George launched himself back into the fray.

George was a blur. His offhand shot out, catching the shaman's throat in a vice grip and slamming her into the ground. Vibrations from the blow rocked through George's arm, narrow eyes staring down at the windless mist-talker. She was gasping, lungs clearly empty and her pale throat was turning pink under the prince's fingers.

Their eyes met. The fury in the shaman's stare was fading and a certain helplessness grew on them. George's grip softened, his mind replaying the dead stare of the man he had killed years ago in an attempt to join the front. The smoke was fading, the energy was disappearing, the magic was fizzing out. Guilt, hesitance.

"George!" Williams called out, snapping George back into the fight but it was too late. The shaman was swinging her arm wide, dagger pointed in. Williams came rushing in from the side. Knocking George off of the mist-talker, the dagger missed the prince, but found a new target. There was a sharp shriek of metal tearing on metal and Williams scurried backwards in shock.

"Oh, fuck..." Williams gasped, gaze stuck on the hilt sticking out of the mail that covered his lower stomach. George rolled to his feet, eyes wide on the glisten of the dagger. Before he could get a word out, the figure of the shaman rose behind him.

A spear whipped by the prince's face and with a loud thunk it caught the shaman in the chest, slamming her back to the ground. George spun to the thrower, Josephine, her arms glittering with bright Stromist magic and her dress torn and bloody. The siblings shared a worried look before splitting off, with Josephine sprinting over to Williams. George, however, cautiously walked over to the fallen mist-talker. The scarlet-splattered shaman was wriggling on the ground and attempting to sit up, the spear impaled through her right side.

Her breath was hoarse and weak, and George could only assume one of her lungs was pierced. He put his boot on her chest and what small force he applied was enough to lay her back down flat.

"Me?" The accent was alien to George, but even still it gave her a seed of humanity that caused George to flinch. This time he didn't hesitate, though, and raised Oathkith, pointing down. He let it drop. A tug and a snap. He yanked it to the side and a spurt of blood shot up at him.

George heard Josephine whisper and turned back to the pair. Josephine was helping Williams to his feet, her face stained with worry. The knight was holding the dagger steady and Imperial guards were starting to swarm, but were giving the trio enough space.

"Cut the horses!" George yelled. The scene froze. The prince's brow dropped. "Cut the horses!" He looked at Josephine. "We need to ride hard to the capital."

"I second that." Williams rasped.

Chapter 17
More Questions

George's horse galloped hard against the road. Josephine rode on Williams' horse, the knight himself sitting in front of the princess, cradled between her arms and the reins. Lagging far behind them, the imperial guards were attempting to keep up with the carriage, the vessel bouncing madly over every uneven stone.

"Mist-talkers!?" George finally hissed out loud. Josephine's eyes narrowed in thought as George continued. "Last I checked, only the Tagist sages knew that magic, and also last I checked all it did was heal wounds and sickness!"

"I know." Was all Josephine managed to muster in reply.

"Well, I'm glad we are on the same page!" George ranted in frustration.

"I don't like this," Josephine said beneath her breath.

George made a face. "Neither do I."

"Same," Williams croaked.

"No, I mean," Josephine started, "during that entire ambush, not a single one of our ambushers targeted me."

"Weird time to be envious," George quipped.

"You dolt," Josephine growled, "I'm saying they were after you!"

"Me!?"

"Seemed to be..." Josephine paused.

Williams' groans and the sound of the slamming hooves covered up the silence. George studied his sister's face in between glances at the road. "Josephine."

"I can't be certain," Josephine continued slowly, "but I don't think we can trust the sages. The mist-talking, the way they've been acting lately, and how they backed sending you to the front."

"They what?"

Josephine shook her head, focusing on the road. "Three years ago, after you ran away to play soldier, the question came up of whether or not you should be allowed to enter the front. A lot of Gavarian and Caldoran nobles seemed to back the sentiment, hoping it would bring more attention to the war and increase Imperial support. But uncle wasn't convinced. It wasn't until a lot of the sages began backing the notion and voicing their own opinions that real pressure was put on the decision. After a lot of backroom talks and suspicious opinion changes, Uncle Caleb was all but forced to pass the decision as his own. Uncle never liked the sages and the sages never liked him, so I thought it was a personal grudge... but now this. But three years later?"

A thought passed George's mind, a memory, when he was fifteen and running from the palace, all the guards were asleep, or were they just stilled by the magic mist? If that was the case, why did the shadow chase him away, he was already in the trap. The prince pressed his lips into a flat line, something else was on his mind, an indisputable fact. "Targeting me doesn't make political sense."

"If any of this is truly linked," Josephine speculated, "No, no it doesn't."

Williams forced his head to the side to look at his friend. "Maybe it isn't political."

"Then what?"

Williams simply closed his eyes. This seemed to get a start from Josephine, who quickly nudged him, getting a grumpy groan in reply. The princess grit her teeth. "Let's just get him to a healer, then we can theorize."

"Agreed." George kicked his heels into the sides of his mount, spurring it even faster.

***

The road came to a halt at the gates of the Gavarian capital of Jornho. Its gate was wide open and any spattering of evening traffic was quickly tossed to the side as George and Josephine came stampeding through. At first the guards went to protest, but upon seeing the bloodstained Josephine they opted to follow them at an urgent pace, shouting for others to cover their posts. Soon, the curious burghers and guests of the city were running after the guards themselves, wanting to see what the fuss was about. George did his best to pay them no mind as he guided his horse through the maze of squat Gavarian buildings and statues that made up the lower city. Williams was bobbing with every gallop, looking more and more pale. The prince did his best to swallow his anxiety.

As the trio sped further into the city, the buildings became more condensed, pushed up against each other, and tall. Stone replaced wood and worry turned into fright. The mad dash finally came to an abrupt end when the prince and his companions blasted into the main courtyard that overlooked the duke's castle. A crowd of people had already pooled in front of the building, sandwiching George's group between them and the commoners who had followed.

Fenric was the first to push through the noble crowd by the castle. He wore rich blue clothes lined with silver. Following close behind was a bald sage wrapped in white robes and a skinny man with a feather stuffed cap, and behind them swarmed the castle guard.

"What is this—George?" Fenric's eyes widened. He looked very much the same, except for a darkness often seen on the face of the restless.

"Ambush on the roads, my retainer needs a healer," George all but barked.

The sage stepped forward first, "Quick then!" He held out his hands as he approached Josephine's horse. The princess yanked the reins, turning the horse from the old man. Confusion spread on the sage's face.

"Is there anybody else who can help us?" The princess called out. The crowd was as baffled as the sage.

"Princess, really." The sage protested with his hands still outstretched.

"I can help!" An old woman shouted from the crowd of commoners. Josephine reared her horse in their direction.

"Quickly, then!"

"Hold on." Fenric held up a hand. "What exactly is—"

"No time," George interrupted and spurred his horse to follow the woman. The crowd began to cleave a way for the trio to pass through back towards the city below. "Follow if you must," George called over his shoulder.

Fenric ground his teeth together and looked at the feather-capped man to his right, who simply shrugged. The Commander leered. "Bring me my horse."

***

Fatty, yellow candles melted slowly in the corner of an otherwise dark room, filling the air with an overpowering stench. There was a window, but just one. It was small so as to keep the Gavarian winters out and as such the group had to settle for the orange flickers cast from the corner. On a thin bed raised on a wooden frame, Williams laid with his eyes shut and lips trembling. His armor was already unlatched and placed on a chair and his wound had already been dealt with. It was now a matter of him healing and regaining lost blood.

Only George and Josephine were left in the room, with Fenric lingering outside. The prince looked at his sister and nodded towards the door. "We should let him rest."

"Okay," Josephine agreed.

George stood and snatched the dagger that had stabbed Williams off of the nightstand. He rolled it in his fingers as he made for the door, turning back only to see his sister leaning over Williams. She was framed in the candle light, her hair draped around his face as she placed a gentle kiss on his cheek. George smiled softly and put his hand on the handle of the door. The sound of the door handle creaking urged Josephine away from Williams and the two exited the room.

"I hope you understand the unorthodoxy of this all." The siblings were met with Fenric's glare. He stood straight and proud, almost a little too much. His stance reminded George of someone trying to keep their head above the water, as if the commoner's house they stood in was something of a swampy pool unfit to touch Fenric.

George raised his brow and continued to fiddle with the dagger, the blade polished clean. It had no unusual markings, and by all accounts was a Vagrant-made blade set on a leather wrapped handle. As the prince pondered how to respond, Josephine cut in, authoritative as ever.

"Where is your father?"

Fenric blinked, a certain emotionless look overtaking his usual scowl. "My father is dead."

"What? Since when?" Josephine eyed George.

"It's only been a few days but he was suffering from his age and sickness for quite a while," Fenric explained.

Josephine made a face. "Why wasn't the Imperial court made aware that he was put to bed rest? We've been without news of the duke for more than a month!"

"Well, I suppose that doesn't matter now," Fenric hissed, seemingly short about the topic, "I'm the duke, and now you have news of me."

It was George's turn to blink, he always knew Fenric would eventually take over Osbert's position, but he never actually could picture it. "Duke Fenric..." he tried out.

Fenric's scowl returned. "Is that so unbelievable?"

Before George could spurt out a 'yes', Josephine intercepted the question. "I suppose not, but I also suppose we should discuss Gavaria's continued need to aid in the war?"

Fenric waved a hand, voice turning oddly cool. "I'll uphold the treaties of my father if you'll uphold the same ones, nothing needs to change."

"That's good news at least," George pinched his chin. A short pause stalled the conversation before George continued, "Are you taking the company of sages now?"

"Not really," Fenric replied swiftly, "a few have come to me with concerns about Nachtism rising in Gavaria..." George raised his brow and Fenric finished, "their concerns are baseless, there is no Nachtism in Gavaria."

"I'm sure." Josephine did her best to hide any sarcasm.

Fenric looked between the two Imperial siblings and tucked a slant into his cheek. "Well, if you have further need of me... find me at the castle... away from..." He waved his hand at the house around him, "*this.*"

The new Duke then turned on his heel and exited the house, door slamming a little too loud behind him. The woman who owned the home and who had treated Williams stood in the kitchen, brow furrowed and eyes caught where the duke was just standing. George noticed this and sighed.

"My condolences."

"It's no secret he's an ass." The surgeon spat.

A rummaging came from behind the door to where Williams was resting, which caused all three attendees to turn to it. Josephine frowned.

"I swear on my ancestors, if you are out of that bed!" The princess knocked the door open to find Williams slouched on the floor by the bed. He looked up at Josephine with big eyes.

"I just wanted a little water." His gaze turned to the clay carafe on a shelf by the window. Josephine softened and marched over to the pot. George hooked a hand under Williams' arm and lifted him back into the bed.

The surgeon put a cup in Josephine's hand, who promptly filled it before tipping it to Williams' lips. The knight knitted his brow.

"I can drink on my own—"

Josephine's stare remained unwavering and she tipped the cup even more.

"For graces..." Williams quickly caught the falling lip of the cup and let Josephine pour him the rest. George stepped away from the bed, nodding at the surgeon to follow him. The two exited the room, leaving the others in privacy.

"My prince?" the woman started.

"First, I just wanted to thank you for your aid. I have no doubt my sister can arrange compensation once she returns to the capital."

The woman's smile caused her skin to crinkle around her pale eyes. "I do appreciate that, my prince."

George smiled back and nodded before turning solemn again. "Just out of curiosity, how soon do you think Williams would be able to move out?"

"I wouldn't suggest moving him until the color returns to his face and the stitching heals over." The surgeon crossed her arms. "It could be a while."

A frown covered George's face.

"Don't worry." The woman's smile returned. "I would not remove a patient of mine so eagerly, he can stay until he is well enough for travel."

"Bill me for each day," George quickly agreed. "Though I have to ask another favor."

"My prince?"

"What is your name?"

The woman let out a surprised laugh. "I suppose I forgot to give you that, didn't I? I am Gertrude Kilnsdot. Currently in service to his Imperial Prince." She gave George a wink.

He smiled. "And I'm forever grateful."

***

Late evening cast its grey gloom outside, dimming the room Williams was laying in to a murky dark, cut only by the glow of candles. Gertrude had long since retired to a comfy chair in the main room, a fact that made George feel guilty, but he was also glad to see his friend finally getting some rest. Josephine sat on the other side of the bed, eyes delicately studying Williams. George smiled, he couldn't imagine what it felt like to spend three years apart like they did. Putting a hand flat on the bed, George chuckled to himself, he could barely stand spending three years without a real bed.

"Something, George?"

The prince looked up at Josephine and shook his head. "I'm just glad everything turned out alright."

Josephine smiled at her brother. "Me too."

"I was thinking about what you said, though," George continued.

"Oh?"

"Yeah." The prince quietly stood up and walked around to his sister. Together the two paced over to the window and hushed their voices, hoping not to disturb Williams. Josephine nodded for George to resume and the prince nodded back.

"If this was some plot against me, why didn't they strike when I was alone with Williams?"

"On the backroads?"

"Yeah."

"Near impossible to decide which backroad you took, I suspect. More still, if they were late in setting up the ambush, it's just easier to strike where they can be certain we will be... or you at least."

"I'm not a fan of your familiarity with the concept."

"Court can be as dangerous as war," Josephine admitted.

George rubbed his chin and fell back into thought. "What about Fenric and the death of Osbert or the sage he was with. Do you think any of this is linked?"

"Could be." Josephine tapped her cheek. "I'm definitely skeptical about Osbert's death, the silence and non-notice of it is too strange to accept, but at the same time I don't think that it is truly linked with the sages and the ambush. I think it would be safe to send a proctor to investigate the duke's demise, but let's keep the mist-talker between us and those we can completely trust."

"Uncle?"

"He will be the first I tell when I get back. If there is a Tagist plot against the Imperial family, he will definitely have a solution."

George winced. "I never thought I'd hear about a Tagist plot against us."

"Anything is possible in the world of politics, but for now it's speculation."

"I don't like being stuck here during all of this," George offered, "I feel like a sitting duck."

"If you hate it now, wait until tonight."

"Tonight?"

"Bedtime? At the castle?"

The prince's eyes widened, "Why would we sleep there if th—if we are suspecting at least Fenric of foul play and the sages of treason?"

"We already caused an upset by publicly refusing the sage, we shouldn't tip our hand any more than we have. Our guards will be with us." Josephine patted George's shoulder.

"I don't know," George rebutted, "I don't like the thought of leaving Williams and Gertrude alone during all of this."

Josephine bit her cheek and sighed. "That *is* a valid concern."

George silently snapped and smiled. "I got it!" he whispered harshly.

"What?" Josephine bounced an eye over to Williams to make sure he was undisturbed before leaning in. George's grin curled.

"We'll go to the castle with only a few of our guards, but then sneak out and have our guards just watch outside the door to make it seem like we are still in there."

"That could actually work..." Josephine looked surprised.

George tapped his head. "The mind of a general." His sister rolled her eyes, but then motioned for him to lead the way. The man suddenly stopped.

"What is it?" Josephine whispered.

"The last time we saw each other, before today I mean," George spoke softly.

A guilty look flushed Josephine's face. "I'm sorry about all of that."

"I'm sorry, too," George said, "You didn't deserve being yelled at like I did."

"Maybe I did," Josephine defended, "I treated you horribly growing up, I wasn't the best sister and I don't really have an excuse..." She closed her eyes. "I hope you can forgive me someday."

"I already have." The prince grinned. "Having my sister at my back is redemption enough."

The princess' face relaxed. "You're one of a kind. Thank you."

Chapter 18
Summer Rose

The next few days crept by at a snail's pace. Josephine managed to fill her days conversing with curious nobles and otherwise sneaking off to be with the recovering Williams, leaving George on his own most of the time. He did his best to avoid eye contact with any nobles, sages, or any other higher-end person who could likely ruin his entire day in a few choice words, be they from them or himself.

Currently, he was moping about in the middle of one of the market squares just after the end of the latest snowfall. It was an open area with wide roads branching out of it at every angle, giving it more of a blob shape than a proper square. From George's understanding, it was an old part of the ancient city and was simply added onto over the years until it turned into the busy monster it was today. There George found himself, leaning against a stone wall that belonged to an apothecary, with two hawkers barking their stands' goods on either side of him. At the center of the mess, George watched with benign amusement as a carriage attempted to inch its way through the crowd and slush to continue its journey inward.

"The best part," a young boy began, having snuck up on George, "is that you just know some rotten rich man is getting absolutely furious in there." George looked down at the smudge faced boy and then back at the carriage and cracked a smile.

"Spoiled, too, I bet," George added.

"Nobles!" The boy shook his head. "That's how my dad says it, 'Nobles!'" Fidgeting, the boy glanced at Oathkith and then back up at the prince.

"Are you a soldier?"

"Sure am," George replied, giving Oathkith a gentle tap. "Captain of the 11th Vanguard."

"Woah." The kid's eyes grew wide. He sputtered a few words before hopping in place with a big grin on his face. "I'm gonna go tell my dad I met you!"

George smirked back as the kid took off into the crowd.

"Captain!" an authoritative voice called out from George's blind spot. The prince panicked and stood at attention, only to relax as the voice turned into a giggling laugh. George spun to meet the voice and immediately turned red. Rosaline was still snickering, a wide smile split across her face.

"You made it!" George pushed to a new topic.

Rosaline poked the man's arm and leaned on the same wall he once was. "Well, my unit was sent here for resupply, so when I got your letter, I figured..."

"Why not?"

Rosaline nodded. "Exactly. So, how's our glorious prince doing?"

"Gloriously bored," George replied with a sigh. "Which to be honest is surprising considering all the—" The prince stopped himself and Rosaline cocked her head. George gave a shake of his own. "How are you?"

"I'm in a similar boat." Rosaline huffed and let her arms droop.

"Are you trying to tell me that resupplying isn't exciting?" George took a few steps from his spot. Rosaline stepped to his side and the two began their walk.

She looked up at the prince. "Hard to believe, I know, but alas."

"What would you rather be doing?" George asked as the two began to cut through some of the back alleys. George had grown accustomed to using them when trying to avoid traffic. Here, only the occasional stand would be wedged between the ancient buildings, but more often than not, there were only scattered groups of playing children and thieving squirrels too fat for their own good. Rosaline tapped her cheek in thought.

"Tough question."

"Got no idea, huh?"

"No, I have too many ideas!" Rosaline's brow fell and her words turned careful and thoughtful. "Imagine sailing the oceans, or making friends with an ancient beast. Finding a lost grove of peace, or simply falling asleep under a shady tree."

"In this cold, I'd prefer a sunny hill with plush grass," George added wistfully. A dumb smile found his face. "And a little snack on the side."

"Blackberries," Rosaline quickly amended.

George cocked a brow. "I recently had some actually."

"Our talks are already rubbing off on you?"

The prince laughed as the pair turned the corner, finding a small untouched pond in the middle of the city. A thick field of snow-dusted grass ringed it and stone benches faced its frozen, mirror-like surface. Rosaline made her way to one of the benches and took a seat before looking over at George. The prince wandered over and sat by her, fidgeting close to the end of the bench. Rosaline gave him a studying look and a small smile before looking over at the pond.

"So, you're really the prince, huh?"

A small tinge of anxiety reared in George's stomach. "Yeah."

Rosaline shook her head and laughed to herself. "The prince of the entire mortal empire? All of Jerrovia?"

"I believe so." George rubbed his chin. "But mostly I just use it for storage."

This urged another laugh from Rosaline, one heartier and truer than the last. She looked back at George, catching his eyes with her own. "I don't think I could have approached you if I knew."

"You didn't," George corrected, holding her gaze, "I was tossed rather roughly in your general direction." Rosaline's eyes crinkled as her smile grew and George's face burned at the sight, forcing him to look away at the pond.

"You know what I meant," Rosaline continued.

"I get it," George assured, "but I'm glad you did."

"Me too," Rosaline agreed," I enjoy your company."

"All two times?" George grinned.

Rosaline held up two fingers. "All two times."

"Find me a sunny hill and we can make it three."

"A shady tree and how about four?"

"Deal!" George broke into a big smile, one that Rosaline mirrored.

"I suppose we still have to finish this time first, though, huh?"

George nodded. "That makes sense to me."

Rosaline scooched closer to George. "Maybe I ruin the silly mood with a serious question?"

"Maybe." George turned to meet her gaze again, lingering longer on it than he expected to.

Her studying look didn't waver. "How do you feel about the war?"

The question pulled George away from the stare, taking his mind from studying the little lines of color in Rosaline's eyes and stamping it on his experiences with the war. He made a serious face and looked down in thought. He smiled briefly, if only politely, before looking back at Rosaline.

"That's a hard question..." His face was set in thought. "I actually ran away to join the war when I was a kid, back then I only had my Uncle's war stories to go off of. After being at war, though, and..." He tucked a slant into his cheek. "War is nothing to be proud about."

Rosaline looked on with soft eyes, nodding slowly. "I wish more people thought that way."

"It's tough," George continued, "because even in my position and rank, I sometimes wonder why the war even exists. I know it's a land dispute between Gavaria and the Vagrants, but where did it begin, who actually owns it..." He paused. "And where will it end? I have no idea."

"I don't think anyone really does." Rosaline leaned forward, elbows on her knees. George mimicked the action before giving her a nudge.

"What about you?"

It was Rosaline's turn for her face to twist into thought. "You'd think I'd have an answer for my own question."

"I'm sorry," George said.

"No, no," Rosaline corrected, "I think my feelings on the war sort of stretch way back."

"What do you mean?"

"Well, in a way I grew up around war." Rosaline looked away to the lake.

George knitted his brow. "I thought you grew up on a vineyard."

"I did... Do you know the story of the knight, Harris Von Rugosa?" The woman snapped her eyes back to George's. There was an intensity behind them.

The prince blinked, eyes caught on hers. He pinched his chin in thought. "Harris Von Rugosa..." George's eyes lit up. "The Hero Harris of Fransberg! He fought in the Great Northern War."

"I know," Rosaline leaned in, as if conspiring. "He's my father."

George leaned along with her, catching the serious glint in her visage.

The medic continued, "After he was awarded for Fransberg, he settled in Barcena with his new estate, the vineyard. He met my mother and well you can guess what happened next, but the point is that all that time and the war was still fresh in his face and always on his mind."

"What do you mean?"

"He was always worried. He'd tell me all the war stories as if they made him feel better, but every time he did, he would just grow paranoid. It was like he felt as if something was always going to jump out at him, or worse, his family." Rosaline clapped her hands together, causing George to flinch.

"That's horrible!" George squared himself. "That's no way to live."

Rosaline held up a finger. "Worst still, when I was just a little girl, he would take me outside and have me train with him for hours. He kept telling me that it would protect me and as I grew up, if it wasn't berries, it was swords. He taught me everything, but mostly he inadvertently taught me what war can do to even a strong mind."

George stared at Rosaline, her face secure and eyes set right. A certain awe overtook the prince as she continued. "So that brings us to this war. I knew it was raging, and I knew that I was prepared for it, but I couldn't help but feel wrong."

"Wrong?"

Rosaline sat up straight, her voice firm. "I couldn't help but feel like the whole ordeal was the result of someone's greed, be it hidden or in plain sight, and I couldn't just sit by. I wanted to help, not the war itself but rather the people caught in it. So, I joined the Auxiliary. If that's where I could prevent people from suffering like my father does, then that's where I wanted to go."

"Admirable compassion." George sat up along with her. "You're more of a soldier than... I don't even know." His eyes fell off of Rosaline and down into a deep thought.

"Do you feel guilty?" She asked abruptly.

"Sometimes."

"But you stayed."

"Because I couldn't leave this undone," George defended, straightening his back and squaring his shoulders. "I have that luxury of leaving, all nobles do, but war isn't a game that you should just ignore the moment you don't want to play anymore. So many are stuck in this reality, people who I'm supposed to lead whether they want me or not." A sad look overtook George's face. "People are trapped in this bloody mess, the most I can do is be there with them."

Rosaline shook her head. "That's compassion, too, George."

The prince's shoulders relaxed and a long breath escaped his mouth. "Thank you. I didn't mean to turn so quickly away from your answer, either."

Still shaking her head, Rosaline swatted the words away. "You have fervor."

"Is that a bad thing?"

"Depends on what about," Rosaline answered honestly, "but about the happiness of the people around you? I can't see why it would be."

George nodded in thought. He pushed a breath through a sudden smile. "Boy, I wasn't expecting such a hard-hitting conversation."

"I'm sorry, did you want to talk about the weather?" Rosaline gave him a funny look.

"No, no! I like this, it's provoking."

Rosaline smiled. "Me too."

"The weather's good today, too," George managed to get out before a soft punch landed on his shoulder.

"I'm not sure Gavaria has good weather."

George arched his brow. "What about snowstorms?"

"As long as there is a warm fire after exploring them, I can get behind that notion." Rosaline jabbed a finger into George. "Mm! But do you know what's the best?"

"What?"

"Summer rainstorms."

The prince looked down at his boots, frost clinging to the sides. Tufts of grass that surrounded him were also stiff with cold and the pond itself was still as frozen over as ever. Despite the warmth of his company, he was quickly remembering how cold it was. "I could use one of those right about now."

"Yes!" Rosaline continued, "The rumble of the skies as warm rain pours down in grey sheets." Her face turned dreamy right before a shiver ran down her jaw.

"Cold?" George guessed from experience.

"Graces be damned, I'm cold."

George looked down where the only bit of warmth was seeping into him, by his leg where his knee was pressed against Rosaline's. Looking up he caught Rosaline also sneaking a peek. A bashful look spread over George's visage, mirrored by Rosaline while they stared at each other. The moment lasted longer than expected, and it would have been uncomfortable if time didn't seem to slow long enough to make this shared study of each other's eyes strangely familiar. Both of them looked all about, as if searching for something along the colored rings of each other's gaze until finally George's face was too bright with a blush to hold it any longer. He looked away, a stupid smile growing on his face.

"George?" her voice came.

"Yeah?"

"If I get my tasks done early tomorrow, would you like another walk?"

A happy flutter filled George. "I would."

***

"I'm not telling you what to do, I just don't think it's safe," Williams pleaded. He stood across the main room of Gertrude's home with Josephine on the other side. A little over a week had already passed and he was standing firm. The princess chewed on her cheek as she soaked in Williams' words while George stood silently in the corner.

"What would you have me do?" Josephine debated, "Go with you to the front?"

"No! Well, maybe? I don't know." Williams looked over at George for help. The prince turned to his sister.

"Williams is right though. The capital is a snake's den. Whoever backed the ambush likely knows it failed."

Josephine rolled her eyes. "That's obvious and doesn't really give me any other option here."

"Why don't you go with her?" George looked at Williams.

Williams looked shocked. "I'm... *your* retainer."

"No, you're my friend and she's my sister," George insisted, "I have the entire 11th to protect me, all she has is... Reginald."

"Reginald is no push over," Josephine quickly added, "not to mention the palace guards and our uncle. Besides, if the ambushers were really after you, and if the sages had a plot to keep you out here, maybe it's best if you did just come home."

"You know I can't do that, Josephine."

"Well why not!?" Josephine nearly growled. "Having you nearby would make all of this so much easier."

"For the conspirators maybe, for you maybe, but I have a duty out here that I need to see complete." George shook his head. A gentle knock sounded at the door that forced George straight up.

"Rosaline?" Josephine questioned as George walked over to answer the door.

George swung the door open to a waiting Rosaline. The sudden catch of each other's gaze forced a smile on the pair's faces, one that only faded when Josephine crossed her arms.

"Hello Rosaline."

"Princess Josephine." Rosaline tipped her head before turning back to George. "Am I interrupting? I thought we could go for..." She let her words trail.

"We can!" George swiftly answered, "we were just discussing our next course of action now that Williams is feeling better."

Rosaline looked over at the knight and gave him a warm grin. "I'm happy to hear it."

"Thank you, Lady Rosaline." Williams smiled back before turning to Josephine. The princess looked between everybody before raising her eyebrows in faux defeat.

"I'll be leaving for the capital tomorrow morning. I already sent word to General Jonsberg, who dispatched two groups of regulars from a fort south of here. One will augment my guard on the way back south and the other will accompany you two back to Korku to resume duties under Commander Darius."

"You did this before we even had this conversation?" George frowned.

"I figured I would be stubborn," Josephine quickly responded, "and I was."

George gave an agreeing nod. "That's a safe bet."

Williams opened his mouth but then seemed to think better of it. The room fell into silence, only to be broken by Rosaline. "I really hope the room was this somber *before* I showed up."

George shot a laugh through his nose and Josephine cracked a small smile, only for it to suddenly droop. Williams was studying Josephine's face as the usual lines under her eyes grew heavier and darker. The princess' eyelids drooped and closed for a moment and her body wavered as if deciding whether to stand or collapse.

"George." Williams stole the prince's attention from Rosaline. George sucked in a small gasp and braced an arm around Josephine just in time to catch her. His sister's muscles seemed to go tense for only a moment before completely relaxing and her breath slowed down to the shallow calm of sleep. Williams shot a concerned look and George mirrored it.

"Is she okay?" Rosaline asked. George shrugged more of Josephine's weight onto his shoulders and lifted her entirely into his arms. Cradling her, he walked her into the room where Williams had recovered. His arms tensed as he slowly laid her on top of the plain linen sheets. Josephine's hair crowned around her head, eyes twitching with dreams.

Only after quietly exiting the room did George answer, "She is."

"What was that?" Rosaline was still confused.

George looked at Williams before looking back at Rosaline. "Sometimes she will fall asleep, seemingly at random. She never can seem to find rest in her sleep either."

With a squint, Rosaline found the word for George's description: "Narcolepsy?"

The prince nodded, heading towards the home's front door. "We should leave her be, if nothing else, a little quiet should help."

"I'll stay here, if that's alright," Williams queried, "as a retainer."

"That's a good idea," George agreed.

***

The Winter evening had already brought the stars out of hiding, blanketing the city in a twinkle of constellations. George and Rosaline were walking under them, accompanied by the orange glow of braziers lined about the streets. The pair's shadows danced on the cobbled walls of buildings as they walked along. As thought took over George and Rosaline, the early winter evening put the rest of the city to sleep. Only huddled pedestrians and grim looking watchmen were outside.

Rosaline kept her face upward, the stars reflecting off her reddish eyes as she studied them. George in turn watched her with the same curiosity she had for the night sky until finally the medic pointed a finger upwards.

"IAO."

"What?" George looked up at the cluster of stars.

Tracing with her finger, Rosaline did her best to point out the constellation. "IAO the warrior, right there next to the falcon."

The prince squinted and the cluster seemed more random to him rather than the pictures Rosaline was suggesting. "I'm… not quite…"

"Right there!" Rosaline stabbed her pointing finger at the sky. George tucked a determined slant into his cheek and stepped closer to Rosaline's finger in an attempt to use it to aim.

"There." She stabbed again and the prince let out a huff, his frustration provoking a laugh out of Rosaline. George's eyes widened as his mind slowly pieced the stars together.

"Oh yeah!" he finally exclaimed, all but pressed entirely against Rosaline's side, cheek resting on her pointing arm. Rosaline rolled her eyes and let her arm hook around George's shoulders, only to fall to his waist when he stood up straight. A smile hummed on

George's face and he put his own arm over her shoulder as they continued their walk.

The evening grew darker, and as it grew darker, it grew colder. A slight breeze began to wind through the streets, but with every chill it sent to the pair, they simply held on to each other tighter. Finally, they had walked all the way to the pinnacle of a small arcing bridge which allowed passage over a gutter that in the spring held a tiny brook. With the cold of winter still being around, it was dry and sparkling with crystals of frost. Together, the two let loose a combined foggy breath before looking over at each other. Their eyes wrinkled with their smiles.

A boot scuffed behind them and they spun around. Standing tall with an expressionless face was Fenric, elbows square behind his back and the moon crowning his head. George arched his brow.

"Duke Fenric?"

"Am I interrupting?" His voice didn't hold any sincerity to it. George opened his mouth but before he could speak, the duke continued, "George, could you walk with me?"

Holding his tongue regarding any wise cracks, George looked over at Rosaline. The medic shrugged before adding, "I'll be fine, the barracks aren't far."

Squeezing her hand, George parted ways with Rosaline and fell in step beside Fenric. The young Duke walked with a certain urgency, his face now scrambled in concentration. It took a few skips to catch up with him initially, but after, the taller George found it easy to keep to his side. Looking ahead, George noticed they were both walking straight towards an old brick temple, the yellow of candlelight spilling out of its windows.

"Is it really Graces'day already?" George exclaimed.

"And evening mass," Fenric replied, "I was hoping you would accompany me."

"Why?"

Fenric stopped and turned to George, the prince mirroring the motion. Sucking in a breath, Fenric explained, "George, I know we had our ups and downs growing up but we are both leaders now..."

George blinked and Fenric frowned. "It's about time we talked as equals."

"At mass?"

"I have a balcony high enough up that we will go unheard, and besides, the Tagist chants and music makes for a good ambience. On top of that, what better place for mediation than in the house of the Imperial religion?"

George felt his gut tighten and his sword hand clench. "Right, after you, then."

***

Fenric's balcony was indeed high above the mass. It was at the pinnacle of the ceiling itself and only accessible by an ancient staircase as beaten as the one in Caleb's tower. In the balcony itself, not much was special. The structure's solid rail was lined with plush fabric to allow comfortable leaning, and a cushioned pew behind was ready to catch anyone too tired or lazy to do such a thing. George himself found leaning to be more comfortable, especially when Fenric was right next to him doing the same.

From their vantage point, George could see the entire mass hall. Unlike the brick outside of the building, the inside was plastered solid and painted with murals of the Graces and their favored sages throughout the ages. Behind a simple wooden altar, a sage dressed in white robes thumbed a quiet, stringed instrument. In front of the same altar was a sage dressed in blues, a sermon in her throat, and in front of her was the more pious of the city, those willing to brave the evening chill to hear the words of Tagism.

Today's sermon seemed focused on loyalty and was being presented with various parables and fables George had heard too many times. The parables always irritated George somewhat, not for what they were or the purpose they held, but how they themselves seemed to be the object of worship instead of the lesson they preached. Either way, George wasn't obligated to listen, especially not since Fenric looked as if he was about to burst from thought.

"I need to know," Fenric began cryptically.

George tilted his head, not sure he wanted to hear the answer to his coming question. "Need to know what?"

"The stories about your mother. I need to know what actually happened." Fenric eyed George. "I know I used to taunt you with the rumors, but surely you have an inkling of what truly happened."

"She fell." George's face grew reserved. "Simple as that."

"No." Fenric turned to George. "Before that... What happened to her and your sister?"

The prince's eyes widened in surprise before settling. "What do you mean?"

"George." Fenric closed his eyes. "I want to be able to understand."

A wrinkle formed on George's forehead. "You actually mean this? You really want to bury our rivalry?"

Fenric's shoulders dropped. "I think so."

George shook the surprise from his face and he looked back down at the mass below. "Three years before I was born, when Josephine was a baby, she and my mother got sick. Scarlet lung."

"So that much of the story is true, then." Fenric pinched his chin. "But scarlet lung is a death sentence, not even mist-talking can solve that disease."

George shook his head. "And it didn't."

Fenric stood up straight. "Nachtism? A deal with the Dweller?"

"No." George knitted his brow. "No, that is where the lie always starts. My uncle worked with a Sage to find a cure and it worked."

"But if that was true, why didn't they make the cure public? Why hide this part of the story?" Fenric pushed.

"The sage went missing shortly after, he ran away with it... Supposedly paranoid that if the cure didn't take, he would face the wrath of my father."

"But it did take, why not come back after?"

George shrugged. "I wasn't alive, that's all I know of it."

"Hm." Fenric fell silent, his eyes flickering with thought. "Thank you, George."

"I guess I should thank you, too," George replied.

"For what?"

"I suppose I never expected you to attempt to hear my side of everything," George added, hesitantly "it feels... nice."

Fenric looked down off the balcony. "Well, you're lucky to have your sister. I suppose I was jealous of that."

"Oh?"

Sincerity seemed to stream in Fenric's voice. "My brother is dead and I grew up in his grave, you never had that."

George opened his mouth to correct Fenric but then thought better of it. Fenric continued, "My father didn't want me, he wanted him. But your father always wanted you *and* Josephine." Fenric's fingers tightened around the rail. "Even my father wanted you."

"I'm sorry." George frowned. "And for his passing."

"Don't be." Fenric's voice was low. "His health was gone, it was only a matter of time." A grim look cast shadows over Fenric's visage. "I'm glad we are friends, George."

"Friends?" George was shocked.

Fenric frowned. "Aren't we?"

"Sure," George agreed, if cautiously. Something was strange about Fenric, something he had noticed when he first saw him a bit over a week ago. Something's changed, a darkness was in Fenric's eyes as he stared at George, seemingly contemplating George's answer.

Looking away from George, Fenric continued. "I respect the emperor. He'd do anything for his family."

"You're still skeptical?" George put the pieces together.

Fenric looked down off the balcony and into the mass below. "Maybe. It just wouldn't surprise me if the Dweller was involved."

George bit his cheek, hating that he was going to ask what he was going to ask. "What do you mean?"

"She's common enough," Fenric answered, "she even shows up in dreams."

George's eyes widened, and Fenric turned to stare him down, a dark seriousness in Fenric's visage. "Did you know that? She shows up in people's dreams. Being trapped in the void, it's all she can really do to speak to us."

The duke smiled at George, unnerving the prince. "I wonder what she wants. Such a strange yet prominent figure in our history, and none of us really know what she wants."

"Something for the smarter people to think about," George cracked a weak grin, but Fenric's smile quickly faded. As it did, George noticed the darkness in his face, the sort you might get from restless nights. Could he also? The duke's voice cut off his thoughts.

"You know, I had another question for you."

"What's that?" George said.

"First forgive me for eavesdropping, but the other week I was out enjoying some air in the trade district and I couldn't help but spot you by the pond with your auxiliary friend." Fenric's eyes were unblinking.

"Oh?" Anxiety was curling in George's gut.

"I remember you saying that you came up north to live out your childhood ambitions of soldiery and glory... but..." The duke was studying George's face. "...that can't be the whole story, can it? Something so simple? There's nothing more?"

The red door planted itself in George's mind and an eerie voice echoed in his consciousness. He closed his eyes, breaking Fenric's stare. Safe behind the underside of his lids, George found composure, as shaken as it might be. "No, I think that might be it."

He felt Fenric's gaze leave him. Opening his eyes again, he saw Fenric's back. The duke was leaning over the rail again. A moment of silence passed between the two, letting the sermon take over the scene. Eventually the duke shook his head. "I see."

George felt the wall growing between him and Fenric all over again. He sucked in a breath and found his courage. "I think I need to go. I need to start packing."

Fenric's eyes snapped to George, the man twisting to face the prince. "You're leaving?"

"In a few days," George lied, startled. The feeling of the lie was thick on his tongue, but not as uncomfortable as the scene around him. "Goodnight."

The duke frowned and turned from George. His voice dropped low, as if disappointed. "Goodnight."

Chapter 19
White Pines and Red Stones

"And there they are!" Franklin put his fists on his hips, a huge pout on his face. George and Williams' journey back to Korku was swift and uneventful. The winter sun didn't rise until just a few hours ago, shading most of the journey in the morning darkness. It was the sort of journey that seemed trapped in a shade of night, creating a certain illusion of infinity only dispelled by the eventual rise of the sun. But now George and Williams were at the outer gate of the keep itself, with the noon-time sun peaking over the pines and one grumpy-faced Franklin looking up at them upon their mounts.

He stood with his Captain's badge clasping a new solid-red cape around his shoulders. George went to speak but Franklin interrupted. "Hector was gone, then you two, without a word, I might add, leaving me alone with the Commander as the sole officer of the 11th!"

"But you do have a nice cape though," George remarked, "a gift for all your hard work?"

"Self-gifted." Franklin's usual mischievous grin reappeared on his face. "If I'm going to be the only captain here, I figured I might as well look the part."

"The part of a parade perhaps," Williams added.

"Get the void off those horses and let me reintroduce you to our own personal Dweller." Franklin turned to walk through the gates. George and Williams demounted to catch up to his side, a pair of stableboys taking the horses behind them.

"Is Darius really that bad?" Williams pressured as the group was suddenly subjected to the activities of the castle fort, with all sorts of faces and tabards rushing across the dirty grey snow. It was a color that matched the stones of the buildings and walls.

Franklin scoffed, a sound visible by his frozen breath, "He's been on something lately, maybe the lull is finally getting to him... or... you know... maybe I'm just getting three officers worth of flak instead of one."

"Speaking of terrible things, I caught up with Fenric," George mentioned.

"Duke Fenric," Williams added.

Franklin raised his brow. "I can't imagine *that* was fun."

"It was strange." George crossed his arms as they walked.

"Fenric's strange." Franklin gave George a face, "what did you expect?"

"He was different." George frowned. "He used to just be an ass, but now he is... quieter, grim even."

"I think he is connected to something shady," Williams interjected.

"I wouldn't put it past him," Franklin agreed.

"Welcome home, boys!" Commander Darius' voice rang from across the frozen courtyard. Ranks of trainees stood between the Commander and the trio. George looked over the new soldiers, their faces red and dripping with sweat in spite of the chill. Some things don't change, Darius' training methods being one of them.

The eyes that stared at the group of friends suddenly snapped back to the Commander as he shouted, "I didn't say stop!"

"Ho-AH!"

***

Forced by necessity and Josephine's warning, as well as the lack of intelligence on when and where the enemy would strike next, life at Korku continued on as if nothing had occurred, at least outwardly. With time and daily ritual, the oppressive Gavarian winter passed by into spring. It took only a few weeks from when George and Williams returned for the colder season to give way but when it did, the spring days pushed the white snow north and replaced it with bright greens and a kaleidoscope of early blooms. Wildflowers had taken over the hills and empty meadows by the time Rosaline's unit rejoined the 11th at Korku and quickly she and the prince were in each other's company once again. Though the lull of winter was thawing as fast as the cold, and various questions itched George's waking mind, the two found peace in each other.

Under an ancient white pine tree, the pair spent a lazy afternoon. Surprisingly plush grass quilted the ground below the boughs, much comfier than any soldier's bed. As George laid upon it, Rosaline laid with him, their arms woven together. They were entangled into a single body, happily napping in the shade. Their eyes were closed and their breath in synchronization and for at least as long as this moment, there were no worries in George's mind. There weren't any thoughts at all.

George's head was silent for the first time in his life and in this quiet sanctuary he relied solely on his senses. The scent of Rosaline mingled with the wild flowers, filling his nostrils, his skin was abuzz with the warmth of the day, and the song birds were chirping their melodies loud enough to drown out the distant clamber of Korku's garrison. For now, George was in paradise.

Soon, even those were dulled as the prince sank further into the engulfing embrace, his mind truly shutting off. The rhythmic pull of Rosaline's breath and the soft tap of George's heartbeat was all that was left… until a familiar voice politely cleared its throat from the bottom of the hill.

George peeled his eyes open, wincing at the sudden contact of sunlight. Unceremoniously, he rolled away from Rosaline who in turn sat up in confusion, one of George's legs still trapped under hers. Looking around, the prince spotted a tall woman in the uniform of the Regulars. It was similar to the outfit of the Stromist soldiers, but the plum-and-wine cape of the Vanguard was replaced with a similarly colored tabard of the Imperial Army. A pale green traveler's cloak was tossed over the woman's sturdy shoulders and a wide ivory grin was struck on her face. The golden locks paired with the jolly face was unmistakable.

"Baldra?" George probed.

"George! Or shall I say *Prince George*." Baldra wagged a finger. "Had me fooled!"

George couldn't help but smile. "I was trying to be sneaky."

"By using your own name!"

"It worked," George recalled as he rose to his feet. Rosaline stood beside him, catching Baldra's eye.

"I'm Rosaline." The medic straightened out her black tunic.

"Auxiliary!" Baldra seemed to approve. "I was Aux—wait, Rosaline?" Baldra's eyes studied her face, flickering back and forth. "Rosaline Von Rugosa!"

Rosaline seemed shocked but then it dawned on her. "Baldra! *Baldra!*"

The two clapped each other in a friendly embrace.

"Graces, you got tall," Rosaline muffled from the hug.

"And you got—" Baldra paused, clearly noticing a lack of height. "The same!"

"Do you know each other?" George blinked.

"George, this is the daughter of Ardric! From my father's vineyard!"

"That's right, you did say you were from Barcena way back when," George recalled.

"Daughter of Ardric, huh?" Baldra teased. "Does that mean you told him stories?"

"Horrible, terrible stories," Rosaline held Baldra at arms length.

George laughed. "Quite frankly, I'm disgusted."

Baldra squinted and turned her nose up. "Well I never!"

George snapped his fingers. "Oh, Baldra! How's Lawrence?" George's smile faded as Baldra's turned into a frown.

"Gone," Baldra replied in a low growl.

"He's not...?"

"No, not dead. At least I think so." Baldra looked away. "As good as dead, though."

"Desertion?"

Baldra nodded, her frown deepening. "He never did align with the war, less so with the Imperial side of things."

Rosaline tucked a slant into her cheek. "Well, enough of that. How did you end up in Korku, Baldra?"

"My garrison is joining up with the 11th on some combined effort," Baldra explained, "I volunteered to collect Darius' officers for the meeting. Which reminds me..." She looked at George. "Darius would like to see you."

"Joint operation?" George's face turned serious. "Sounds big."

"I should report back to my own unit," Rosaline cut in, "no doubt they'll have a play in whatever this is."

George nodded. "Stay safe."

"Don't tell me what to do," Rosaline stuck her tongue out.

George rolled his eyes and went to snap back but Baldra nudged him. "George!"

"Right!" George stood at attention. "Let's go."

***

Korku's war room was larger than it ever needed to be. It had a high vaulted ceiling that crept down to circular stone walls. Three large stained-glass windows stretched from floor to ceiling and cast a glittering rainbow across a wooden table so large and thick, George wondered how they managed to get it in the room altogether. What was usually empty space between the table and the dusty suits of armor was filled with the big names of the region.

Commander Darius stood next to General Jonsberg who in turn stood next to a General that George had never met before. Next to this commanding trio was Dame Honora, making it a quad of big names, with Franklin standing short next to them. Honora looked as serious as ever, reminding George of his time as an Auxiliary under her, or rather his time under Rick. Though the lines of stress were even deeper on her face than last he saw her, she looked at George with a seed of respect this time around. Something big was going on, this room was proof alone.

"Prince George," Jonsberg all but announced as the captain made his way to the war table. George tipped his head and folded his arms behind his back, a habit he recently picked up on that reminded him too much of Reginald.

"What's going on?"

"The giants are finally making their move," Darius answered, "a push to retake Kors and unite their front."

"Duke Fenric is pledging his army to aid us just like his father did two years back," Franklin added.

Honora looked down at the table, eyes pouring over the maps and letters. "Should all go well, we will have a repeat of the first battle of Kors and possibly crush their tenacity for good."

"Especially if we take out the giant's new chieftain, same as the old," Franklin was quick to add.

"This one might be a little trickier than the last," Darius admitted, "this new chieftain is claiming to be the Titanspoke and is gathering quite the following."

"What's the plan, then?" George questioned.

Jonsberg stiffened up at the query and looked back down at his map of Kors. "Unfortunately, the angle they are striking in from nullifies the battlefield we chose last time and puts us on a more open field against them, but with the Gavarian forces and the aid of General Tobias as well as an entire garrison of regulars permitted to us, we should be able to surpass their numbers and hit them with more quality than they could ever muster." Jonsberg's face twitched a little.

"No sane general admires the idea of a pitched battle of numbers," the man George couldn't recognize earlier, General Tobias, spoke. His voice was cool and calm, unlike Jonsberg's usual rambling demeanor. "But the arrival of Gavarian cavalry will pinch them in half, giving us two much more digestible pieces to work with.

"Why don't we pick a different spot to meet them?" George wondered out loud.

Honora shook her head. She said, "If nothing else, their self-proclaimed Titanspoke knows how to maneuver the Vagrants and the giants effectively. If we choose a more suitable spot back, we lose a lot of ground and they gain a lot of momentum, and if we try to meet them earlier, we would be in an even worse position and under threat of stretching our lines thin."

"And we didn't pick up on this earlier?" George furrowed his brow, the accusation getting him a tiny glare from Darius.

The Commander cleared his throat. "The time frame was fast and short, our spies got it back to us as quickly as they could."

"But!" Franklin tapped a finger back down on the map. "Our glorious Generals have already concocted a swift battle plan."

Jonsberg made a face. "This is a war room, Captain, show some respect."

"Sorry, sir," Franklin apologized.

George in turn tilted his head down out of respect, waiting for the General to continue. Jonsberg studied the others for a moment, as if routing any more interruptions before speaking.

"The enemy will be arriving from the west and northeast with the majority of the giants coming from the northeast." Jonsberg tapped a finger on the map. "We will intercept the northeastern army in these fields split between the hills and valleys of Kors, a bit more east than our last battle. The marshes that once flanked us will serve to slow the western approach long enough for Fenric's forces to arrive from the same direction, forcing the western army to head back north and down again into the main group, or become flanked by the Gavarians. So long as this pincer works, the 11th and the Regulars should have no issue combating the northeastern approach."

"A solid strategy, general," Tobias praised, "even if the western army decides to push south to avoid the Gavarians, they are still sandwiched between them and us. Their only option is to regroup with the Northeastern."

"And once forced together, they'll be easily managed and executed by our better trained ranks." Jonsberg nodded. "Especially with Gavarian cavalry to provide some flank pressure."

Honora nearly smiled. "If all goes well, the second battle of Kors will be as swift as the first."

"And hopefully the war along with it," Jonsberg grunted, "it's already long overstayed its welcome."

George curled a grin, remembering Jonsberg's words so many years ago when he first saw the man, he was so confident in the war being nothing more than a short conflict. Darius interrupted his reverie with a command. "George, you will be leading the center column with Franklin as your officer, I'll be on your eastern flank, likely taking the brunt of the initial fighting."

"And the west?" George questioned.

"Don't you worry about your western or southern flanks," Tobias held up a hand, "I'll have a column of regulars on each."

The room fell silent as everyone's gaze sank into the battle plan laid out on the map. Through the thick stone walls, the faint sound of training soldiers seeped through, challenged by a loud robin nesting by the window. George could hear the wind brush up against the keep and felt the warmth of late spring fight the cave-like chill of the room. Everything in George wished he was back under that pine tree with Rosaline and something in him told him this wouldn't be the first time he wished that.

"George." Franklin's voice came. The prince looked over at his friend.

"Let's end this war." Franklin gave him a determined nod.

"Let's." George's visage mirrored Franklin's resolve.

"Ho-ah," Darius agreed softly.

***

A field in spring was always a beautiful sight and by all means the fields outside the foothills of Kors were no exception. The grass was mowed low by deer fattening after a harsh winter and where they didn't feed, brightly colored wildflowers sprang up. On the edges of the meadows were the slopes that led into the mountains and on them were the dark green silhouettes of the vast pine forests. Even the sky complimented the scene with a deep azure and fluffy white clouds. George was witnessing the rare window of life present only for so many months this far north. The crest of the hills surrounding him reminded him of that, with frost still glistening on their shady sides.

Summer was nearly here, and it would stay only for a short while. George wished he could enjoy it, but no part of him could, not while sandwiched between his fellow soldiers, awaiting to kill or be killed. He stood in the center column, staring to the empty northeast with a spear in one hand, a shield in the other. Oathkith was tightly tied to his belt and waited patiently for the fray to come.

These sorts of silences always made George feel like the battle wasn't going to happen and that this was all a fluke, a mistake. There never was an enemy and they were just staring at an empty landscape for no good reason.

George's column seemed to copy his own aloof yet alert nature, only to tighten near Franklin's flank, the eastern half. Franklin was no doubt nervous, George figured, but everyone was. Only a liar would say that this wasn't a scary moment to wait for and that standing in a field in preparation to kill someone was just a fine way to spend a day. George scoffed at his own thoughts.

"Captain." Williams, who stood next to the prince, urged George's attention. Looking forward past the empty fields, the prince could see the enemy lines start to blur into sight. They seeped through the trees, both tall giants and fierce Vagrants. George pressed his lips into a thin line. "Flag the flanks."

Williams held up a colored banner and a horn bellowed to George's south. Before long, a line of regular column archers formed in front of George's position. Keeping his eye on the archers, George held onto his next order.

The captain of the archers raised a flag and shouted his own orders. Cool and well-trained, the marksmen readied their arrows and took their stances. Through the lines, George could see the giants getting closer. There were a lot more of them than last time. At the head of the enemy charge, George could make out a giant painted red and adorned with bones. He was bigger than most and the way he moved spoke of a deep bloodlust that George could feel all the way on the other side of the field. He must be the new chieftain.

"Archers at will!"

All the sounds of the meadow were ripped apart and replaced with the snap of bowstrings and the scream of arrows. A shadow flew across the field and the flood of arrows arched. Projectiles pelted into the enemy horde, slamming into flesh and shield alike, but as the wave of arrows approached the spearhead of the charge where the red stained giant was, a bloom of blue mist exploded.

George's eyes widened as the approaching arrows sank into the blooming cloud of mist, slowing to a complete stop and leaving the charging enemy unscathed as the arrows hung suspended in time.

"Mist-talking!" He swore. Other areas of the charge seemed to deploy their own pulses of the magical mist, slowing the arrows and freezing them in the air, only for them to clatter harmlessly as the mist dissipated.

"Hold shields, ready spears!" George hollered. "Advance ten and steady line!" Another flag was shot up and a set of horns repeated George's commands. George's column advanced through the line of archers before digging in. A horn bellowed to the east. Darius' line was prepared to take the brunt of the charge. The archers themselves had threaded back to the southern flank to join the rest of the regulars.

"Shields high!" George called out, anticipating the enemy barrage. As soon as the order came out, the sound of javelins slamming into the soldier's shields overtook the battlefield. The enemy let out a terrible roar and George knew the true battle had begun.

Thunk! George's shield arm shook from the impact of a javelin, the metal tip poking out the back and pointing right at his nose. He quickly tossed it away and grabbed his spear with both hands, slamming the butt end into the ground just in time for the horrific horde to ram into his formation.

His spear screamed and threatened to snap, bending under his hands when an unsuspecting Giant fell on its tip. Horns were blasting from Darius' column, the fighting even more intense than where George stood.

"Damnit!" George growled over the sounds of war. The creaking turned into a crack and his spear broke in two. A dead giant fell off to the side with the important half embedded in their gut. George tossed the handle to the ground and ripped Oathkith from its scabbard. The blade glistened under the light of the sun and immediately found the neck of a rebel.

Golden light erupted all around George as the Stromist magic of his allies blazed. He felt the itch deep inside himself and called to it as he held ground. He yanked his blade from a rebel's chest and moved to hamstring a giant. A cruel maul decorated with finger bones came crashing down, but the prince juked out of the way, the sharp edge of Oathkith cutting deep behind the owner's knee. The giant, dressed in gore and furs, roared as dark, red blood came pouring from the wound. George kicked into it, a small burst of magic pulsing through his leg and hobbling the giant. The huge warrior fell to a knee where George was in perfect range. Capitalizing on a sudden surge of magic, George hacked his blade downwards, slicing the giant's head off in a mess of red.

But where one fell, another appeared. George's magic wasn't complete, he could feel it, that strange pool of blue blocking a chaotic energy deep within. Gritting his teeth, he pushed through with what magic he did have. A rebel came bearing down on the prince, but he was quick to duck and rise with his blade. The tip of

Oathkith ripped through the enemy's neck and with a square knee to the chest, George shoved the enemy off his blade and back into the swarming horde.

Fenric better get here soon. The thought was on more than George's mind. Darius' column was noticeably being pushed south and the enemy army was flooding over them and into the regulars who couldn't do much against any mist-talkers among them. This whole change of direction was isolating George's column, squeezing them and giving them only the west for reprieve.

On cue, a horn bellowed to the west and George risked a glance. His stomach dropped, an entire army of Vagrants stood on the horizon, no Fenric, no Gavarians. The enemy stood fresh and ready to kill, and even with a slight incline in their way, George knew this was bad.

Williams ran his blade through an enemy's heart before knocking another away with his shield. "George!?"

"Williams, request withdrawal. We're about to be routed!"

The retainer fumbled a bone laid horn off of his shield arm, George covering him as he did. With a loud blast, Williams let loose the sound. In moments, Darius' and Tobias' horns replied. It was over.

"Withdraw!" George cried out and Williams blasted the horn a second time, just in time for the western army to slam into the regulars' western flanks, completing George's isolation amid the raging horde. The back troops started a steady withdrawal, while Darius' column attempted to fight more north to aid in the retreat. Even still, George slowly saw fewer and fewer allied faces. Soon he was standing amid an ocean of the enemy, with only his strongest covering the retreat alongside him.

Nearby he saw Franklin fighting to cover the retreat as well, his blade shimmering with magic as he cut down approaching enemies.

"Back!" George ordered and his line fell back a step. Franklin fell in line next to George and Williams. Together they stabbed their blades out to catch a rebel.

"Back!" The order came and the line fell backwards again, this time a giant broke the eastern flank, that portion of the column collapsing into a frenzy. The break forced Franklin away from George, enemies swelling in between the friends.

"Back!" George yelled again, but he knew that what he saw were the only ones left in the fray. He dare not sneak a look behind him to see the status of the rest of the army.

"George." Williams jabbed the edge of his shield into a rebel's neck

"Get out of here, Williams!" George nearly bit off his own tongue as a kicked-up stone bounced off his helmet.

"*We* need to get out of here!" Williams corrected, dodging a hammer swing just in time.

"Go!" Franklin screamed from the flank, face red and forehead bleeding. The line was broken, and the enemy was starting to seep in between the soldiers. George caught Franklin's gaze, both confidence and fear in his eyes. They widened and George felt a sickness creep into his own blood.

All sound seemed to dampen and fear overtook George. Franklin stared back at his friend with absolute terror carved into his face. The air felt fuzzy, almost like static and the prince could feel his body growing heavy. Franklin was mid-dodge, frozen in time, horror stuck on him. Between the two friends was a dense cloud of mist, George didn't even see anyone cast it. They were stuck.

Sound finally stopped altogether and then there was a faint buzzing. Finally, a tick, and a great flash of blue mist exploded out of Franklin, turning the man into a flood of red, his limp body getting thrown to the side.

George regained feeling in his limbs as all of the sound rushed to him all at once. The blast threw him backwards. He landed hard on his back, a piece of metal lunging through his calf and grinding against his bone. George screamed.

The red-painted giant was now in front of him, having erupted from the blue mist. In one hand he held a blade the size of a grown man, in the other he inspected Franklin's corpse. Shaking it as if it was a broken toy, the giant chieftain let it fall to the ground.

"No!" George screamed, golden magic pulsing through his body and springing him back to his feet, impaled leg and all.

"George don't!" Williams cried but it was too late. Stromism blasted out of George's legs, allowing him to leap right into the fray. He landed next to Franklin's body, his front foot on the red caped back of his friend while his back foot held him steady. Oathkith flashed and cut down an approaching rebel, it swung again and lobbed off another's head. It deflected a blade and then cut off the hand that held it. The sword became an extension of George as rage swelled inside him. Quickly it punched through the neck of another enemy. A giant approached, but George let Oathkith slice clean through its knee, then the other one, ending the victim's life by shoving the blade's point clean past the giant's eye.

"Franklin please," George growled as he fought, but there was no life under his foot. Only a pair of frightened dead eyes looked up at him, a mess of dark blood pooling around the mouth and chest.

George felt his chest screw up. "Franklin!"

A hammer slammed into George's back, the force being absorbed by his cuirass but knocking him forward. Another powerful hit from the enemy hammer came again, but this time it crashed into the side of his helmet. Harsh ringing filled the prince's ear and a snapping pain shot up his spine. The prince collapsed to the ground, his face landing beside Franklin's.

George tightened his grip on Oathkith, the other accidentally grabbing Franklin's cape. He shot back up just in time to avoid another hammer swing. Sword in one hand, cape in the other, George yanked the fabric free. It came loose in a flourish, catching a hammer swing. The Vagrant who owned it roared, but George ended them with a stab through the chest.

The prince was ragged and chaos swirled around him. He could barely stand and his fingers were numb. A rumbling laugh boomed, and he noticed a pool of mist encroaching upon him, the red-stained giant just in front. Evil eyes stared at George, but George didn't have the strength to stare back. The cloud of mist held George still.

"This is your end, Cursed One," the giant chieftain, the Titanspoke hissed.

A massive blade came arching down at the dizzy soldier. George felt the mysterious chaos in his chest break free for just a moment, its power pushing his weak arm into action. Black smoke pooled around George's fingers, pushing the mist back and rocketing Oathkith upwards. The Chieftain's blade crashed into Oathkith and the ringing bang sent the prince fast into the air. The world went spinning as George flew from the impact. He landed only to bounce off the ground, skidding, bouncing again and into the treeline. George's body fumbled into the dark woods and then with the crack of a heavy branch, everything turned dark.

Chapter 20
Please

Franklin smiled wide at George, his tunic as white as the snow. George himself was dressed in a dark outfit to contrast but still wearing a smile as big as Franklin's. All around the pair, people swarmed, both joyful villagers of Korku and old war buddies of Franklin and the prince. Hector himself was chatting with Darius by a row of flowers, and the overseeing sage stood aloof by a table of food that was slowly being picked clean. It was a winter day, but the feeling was warm, and no one seemed to mind the snow underfoot in exchange for the festivities. Johanna hung on Franklin's arm with a Cheshire grin and a giggle in her throat.

"I never thought I'd see the day," George remarked with a laugh. Franklin slugged a solid hit into the prince's shoulder.

"What's that supposed to mean?" The tone was friendly.

Johanna simply shook her head. "You two tease each other more than I tease Franklin, sometimes I wonder who should have been in this dress."

Franklin scoffed, "Well not Mr. Shoulders over here. He'd either look the part of a sail or a snake victim."

"You think you're prettier than me, eh?" George raised a challenging fist.

Johanna pinched the bridge of her nose, swallowing a jumping laugh. "I can't be bothered with you two."

"You know we are only fooling." George stood up straight.

Franklin made a face. "Well maybe you are, but I meant it."

The prince snagged one of Johanna's hands from Franklin and clasped it gingerly. A sad look overtook his face as he said, "Good luck, Johanna. I'm afraid he's an idiot."

The bride nearly choked on a sudden laugh, forcing a bellowing chortle from George and Franklin. Franklin sighed happily and looked up at his friend, one brow arched.

"Say George?"

"Mm?"

"Don't you have somewhere to be?"

George blinked. "No."

"George." Franklin bounced his eyebrows. "You know you can't stay."

"Franklin, please." George felt a stone fall in his stomach, a churning sickness swirling around it.

"You need to go, George."

"Please let me stay." A heat swelled in George's face, his eyes threatening tears.

Franklin shook his head. "You need to go."

"Please!" George burst into tears.

"No!" Franklin roared back.

"I want to stay!" George all but screamed, deep sobs shaking his body. "Please let me stay!"

A deep and alien voice rumbled in the sky. "Hinan..."

Something gripped George, but he couldn't see it. The winter was gone, the wedding was gone, Franklin was gone, only darkness, only black. Something held him tight, moving him. He wanted to thrash but he couldn't wake up, a deep pain in his leg and a hollow in his heart.

The voice came again, "Hinan."

It wasn't so alien anymore. He knew that voice. George opened his eyes, or tried to. A blurry image appeared, a great horned figure held him in its arms, moving him swiftly over indistinct ground.

"You cheated death, Hinan," the horned man explained, "be careful, I can only imagine how furious the Dweller must be and we need you alive to end this."

George struggled but two fingers came and closed his eyes again. A blue whir whizzed behind his eyelids and then with a pink flash, the darkness came again.

***

Cold water splashed over George's face. He woke up with a deep gasp and immediately the light of midday stabbed at his eyes. The prince sat on a dirt spot directly in the sun, body sore and riddled with pain. His mouth was cracked and his tongue was dry. A rough rope tied his wrists to a wooden stake behind him and a group of Vagrants ringed his vision. One of the Vagrants held an empty bucket and a wicked grin.

Startled, George squirmed, noticing his impaled leg was completely and strangely healed. His armor was missing, as was Oathkith, but Franklin's tattered cape was clasped around his shoulders. The gambeson he had worn under his armor was stained brown with dirt and already ripping from abuse, matching his own beat-up image.

Ahead of him, one of the Vagrants stepped forward to stand by a blacksmith's grindstone, the only other object in this strange dirt pit. George looked up at the man, squinting into the bright blue sky. The Vagrant wore finely stitched pants and a gold-clasped shirt patterned with swirls and other symbols. Armlets coiled up and down his right arm and a chipped sword hung on his belt. His face was like a Gavarian's: fair, bright eyed, and blonde. A fierce look was etched across it, magnifying as he started to bark in a language that George couldn't understand.

The prince could only offer a terrified and confused silence, one that seemed to anger the man further. He growled at George in his alien language and one of the other men behind him began to pedal the grindstone into a hissing spin. The first man growled his words again.

"I don't understand!" George managed, but the man didn't seem to heed it. Roughly, he grabbed George by the back of the collar, gripping him by the throat of Franklin's cape while another man loosened George's bindings. The rope fell from his wrists and George felt blood trickle back into his numb fingers but he didn't have time to think on it. Angrily, the first man heaved George forward, brute strength putting the prince back on his knees in front of the spinning wheel. George's eyes widened as the rough stone blurred close to his face. He could feel the wind off of it.

The growl came again, but whatever time the man gave George to answer before was cut in half. First, George felt the grip on him tremble with anger, second, he felt the rough tug as he was thrust forward and after that, all he felt was pain. The stone burned a bloody wound into George's cheek, the coarse grindstone smearing as George screamed in absolute agony. He was pulled back from the bloodied stone and the growl came again. George whimpered, but this time, as he felt the man thrust him towards the stone, another voice came that paused the torture.

These words were also alien, but the voice was strangely familiar. A man that itched in George's memory broke through the ring of Vagrants. He wore the clothes of a rebel but had the posturing and voice of an Imperial. George squinted, one of his eyes still twitching in pain. As the Imperial finished talking, the first man from before let go of George, throwing him to the dirt. Air escaped George's lungs and the dust stung his bleeding face. Grumbling, the Vagrants started to disperse, clearing George's view as he laid on the ground.

He finally noticed it, he was in a village of some sorts, one built on the meadows of a large clearing. Simple, squat wooden homes peppered the meadow and smatterings of farm animals and crops filled in the gaps. Women, men and children were working on their daily tasks, though most were staring at the prince.

"George." The Imperial's voice turned to its native tongue. "George, is that you?"

The prince tried to get a better look at the man through his tear blurred eyes. "W-who?"

"George, it's me, Lawrence."

***

Old chains rattled and Lawrence secured a lock on a beat up shed that was clearly once used as storage for the stable next to it. It was an ancient building, but a sturdy one, with thick wooden beams and a tightly sealed door. The roof was thickly thatched and boarded off from the inside to prevent leaks, or in George's case, from him getting out.

The prince stood, baffled and beaten, on the muddy square floor of the empty shed with the only light being that which filtered in through a cut out eye-slot in the door and a small hole off to the side, clearly gnawed open by some sort of rat or mouse. George had his face pressed against the slot in the door, sucking all the air from the outside in an attempt to save himself from the damp, dirty air of the shed, but more importantly, to meet Lawrence's gaze.

Lawrence gave George a sorry look, clearly disturbed by the beaten face staring up at him. His eyes often bounced to the already crusty and bloody scar forming around George's left cheek.

"I don't understand," George said, his voice hoarse. "You save me from one torment just to throw me into another?"

"The Village Lord ordered this, not me." Lawrence shuffled in place.

"Who cares?" George spat. "You're not even a Vagrant, you're—"

"Ulmi."

"What?" George squinted.

"We aren't Vagrants, we are Ulmi. The Ulmi people."

"We? Ulmi?" Frustration boiled in George's stomach. "You're a fucking Imperial!"

Lawrence scowled and slammed the tiny slot closed, locking George into the darkness. George felt his anger boil and he slammed his fists into the door.

"Lawrence!" he bellowed, ramming his knuckles raw. "Lawrence, you're a damned traitor!"

George felt blood rush to his face and he gritted his teeth as he continued his barrage. "Lawrence! Lawrence!" Finally, the prince let out a deep roar, rattling the door as he pounded. Stopping,

George sucked up another breath before screaming again, tears stinging his face wound. He let out another scream, this one turning into a hiccupping sob at the end, until finally his screams were loud tearful cries.

Lightheaded, George fell backwards to the soil below. There he laid on his back, staring up at the darkness and trying not to choke on his whimpers. He grabbed the ends of Franklin's cape and pulled it up onto him, his only shield against the dirt and cold.

***

"I didn't tell them who you are." Lawrence's voice came from past the door. George was still on his back, mouth open and dry. He didn't know how long he had laid there, but his stomach was an empty pit and his throat was on fire. The prince blinked in the darkness, unsure how to respond.

"They found you in the woods, so they think you're just some sort of spy who got lost."

George didn't move. He stayed where he was, staring at nothing. "The woods? I was at the battle of Kors."

"Well, you must have walked very far from it. They found you in the woods wrapped in your cloak and broken armor."

"And my sword?"

"None," Lawrence replied, "All they found on you was your field knife."

Silence.

"How long will they keep me?" George struggled to sit up.

Silence again.

"I don't know."

George frowned, his voice low. "I'm sorry, Lawrence."

No response came from the door and so George continued, "I know you are just trying to help."

"It's alright," Lawrence replied. "I'm more sorry than you are, I think. I wish this wasn't how you got to know the Ulmi."

"How did you come to know them?" George wondered out loud. The slot in the door opened, a beam of moonlight coming through. Even the light of the night was enough to make George squint for a moment in recoil. Lawrence's hand came through the slot, a waterskin dangling in his grasp.

Crawling over, George snatched it from his hand before collapsing with his back on the door. Ripping the stopper off the skin, George guzzled the water. The fluid washed down his cracked throat and brought feeling back to his mouth. He could feel the cold water travel through him, and he drank until the skin was empty.

George felt Lawrence press up against the other side of the door, the man's voice coming through at the same level as George. "I suppose I just wanted to. I couldn't justify the actions of the Imperials anymore, I couldn't be a part of that, and so I left... only to find my way here. I didn't mean to, not consciously anyway."

"And they accepted you?" George squeezed the skin, forcing a final drop out of it.

"Not at first," Lawrence admitted. "Fate was on my side, and while I dwelled in the outskirts like an animal, I caught the eye of the local Lord's daughter."

Pulling his knees up to his chest, George cocooned himself in Franklin's cape. Thoughts buzzed on his mind, trying to picture Lawrence's story.

The deserter continued, "Well anyway, I suppose it started when I stumbled upon her gathering dandelions in the fields. She was curious enough to attempt to talk with me, which didn't go very well."

"I can't imagine it would." George replied.

Lawrence shuffled on the other side of the door, as if getting comfortable. "No, no it didn't and I would be a liar if I didn't say I was frustrated enough to give up on communicating with her, let alone the Ulmi people after that. I felt like a beast unable to relay my simplest thoughts, but Yulna wasn't so easily dismayed. She visited me a few days each week and slowly we learned to talk with one another. I'd help her with her tasks, and she'd teach me new words."

"And this all led to where you are now?"

"Give or take," Lawrence agreed, "the simple kindness and curiosity of one person helped me build a new home here. Two years have passed since then, and now I am a father, a husband, and an Ulmi."

"I'm glad you found peace," George muttered.

Lawrence paused, as if weighing his next words carefully. "You could too."

"I can't stay here," George answered softly, the image of a white pine and a brilliant smile playing in his head. Next came the vision of Franklin, and then Williams and Hector. Jonsberg and Darius appeared in his thoughts, only to vanish as his mind turned to darker subjects. The conspiracies, the horned prophet, the Dweller, *Fenric*. George clenched his fists. He spoke through his teeth. "This isn't where I need to be."

"You don't know that—"

"I do know!" George growled. "I'm sorry, but I do know."

Silence.

"You're probably just hungry."

"And trapped in the dark." George didn't mean to hiss as harshly as he did.

Silence again.

"I'll talk to the Lord about it in the morning, maybe he'll let you out."

Looking up at the beam of moonlight, George sucked in a gulp of the fresh air that fell from the open slot. "Can I make a request?"

"Hm?"

"Leave the slot open."

George felt the door vibrate as Lawrence stood up, the man's voice coming from up high now. "I can do that, sure."

"Thank you."

Lawrence's voice was softer, as if he was already a step away. "Of course."

"Lawrence." George called back.

"Yes?"

"What did the Imperials do that was so awful that you needed to abandon Baldra?"

The man's voice was close again. He clearly hesitated at the mention of his old friend but eventually he answered. "It's not so much what the Imperials did, but what they've been doing."

George was silent.

"You see," Lawrence continued, an ambient passion in his voice. "The Ulmi people never accepted the reign of the self-proclaimed Mortal Empire, or the idea that the Jerrovian Empire was the sole authority of the continent, and so they've been at odds with the Imperials ever since. Land disputes, unwarranted or out of jurisdiction arrests, sending Proctors and spies to sabotage Lords and alliances. Your own grandfather even broke a treaty to completely indoctrinate them by force and attempted to annihilate any refusing holds."

"My grandfather was a madman who only saw the Ulmi as the cause of raids and unrest in the north." George frowned. "My father and uncle put a stop to him."

"But not a stop to the problem," Lawrence pressed. "There is still no love between our two peoples. A simple land dispute over farms in Gavaria led to this entire blown out war, that alone should be a sign enough that this is a festering wound. Dweller be damned, most of the Ulmi joined the war and Giant alliance out of fear that the Empire would attempt another annihilation."

"How do we close the wound, then?" George stood up to put his face through the slot, finally catching Lawrence's gaze. The two stared for a moment before George continued. "Give back the farm land?"

"No," Lawrence frowned. "That would just upset the Gavarians and likely cause another conflict."

"Keep the farmland, then?"

Lawrence furrowed his brow.

George mirrored the look. "What action could I do to help end this war and prevent conflict between our two peoples from arising again, how could we live in cooperation?"

"I think..." Lawrence was hung up on his own words. "I think the Empire needs to dissolve, first."

"And open them up to Gavarian influence, solely." George pursed his lips into a line. "Either side can make the argument that ending the other side would solve the conflict, that's what my grandfather wanted to do, but I'm starting to think that the only way to end the conflict is if both sides want to cooperate to begin with."

"That sort of cooperation can't be found in this war." Lawrence frowned deeply.

George sighed. "Unless the leaders of it can be made to reason..." A thought passed behind George's stare and he opened his mouth. "What if there was another reason this war started?"

"What?" Lawrence furrowed his brow.

George steadied his gaze as best he could, his knees wobbling. Seriousness seeded in his voice as he thought out loud. "What if someone wanted this war to happen?"

Lawrence took a step back, as if pushed by George's intense stare. The bloodshot grey eyes of the prince dug into Lawrence, studying the man. George's mind was already screaming with pain, and now it was twisted with the puzzle of the conflict. He felt a little guilty, but he also felt slighted, and angry, though most of all he felt tired, tired and hungry. Even still, his mind was restless.

The prince spoke again. "What if the Dweller started this war?" A long pause followed the accusation. Lawrence simply stared at George with pitying eyes, as if he thought George had gone insane. The buzzing of night insects captured the scene as both parties stared quietly.

"George," Lawrence broke the silence. "I'll bring you some bread, but then I think it would be best if we continue this conversation after I speak with the Lord about your situation."

Anxiously gnawing on his cheek, George receded from the slot in the door. "Very well."

The rest of the night was a long one. George's stomach made quick work of the bread that Lawrence had brought and was grumbling just mere moments after. His nose seemed to be in cahoots with his stomach and every time George stuck his face through the slot for fresh air, he swore he smelled the pastries he used to steal back at the palace. The hungry reverie would only last in spurts though, as his body would eventually groan about being tired and before long George was having a spotty sleep on the dirt floor of the shed, his only blanket being Franklin's torn cape.

Eventually he gave up on sleep, unsure if he ever truly fell into a slumber or if he just uncomfortably drifted for a few hours. Unfortunately, being awake meant being a slave to the processes of his body and after putting it off as long as he could, George picked a corner to relieve himself in, only for the shed to generously accept the smell of urine as its new odor. This new turn of events brought George to the tiny hole chewed into the wall, as he was too tired to stand up by the slot for fresh air.

First, George stuck his finger in it and when nothing bit it off, he stuck his nose through. Immediately he was hit with the smell of horse and hay. The prince shuffled to get a better angle and snuck a peek. He was met with the sight of a strong horse's leg standing right by the hole. The leg was a speckled white that was dulled with age. Whoever the horse was, George could only assume it had already lived its glory days.

"Psst!" George whispered through the hole. The leg stamped, clearly confused.

George grinned, happy with the distraction. "Down here!"

A snowy muzzle blocked the hole, a huge snort blowing a muggy sneeze into George's face.

"Hey!" The prince leaned back. A subtle scraping sounded in response, clearly the horse's head bumping the wall. The bump took George's eyes and sent them up the wall and, for the first time, the prince noticed a second even smaller hole rotted from a knot in the wood. For a moment George figured that meant the wall could be busted through, but testing his weight against the wood quickly destroyed that idea. The wall was definitely braced with cross planks on the stable side.

Shaking his head, George peeked through the higher up hole. The horse was staring right at him with intelligent black eyes. Definitely older, the animal was a milky white with speckled grays and a tiny crest of reddish brown on its forehead. George gave the horse another quick study. Something about her forehead itched his memory.

"Hello." George's words caused the mare to steady, as if awaiting further commands. The personality was already clear to George. "You were a warhorse."

The mare stamped her hoof and dipped her head. As a shaft of morning sun caught the head of the horse, George could have sworn the reddish-brown crest looked more of a blazing crimson red. Remembering his conversation with Lawrence all those years ago, the entire sight reminded him of IAO's reddish mount of legend.

"You're a pretty horse, you know," George complimented, "care to be friends?"

The mare stamped again.

"George." Lawrence's voice made George jump. Quickly, George turned from the hole with a guilty face, as if worried someone will take the tiny reprieve away from him. Lawrence didn't seem to notice, but otherwise stared at the prince with a grim look.

George's stomach sank at the sight and as he approached the slot, he had a bad feeling.

"What did the Lord say?" George felt he already knew the answer.

"I..." Lawrence hesitated. "I'm sorry."

"He said no?"

"He is convinced you are a spy," Lawrence hastily explained, "I tried to tell him you were just lost, but he didn't believe me. The armor you were wearing proves you were military, and why would a military unit be lost in the woods so close to his home other than for nefarious reasons? That's how he is going about it."

George let out a long and frustrated exhale. "So, what are we going to do about it?"

"What do you mean?" Lawrence raised a brow.

Making a face, George explained, "The Lord didn't work, I'm just going to have to escape somehow. How am I going to escape?"

Lawrence tilted his head. "I can't help you escape."

"What?" the prince hissed in surprise.

"I can't just let you go, that would betray the trust the Ulmi have put in me. They are already suspicious enough at how I keep defending you."

"Lawrence, please." George stepped forward. "They can't keep me here forever, and you know when they find out I don't have any information, I'm as good as dead."

"I really can't." Lawrence's face was guilty. "I don't like it but I can't."

"When you didn't like something the Imperials did, you went against it. Can't you do that here?" George felt frustration rise in him.

"No, this is different." Lawrence was shaking his head. "I can't betray the Ulmi."

"But you can betray me!?" George was hurt, talking louder than he probably should have.

"It's not like that."

"Well, it seems like that!" George growled.

"I have a family!" Lawrence growled back. "It's not just me I have to think about anymore, it's not just me!"

The prince recoiled, surprise dripping into his frustration.

"You can't ask me to go against my family."

George couldn't help but growl, "What am I supposed to do?"

"I don't know," Lawrence admitted. He turned away for a moment, looking at something George couldn't see. The prince noticed a look of care and thought reflected in the man's eyes as he did though. Lawrence turned back to George.

"I'll go get you food and water, but then I don't think I can speak with you any more... it jeopardizes both of us."

Silently, George nodded, a burning anger bubbling inside of him.

"And George."

The prince locked eyes with Lawrence, the man continuing, "I'm sorry."

"What do you want me to say to that?" George pressed between his teeth.

Lawrence nodded his acknowledgement, face twisted with guilt, and awkwardly turned away from the slot.

"I'll leave the slot open."

George couldn't bring himself to say anything.

A few moments later and silence reigned. George stood alone in the dark, too afraid to attempt sleep and too uncomfortable to lay down. He shoved a hand in his pocket, face turning to one of surprise when his fingers found something. Rolling the object in his fingertips, George procured a piece of pink wood out of his pocket. Staring down at the trinket in surprise, George gripped it tightly in his fist and sat down.

The prince rolled it in his palm for a while before placing it mindlessly on a rough rock that stuck out from the mud. With nothing better to do, and his thoughts too harsh to dwell on, he started to rub it against the rock, smoothening it out into the shape of a raindrop.

Chapter 21
The Altar of Harmony

Four days of silence followed George and Lawrence's last conversation. Each morning someone would toss in food and water, and each afternoon George tried to make it last until he fell asleep. Three days of this started to make the shed stink, and the wound on his face began to scab in such a way that it felt like a burn was spreading over his cheek. George's skin was under a layer of dirt and his cape was a dull red mottled with damp spots and a moldy smell. Four seemed like such a small number and yet four days in the shed was more than enough.

On the fifth day, George found himself standing by the slot, face pressed out of it in an attempt to escape the smell of urine and filth. The sight outside was always surreal. Groups of people were going about their daily lives as if he wasn't watching, as if some crusty, beat-up man wasn't hungrily looking on with teary eyes. Children played, men and women went about their work, and warriors trained. There was a whole life outside the shed.

"Look at 'em, Ai." George called just loud enough for the stable next to the shed to hear. A thump sounded in response. George furrowed his brow. "I know."

A dampened snort came from behind the wall.

"I can't help it," George defended himself. The prince pressed his lips into a thoughtful line and stepped back into the darkness of his cell. Finding the wall with the holes in it, he leaned against it. A nuzzling sound scratched at the other side and George knew Ai was there.

George slapped a palm against the wall. "I need to get out of here." He laughed. "I *need* to get out of *here!*"

He closed his eyes and his palm turned into a fist, banging with each word. "I need to get out of here!"

His final bang was overshadowed by a bigger one, as someone slammed the slot to the shed closed. The rattling of the lock clicking into place quickly followed after. George's eyes widened in the darkness. "No."

"No, no, no!" George rushed to the door and slapped the back of the slot's cover. "No! No, open this please! No!" The prince slapped and pounded until a warm trickle poured over his knuckles. "No, no, no!" Both hands slammed into the whole door. "No!"

Falling to the soil in defeat, George began to shake. He pulled up his knees and coddled himself under Franklin's cape. Letting his face fall between his legs, the burn in his eye turned to drips of tears. All George felt was the cold of the shed, the chill of his own emotions, and the warmth of the tears sinking through his pants.

A whinny called out from behind the shed wall.

George cracked a sad smile. "Thanks, Ai."

***

Unsure how long he sat there, George found his knees creaking and popping when he finally decided to stand up. His eyes had adjusted to the darkness of the shed but even then, he couldn't make out anything beyond the tiny holes he would speak to his last remaining friend through. Running his cleanest finger over the ridges of his facial scar, he fell into thought.

With each breath, his emotions changed. Rage, hate, frustration, sadness, fear and even melancholy danced in his mind, eyes blank. His dry lips trembled. "Why."

Franklin's eyes stared at him through the dark, glossy and lifeless. Behind him, his sister was in danger, the sages laughing. George felt tears roll down his cheeks and his sword hand clench. The sounds of war rang in his ears, the pang of his helmet being smashed, the hiss of the magical mist, the stare of the woman in his nightmares. So much was happening, but it was so hard to answer... "Why." The word choked on a sob.

The only answer was the soft snort of Ai in the room next to his, and the gentle sounds of the outside world. George closed his eyes, as if it made a difference. Plopping down onto the ground he tried to focus on happier things. His nose twitched, emotion still swirled inside him, but he forced it down. A cold stuck to his cheeks where his tears once were, making him feel naked. He screwed his eyes shut even more, attempting to go deeper away from where he sat but a noise pulled him back out.

Squabbling sounded outside and the tranquil sounds of the village were overtaken by angry shouts and the rattle of chains. George's eyes shot open and he sprung to his feet. He took a stance. If this was the end, he was going to go out like a soldier. The noise came closer and closer and by time it was at the shed door, George recognized one of the voices.

A harsh Kafshe voice cursed at the Ulmi outside and when the door was wrenched open, George was blown back by the sudden burst of light. Steeling his gaze through the evening light, the prince saw a mob of Ulmi trying to push Opane into the shed. The Kafshe was covered in chains and bruises, but still she pushed back at the mob. Her fingers crackled with freezing ice—

"Opane?" George croaked.

Spinning to George's voice, Opane's amber eyes widened. Taking advantage of her shock, the Ulmi finally pushed Opane into the shed before slamming it shut behind them. The Kafshe stumbled forward into the dark.

"George?" Opane held out her hands to catch himself.

"Yeah." George put a hand on Opane's shoulder, securing her in place. "What are you doing here?"

George could hear a sarcastic scoff come from Opane. "The Kafshe never forget a friend."

***

The only sound was the chorus of summer crickets. Their chirp was dampened by the walls of the shed but still they provided a break from the silence often found late at night. The slot once again was locked shut, leaving the Kafshe and the prince alone in the dark. George could only assume there was no moon that night, since usually at least some starlight would leak through the holes that lead to Ai's stable.

Facing each other, the imprisoned pair both sat with their legs crossed. Opane was deep in thought, George could tell. George himself was a scattering of thoughts. Between his wishes to experience the summer night outside and his desperation to escape, he found a seed of doubt that anchored him to his spot. It swirled with sadness and depression, fortified by dreams of Franklin's dying eyes and the loss of Kors as well as his inability to know what to do next, what to do with everything he now knew. His decisions up until this point led him here, and led those he cared about to despair. He felt stuck.

Opane fidgeted and George snapped out of his thoughts. Even in the dark, George could feel the Achian eyes staring at him. Opane's voice came out quiet, almost hissing. "George."

The prince copied the hushed tone. "Yes?"

"It's a beautiful night out, no?"

The question stood out as odd. "Yes?" George answered with a hint of surprise.

"Then why are we still in here?"

"We are prisoners."

"Only in name," Opane quickly answered. "We are held by a rotting shed, why are we still here? Why were *you* still here?"

"As if it was that simple." George fidgeted.

"Why isn't it?"

"Even if we do break out of the shed, there is an entire village waiting for us. There are guards, wilderness, and scouts. I'd never make it back to the front," George did his best to explain.

"Of course you wouldn't, not in this shed." Opane exhaled sharply. "You are a Stromist, I have seen your power. These people cannot hold you, they cannot hold me."

"I can't just fight them." George felt his gut tighten.

"Why not?"

"They are just people trying to live," George explained, even if the hate in his stomach refused to accept the words. The Kafshe groaned skeptically.

"No, there's something else binding you."

Frustration welled in George's chest but he didn't say anything. Opane pushed, "tell me why won't you make a decision?"

"Is it the right one?" George snapped. "My decisions already brought all this pain to me and those near me... maybe I should spare the rest of the world my decisions and dreams."

Opane fell into a thoughtful silence. "As if you can just stop making decisions. Others need you, George, you cannot sit here and wallow in the hopes that things will fall into place. You have to make a decision, the world will move without you if you don't, you have to escape this place."

"I'd only reinforce the village's belief that the Empire is a monster," George debated, shifting the blame.

"The Empire *is* a monster, but so are the Ulmi, so are the Kafshe, the Paleskins. If you group people in a big enough net, you will find a monster. *George* is not a monster, neither is Opane, but we are alive, and we are being denied our lives, and we have people who need us. We do not have the luxury of being prisoners." Opane paused. "You have learned to be helpless in this shed, you turned the wooden walls to steel and have trapped yourself in your emotions and worries."

George felt heat in his eyes and looked to the ground. Opane continued. "It's time to stand up and come home. You need to set things right."

"Why me?" George sniffed.

"Because of who you are," Opane answered, "you are an Imperial with the heart of a Kafshe, a rare breed. You have shown compassion, even to your captors, even to those who have slain your friends."

George winced. "But I still hate them."

"And still you have shown compassion in your actions," Opane quickly defended, "only now it is time to show that same strength to yourself, for the good of yourself, and for the good of Jerrovia. You will go on to do great things, I have felt this." Opane was putting a deep passion in her voice, as if she had practiced this speech. It was enough. Her poetic way was moving and George knew even without the frills that she was right, as always.

"Then we escape." George cleared the tears from his throat. "But there is another obstacle."

Opane hummed, "Hm?"

"The Stromism you are betting on being our key out of here isn't exactly what you think it is."

"What do you mean?"

"I can't..." Embarrassment pushed through his dense emotions.

"You can't?" asked Opane.

"I can't use my magic on command, it only comes when it wants to come." George said, "I have tried countless techniques with both my uncle and Commander Darius."

"Mmm..." Opane groaned, doing her best to remain the impartial teacher, "I suppose that makes sense."

"It does?" George blinked.

"You have quite a large Altar of Creation, I can see how it could be difficult to wield."

The prince dropped his brow. "A large Altar of Creation?"

A condescending chuckle came from the Kafshe. "So many years since the days of IAO and still the Imperial magicians have yet to accept the concept of the Altar. The sages' doing, no doubt."

George scooched closer. "But what is it?" He was now close enough to just be able to make out Opane's face. Her eyes crinkled as he asked his question, as if amused.

"Everything in the world, all matter, is made of two primordial forces," Opane explained, putting two fingers between them. "In everything, even the air itself, these two forces interact in harmony to create the seen and the unseen. We, those who still hold the teachings of old, call these two forces the smoke and the mist." A small chiming sound sparked in George's ear with the mention of each. It felt familiar and his mind itched as the words carved across his consciousness.

Opane paused as if she had heard it too. "If there is so much of the smoke—" The chime again. "—then there should be as much of the mist. When these two are balanced, even if just for a moment, a field of harmony is created between them where anything could become reality, this field is known as the Altar of Creation. In other words, the primordial forces work behind the scenes and combine to create matter, from stones, to air to living things such as you or me. The power of creation lies in the Altars created by the interaction of the two forces. Kafshe sense the Altars in the world around them and use their own will to create upon it, such as ice or fire from air. The Stromists have the miraculous ability to manipulate their own Altar of Creation that serves as their life force, slowing down any undulations of smoke or mist and leveling them perfectly to create strength. Such power is strong enough to balance the body's smoke and mist from outside forces."

George was immediately reminded of when he broke through the mist-talker's embrace. "So, a Stromist controls the balances of smoke and mist inside of them and around them?"

"Immediately around them, yes, which brings us to you," Opane explained. "Since I had first met you, I could feel an incredible altar of creation within you. I do not know how to explain it, but you're dense."

"Geez, thanks." George frowned.

"No." Opane waved an invisible hand. "I mean to say that the levels of the smoke and the mist within you are incredible, larger than anything I had ever witnessed before, and because of such a volume, when both sides balance, it creates an incredibly large Altar. It makes sense to me that you cannot balance it, not with traditional Stromist training, especially when the Stromists won't even recognize the existence of the harmonic balances. Odd, seeing how you Imperials use the mist so often in your sage magic."

"So, what am I going to do, then?" George crossed his arms.

"I'd say you should train like a Kafshe, but that would be equally as useless, because you are not." Opane fell into thought for a moment. Her fingers tapped at the dirt below as she thought. "But there is one Stromist technique I do know, passed down by the Kafshe from an unwritten age where Stromists and Kafshe fought side by side. It is how I could feel your Altar, though I imagine a Stromist could use it much better than I could."

"What do I have to do?" George's excitement was leaking into his voice.

"Close your eyes, fall into meditation and attempt to reach out to your Altar of Creation and when you find it, try to feel the flow of smoke and mist, see how it interacts within you, and try to understand the nature of each of the forces."

George went to speak but Opane held up a finger. "Once you find it, reach outwards, and feel the smoke and mist of the world around you push and pull on that which makes you. You'll feel where it cloves, where it joins, and eventually you'll see where it balances. Perhaps then, you can see what you need to do to balance your own Altar, to wield it." Opane cleared her throat. "You should already be familiar with the Stromist technique of centering yourself."

"It's how most Stromists activate their abilities," George answered.

"But not yours, I wager. Centering dampens the chaos of the smoke, which is fine for small Altars, but what of the mist when there are larger quantities, it doesn't account for the mist! Use the centering technique in your meditation, but try to reach out to both natures of harmony."

George closed his eyes, while Opane continued her lecture. "Smoke, chaos and freedom. Mist, stagnation and peace. Harmony, freedom in peace. Find freedom where there is stagnation, and incorporate order where there is chaos. Reach inward and find your balance."

The Kafshe's voice drifted off as George fell into meditation, his mind a flurry of thoughts and body aching from the cold soil floor. He held his breath and felt his heartbeat until finally he found a thought to follow: Summer rain.

***

Days had gone by and so had the nights. Summer rain pelted the shed and kept the Ulmi inside their homes. Plates of rotten food piled up by the shed, all untouched. Skins of water remained undrunk, and the slot was never opened. The guards attempted to feed the prisoners within the first few days, but gave up quickly, and found themselves unsettled.

Inside the wooden prison, George sat in meditation. He was unmoved from his place days before, and Opane sat beside him in just as deep of a concentration. A gentle hum was all that would occasionally arise from the pair, almost always in synchronization. They didn't seem malnourished, nor dehydrated, but held the appearance as if they had just begun their near weeklong meditation. It was a phenomenon that Opane had explained prior to the start of their journey.

As strangely calm as the scene was on the outside, George wandered a dangerous battlefield inside. He felt all the pieces that made up who he was, all the memories and experiences, all down to the base of who he was. Every bit flew by him and danced in a mess he could barely put together. In there, he found a deep desire to avenge Franklin, and to end injustices on all sides. George wanted to protect others, fight for others, be there for others, but he also wanted to do what was right for him.

The prince's head was a swarm of quotes and voices. He could hear his instructors in the past explaining how to center himself, to curb emotion and find peace to activate his magic, but that didn't feel right anymore. Why couldn't he use his emotions, if they were what gave him breath and gave him ambition and strength? He could see the mist inside himself flare at the thought, swirling devious and blue.

It was an incredible pool of mist, still and overtaking. Even if the smoke inside him burned coal black, it couldn't escape this immense sea of mist. Sucking in a breath, George let himself feel. He broke the barriers, the defenses. Tearing down the walls within him,

George let himself be vulnerable. Without thinking, George ripped at all that stabilized himself, all that he told himself he needed to be. Opane's voice echoed in this chamber of destruction.

"You cannot tell a flame where to flick. It will, as you will. Let it, let you."

With the dam broken, George could feel his hate flush inside him, his sadness, his happiness, his joy and fear. He felt all that came off of him, and he followed these strings of emotion to its source: the real him.

Pushing past the sea of mist and the fresh torrent of smoke, George found a golden meadow. It wasn't quite still, with the wind ruffling waves through its grass, but it wasn't quite chaotic. The air was somehow tranquil in its gust, warm and sweet. There was a hill and George found himself on it, sunny and comfortable. Rays of heat tingled his back as he laid staring up at the blue sky and lazy clouds. The sensation grew and grew until he felt it in every inch of his body. The prince's eyes sprung open.

"Ah!" George sucked in a gulp of air, his heart speeding to catch up with his newly awakened state. Opane opened a single eye.

"I feel it," George nearly giggled.

"Do you feel the others?" Opane questioned.

George furrowed his brow. "I feel you, calm and cold, like winter." The unseen natures of harmony pushed against George's Altar. The prince's eyes widened. "Wait."

Opane's face split into a proud smile. "You feel the third?"

"I do." George was in shock as a powerful Altar pushed through reality and lapped at him. He turned around to look towards the stables. His eyes widened as the immense power flowed from Ai's stable.

"She is something of a coincidence, or perhaps exactly what was meant to pass." Opane explained slowly, "Such an Altar to match your own."

"Ai," George whispered. A soft snort came from the other side of the wall. George frowned, the tips of his mouth trying desperately not to curl into a smile. "I knew you were a beautiful horse!"

"Come," Opane shushed, "You're not quite ready, let's keep practicing."

Chapter 22

IAO reborn

The next day was the rainiest day that the bloated grey sky had to offer. With cracks of lightning and blasts of thunder, the shed was a soggy echo occupied by two drenched prisoners. Intense concentration was plastered on their faces and a humming vibrated from their throats. Even Ai was strangely silent for such a stormy day and the only noise other than the pattering of rain was the whispers of the Ulmi villagers.

That morning, the warriors of the village had dragged out the old grindstone and put it in front of the shed alongside fire pokers and smithing tongs which hissed against the rain. Unlike the first time the warriors tortured George, this time they were clearly nervous. Routinely, they had been opening the slot on the shed door, sending the overcast light into the dark prison, only to shut it up again and resume hushed conversations.

What was going on, George had no idea. His mind's eye lay amid a swirl of smoke and mist, watching the natures of harmony dance with one another. From this place he could see the small altars of those around him. Opane's calm mist-filled altar sat beside him while the large and balanced altar of Ai laid through the wall. Even the small altars that made up the warriors outside shuffled into view here. George could tell Lawrence wasn't with them.

From his meditative state, George could still hear the slot open again, except this time it didn't close. Instinctively, the prince's ears perked at the sound of the door itself opening and coming through he could feel the altars of the warriors. The prince kept his eyes shut and his breathing steady, eager to maintain the balance he had accumulated.

A musty wind passed by George's face when the warriors stepped past him. The slap of gloves on flesh sounded and Opane's humming abruptly stopped. The warriors had grabbed her. With a rustle, Opane was silently yanked to her feet. The Kafshe remained eerily calm. When the warriors pushed Opane past George, the Kafshe whispered, "Are you ready?"

George's face screwed up in concentration, his will spreading over the harmonies within. Tendrils of blackened smoke hissed from the air itself and streamed into George's body and his humming stopped. A single altar belonging to one of the warriors seemed to pause, watching George as the others dragged Opane away. The sound of Opane being thrust to the ground entered George's ear as if it were right next to him, and when the whetstone started to spin, George had heard enough.

The warrior in front of George gave the prince a puzzled look. With curious eyes he poured over the meditating man, hand tight on the hilt of his blade. The smoke continued to seep from the air and into George, and as it did, a deep crimson stain started to appear on the prince's fingertips. Slowly the stain started to grow outwards, consuming more and more of George's hands and then his arms. Shocks of white began to bleed through his black hair and just as the warrior was about to reach out to the prisoner, George's eyes snapped open.

The prince's grey stare was a storm. An unbelievable amount of power rushed through his body and pounded across his heart. He felt like he was floating, and that the world around him was made of wind, unable to restrict him in any way. But the Ulmi warrior tried, igniting a deep red anger inside of George.

Perhaps out of blind fear, the warrior swung at George but to the prince, the swing was more of a crawl than a strike. George's hand shot outwards and grabbed the warrior's wrist with such force that the man was ripped from the ground and thrown into the wall of the shed. The wood cracked behind the man but already George was through the open door, nostrils flared and steaming.

Shouts erupted as other warriors came flooding to the scene. Unarmed villagers ran from the sight and screams cried out in fear at the reddened George. *"IAO!?"*

Opane immediately took advantage of the situation and slipped out from under the two interrogators who had stood over her. By the time they noticed their prisoner was free, Opane's hands came clapping down, one glowing palm on the side of each of their heads. Shards of ice grew out of their skulls and they roared in pain before collapsing to the ground. The Kafshe met George's furious gaze and hesitated, clearly surprised.

Before Opane could study further, a swarm of Ulmi warriors descended on the pair. One lunged at George with a spear while another came from the side with an axe. The prince was a blur, his crimson hand grabbing the arm of the spearman and yanking him forward. The force of the pull ripped the spearman's arm into a spray of blood and rocketed the spear into the axeman. Deep down, George was horrified, but the only emotion that could bubble forward was a dark bloodlust. His flesh was red and his vision focused like that of a predator.

"Balance!" Opane cried out to George, the word blurring into a gurgle by the time it entered George's enraged mind. An arrow whizzed by Opane, the Kafshe responded with a snarl before tossing a shard of ice at the marksman. The archer was launched off his feet from the blow and pinned to the closest cottage.

George could hear Opane's next words but the raw energy stampeding through his body presented it to him as a muffled blur of sounds and images. The chaos in him was raging, unbound and raw as it fed immense strength to his body. Flashes of the enemy warriors played across his vision, but each one he smothered in fractions of a second. They were shadows, the world was shadows, and he was there to enact his revenge.

An axe flew for his head, but he was already off to the side. Swords bit the air where he used to be and arrows peppered the ground harmlessly. The prince's hands were caked in gore, one punch slamming through the chest of a warrior. George wasn't sure who he was fighting anymore, when a black blob appeared behind him.

A desperate mob of Ulmi soldiers were forming by the stables, and another formed behind Opane, surrounding the pair. The Kafshe's hands crackled with freezing air and George's breaths were power filled growls.

"Control the smokeform," Opane hissed under his breath. "Stabilize it!"

Before George could reply, the sound of splintering wood cracked and Ai slammed through the walls of the stables, whinnying and bucking. The speckled horse was a deep crimson, and the same rage of George's was present in her eyes. When the horse's hooves plowed into the ground, the earth itself shook. The Ulmi staggered, struggling to remain standing but Ai bowled through them anyway.

As the horse came crashing by George, the prince threw out his arm and hooked himself onto the beast's back.

With stormy eyes, George looked down at Opane. Nodding, the Kafshe hopped behind George. Opane slapped Ai's rump. "Go!"

Ai wound up and as its legs hit the ground, the world turned into a speeding mess of colors. Red shimmering crackled over Ai's limbs and the beast cut through the land.

***

The world was pinstripe blurs around George. He could see Opane's mouth moving behind him but he couldn't hear her words. Opane's usual grey face was turning red and vascular, the kafshe clearly trying to scream something at the prince. George furrowed his brow and looked forward again.

Strength still pumped through George, his body flexing with incredible power. The rush was a divine buzz in his heart, but his head was sharp with pain, aching from the chaotic rush of emotions and thoughts. George's gentle and compassionate nature fought against the immense animalistic rage invading his heart. He never heard of Stromism like this one, and by Opane's reactions, George would wager the kafshe never saw it before. Before he could think on it further, his keen eyes snapped at a quickly approaching target. Ears perked, George could hear the sounds of an approaching battle even through the wind.

With things moving so quickly, George could only see in snapshots, but it was enough to confirm what he sensed. Ahead, an army of Ulmi were fighting Imperials. George recognized the plum-and-wine filigree on the Imperials. They had the Ulmi beat in skill, but the warriors of the free men smartly put their backs to a hill, giving them the high ground. George yanked Ai's mane and the horse turned towards the battle.

The shouts of battle turned to screams of surprise as Ai came blasting down from the hill and exploding into the back flank of the Ulmi. Ai's gallop sent shockwaves through the ground, leveling crowds of Ulmi. George launched himself from the horse and landed in the depths of the enemy lines. They roared in fear at the sight and in moments George had already ripped a blade from one of the warriors, his mind once again drowned in battle.

Cries of *"IAO!"* filled the air, and the enemy army was shaken. A dense *"HO-AH"* sounded from the front and George knew the Imperials were taking advantage of the confusion. Splitting, the enemy began to retreat but George kept swinging. His stolen blade snapped in half, breaking halfway through the shield of a terrified opponent. Quickly George followed up with a punch that caved the enemy's helmet inward and sent them into the air.

Imperials began to appear in the fray as the enemy lines thinned to desperate survival, but George kept his momentum. The armor of an Imperial flashed by George and he nearly struck it out of habit. It wasn't until Opane jumped on his back that the prince recoiled in surprise. Opane slapped a hand onto his cheek, a cold blast sobering him.

"Balance!" Opane cried as she slapped another cold chill into George. George stared into Opane's amber eyes, mouth agape. Opane's hand fizzled with more magic and George shook his head, the crimson on his skin starting to fade. The great density of rage and chaotic emotions seemed to settle as George felt himself trickle back to the fore of his mind.

The prince stumbled onto the ground and Opane rolled away from him. The army of Imperials surrounded George, Opane, and Ai, who had taken to grazing between the corpses.

Mutters came from the Imperial soldiers. "IAO? IAO?"

"Nah!" Another mutter came.

"It's the prince!"

"The prince!" A cheer started, realizing the victory at hand.

"No!" A familiar voice cut through the infant cheer. Darius pushed through the lines, eyes stuck on George. "It's Georgie boy!"

"HO-AH!" The army roared. "Georgie boy!"

George's lips shivered into a smile before dropping into a pout. The strength from his body faded and he felt the burden in his chest lift. A warm sun was on his head and familiar faces were cast around him, even Williams' stood smiling at him from the crowd. A wetness began to well in George's eyes and a deep sob choked in his throat. He sat amid the slaughter, covered in dirt, blood, piss, and wounds. His cheek was crusty and infected, stained further by a now endless stream of tears.

Darius stepped forward and as soon as he knelt to inspect the prince, George embraced him. The prince's body shook with each sob. Williams' hand came next, placed softly on his back and finally another hand came to tap the top of his head. Looking up with blurry vision, George saw Uncle Caleb's chestnut eyes looking down at him.

"You're alright now." His uncle smiled.

***

George was shaking, he couldn't help it. He was shaking at the battle and all the way back to Korku. He had a bath that turned clear water into colors he wished didn't exist and had his face cleaned with ointment, stitched closed and bandaged. Now he was outside (as per his request) sitting on a tabled bench under a gazebo, still shaking. It was like his body was frozen, but the summer sun was generously draping the entire structure in its heat. Opane sat across from him, more rigid than George, with an alertness in her sharp eyes that reminded the prince of a rabbit. Next to him, and perhaps the cause of Opane's nervousness, sat Caleb Heinrich, Imperial Regent of the Jerrovian Empire.

The gazebo overlooked the garden where George and his friends liked to spend their free-time, but now all that was in it was Ai, happily grazing and back to her usual speckled grey coat. Williams sat near the horse, bouncing his eyes between the beast and the gazebo, clearly wanting to talk to George, but Caleb had requested privacy., even if Williams was still in earshot.

"I'm glad you're back," Caleb began. "It had been a worrisome few months without you."

George's eyes twitched. "Months!?"

"Well," Caleb corrected. "Only near two."

Hands shaking, George caught his head. "I thought it was only a few weeks at the most."

"Since I had found you, it was maybe a week," Opane offered, "but before that it was quite some time since the second battle of Kors."

"Wait." George gulped. "So what month is it?"

Caleb looked up at the ceiling of the gazebo. "Month of Jubilation."

“What day?”

“The twenty-six.”

George blinked. “I’m nineteen.”

Caleb tucked a slant into his cheek. “When your birthday came and went, it just made me more worried about you.”

“Is that why you’re here, at the front?”

“Mostly.” Caleb shuffled forward in his seat, planting his elbows on the table. Clasping his hands together he continued, “though a few things have changed since you were captured.”

“Like what?”

“Firstly...” Caleb trailed. Frustration knit his brow and he continued. “Well, I don’t know how to tell you this so I’ll just say it: General Jonsberg has passed away.”

“What!?”

“Hold it!” Caleb held out a hand. “Before you ask, he died in his sleep. Complications of age, but he died in peace. I came to the front to take his place and to find you, of course. But what surprised me is that it wasn’t any of my agents who found you, but—”

“A Kafshe?” Opane interrupted.

“I was going to say Achian,” Caleb replied, “I didn’t want to assume.”

“George had proved himself a friend of my people, and when we heard he was missing, the Paleskins and I took to the trails.”

“Well, on behalf of the Empire, I thank you, but as his uncle, I thank you more than I could ever express.”

Opane lifted a brow and pursed her lips in thought. “Perhaps this thanks could translate into better relations moving forward.”

“I hope so,” George interjected.

Caleb gave an approving nod. "Me too."

The table went silent and Caleb let his fingers tap the table. Slowly he looked over to the Kafshe, who closed her eyes.

"You saw it as well?" Opane offered.

Caleb made a face. "Of course I saw it, everybody saw it!" He looked at George. "What was that?"

It was George's turn to make a face. His face was plastered with anxiety, he knew what they were talking about, but he couldn't bring himself to start the conversation. He wasn't sure how he felt about what just happened. Should he be excited that he mustered such great power, or worried he couldn't control it in the slightest?

"That power," Caleb pushed. "You looked like something out of one of my books."

George blinked. "It was Stromism, I unlocked my Stromism."

Caleb shook his head. "No, that wasn't *just* Stromism. Stromism is more precise and shimmers with golden magic. That was IAO's Stromism."

"Smokeform Stromism," Opane corrected. Caleb looked over at the Kafshe and Opane continued, "As far as the stories go, your IAO of the past was the only one to ever use it... effectively at least."

"He literally founded Stromism, of course he could use it," Caleb's words were clouded with a slight uncertainty as he looked over George carefully.

"Yes," Opane concurred with Caleb, "I suppose that's true."

"IAO not only founded the magic, but he created new branches of it as he lived and served the Empire," Caleb continued. "His most fabled branch was what he deemed his own Stromism, that which turned him crimson and gave him strength no normal Stromist could muster."

"Indeed," Opane agreed again, "But here is where our stories differ. The Paleskins first called his creation Smokeform Stromism because of the change in his altar of creation."

Caleb flinched, causing Opane to smile. The Kafshe goaded, "you know about the altars of creation, don't you?"

"Oh, you mean that topic which is often found in forbidden occult books, yes, if no sages are around, I sure have." Caleb gave Opane a wicked smile that wiped the Kafshe's own smirk away. "You're telling me that it's called smokeform because it creates an imbalance of smoke in the harmonies that make up the altar, no?"

"Not quite." Opane got her smile back and George rolled his eyes.

"Can we jump to the point?" The prince begged.

Opane frowned. "George has an incredibly massive altar of creation sandwiched between an abnormally large sea of mist and an average, let's say pond, of smoke. When I had him balance his harmonies, his body dragged more smoke inwards from around him, creating an influx of smoke his body and altar are not used to... giving him the smokeform. It's an overload of chaotic smoke energy, only George couldn't quite figure out how to stabilize it from there."

"That explains why he nearly chopped my head off." Caleb shot George a look.

George recoiled. "I don't even remember that." The truth was, his memory of what happened was mosaic at best.

"Let's just say you can do Stromism now." Opane waved the topic away. "Causing your usual balance of harmonies to stabilize is enough to create what I'll call true Stromism, and now that you know what your balance looks like, I wager you may have better control over doing it on command. Shimmering golden ribbons and all."

"And the smokeform?" George questioned.

"Stay away from it for now." Caleb looked worried. "If the altars theory is correct, which to be honest is starting to sound better than the pacification theory that the sages spout every damned second, then you'll need to balance the smokeform by bringing in even more mist to stabilize the chaotic energy at the level you wish it to be at or somehow perfectly balancing your current levels against the smoke, but if you can't manage to do that on the spot..."

"Then you get the massacre at the Ulmi village, and what nearly became a bad case of hurting friends at the battle," Opane finished.

George looked down at his lap. Opane called it a massacre, and George couldn't agree more. He had to do what he did, he only wished it was fueled by merciful pragmatism and not whatever that blind, lusting rage he felt was.

Opane sighed, as if reading George's mind. "They were soldiers and enemies... but let's avoid doing it again."

George fell into a thoughtful silence, to think he had such a monster inside himself. Opane cleared her throat. "If it's alright with you two, I have a family of my own that I haven't seen in a week or two."

Caleb waved a hand. "Of course, and thank you again."

Looking over at Opane quickly, George gave the Kafshe a stern look. "I don't think I would have survived without you showing up when you did. You'll always have my friendship."

"And you'll have mine." Opane dipped her head.

"Friend to a friend, then," George queried, "maybe when you have the time, you come back to teach me a little more about all of this."

Opane stretched to her feet and looked over at Caleb. "I may, though I think you might already have a worthy teacher."

"Now that I know what I'm dealing with," Caleb grunted, "maybe I *can* make a Stromist out of you at last."

George gave a sheepish grin to them both, that made him feel a little better. After all, a monster is just a hero that hasn't yet learned to control itself. He would solve the mystery of controlling the smokeform, if not for all the good he could do with it, then for the sake of those who died in anguish because of it. The prince shuddered, he could still feel the prickling rage, now swimming in wait in his stomach.

Chapter 23
George Reborn

After his meeting with his uncle, George hazily made his way to one of the castle Kalvin's bedchambers. Of course George wanted to finally confide in his uncle about his theory on the Dweller, which ultimately meant he had to come clean about his dreams. Though if it meant ending a war and bringing light to the shadows that had haunted him these past few years, let alone potential assassins, he was ready... or he would have been if he wasn't so tired. George knew that if there were going to be any more deep conversations and plans, he needed to get some rest first. His hand pressed against the door.

Uncle Caleb let him use his bedchamber instead of the barracks and George was too tired to be humble. It had been four years since George slept on a proper bed, and yet he would have settled for his old cot after his time in the Ulmi peoples' shed. Either way, he fell asleep as soon as his head hit the pillow. Blackness overtook his entire night, not one dream or nightmare able to flitter from his exhausted head. The only thing that managed to wake him momentarily was his back and hips popping with a painful relief, perhaps celebrating being aligned on something other than a dirt floor.

George missed the morning completely and awoke in the afternoon, having slept almost an entire day. Normally he would have been ashamed, but no one, not even the most vicious tongues of the soldiers blamed him. His first conscious action was to put on some real clothes, and luckily he was the same size as his uncle now. He put on black trousers and a midnight blue buttoned shirt with grey boots. George took one long look at the grey cloak and silver clasp that went with the outfit, but happily flung his tattered red cape over his shoulders instead, using the simple toggle and captain's badge that Franklin installed to keep it secure.

Looking very much in between a battered war hero and a noble, George made his way outside, already sick of being indoors. Today was definitely not a day for training so George made his way back to Korku's gardens, hoping to catch Uncle Caleb in between his meetings. A single thought was bothering him, though, now that he had time to think about it. When he was captured and talking to Lawrence, he had thought it and even said it out loud, could the Dweller actually be involved in the war? What would her motive be, what does she want and what does she want with *him?* He pinched his chin in thought, and what of the mist-talkers of the enemy, and Fenric. He shook his head, he'll definitely need to have a talk with his uncle about it.

Finishing his journey to the gardens and putting the heavy questions on hold for a moment, George walked out into the golden sunlight of the grassy area. Ai was present amid the summer scene and already nuzzling his side. George smirked and laid a hand on the old mare's snout. "Hey."

"George!" Williams called out. The knight was in his usual uniform, but wore a smile that stretched to each eye. In his hands he held an incredibly well-made sword with a white handkerchief fluttering from its handle.

"Oathkith!?" George gasped in surprise. "You're the best."

A bashful look overtook Williams as he handed the blade over to George. The knight looked down at the ground. "After the battle, I went back with a scouting party to find you and any survivors... When I found Oathkith but not you, I knew you must've been taken."

George nodded. "Thank you, Williams." The prince tied the scabbard to his belt, and Williams continued. "I knew you'd be back. Some of the others thought that since you were the prince, you would have been executed on the spot, others figured we would receive an ultimatum from the giants, but when no confirmation for either possibility came, the others began to think what I thought: that you were as alive as ever. I never gave up on you."

The prince's eyes turned soft. "I never would have expected you to. Void, I could be buried six feet and you'd be standing at my grave waiting for me to dig myself out."

"Only because I would assume it was an elaborate step to some stupid plan you and the others cooked up." Williams laughed, catching George in a chuckle.

A thought lingered between the two and their faces turned solemn. Williams cleared his throat. "Speaking of the others, I got something else for you."

George looked up. "Oh?"

Fidgeting, Williams pulled a shield off from his back. Unlatching the piece of lacquered wood from its spot, he presented it to George. It was a standard shield of the Imperial Army, tall with a tapering bottom. The layers of wood were glued together nicely and a dense leather case protected its face, though it was worn with use. The symbol of the Imperial falcon over an elaborate '11th' was painted on it, and underneath was a piece of graffiti. In terrible handwriting, someone had written "Rook" in black lettering.

"Franklin's shield." George felt a heat behind his eyes.

"You lost yours in the battle," Williams explained, "I figured Franklin would want you to have his."

Without thinking, George took the shield and strapped it to his arm. He held it up to the dewy sky and flashed a melancholy smile. "Thank you."

"He's being rested at the Imperial city," Williams inserted. "Hector is coordinating with his family back home."

George nodded. "I'm sure that's what he would have wanted."

The two took a moment of thoughtful silence before George continued. "Did I miss anything else?"

"Not as much as you'd think—oh!"

George's eyes widened. "What?"

"Tonight!"

"Tonight?"

Williams shook his head. "Yes, sorry. When I sent a letter to Josephine telling her of your return, I also took the liberty of sending one to Rosaline."

George cocked his head, and while he tried to play it cool, he could feel his chest swell. "What does that have to do with tonight?"

"She wants to meet you, by the bridge near Gable's farm."

The concept both sent chills of excitement and anxious anticipation through George. "When exactly?"

"Before the last bell." Williams paused, "and George."

The nervous prince looked up from chewing a nail. "Yeah?"

"She's happy you're back and can't wait to see you, so expect good things."

George shot a laugh through his nostrils. "I can't imagine a world without you, Williams."

***

The bridge by Gable's farm wasn't much of a landmark. It was an arched wooden structure with low railings which allowed travelers to walk over a small unnamed stream that babbled below. Often Korku's residents used it as a quiet place to meet and as such at some point someone placed a simple stone bench by the road that led to it. It was there that George sat, staring onward towards the castle itself.

Because the summer night was already turning the sky purple, the silhouette of Korku was a blackness that marked the end of the tamed green pastures between itself and George. Only cottages dotted the farmland in between, opening the sky and giving George a grand view of the many stars.

Of course, now and again a patrol would wander by and their torch light would reset George's vision, but otherwise he was in a single scene conquered by the peace of a cool summer's night. The tiniest breeze swam around him and a chorus of crickets put music on its waves. In any other scenario, George would wager his own heartbeat to match the calm rhythm of it all, but in the case of waiting to see Rosaline, he couldn't help but be anxious.

Admittedly, George had arrived much earlier than the last bells out of sheer anticipation and now he was stuck there. Now and again, he'd find himself sinking into the scene and daydreaming, but every rustle made him jerk to attention, expecting to see Rosaline.

He'd been in such a situation once before and now he was starting to dislike waiting.

"Patience," he spoke to himself while trying to focus on Williams' encouraging words, but George's anxiety was persistent. He coughed, hoping to force it from his chest, but as the sky grew darker and the final bell tolled in the distance, George could only feel his chest sink.

Boots scuffed behind George and he nearly threw up from a sudden burst of anxiety. Twisting around he was met with the orange glow of a torch and Darius' face. The commander blinked as he studied George's surprised face.

"Doing something you're not supposed to be doing?"

"What?" George furrowed his brow, waiting for his heart to settle down.

"You look like a criminal caught in the act..." Darius droned as he scanned the area. "What are you doing out here?"

George wringed his hands between his knees. "I'm waiting for someone."

"As pale as you are, is it the mortician?"

"No, my girlfriend."

"Wife was my second guess." Darius smirked and took a seat by George. He stuck his torch into the soft soil and let out a long sigh. "Rosaline, yeah?"

"How'd you know?" George looked over at the commander with wide eyes.

"You're not sneaky, figured you knew that by now." Darius watched the flames of his torch. "I've seen that face on you before, though, haven't I?"

"This won't be like that time," George quickly defended.

"I bet it won't." Darius offered a smile. "But just know..." The commander furrowed his brow. "Well look, George... I was just a kid when I joined the army. I fought in the Dwembin Isles during the Nachtist boom back when you were probably only a small boy."

As Darius spoke, George was noticing the grey hairs that curled hidden on Darius' head for the first time. So much time had passed since he first met this man, never did he expect to be sitting next to him, feeling almost like a son.

"...But anyway, the point is my scouting party was captured and I was too scared to struggle until death like the others, so I was thrown in a hole in the ground." Darius looked onward, as if envisioning his story. "Well, I was terrified. I heard of all the terrible things the Nachtists did to their own, let alone prisoners... blood sacrifices, cannibalism... anything to please the Dweller. The only thing that got me through was thoughts of my wife back home. I was going to go home after that, quit the military and buy a farm with her somewhere in Embla and never look at a sword again."

George frowned, seeing where this was going.

"Well, scarlet lung was ripe back then and she wasn't much of an exception. She died when I was in the hole, and so I felt a piece of me die along with her when I found out." Darius straightened his lips into a line and gave George a stern look, just like a commander. "But here I am, a whole lifetime later. It hurts, it's a wound, but I still have to live."

Heat returned to George's eyes, and he could see the same heat in Darius'.

"I know you're feeling loss and you're scared of more loss, and I wish I could be the one to tell you that such things never happen twice, but loss will happen." Darius stabbed a finger into

George's chest, his voice deepening. "But George, the world will never take anyone from you and neither will death because for something to be taken, you first have to own it. The world is ocean waves and all we can do is love the islands we find, when we do. Franklin was a good person, and so is everyone else you hold dear. If you love them like they are still here, then they are never really gone, yeah?"

The commander hooked a finger under his cuirass and pulled out a simple string with a wedding band on the end. "You got me, George, for as long as the world will allow."

George gaped, unsure of what to say. A tiny croaking noise came out instead and a smile broke on Darius' face. Snorting a laugh, the commander spoke again, "Well, enjoy your night. You'll need to be in good spirits for tomorrow." The man stood up and snagged his torch. "Have a good night, general."

"Wait, general!?" George all but shouted, but the Commander was already sauntering away with a laugh vibrating from his shoulders. George watched him fade into a bob of orange light.

"George!" Rosaline's voice made the prince's heart jump into his throat. Before George could even turn to see her, the woman collided with him and knocked him off the bench. Rolling into the grass, Rosaline's arms squeezed George tight, her smell filling up the prince's nostrils.

Squeezing back, George could feel her heartbeat against his, both jumping with excitement. He closed his eyes, at a loss for words and sank into the embrace. The sound of crickets was all that was left, the two silent in the grass. Little flickers of fireflies danced by, but when the pair's eyes finally opened, they were stuck on only each other. George smiled, and Rosaline smiled back even bigger.

"I'm not letting go," she threatened.

"Please don't."

Chapter 24
The Plan

Caleb's assigned office was the quietest and most private place in the entire castle, which made the Regent perk a brow when George requested to meet there with Williams and Rosaline. The room itself was large enough for the meeting, dominated by a pragmatic oak desk and several stiff chairs. There wasn't much decoration beyond a few drapes and the only light that found its way in was from three arrow hole windows off to the side. The door was propped open ever so slightly for George's comfort.

The trio stood in silence for a moment, all eager to hear what George had to say. The prince himself mulled over how he wanted to approach this topic. He had his most trusted friends and family with him, and he wanted them all to know what was going on, at last.

"Williams already knows this," George admitted, "but it's about time I tell you, Uncle." George glanced at Caleb before looking at Rosaline. "And out of respect, I want you to know this too." His dire words put anxiety on everyone's face.

"As you three know, there was an attempt on my life last winter on the road to Jornho. The assassin was a mist-talker, and that spring, we encountered an army of mist-talkers fighting for the enemy."

"Correct," Uncle Caleb answered. "I've already put my most trusted proctors into investigating the sages. Josephine is coordinating with me back at the palace." He folded his arms behind his back, giving Williams and Rosaline a hesitant look before sighing.

"We've also opened an investigation against Fenric, for the murder of his father and for suspected treason."

George flinched. "Suspected?"

"He claims he was held up by an enemy ambush," Caleb explained.

Swallowing the Prince kept the conversation on track. "I have a theory about this war."

All eyes were on him. "I believe that the Dweller is behind it."

Williams didn't react, but Rosaline and Caleb both were taken aback by the statement. Caleb looked grim. "Why?"

His question had a tone to it, one that said he didn't doubt it could be the Dweller. George frowned. "I've been having dreams."

Caleb paled at the revelation. "Dreams?"

"Since I was fifteen. I know now that it was the Dweller. She was asking me to release her, not that I really understand how I could do that. Either way, I have a feeling she started sending assassins after me at that time, and I managed to escape them and join the war, where she once again tried to have me killed."

"But the war had already started by then," Rosaline pointed out, having regained her composure. "The war couldn't be an attempt to kill you specifically."

"Lastly, what does she even get out of this," Caleb wondered out loud. "A war between Imperials and Ulmi, as well as the second born dead."

George fell back on his uncle's words, a question of his own forming.

"What does the Dweller want?" George felt himself repeating the words of Fenric. A guilty look flashed on Caleb's face for only a brief moment before he closed his eyes and steeled himself.

"It doesn't make any sense, yet," Caleb concluded, but George couldn't help but see the red door in his mind, and hear the words of the woman trapped behind it.

"She wants someone to open the door." George said blankly. "She wants to be let out."

"Let out?" Caleb furrowed his brow. "She's trapped in the void."

"How did she get there?"

Caleb bit his lip. "I don't know."

A pause.

"She started the war," George confirmed, "and when she couldn't kill me separately, she tried to have the war kill me." An idea slowly emerged. "Because... Because if the Dweller ever found her way out of the Void, what stands in the way?"

Caleb looked somber, as if he had already thought this through. "The Empire."

George nodded, his mind now running with the idea. "I think she started it to weaken the Empire. I've heard rumors that the Titanspoke who served as the catalyst and now the chieftain of the rebels was having strange dreams. I think it was the Dweller. And I think when I avoided her assassinations, she pushed me further into the war to kill me at the Battle of Kors."

"I just want to remind all of you," Williams finally spoke up. "That it was the Tagists who pushed George into the war."

"That's right," Caleb pinched his chin. "There's no way the Tagists are working with their arch nemesis, is there? Then again, knowing them…"

"We would need proof," Rosaline added.

Caleb eyed her. "Of course. I can't go condemning the sages on a whim, or I would have done that years ago." He shook his head. "I still don't get what they would achieve by assassinating you, or why Tagists would work with Nachtists."

"A common goal?" Williams offered.

Rosaline perched a brow at that. "Sounds like the Dweller just wants to escape the void, how would the Tagists benefit from that?"

The Regent's eyes slowly opened wide at the thought until they were like saucers. "I know a heresy that might answer that."

They turned to him and he gave them a look that asked them never to repeat his words, the kind of look only an Uncle could give. "There's a chance that the Graces themselves do not live in the shrines, but actually in the void, the same as the Dweller."

George furrowed his brow. It was a heresy, that was for sure, and surprisingly one he never heard before. "I don't like what that means if the war succeeds in destabilizing the empire."

Williams pinched his chin and hummed. "It would mean that the Dweller can move safely onto the next part of her plan."

Rosaline leaned back until she was pressed against the wall, her head clearly spinning with thoughts and sudden emotions. Despite it all, she seemed calm enough to stand by George and his trusted family. She scrunched her brow. "Then I guess all we can do for now is to end the war, huh?"

"End the war, and get enough evidence to shut down the sages. Maybe even shed some light on the whole mess," Caleb added. A pause. "George, the war council will be meeting this afternoon, but leave these details between us as much as possible." The regent looked at Williams and Rosaline. "You as well, don't breathe a word, and never repeat what you heard here." His voice fell low. "Especially regarding any dreams of the Dweller."

"Of course," Rosaline nodded. Williams tipped his head out of respect. Caleb returned the gestures.

"Good," he said. "Now if you don't mind, I'd like to speak with my nephew in private."

With a few words, the other two filtered out of the room, leaving George alone with his Uncle. Williams made sure to leave the door open just a crack for his friend. The prince looked over at Caleb, who let out a long sigh.

"Since you were fifteen, huh?" Caleb crossed his arms and sat on his desk. "You could have told me."

A sheepish grin found George, one that hadn't split his face since he was a boy. "Well, you know how thinking doesn't quite work at that age."

"Oh?" Caleb leaned back to evaluate his nephew skeptically. "And you've fixed this discretion?"

"I told you the truth, didn't I?"

A smile cracked on Caleb's face. "I know, I'm just teasing. You did well despite it all."

"I figured you felt that way," George chewed his cheek. "After all, I heard you made me a general."

"Against the idea?"

"Absolutely," George answered quickly. "Or I would have been before Kors."

"And now?" Caleb was watching him closely.

"Now I want to step up and finish the fight Franklin started."

Caleb nodded. "You'll have your chance, just be careful. I wish you told me about the Dweller sooner. I could have planned better."

A thought crossed George's mind, a thought he had held onto for a long time. Being a man, he finally had the courage to turn it into a question. "What do you know about the Dweller?"

Caleb didn't even flinch. He just stared, as if he was waiting for that question, as if he had been waiting for that question for a long time. "Let's finish the war first. One thing at a time, I can't have your focus split in too many directions."

George frowned ever so slightly. "Should I be worried?"

"No," Caleb shook his head. "Just focus on the war for now, I promise I'll tell you anything and everything you want to know from my studies after."

"Deal," George agreed, though not right away. Even though he had to admit his curiosity was dangerous, he always wanted to know exactly what his Uncle knew and what he was doing up in his tower, but for now, there was a war to win.

***

It had been a while since George stood in Korku's war room, and not much had changed in that regard. The ceilings were still high and vaulted, the windows stained and tall, and the center of the room still had a dominating wooden table. One of the few differences that George could definitely feel was the number of eyes on him as he stood staring down at a map of the region. Even Darius was looking at him differently.

"General," Daniella, a short, bright-eyed captain who had replaced Franklin, started, "the giants have unified a front across the region of Kors allowing them to strike to our northeast, northwest and north at will. Since the second battle of Kors, we have been stuck on the defensive. Their Titanspoke Chieftain is showing immense military resolve."

"They know they have control of the region." Caleb stood behind George, almost like his shadow. "This means they can safely avoid meeting our offenses or pitting themselves against us in open battle. Even if we try to strike them in a vital area, we would overextend and find ourselves overwhelmed on three sides."

"They've dragged us into a war of attrition," General Tobias agreed, "even if we send for reinforcements from the south, they will just be sponged away with time and supplies."

George frowned. "Well, it's not like we can just say we give in, they outplayed us."

"I don't think anyone here is thinking such things," Honora gritted her teeth. Frustration was evident in her face, it was evident in everyone's face.

"If Kors was anywhere closer to the Imperial Province, they'd be dust by now," Darius mused out loud.

"Then let's make them dust." George grew stern. "The longer this war goes, the more injustices pile up and the more hate grows. I think we need to bait the giants and the Ulmi into one final battle to end it." Caleb and Darius nodded at George's words.

"Shall I send them an invitation?" Honora gave George a look.

"This is a war room," Caleb reminded. His voice caused everyone to stand a little straighter. "Let's have some respect."

"Apologies." Honora closed her eyes. "The war is sapping more than just our supplies."

"We need a bait," Tobias announced.

"And I think I have one," George concluded. All eyes turned to him in anticipation. Thinking carefully, George slowly explained without tipping too far into his secrets. "My sister, Josephine, has provided me with some intelligence regarding the motivation of maybe not the war, but of some of the enemy's secondary objectives. I think we can dangle one of their secondary objectives in front of them and force them to move into a battlefield of our choosing."

"And what exactly is this intelligence? What's this objective?" Darius looked at George with a certain skepticism.

"There is reason to believe that the enemy has been tasked with the termination of my life. If I were to challenge the enemy and showcase that I would indeed be where the battle is, they would come in full force to see me dead."

"How do you know this?" Honora asked.

Caleb held up a hand. "I have reason to believe this motivation as well."

"You can't just leave us in the dark, banking the war on something so secretive," Tobias argued. George bit his lip and slowly nodded.

"What I'm about to share is only for this war room, it is sensitive information," George warned.

Caleb stepped forward, eager to cover for George. "I will see any attempts of relaying this information outside this circle as treason. It is pertinent to a proctor investigation and the security of the Imperial Family."

The room fell silent after Caleb's words. Daniella was pale, and looking at Darius helplessly. Darius shot a sigh through his nostrils. "Captains are dismissed."

"And retainers," Honora added. Guards, retainers, captains and anyone under the rank of General slowly shuffled out of the room, except for Darius, who George gave a reaffirming nod.

With the war circle smaller, George cleared his throat. "Princess Josephine was the first to put it together, but there may be a small sect that has taken over the leadership of the enemy armies after the first battle of Kors, if not before. The Giant Chieftain who controls the enemy is suspected to be a member of this sect."

"What is the purpose of this sect?" Tobias asked, stepping closer.

"We aren't sure," Caleb added, "But once again Princess Josephine was the first to notice that this sect does have the goal of terminating Prince George and have sent agents in the past to do so. They may have also been responsible for the push to send George to the front in the first place after he was made to stay in safety at Torskyla."

"How did Josephine even identify this sect?" Honora wondered out loud.

George opened his mouth but Caleb answered first. "That much is still sensitive."

"I understand." Honora showed uncharacteristic grace. "So, you're certain that dangling George in front of them will be enough to provoke a reaction?"

"Provoke is a good word," George cut in. "For this plan to work, I'm personally going to need to provoke them so they believe without a trace of doubt that I'll be where we want them to be."

"How do you plan on doing that?" Tobias asked as Caleb fell into thought.

George dropped his brow sternly. "I'll lead a small covert team right into the high Chieftain's camp and issue the challenge. We will go in unseen, provoke the Chieftain, and escape before they can retaliate."

"George, you aren't sneaky," Darius quickly brought up. "Why can't we just make it obvious that you'll be at a certain location and hope they take the bait?"

"Too much risk in them just not showing up, but they will have to answer to a direct provocation." George rolled his jaw in thought. "When I was a prisoner, the Lord who had captured me decided to torture myself and Opane even after realizing we not only couldn't communicate but also couldn't provide any useful information. It was a show of pride, because otherwise showing mercy would have been seen as soft on the enemy. Humiliating them with such a plan, with myself personally as the lead, would be far too grave an insult to ignore. On top of that, I'll talk directly to the high Chieftain, he won't be able to ignore the chance at my life."

"Then why not just slaughter the high Chieftain in his sleep? I mean if you're already going into the camp unnoticed." Tobias scratched the back of his head. "Cut the snake's head off."

"Unfortunately, this snake is liable to just grow another one," Honora quickly intercepted. "And can we use the high Chieftain's name? The amount of Chieftain'\s among the enemy is confusing enough."

"What is his name?" George felt the question in his chest; he was requesting the name of Franklin's killer.

"Galmun," Caleb answered, "Galmun Blue-Breath."

The name repeated in George's mind, locking in place before he nodded in agreement with Honora's theory. "We need to crush the army as well as all its leaders in one swoop. Then when they are weakened, we can end the war altogether."

"I don't like it," Caleb finally admitted, "but you're right."

"Then it's agreed?" George looked around the table.

"We can discuss the strategy for the ideal location to drag them to and what forces we can muster for it," Tobias mentioned, "But otherwise, I agree."

"I agree as well," Honora added.

"You have the 11th," Darius gave in.

"Good." George gave a serious nod.

***

Hours of discussion crawled by after that. The colorful light shedding through the stained windows went dark eventually and the carafes of refreshments brought in by castle servants started to pile up nearby. Darius was clearly grumpy near the end, likely brought on by his continuously growling stomach that no mere snack could seem to satiate. Honora wasn't doing much better, butting heads with Tobias at almost every turn when talks about logistics were brought up. Only the calm head of Caleb and George's ambition kept the table moving forward.

Finally, George stabbed a finger at the map splayed across the table. All eyes were pinned to where he pointed before slowly rising up to meet his gaze. Darius grinned.

"Boy, you have come a long way."

Tobias seemed surprised. "That... will actually work just fine."

"I agree." Honora nodded.

Smiling, Caleb closed his eyes. "Creative, I'm certainly proud."

"We can only do it once, though," George warned, "And no one can catch wind of this until it's too late, or this little trick is as good as our grave."

"That makes me wonder, would the enemy know about this?" Darius looked at Caleb.

George replied. "No, fortunately or unfortunately the enemy is ignorant to these sorts of things."

"Then it'll be quite the surprise." Caleb blinked. "Let's set it in motion."

The bickering turned into a round of compliments and small cheers until Darius' stomach growled loud enough to remind everyone else's stomach that dinner had come and gone without them attending. Quickly after, the room filtered out with the secret plan securely locked in the attendees' heads. Only George and Caleb remained in the war room.

"How do you feel about it?" George questioned his uncle. Caleb raised his brows, an approving look on his face, but before he could answer, the war room doors swung open. In the doorway stood Fenric, face serious if not slightly perturbed and his armor already donned: chain covered by a breastplate and a green cloak.

George's fingers instinctively wrapped around Oathkith's handle. Caleb in turn looked surprised. Fenric took a few steps inside until he was mere feet from the pair. With each step he took, a frown seemed to deepen on the duke's face, only to turn into a snarl when George's free hand knocked any markers off of the strategy map.

"Why wasn't I summoned for the war council?" Fenric plied.

"I appreciate the fervor, but I decided that my forces alone can handle the next step," Caleb answered just as sternly. Fenric's eyes flickered to George.

"This is Gavaria's war, I need to be informed of these things."

"For Gavaria's war, your army seems to have a hard time showing up to it," George hissed back.

"Are you calling me unreliable? My forces were occupied during the second battle of—"

"I'm calling you incompetent." George's words caused Fenric to flinch. "As General Lieutenant to the Regent, I reviewed your report. An entire Gavarian army delayed so heavily by a single skirmish that never even had reason to happen. You attacked the Ulmi village resulting in the delay, the enemy army was already out of the area."

"You weren't there," Fenric grit his teeth, "You have no idea."

"I know that your report was suspect enough to warrant an investigation." George stepped forward, fingers tightening around the hilt of his blade. He didn't want to admit it to himself, but the sizzling anger of the smokeform was scratching at its cage. "And I know a lot of people died because of you."

Fenric hissed, "You still had the upper hand."

Anger rushed further into George and he stabbed a finger, that was subtly reddening, into Fenric's chest and pushed the duke back half a step. "You were supposed to be there!"

Fenric's eyes narrowed and a strange darkness swirled in them. A grim look on the duke's face sent a chill down George's spine, right into his anger filled chest. An unsettling silence sat between the pair while George grew even more irritated.

"We're always supposed to do a lot of things." Fenric's voice was quiet, uncomfortable.

"You were supposed to be there." George repeated, jaw clenched. "People died."

"Franklin died," Fenric corrected. "Don't pretend you care about anyone more."

George's eyes widened with surprise and fury. "Don't try and justify yourself."

"Am I wrong, then?" Fenric took a step closer.

"Yes," George growled.

Caleb interjected, "That is enough."

"If only such words could really stop things," Fenric added quietly, "but it's useless. It's all useless." The duke paused long enough to stare deep into George's eyes. The prince found a cold anger in them. "Franklin's death was useless."

Oathkith screamed out of its scabbard and slammed into Fenric's own blade. Metal rent, Fenric just having pulled his sword in time, the clash mere inches from his nose. George's sword had bit almost completely through the metal of his own and reddish-gold strings of magic danced down the prince's arm, his fingertips red and a faint smoke in each breath.

"George!" Caleb stepped in.

Fenric's eyes were wide, arm shaking from the force of the blow. He swallowed hard. "You play a dangerous game. An Imperial prince striking at a duke."

"I don't see a duke." George yanked Oathkith away, the tug severing the two halves of Fenric's blade. The top half clattered on the ground and George pushed Oathkith back into its scabbard. The prince turned from his nemesis, closing his eyes and swallowing the monster back into its pit. "Get out."

Fenric snarled and stomped out of the war room, only to poke his head back in and shoot a finger out at George. "I won't forget this."

"Eat shit," George barked back. The duke spat on the floor before slamming the door behind him.

"Well said," Caleb looked over at George with sharp eyes. The prince could feel himself withdraw under the gaze of his old mentor.

The Regent pinched the bridge of his nose. "I suppose your temper just doesn't go away when you get responsibility. Let's hope your diplomacy skills don't come back to bite our asses."

"We have bigger things to worry about." George looked back at the war table.

Caleb sighed. "Someday, you'll see how things connect."

"Speaking of connections, do you think Josephine will be safe in the capital?" George quickly changed the topic.

"Let's just do what we need to do here and then get back to her," Caleb answered, "not that I have any doubt she can defend herself, either politically or physically. She has her father's Stromism, that's for sure, and her mother's wit."

George snorted. "No wonder I wasn't left with anything."

Caleb rolled his eyes and let them fall on the messy war table. "You got something, kid. You got something."

Chapter 25
Final Hunt

"Make sure this gets to Opane," George ordered. He stared down a messenger who nodded quickly before snatching George's letter.

"Yes sir."

It was a sunny day. The trees that surrounded the castle were teeming with the songs of various birds, not that they could be heard very well. Under the blue and white sky, the entire garrison was a cacophony of movement, preparing for a march. Tobias' agents sped away from Korku the night before, eager to get the region's entire garrison ready, giving George two units of regulars while the rest kept the peace across Gavaria. Of course, George also had the 11th Vanguard. Caleb had hoped to pull the 10th Vanguard from Caldora, but there wasn't enough time for them to arrive, though they were sent orders to be on standby in case of the worst.

"George." Johanna broke the prince from his thoughts. He blinked, looking over the widow. Her eyes seemed dull compared to how they used to sparkle, and the joy that often played with her smile was replaced with sorrow. It hurt George's heart to see the woman like this. From head to toe she was still dressed in black, even on a sunny day such as this.

"Yes?" George replied softly.

"Please..." She trailed. "Give those bastards a few for Franklin." She forced a smile and George offered his own.

"He'll be fighting alongside me." George tugged on his tattered cape. "They won't know what hit them."

"Good." Johanna seemed relieved, if only a little bit. "Just make sure to come back yourself."

"Oh, he will." Rosaline's voice called out from the side. She stood in her uniform, the black tunic of the auxiliary under a light cuirass of equally black cloth and hidden metal plates. She kept a short sword on her side next to her dagger. Any usual spots for chainmail or greaves were removed to presumably lower any noise and keep the wearer obscure. George raised a brow.

"You look ready for a covert mission."

"I have one in particular in mind." Rosaline stood up straight. "Pending the general's approval."

George himself wore very little under his cape, with only a similar dark coat of plates protecting his torso and thick leather vambraces covering his forearms. High dark boots covered almost up to his knees, where loose grey trousers were tucked under. He furrowed his brow.

"I don't know."

"Listen." Rosaline stepped forward. "I'm not sitting around while you go into battle again. I'm a soldier, the same as you, and I did warn you that I'm not letting go. Besides, I may have finally found something to put my father's training towards."

George cocked his head, not yet putting the dots together. "Oh?"

"If the skills he taught me can help end the war early, all the more people will be saved from suffering." Rosaline gripped the end of her sword and gave it a rattle. "I'll draw my blade for peace."

George blinked. "Valid points, soldier."

"General." Rosaline dipped her head sarcastically.

Johanna smiled. "A team to be reckoned with."

"A trio it is!" Baldra's voice boomed as she approached the group. She too was dressed for the mission. As Baldra came into the circle, she slapped her boots together and stood in salute. "Volunteering for the mission that no one was supposed to know about, sir!"

"Dweller's mug," George shushed.

"This is the worst group for a silent mission I've ever seen," Darius judged from the sidelines. A blush grew on George's face.

"It'll work," George resigned. "It has to work."

"Well." Darius pinched his chin. "In case it doesn't, I ordered your retainer to see you all through." The commander pointed behind the group.

"What?" George spun to meet Williams' gaze. The knight was dressed the same as everyone else, though he also wore a big smile on his face.

"Didn't hear me coming, did you?"

"Well now the mission *can't* fail." George slapped Williams' back. Rosaline smiled and Baldra copied the grin. Johanna stared at them all with big eyes. The widow sighed with a hint of happiness.

"I think I see an end to all this madness."

***

"So, after we get their attention, we run where?" Baldra asked for the third time. The group was already half a day away from Korku, having spent the entirety of the day prior riding hard on old paths through the winding peaks and valleys of Kors. Of course, they were exhausted after thrusting themselves so far into enemy territory, so they spent that evening resting in the thick of a pine forest without a fire to keep them warm. Now they were on the move again, very close to their target destination and straddling the earliest hours of the morning. All about them were quiet stones and tall, prominent trees. Dewy slopes caught the sun between the branches and gullies were hidden by shadows. Even the birds were just starting to wake, with the distinct smell of summer morning finishing the scene.

George slapped his own face upon hearing the question repeat itself. Williams closed his eyes in anguish, leaving Rosaline the task to answer the man. She herself was having none of it, the exact amount of comfort expected from a night on a forest floor present on her face.

"We instigate the camp and issue a challenge." Rosaline looked behind her, her vision swallowed by the oppressive forest. "Then we head south to a valley cut between sheer rock faces and that's where we will meet them with our full forces."

"One of the walls of the valley has a plateau above, that's how we will recognize the correct one," George added. "Up there, Darius will have smoke signals for us to follow... as clear to us as it will be to the enemy."

"Oh." Baldra pinched her chin in thought. "Right."

"Here's hoping they give us the time to reach there," Williams threw in.

George furrowed his brow. "I think so, they'd be mad to rush after us without accumulating all their forces first." The prince paused. "Speaking of." He held a finger to his lips. "We *are* in enemy territory, let's keep the talking to a minimum."

Nodding along, the group fell into a silence and continued their trek. If all went well, they'd locate the enemy encampment before dusk, steal an hour or two of rest, and be able to sneak in under the cloak of the night. The entire scenario played over and over in George's head, attempting to think of every possibility. Some thoughts made him grin, others made him grimace. A branch snapped, pulling George back to reality.

Baldra had stepped on a twig and was holding her nose in the air. "Smell that?"

"Storm," Williams answered. "The air is getting thick."

George blinked and looked directly up through the canopy. The sky was already a slate grey, swelling with rain.

"Summer storm," Rosaline added.

Nodding, the prince replied, "This could prove useful, it could mask our approach."

"Or soak us through and then leave us before we even find the camp." Williams frowned.

"Then we move," George ordered, "and hope for the former."

Silence reigned again and the group wove through the high pines. Their only sense of direction was the general location provided by Uncle Caleb's spies and the occasional sign of passerby. Lucky for the group, the giants weren't subtle and soon they were skirting the periphery of a set of giant tracks that were pounded through the landscape.

Rare drops of rain were already starting to fall, the fat drops of water bouncing through the pine boughs and making a distinctive sound as they hit the forest floor. George went to pull his cape tighter against himself only to remember he took it off for the mission. Frowning, he settled for crossing his arms. Warmth pressed against his shoulder and glancing over he saw Rosaline walking against him ever so slightly, a coy smile curling the edge of her mouth. Grinning, George focused forward.

The rain slowly began to pick up until it was a steady pour, whipped by growing wind and kicking up an aroma of soil and pine. An electric smell was also dense in the air, making George's hair stand on end. Williams was definitely right, there was a summer storm approaching. Looking up, the prince could at least appreciate the cover of the dark clouds.

A muffled snort made George's ears twitch. Tuning in, he could hear loud scuffling in the rain alongside a gross chorus of gobbling sounds. He held out a hand and the group halted.

"What is it?" Rosaline whispered into the prince's ear.

George scanned the horizon but the rain was starting to fall in grey sheets, limiting the distance of his view. The prince reached out with his altar of creation, his eyes useless against the rushing water. As he felt the ebb and flow of the mist and smoke of reality, he eventually pinpointed the telltale push of living creatures in the distance. Silently, George gestured for the others to follow him.

Eventually the soaked-through group found their way to a tree that had fallen a long time ago. Its roots had collected enough dirt and debris to form a miniature hillock in the woods. Hiding behind the crest of the natural earthwork, the group peered down into a small glade.

Through the rain they could see a nest of pigguts chewing on what looked like the mutilated remains of a lost Ulmi man and child. Baldra closed her eyes, a swear hidden on her lips. George sucked in a breath, steeling himself at the unexpected sight. One of the pigguts was already trying on the bloodied clothes of the deceased, terrible things hanging from its saw-like teeth.

The dopey smile of the victorious piggut was quickly wiped away as it turned into fear. A massive piggut nearly as tall and definitely twice as wide as a small man came swaggering onto the scene. It wore a misbuttoned shirt that couldn't contain its greasy, protruding gut and held a crude yet effective battle axe. The beast stood twice over the other pigguts, who cowered in subservient terror and let the larger one take over their spoils without question.

"A warlord," Williams recalled.

"Never thought I'd see one," George answered, glad the rain kept the scent of the scene away.

"I wish I didn't." Baldra was already backing away from the crest, having seen enough.

Rosaline nodded. "Those poor people."

George pursed his lips, giving the scene one last look. "Unfortunately, there is nothing we can do about it now, we have a mission to complete."

"Right," Rosaline agreed.

***

Noon came and went, and it was raining so hard that George could barely see past a stone's throw distance in front of him. The world was grey, cloaking the group in a massive storm. Even if the rain didn't drown out all the sounds of the forest, the rumbling sky above surely did. George nearly called for the group to stop their search and to wait the storm out, but just before he could make such a decision, Williams spotted the orange glow of a defiant fire in the distance and sure enough, the camp was there.

Now the group stood on the outskirts of the encampment, keen on using the oppressive storm for cover rather than waiting for the night. Large balls of orange fire were all that illuminated the giant's camp, but even they in their massive heat were losing a hissing battle against the rain. Using what remained of the bonfires, the group was able to deduct the area of the camp. It was massive.

"To be expected of giants," Williams had defended. To even speak through the sounds of the storm, he had to be right up next to George. The prince nodded, formulating his plan of approach. Keeping an eye on the large silhouettes that bulged out of the sleet of rain, George motioned for his group to follow him.

They crouched alongside a palisade wall. The logs were bigger than any human-made palisade and following it tightly, they snuck around to where the palisade opened up to allow traffic in. Naturally, a giant stood at either side looking outward and away. They were clearly perturbed by how soaked they were getting and taking advantage of the distraction, George slipped behind one and into the camp.

Turning too sharply, George nearly bumped into an Ulmi warrior who was utilizing some bushes on the other side of the wall to relieve his bladder. The warrior froze at the seemingly spectral shapes in the rain but before he could react, Rosaline pushed forward and covered his mouth with one hand, the other on his throat. George watched as she gently laid him on the ground, quiet and still. Not wanting to leave the man in the open, George and Rosaline pulled him into the bushes. Baldra snickered, assumedly at the irony.

Williams tapped George's shoulder and motioned ahead where large shapes were apparent through the blanket of rain. Thunder rolled above but the telltale pattering of the storm on canvas told George that he was looking at tents.

Thanks to the storm, not many of the enemy were walking around, making the journey to the tents easy. The group ducked behind the shelters and slowly bounced from cover to cover as they searched for the Galmun's abode. Some of the tents had barrels of arrows by them while others had racks of bows, spears, and swords. It was hard distinguishing the tents other than by size, but a large tent only meant it was a giant and not an Ulmi, but not particularly the high chieftain's.

While the group was thinking about their next move, the flap of the tent they stood by wafted open. Hugging the shadows of the next closest tent, the group held their breath. Lawrence, his face illuminated by a light, strolled out of the tent, hands on the strings of his pants.

Baldra lunged, but George's swift hand pulled her back by the collar. The prince gave the soldier a stern look before letting go. It bothered George as well. Lawrence's Lord must have joined forces with Galmun. Shaking the thought from his mind, George motioned for the group to continue.

At last, the group happened upon a tent made for a giant, with Ulmi guards posted outside of the entrance. They were drenched through and uncomfortable, so much so that they didn't notice Baldra and Rosaline round the back of the tent and slip behind each of them. Using their short blades, Baldra and Rosaline slit the guards' throats with little fuss.

The inside of the tent was illuminated enough to cast shadows on the canvas walls, showcasing a single massive figure and two smaller ones. George snagged two bows from a nearby rack, strung them both against his knee and tossed one at Williams. Nodding, the knight knocked an arrow and pulled back. George waited until his and Williams motions were in sync and then after a brief mental countdown, he let his own arrow fly, Williams' zipping shortly after.

Thunder drowned out the sound of the snapping strings. The arrows punched through the canvas and slammed into the two smaller shadows, their hazy figures collapsing to the ground. The larger figure straightened in possible panic, but the group was already rushing into the tent.

Inside, two enemy warriors were laid on the ground, blood gushing from each of the arrows stuck in their throats. The only other person in the tent, Galmun himself, stood fuming, eyes wide and glaring. George froze as he entered the tent, the face of the Chieftain already burned into his memory when he watched him slaughter Franklin. A deep hatred boiled in George as he stared up at the giant. He could feel the smoke hissing into his fingers.

Williams nudged George and the prince snapped from his growing anger. Through gritting teeth, George growled, "South of here there is a valley by a plateau, meet me and my army there by smoke, it will be your one and only chance to slay me."

Galmun bellowed a laugh, clearly hissing with anger of its own. "A bold statement."

"I know you're after my life," George asserted, "but I won't give it easily."

"Do you?" The Chieftain's eyes narrowed. "We have been called to a higher purpose and so we cannot fail. Easily or not, your destruction will help open the path."

"Path?" George narrowed his eyes, could he mean a path to the void. "Who is 'we'?"

"Do not worry your head, baby prince," Galmun mocked, "I will cleave it free of worry soon enough."

The giant Chieftain reached for his weapon but George drew back his bow. Magic shimmered in his arm and with amazing force he loosed an arrow using enough strength so that the bow snapped on launch. In the blink of an eye, the Giant spewed mist from his mouth, the magical haze catching the lightning-fast arrow just in time. The tip of the arrowhead still managed to sink a few fractions into the Galmun's chest, just cutting the skin. Surprised, the Chieftain's eyes were furious.

Still staring down Galmun, George slapped William's chest with his off hand. "Withdraw."

With the first part of the mission completed and the challenge issued, the second half began. The Chieftain roared his hate and gripped the massive blade leaning against a rack but the group was already dashing out of the tent.

Galmun's growl was at their heels only to fade as the group was reunited with the thunderstorm outside. Flashes of lightning fuzzed their vision as they began their retreat through the downpour. Behind them the chieftain was barking orders and the camp was stirring to life. Adrenaline pumped through George, and the group ran on their toes, sprinting like mad through the swarming nest.

George let his voice rumble from his chest as he ran. "South, my army waits to crush you once and for all. Scatter now and be spared! Your Titanspoke is a fraud and will lead you to destruction!" George knew the challenge would sit like hot nails under the skin.

Already the giants and the Ulmi were shouting back, some in the Jerrovian language, some in the Ulmi tongue. All George knew was that the camp was awake, aware, and furious. Would they actually fall for such an obvious trap, George didn't know, but he did know as obvious as it was, the enemy's pride was on the line as were the secret goals of the Chieftain. Any further thinking was cut off by the approaching enemy.

Behind the sprinting group, the Vagrants had already formed a posse, nipping at their heels. The opening in the palisade was just ahead, but the giants were gaining on the group and there were still the two guards posted ahead. Normally Stromism would be able to launch George out of trouble, but with his non-Stromist companions, all he could do was grit his teeth and fall back on a plan he had formed earlier that day.

"Williams! You take the right." George barked his order and ripped Oathkith free of its scabbard. The knight nodded and knocked another arrow into his stolen bow. As predicted, the two guards of the palisade appeared to cut the group off from escape.

An arrow shot out from Williams' bow, catching the rightmost guard by surprise as it snapped through his eye. The giant dropped dead, a rag doll before he even hit the ground. George on the other hand kicked off the ground with golden ribbons powering his leg and launched himself into the air at breakneck speeds. George landed on the shoulders of the left most guard, Oathkith sinking in and out of the warrior's neck. He leapt off in fluid motion before the guard had the chance to react. Crumpling to the ground, both the guards were dispatched with ease, leaving the exit wide open.

Now having a clear getaway, the group dashed out of the camp boundaries. Unfortunately, they weren't the only ones. A stampede of enemy forces was right on their tail. George pumped his legs and took a hard turn, the others following him. Confused and terrified looks were carved on his companion's faces, only softening upon realizing the direction they were heading.

Down into the pine forest the group charged and the shouts of the enemy broke over the storm above. Branches and bushes slapped at them as they darted through, hopping over loose stones and outcropping roots, until the ground itself seemed to give way.

With a leap, George hopped right into a glade set in a depression of the forest. Angry squeals of pigguts sounded immediately as the group darted right through their gathering. The piggut warlord let out a grizzled growl, only to suddenly have an unlucky Ulmi warrior run right into it. A shallow grin formed on George's face and he kept his trajectory, sprinting out of the piggut den with his friends in tow.

Sounds of an impromptu battle exploded behind the squad as they made their getaway deeper into the woods. Visceral screams of pigguts being slaughtered and men being eaten alive curdled the rain and sent chills down George's spine, only to be startled by a clap of thunder above.

The adrenaline of it all was still in their veins as the group took a few quick turns and attempted to put as much distance between them and their pursuers as possible. Just as George was thinking they were in the clear, a sudden shout sent the entire group spinning in shock. An Ulmi warrior and a giant were still on their tracks, stragglers from the group that got caught in the piggut den.

George squinted through the rain and his heart froze over; that wasn't an Ulmi warrior.

"George!" Lawrence cried out, a voice of desperation and fury. The giant wasn't as keen on dialogue and immediately broke through the space separating the two parties. Rosaline quickly intercepted the giant and ripped her sword from its scabbard. Attempting to push past the soldier, the giant sent a lazy swing of his log sized mace, but Rosaline bounced out of the way. She instinctively countered the attack, swinging at the giant's leg and dragging the edge of her blade down the back of the knee.

The massive warrior howled in pain, twisting to strike at Rosaline again, but Williams was already on the giant's other side. George and Baldra ran to help, but Lawrence stepped in their way.

"I did all I could for you!" Lawrence was foaming with anger. "And you slaughtered my people."

"I didn't want it that way," George held up a hand, shaking his head. "I didn't want any of this."

"Well, you got it!" Lawrence spat.

"Lawrence!" Baldra muscled between the two. "I'm placing you under arrest to be tried by the Imperial Courts for treason and desertion." The woman's voice was rough with an anger of her own, blasting through the roar of rain. Pain cut into her tone.

An incredulous look washed over Lawrence. "You're insane!"

Baldra went to grab Lawrence but his old friend pushed her hand away. Scowling, Baldra hissed, "Am I?" Thunder boomed. "I'm not the one who ran away when things got ugly!"

"The Imperials have you brainwashed!" Lawrence jabbed a finger in the air.

Baldra's face twisted with irritation, water drizzling down the lines of her visage. Her eyes were stained pink. "You stole my best friend from me."

Lightning flashed above and another crash of thunder kept the scene alive. In the back, George could see Rosaline standing on the chest of the giant, the warrior having been toppled by her and Williams. A stream of dark blood poured from the defeated giant's neck.

"The battle is over!" Rosaline shouted, causing Lawrence to jerk. The traitor quickly pointed his Ulmi blade at Rosaline, who leapt back. George flinched but Baldra snagged Lawrence's attention once again.

"You heard the soldier," Baldra yelled, "It's over."

"Void," Lawrence swore and held his sword in a high guard.

Baldra gripped her own blade with both hands. "Lawrence..."

"The only one who will be taking your supposed best friend from you, will be yourself and your own actions!" Lawrence swung

"Wait!" George called out, but it was too late. Baldra quickly parried Lawrence's blade, bouncing it upwards and opening the traitor up. Twisting her own blade and redirecting the momentum, Baldra let the point of her sword punch into Lawrence's stomach. A burst of red plumed and Baldra yanked her sword free.

Croaking, Lawrence fell to his knees. His hands were lazily trying to push the blood back into his stomach, while his eyes were wide with shock. Baldra had her own eyes closed as she positioned herself behind her friend. Bringing her sword down in an arc, Baldra ended his old comrade's suffering. Lawrence fell to the side, a bloody mess.

"Baldra..." George was frozen in surprise.

The soldier refused to look at what she had done. "I serve the Empire."

Williams cut in. "We should move."

The prince nodded and the group started up a hesitant trot. This time it was quieter than before, haunted and empty. Even the storm seemed quieter, unsure. George didn't like this, he never wanted it.

Chapter 26
For Franklin

The storm was coming to an end and the sun was now blazing through the dispersed clouds, heating the rain-soaked valley and summoning a humid musk. George and his group had made it to the rally point without any further trouble, having spotted the smoke signals rising above the pine trees. The forest cleared into an overgrown meadow that stretched an incredible length, dipping in the middle as usual of a valley. As George previously imagined, the to-be battlefield was massive, with a steep rocky slope on one side that led to craggy uneven peaks, and a nearly straight up rock-face on the other. Topping the rock-face was a great plateau which the smoke signaling team abandoned quickly after George arrived. All along the rock wall were tangles of vegetation and behind them hid ancient caves that Opane had once told George about, saying they were old holy sites for the spirits of Kafshe.

Saturating the valley itself was an army larger than George had ever seen. Columns upon columns of regulars and the stromists drilled for battle while auxiliaries sharpened blades and manned cooking tents. Such a massive crowd had turned the lush green valley into an ever-moving sea of plum-and-wine. If the challenge worked, then the enemy would be shortly behind George, assuming they could muster quick enough.

The prince pushed through the rush of activity, through the men and women gearing the horses and through the long lines for food, all the way to the command center that was set up by the rock face. With his eyes peeled for his uncle, George's ears caught Darius' voice through the assembly of sounds.

"They could simply wait us out," Darius was complaining.

Turning to the voice, George saw the Commander standing by his uncle, the two under a plain canvas roof held up by four stands. A small map of the valley laid between them on a simple table.

Caleb held a scoff, "If it came to that we'd just leave. I managed to get a hold of the 12th and they're already marching to cover a withdrawal, assuming they could be late. We also have a set of regulars already covering us with reinforcement lines from Korku."

"No provincial army?"

"The duke can't be trusted with any of this," Caleb quickly answered. "So, either the enemy meets us here, or the war continues."

"And I don't think any side wants that," George cut in. Caleb looked over, immediately smiling at his nephew. Darius shared the happy surprise.

"So, it was a success?" Caleb turned his attention over to George.

George looked down at the map. "They'll be here."

"Then prepare yourself," Caleb ordered, "We have at least half a day, at the most two days, before the battle begins."

"If it does," Darius warned.

Caleb cocked his head to the side. "Have faith in your old ward, he knows what he's doing."

Darius tucked a slant in his cheek but offered George a proud gaze. "True enough."

"Besides." Caleb looked at the empty plateau. "I have a feeling they'll assume they have the upper hand."

"Lord Regent," Williams interrupted. He stood behind George, one hand under the collar of his coat of plates. George spun to look at his friend, and cocked a brow. Caleb copied the surprise.

"Yes, Williams?"

The knight pulled a soaked letter out from under his armor and held it towards the regent. "I discovered this inside of Galmun's tent during our mission. I recognized the imperial alphabet on it and thought it pertinent to our investigation."

Caleb pinched the letter and took it from Williams. He peeled the paper open and scanned its contents. "Encrypted, but no doubt useful." A thoughtful hum snagged in his throat.

"I have a feeling a lot of things are going to come to light very quickly." He folded the paper and crossed his arms. Looking back at the to-be battlefield behind them, Caleb put on a serious face. "You all should rest up while you still can."

***

George sat in silence. In his fingers he rolled the pink wood he had carved from the roots of that tree so long ago. It was still smooth from his time in the Ulmi shed and as he held it in his hand, he could feel all that he went through with this small piece of nothing in his pocket. Though he supposed now it was something. It was a piece of him in a strange way, having held it for so long.

Around him the army was in chaos trying to settle everything before the enemy came, but on orders from his uncle and good sense, George sat on a wooden bench under a white canvas tarp, staring at the tiny wooden raindrop in the palm of his hand. His legs only just stopped burning from his sprint and with all his will, he was resisting the urge to listen to the groans forming in his muscles.

Regardless, his mind was stuck on recounting everything that brought him here. He cocked a brow, so many things and none of what he ever expected. The prince rolled the piece of wood over to look at the other side, a river of grain showcasing the way the wood fit back in the root it came from. George rubbed his thumb over it and furrowed his brow. He wasn't through with it all just yet, and there were so many more questions to answer.

"Hey George." Rosaline's voice came from a bench nearby, the woman looking over at the prince with curious eyes.

Peering up, George smiled. "Yes?"

"I was thinking about what the High Chieftain had said." Rosaline pinched her chin. "I don't know what to make of it."

"About the higher purpose?" George slid the wooden trinket back into his pocket. "I have no idea, but I know it's linked to the sages, it has to be." He remembered the woman from his dreams. "And the Dweller."

"But what do the sages get from any of this?" Rosaline questioned, "I mean, hijacking a war, sowing disorder in the north? For what?"

"Let's not forget their desire to assassinate George himself," Williams added from the sidelines. The retainer was leaning against one of the posts for the canvas roof. "And apparently having that in mind for four years now."

"That makes the least amount of sense," George agreed, "I'm not even the heir, so it wouldn't make sense for it to be a political move on their part."

"It throws me for a loop, too." Williams rubbed the back of his head. "The disorder and war, I can justify a coup, but the assassination? That has me stumped."

"Though, Williams." George was cradling his chin in thought,

"Yes?"

"Back on the way to Jornho, you mentioned that maybe it wasn't a political move... what did you mean?"

The retainer blinked. "Well, I may have been delirious from the blood loss at the time, but... I suppose I was thinking that the sages deal with so many things outside of politics, maybe it lines up with one of their other aspirations."

It was Rosaline's turn to ask questions. "Like..." Her voice dipped into a low whisper. "The heresy?"

"Maybe," Williams admitted. "They can be so secretive with their order, it could be anything."

George fell from the conversation as his mind wandered into the possibilities. Why were the sages working with the Dweller and what did he himself have to do with that? It wasn't a political motivation, it had to be a different sort. The Dweller wants to be let out, but what do the Sages want, did the Graces exist in the void too? The war will help the Dweller when she escapes, but this isn't how she will escape, that's the next step George had to figure out, how she intended to breach the void. Between his dreams, his past, and the stories of the wild prophet, George could feel an answer itching at the forefront of his mind but he couldn't quite grasp it just yet.

Rosaline rolled her jaw in thought, her words pulling George back to the camp. "Well, whatever it is, we'll put a stop to it today."

"Here's hoping," Baldra finally chimed in from behind everyone. She had been sitting silently with her eyes to the ground in thought.

"We'll put an end to it," George reaffirmed, though he had a feeling that they were standing at the first step of a long road. "Now and forever."

Williams smirked. "Ho-ah."

"Ho-ah."

***

Oathkith was firm in George's hand, and Rook was tightly fastened to his shield arm. He wore the polished armor of the Imperial Stromist Vanguard, and around his neck and shoulders, the tattered red cape of Franklin fluttered in the breeze. He sat atop Ai, his warhorse stamping the ground eagerly. It had been a day since the storm, and the morning summer wind was sharp and warm. A cloudless blue sky heated the valley and across the field, an endless swarm of giants and Ulmi globbed.

Behind George stood the rank and file of the 11th and on their flanks were the regulars. This was going to be a pitched battle, with George and the 11th leading the spearpoint. To George's side sat Williams on his own horse, and slightly ahead sat Caleb on his. The entire front line of the 11th was mounted, chargers hemming and hawing for what was to come.

"A lot less of them than I thought there would be," Williams remarked.

"I agree," Caleb answered from his horse, "let's hope they aren't up to anything sneaky." His words were sweetened with a hint of sarcasm and a grin. George couldn't help but grin back, leaving Williams confused.

Turning serious, Caleb hit the pommel of his blade against his helmet, ensuring it was tight in place. "Alright, remember they toss their javelins first. Head straight, bank right and then hit them closer to the flank, and keep your shields up."

"Got it." George checked his own helmet before lifting his sword. Williams copied the movement and as Caleb lifted his higher, the cavalry behind them readied their lances.

The horde ahead was a solid mess of Ulmi and giants. Thousands of angry eyes stared down the Imperials and staring back was just as many Imperial hearts burning for vengeance. George's own heart burned bright, eyes scouring the black line for any sign of Franklin's killer. The prince could feel his fingers tighten on Oathkith and the pulse of Stromism tickle his muscles.

"*For the Empire! For Jerrovia!*" Caleb's voice came booming...

"*CHARGE!*"

A uniform shout erupted past the command and a flood of cavalry spilled onto the battlefield with the Imperial Regent, the prince, and his knight at the point. Their cry shook the ground as they stampeded forward, swords and lances pointed ahead and violet capes snapping behind them.

Wind burned in George's eyes as his steed bolted across the valley. The enemy line was coming up quick, and George could make out the fear and hate in them. They wound up their arms and, in an instant, the sky was peppered with javelins. Quickly, the cavalry formation banked right, having kept at the maximum distance until then. Baiting out the throw worked and most of the deadly shafts plummeted harmlessly to the empty ground, the formation rounding back towards the enemy flank.

Ulmi Mist-talkers rushed a defense, their alien chanting summoning a cloud of mist in an attempt to stop the advance but it was too late. George and the other Stromists were shimmering with magic and enchanting their mounts. With ease most of the Vanguard cut through the blockade and slammed into the enemy lines.

Ai fearlessly crashed through the round shields of the Ulmi warriors and just as quickly as Ai broke the line, George sent Oathkith down in an arc. Spurts of blood flew back in return, only for George to switch sides, hacking at any approaching challenger. Just as soon as George made contact, the bulk of the charge splintered into the enemy flank and signaled the start of the true battle.

In moments, the rest of the army had clashed, the front lines of both camps raging against each other. With the elite Stromists used for the initial cavalry charge easily counteracting the mist-talkers and the other Stromists peppered along the front lines keeping the rest of the magic users in check, George was able to sink deeper into the enemy lines.

More and more, the grass below was turning slick and sticky with blood. All around George, the battle waged and churned with violence. Shields were split and spears broken, swords were drawn and vicious mortal combat raged. The prince scanned his surroundings, parrying and countering any incoming attacks with ease. He wasn't concerned with the average warrior.

Finally, his eyes found Galmun Blue-Breath, the warlord standing tall with his giant retainers. He was dressed in his battle garb, a terrifying mix of tattoos and bones. He looked exactly as he did when he slaughtered Franklin. George kicked his heels into Ai and the horse bolted towards the target, but no sooner than when the prince began, did Williams break into view.

The knight was also darting towards the Chieftain with a spear couched under his arm and his horse galloping. One member of the Chieftain's retinue went to intercept Williams, catching the knight's spear on his massive shield. Williams' weapon exploded into splinters, but the knight wasn't disheartened. He drew his sword and leapt off his horse in one motion, his free hand catching the top lip of the giant's shield. Surprised, the enemy wasn't quick enough to stop the knight from thrusting his sword over the shield and deep into the giant's throat.

George watched as Williams rode the giant all the way to the ground, a geyser of blood shooting from the fallen foe's neck. Quickening his pace, George galloped to aid Williams, his heart suddenly stilling as Galmun began to chant. A cloud of mist started to form around the knight, but Williams was quick to roll away. The hammer of one of the other bodyguards came crashing down but again Williams just managed to roll out of the way.

Angry chanting erupted from the Chieftain and this time instead of a cloud, a dart of condensed mist rocketed out of his mouth and caught Williams off guard, the projectile slinging into his face. Williams snapped backwards from the strange blow and collapsed to the bloody ground. The knight's body began to tense up until Williams was completely paralyzed. Again, the giant's hammer came crashing down to squash its now stilled victim.

A horrible scream curdled from the giant bodyguard who held the hammer. A flood of blood poured from his shoulder and his arm twitched on the ground, hammer still tight in its grasp. Williams laid safe in the shadow of George, the prince glowing with magic and his blade dyed red with gore. The giant looked down at George with absolute terror, only to pale and fall on their back, blood now only drizzling out of the wound.

"Cursed one." Galmun growled behind the prince. Quickly, George positioned himself between the giant and his struggling friend. The two leaders locked eyes, one grey and split with vengeance, the other yellow and burning with hate. Around them a ring of battle contained the pair, laying the boundaries of their fight.

Raising Oathkith, George spoke, "Mist-talking, explain!"

Curling a devious smile, the giant bellowed. "A gift from your Graces, of course!"

"Impossible!"

"Oh?" the Chieftain cackled, "it would appear the Graces of your people no longer favor the Empire, but require something much more grand."

"You work for the sages?" George snarled.

"No, lost prince." The Chieftain raised a sword as big as a man. "They work *with* me." Summoning an air-splitting sound, the sword came crashing down.

George dodged out of the way and closed the gap, only for the chieftain to back up and shoot a cloud of dense mist in between them. George stopped just in time. This mist looked thicker than the others.

"Why would they do that?" George grit his teeth, staring at his enemy through the shroud. "What do they have to gain?"

"The sages or the Graces?" Galmun teased, letting loose soft chants in between his words. "If you can't see the goal, then you are more lost than I could have imagined."

"Tell me!"

"I'll grant you one mercy, cursed one." Mist hissed from Galmun as he spoke, the thick vapors threading between his teeth. "Something for you to ponder while you die: where do the Graces dwell?"

George's guard briefly lowered. It was true.

Galmun's fingers tightened around his massive blade. All at once, the chieftain blasted from his spot, a torrent of mist spiraling around him as he darted for the prince. George's eyes widened and a burst from his left foot kicked himself out of the way of the ensnaring charge just in time. He couldn't aim the leap well and was sent into a roll, only just managing to bounce back to his feet in time to meet Galmun's gaze once again.

A roaring cheer erupted among the enemy and George glanced behind him. Atop the plateau, dark figures were forming—enemy marksmen. George refocused on the Chieftain, the two fighters circling each other once again.

"It would appear you have lost," Galmun gloated, "It was foolish of you to bring your entire army to such a place."

"Entire?" George hissed, and an uncomfortable look etched on the Chieftain's face.

Behind George, a massive explosion of ice ripped across the top of the plateau, followed by bolts of fire and cracks of lightning. The giant froze. Paleksins and Kafshe were spilling out of the very rock walls under and on the plateau.

Galmun twitched. Roaring ferociously, the massive warrior spewed an ocean of mist, blocking George's view of the warlord completely. George slammed his feet into the ground and leapt over the cloud. With both hands he aimed Oathkith and came plummeting down. The Chieftain sidestepped, getting out of the way just in time. George landed with an explosive crack that punched a crater into the ground. The ribbons of magic that swirled around the prince bled red.

"I will gut you." The Chieftain gnashed his teeth and barreled towards the prince. His blade swung and George's raw strength caught it on Rook's face. The prince's eyes were full of fury and his gut full of hate as the two stared each other down past the lock. The monster inside of him wanted out, but George knew it would be too early for that. Yet even so he knew he needed to let some of his power bleed through. Feeling a pulse rush into his arms, George's muscles swelled and he managed to push the giant backwards from the clash.

Surprised, the Chieftain began to chant. George readjusted his fingers on Oathkith, rolling the hilt and itching for the final blow. The prince knew the Chieftain's mist was too thick for his Stromism to counter. George's eyes snapped wide as an idea passed through his mind.

With a final word, a burst of mist fogged the area, spilling from Galmun and engulfing George entirely. The blue was so dense, George wasn't visible from the outside. A wicked smile formed on the Chieftain's face. Heartbeats counted the moment, with Galmun raising his towering weapon over the trap, eager to split George in two. Another heartbeat and Galmun's smile faded. Smoke was swirling around the sea of mist and a red glow coming from within was turning the mist purple. An ear shattering sound clapped across the battlefield and a crimson blur burst free.

Galmun barely had time to defend. Oathkith bit right into his blade, shrieking as it ripped into the metal. George himself was stained red in Smokeform, face twisted in hate and yet the monster chained or more accurately, balanced with mist. Gritting his teeth, the Chieftain pushed away. George landed, Oathkith swinging into an offensive stance. Shimmering golden magic began to form on the Chieftain's arms and legs, anger seething.

Magic screamed as the Chieftain unleashed Stromism through his legs. The ground caved in as he kicked off towards the prince and despite his mountainous size, the Chieftain was a haze as he moved. George snarled and shot off as a blur of his own.

A thunderous bang sent a shockwave across the arena. The Chieftain's blade collided with Rook, only the byproducts of George's magic keeping it intact. Past the 'Franklin' carved in the back lip of the shield, George caught the gaze of his enemy. The fighters landed and already George was leaping back through the air.

Ready for the strike, the Chieftain arched his blade, catching George. The blow pounded against Rook, which was pushed back and slapped against George's chest, sending the prince flying. Shooting through the air, the prince slammed into the battle that raged, knocking over a group of warriors. The landing skipped George a few times, leaving a trail of indents before he managed to find his feet. Not losing a second, the red ribbons of George's magic roared to life and the prince was charging back into his fight.

Guard up, Galmun held at the ready, but as George came into range, the prince stopped, ducked the Chieftain's sword, slammed Rook upwards to push away Galmun's guard, and punched forward with Oathkith. The Chieftain just barely managed to juke the point of the blade but was unable to avoid the tearing edge, leaving a deep bleeding cut on his side.

Galmun groaned furiously and used his free hand to grapple George's shield. George dropped Oathkith into the ground and used his now liberated hand to grab the Chieftain's. The giant's eyes widened when an explosive strength traveled along the grapple, George yanking the Chieftain down towards him. As the Galmun fell forward, George bucked out with his helmeted head, crashing it into the Chieftain's.

A burst of blood popped from the giant's nose and he spasmed to the ground with a bang. George grabbed his blade and swung, but the Chieftain rolled out of the way and back to his feet. Snatching his own sword, the Chieftain threw out an arching slash. George caught it on his shield and stabbed out with Oathkith, but the Chieftain quickly parried with the flat of his blade and punched out with his pommel. Dodging, George got to the side of the Giant, only to be countered with a swift punch.

George ducked below it, rising with another swing of Oathkith. The two were a flurry of blows and strikes, their battle creating a storm of thunder that started to drown out even the war surrounding them. Many eyes were watching them as they fought, until finally the Chieftain parried one of George's swings and riposted with a high arch of his own.

The prince was prepared for it, though, and bounced the enemy blade off Oathkith as if it were a knife, then struck out with the edge of his sword. Oathkith swung wide with a stream of blood, the blade sinking through the Chieftain's knee and severing it. George was lightning and renewed the swing at the other leg, again cutting the Chieftain's leg clean off. Red exploded and Galmun began to topple to the ground, eyes wide with death and fear. As he passed by George's battle-furied stare, Rook came shooting forward, the metal edge cleaving into the enemy's skull and rocking Galmun to the ground with a loud bang.

The dust slowly cleared from the impact, leaving George standing tall above the crumpled mess that was his enemy. "For Franklin," George hissed. Almost immediately, the red on George's skin began to fade and his chest heaved with exhaustion. A gauntleted hand gripped his shoulder and he spun to meet it, blade ready.

George paused, Williams stood grinning at him, and behind him was Caleb. Blinking, George looked past them to see the faces of the 11th. Just realizing, George noticed that the sounds of battle were almost gone. The prince opened his mouth to speak but nothing came out.

All around laid the bodies of Imperial and Ulmi alike. The valley was carved by war and magic, with the area around George a maze of craters. Magical fire still burned some of the grass in the distance, a fog of frost hung over the plateau, and even some clouds of mist still lingered. A few regulars were being carted away, blue crystalline lesions scabbed on their skin from intense exposure to the mist. There were more Imperials standing than the enemy, though, with most of the enemy dead, captured, or retreating. Several noticeable Vagrant Lords laid in pools of blood, and any captured ones bared downcast eyes.

Caleb turned from his nephew to look at the scene. Clearing his throat, he declared, "Jerrovia has won!"

A thundering roar filled the valley, the force vibrating off of George's chest. A heat sunk behind his eyes as if a dam was finally being relieved of its burden. The war was over. It was truly over.

"So, you used the enemy mist to stabilize the smokeform?" Caleb pinched his chin. "I have to say, I don't know when you got so clever."

George grinned weakly, his body feeling the effects of his fight. He sat slumped in the back of a carriage, almost at the gates of Korku. He was bruised and tired, but alive. His breastplate had cracked during his fight with the Chieftain, leaving a welting purple on his chest and his helmet was never to be used again. Oathkith and Rook, however, seemed better off than even George himself. His uncle explained that the side effects of some magic can echo in the user's personal equipment, something George was pretty sure he already knew.

"I guess I had a good teacher." George smiled.

"A good many, that is," Caleb agreed. "It took a literal army to train you, but I can't argue with the results." The Imperial Regent sat back proudly. The carriage lurched to a stop and the sound of cheering could be heard outside.

"I think we are here." Caleb sucked in a breath before putting on a fresh smile. "Let's go greet a peace filled Empire, no?"

"Before we go." George reached out a hand to keep his uncle from opening the carriage door. "I think I learned more about the hidden enemy, and I'd like to discuss it with you."

A serious look found Caleb's face and he nodded. "After this, absolutely. One of the Lords we captured has a few words to say on it as well... but first, we have to make our appearance. *This* war is at least over, let's go punctuate that."

George nodded and let go of the door. Opening it, Caleb exited into the stream of daylight that leaked in. Steeling himself and finding his resolve to stand up, George followed after him. A rush of light blinded the prince at first, his ears perking to the chanting of his name and loud blessings for a peaceful empire. When his senses finally returned, George was walking the path to the castle, crowds on either side of him.

He couldn't help but smile back at all the relieved faces and beaming grins. The people of Korku were ecstatic, even throwing bits of flowers into the air, creating a slow colorful rain. Some were calling out to Caleb and blessing his name, others were crying for 'Georgie Boy' and even a few were calling for George 'Iron Will' Heinrich, but mostly people were cheering for the end of the war, to which George cheered back.

The road through his victory ended at the gates of castle Kalvin, where Opane stood next to Williams, the two talking. As George approached, they both stopped to smile at their friend.

"George!" Rosaline's voice shot through the air as the medic came pushing past Williams. She herself was bruised from the battle, and hailed the savior of one of the medical stations near the valley that was ambushed during the fight.

"Rosaline!" George eagerly wrapped his arms around her, squeezing her tight.

"What about me?" Baldra's voice came in from the side and George laughed. A final hand came in from his peripheral and gave George a proud shake. Looking over at Darius, the Commander was grinning wider than he ever had while sober.

"The enemy leaders are already surrendering," The Commander announced.

George nodded, seriousness finding him. "What happens to them next?"

"That's the capital's decision," Darius informed, "But I feel that the capital has a few bright heads for once." He winked.

"Speaking of," Caleb cut in. "We leave for the capital tomorrow."

"Already?" George was more shocked than he should have been, already expecting this. Perhaps it was just because he hadn't seen home in so many years that it started to feel like it didn't exist, or perhaps it's because he found a new home up here.

Caleb shot a chuckle through his nose. "Well, we can't stay in Korku forever."

"I'll visit." Rosaline put a hand on George's arm. "As soon as I can."

George smiled at her before looking over at Williams. The Knight was grinning.

Williams chanted, "the only way out was through."

"The only way out was through," George repeated.

***

As the celebrations bled into the night, George was whisked away from the festivities along with his uncle. The two were brought to the depths of Castle Kalvin, reaching places George had never seen before. They had walked the damp stonework deep underground, the only sounds being the flicker of candles and the drumming of some loose drops of water dripping onto the floor from some unseen source. It was cold down here, even in the summer. George was uncomfortable.

The winding hallways were winged by rows and rows of empty cells, each with an Imperial guard standing watch. George was reminded of the power of his uncle, who had commandeered the dungeon and already it was filled with his personal guard. Caleb mentioned that it was for the safety of their prisoner. Finding the final cell, George met the man Caleb was talking about.

Sitting on a lonely stool above a threshed floor was one of the Ulmi lords. He had a bandage around his head and his left arm was cast in a sling. Once fine cotton garments, dyed burgundy and blue, were now tattered, and any sense of decorative jewelry the lord usually wore was missing, with only reddened imprints left on his pale skin to betray that they ever existed. He had a bowl of fresh water, and a bowl full of dried fruits, perhaps as a sign of hospitality for the prisoner. Questions were being paddled back and forth between the lord and the imperials with each drawing George deeper into his own curiosity.

"And how did the war begin?" Caleb asked.

"It was indeed a land dispute," the lord said. "I was there during the first conclave that suggested action, I knew the lord who brought it up even."

"Who was he?" George followed up.

The lord shook his head. "It's not worth cursing his name now, he's long dead. He died in the first battle of Kors."

"So why bring him up?" Another question from George.

Tilting his head, the lord looked straight at the prince. "Because your assumption was right. He did have a dream, one he used to tell me about. I would shush him every time, but he would go on and on about it. He dreamed of a voice, a woman's voice. She would tell him, no, goad him to take action. It helped light his already growing hate for the Gavarians, and with the land dispute as his proof for war, and his dreams to keep him angry, he convinced so many more that it was about time we took our due. Then came the Titanspoke."

A thoughtful silence fell on the room, the lord seemed to be choosing his next words carefully. "The Titanspoke, Galmun, was the one who struck the alliance with us and the giants, but the leader of the giant conclave he represented died in the first battle of Kors along with the Ulmi Lord... his vision was done. I swore the united army was going to collapse on itself, but then... Your priests came to Galmun, the lieutenant of the giant conclave, and helped him wrestle power among the leadership. They were the ones who fabricated a story about how he was a Titanspoke in the first place, it was hardly a secret among some of us Lords, but he inspired us through both words and violence to continue the fight. He convinced most of us that there was something to be won here and that it was the will of the Titan. I guess I even started to believe him at one point, but..."

A forlorn and guilty smile spread over the lord's face. "There wasn't, there never was. Nothing for us to win, at least. Nothing for us."

"Then for who." Caleb looked at George.

"And to what end," George said back.

"I said all I know," the lord let his eyes fall to his lap. "May my dead kin forgive me."

"This may just help us end any further fighting," Caleb assured, "they will forgive you openly. Come, George."

The two imperials stepped out of the cell and back into the candlelight of the hallway. With shadows flickering over their faces, they hunched in the corner to speak softly.

"Think quietly on his words, George, but remember he is telling us what he thinks we want to hear." Caleb rubbed his chin. "Though it sits uneasy in my gut."

"The sages continued the war after the Dweller's attempt failed," George said, his own gut swirling with anxiety.

"To also reap the reward of a weakened empire?" Caleb furrowed his brow.

"Probably," George agreed. "For when they escape the void?" George looked at his uncle, the older man looking off put by the sudden question.

"How in the world can anything do that?" Caleb huffed sarcastically, but his eyes betrayed his own curiosity..

"I don't know."

Caleb squinted. "If the Dweller's goal was to leave the void, it makes sense that the Graces would pick up where she left off if they too want to leave the void... but that means the Dweller had a plan beyond the war, because a war alone won't free either of them. It was a vehicle to make it easier." As the Imperial Regent explained, his face grew dimmer and dimmer, thoughts flashing behind his eyes.

"And my death?" George finally asked.

"You being alive must stand in the way of their release, somehow," Caleb surmised. His thoughtful look collapsed. "It's the same reason why they attacked the empire: it too is in the way." Caleb gritted his teeth and swore. "If both the Dweller and the Graces are threatened by a united mortal front, then I can only surmise what apocalyptic plans they must have in store." His eyes turned deadly serious. "We need to get back to the capital. I don't like being in the dark like this. We'll leave tonight, and once there and rested, I'll begin gathering all the information I can. You should focus on acting like everything is normal, and remain safe. We can't pounce before we are ready. We foiled this part of their plans, we have time while they pick up the pieces."

The prince was staring in shock as his uncle spouted the plan, unsure on what to make of it all. He already came to peace with the idea that some strangers wanted to kill him, but the idea of having to live in that reality in his very own childhood home and then pretend it wasn't happening was unsettling to him. Uncle Caleb seemed to push past the hesitancy with his own urgency, grabbing George by the shoulders.

"Understood?"

"I understand," George finally agreed.

"Then I'll meet with you in a few hours by the carriages, pack quickly."

With little else, George's uncle swiveled on his foot and marched down the hallway, leaving nothing but the echoing calls of his footfalls and a hurricane of questions for George. The prince stood there stunned, the war was over, but something else was just beginning.

Chapter 27
Back at the Old Elm Tree

George sat under the old elm tree that dominated the Imperial Gardens. His stomach was fuzzy with anxiety and his fingers hadn't stopped shaking since he returned home last night. Being far away from the action he had grown used to was weird for him, and the stagnant silence of the palace put him at odds. Already he had gotten the ire of the newest palace staff the night before when he refused to put Ai in the stables, instead allowing the horse free roam in not just the courtyards, but the interior itself. After all that he and Ai went through, no piece of George could put his friend in a closed space ever again.

Behind the prince, a barber was cutting his long, overgrown hair and trimming his beard to match. Watching the black strands fall to the ground, George knew the war was really over. So much had changed in the four years he was gone, and he wasn't sure he liked it, or maybe he did. George didn't know. He curled his fingers into a fist. He knew he was glad that it was over, but he was also sad.

"George," Hector called out. A soft smile formed on George's lips at the sound. The latest elected Imperial Marshal of Stromism walked into George's view, dressed in ornamental armor.

"Hector." George grinned.

"Me and Williams were talking." Hector smiled back, turning slightly melancholy as he continued, "Well, we were going to visit Franklin's grave tomorrow since you two couldn't make it for the funeral, and I was wondering if you wanted to join us."

"I would like that." George nodded, only to have his head rectified by the barber's stern fingers. George rolled his eyes, "I'll come see you in the morning."

"Don't be a stranger before then," Hector chuckled, "I need my friends now that you two are home, it's been lonely."

"Surely you had Josephine to bother you?"

"She scares me," Hector admitted, "I can't tell when she is serious or joking."

"Only Williams can," George laughed, "but sure, I'll come see you after this, even."

"Great!" Hector nodded. "Then I'll leave you to it."

The man wandered off, leaving George alone with the sounds of scissors and birds. A gentle wind wafted through the flowers, providing some peace, with the smell reminding him of Rosaline. Closing his eyes, he tried to picture his time under the white pine back at Korku, only to be broken from his memory by a gentle tap to his shoulder.

"Finished."

A silver mirror was placed in George' hands and he had a good look at himself. He sat in a chair, dressed in a black doublet and trousers, Franklin's cape still draped around his shoulders and a trimmed beard was on his chin. Above his beard he could see the deformed scar on his cheek, gifted to him by his Ulmi captors, as well as a fresh notch on the corner of his mouth from the final battle. His hair was cut short again, tamed by a princely crown of gold. His grey eyes that once sparked with youth were ever bright, but now held a deep sorrow in them.

George stared for so long that the barber up and left after cleaning his shoulders, leaving the man alone with his thoughts and an image he barely recognized. Beyond that, George couldn't help but remember that none of it was truly over. The war was finished, but what of the sages, the mist-talkers, or even Fenric. Furrowing his brow, George fell into a deep thought, replaying his time in the war over and over, trying to find any answers he might have missed. What exactly about his existence worried the Graces and the Dweller enough to try and kill him? Is this why they called him the cursed one? Cursed how? Well, he supposed he was looking for ways to keep them from leaving the void, or at least he will be once he figures out how they intend to do it.

It was only when a warm plate was placed on his lap did George pull away from the mirror and his thoughts. A perfect white plate sat on his pants with four jelly filled breakfast pastries steaming atop it. Looking up, George saw the smiling face of his father. Behind the nest of wild golden hair, George met his father's blue eyes. The prince sat in bewilderment at the sight of his father, the hurried thoughts and worries in his head ceasing long enough to appreciate the gentle grin his dad was wearing, and the happy glint in his old eyes.

"Happy birthdays, son." A voice the prince had missed.

George smiled. He knew he wouldn't be alone in this.

"Thanks, Dad."

Epilogue
The Emergence, Book Two!

"Check." Reginald said with such modesty that made it seem like putting George into check was as simple of a task as sweeping a room. George gritted his teeth, pouring his eyes over the chessboard. The two sat in a lounge of the palace, the door wide open on George's request. Outside the door, Ai could be seen wandering the halls, but at this point the palace staff knew better than to question it.

"It took you four years to give me the game you promised." Reginald's face was stern but his words had comedy in them. "The least you can do is survive more than five turns."

George's piece clacked against the chestnut wood, saving his king. A proud smile formed on the prince's face. Josephine snickered from her seat off to the side and George scowled.

"What?"

"Hold on," the princess said from behind the lip of a tea cup. Taking her time, she sipped at the drink before gingerly setting it down. Clearly frustrating her brother, she took her time swallowing and smacked her lips at the taste.

"Jose—"

She held up a finger and cleared her throat. "You fell into Reginald's trap."

"No I didn't!" George looked back at the board, only for Reginald to pluck George's king from its roost.

"Checkmate."

"You're too good at this game," George slapped his own face. Reginald shook his head.

"So I hear."

"Hello!" Caleb's head poked into the lounge. His eyes were swollen as if he had a sleepless night, likely one filled with books, and the clothes he was wearing were the same as yesterday's. The trio looked up at the Imperial Regent, but before they could answer, Caleb nudged his chin at George.

"Mind if I borrow the defeated?"

Reginald grinned. "By all means, your grace."

George slapped his pants and stood up. Caleb eagerly nodded him along until the two were walking down the hall away from the lounge. Caleb remained silent, tapping his lips as the two walked. George knew better than to question it just yet, he could see the thoughts racing behind Caleb's eyes. He must have discovered something huge.

Only when they turned off the main hallways into an older part of the palace, did Caleb speak. Keeping his voice too low to echo, Caleb began, "I have a lot I want—that I need to tell you."

Furrowing his brow, George waved a hand. "Go on."

"Listen close, George and don't repeat this to anyone, except for Josephine."

George only had time to tilt his head in confusion before the Imperial Regent began. "I had been reading."

"I can see that."

Caleb shot a laugh out of his nose. "No, I had been *reading*. It started with the old books Opane gifted me, and they led me deep into the forbidden books scattered across the Empire, until I stumbled across a mention of an old study in Alconia. Naturally, I went there."

"I thought you were going there to cement the peace after their civil war," George arched a brow.

"Both," Caleb was quick to answer. "But George, listen."

The two stopped walking. They had made it to a quiet part of the palace populated only by old relics and spider webs. Caleb turned to face his nephew directly.

"A lot is about to happen, I can feel it, so much is going on under the rug. The war in the north was only a symptom of what's truly going on, and something much bigger will take place."

"What do you mean?" George questioned.

"I don't know... yet," Caleb admitted, "and while we already knew the sages were up to something..." He pulled a folded piece of paper out of his pocket, and George immediately recognized the rain-stained paper.

"The letter Williams recovered?"

The regent snapped a finger against the malformed missive. "Decoded, and now we have concrete evidence that they were indeed connected with the war and *did* in fact aid the giant's mist-talking. They are without a doubt guilty of treason and conspiracy in not only working in conjunction with the enemy to assassinate you, but to also destabilize the empire."

"If we have evidence, can't we convict them?"

Caleb shook his head. "We could only convict the ones whose names are connected to the letter, but I fear this runs deeper than a few outlaw sages. Convicting them now would only tip them off that we are on their trail." The Imperial Regent paused and shook his head again. "No, we bide our time, get them all at once."

"*All?*" George repeated in surprise.

"All." Caleb sucked in a breath. "This runs deep. This is also somehow connected with Osbert's death and Fenric's rise. The proctors sent to investigate have gone missing, which doesn't ease my mind... though I don't know if the sages were behind this one directly."

"The Dweller?"

"Nachtists," Caleb nodded, "they are on the rise in the Dwembin isles again and even in Caldora now. I believe Fenric may be linked with the Dweller."

"I knew it." George could feel his fingers curl. A hate sat in his chest for Fenric, and this would be all the more reason to strike out against his rival. The thought made George pause, it was a violent thought and he couldn't help but wonder if it was his own, or the growling creature of the smokeform. Caleb's voice pulled him out of his thoughts.

"I'm not sure yet, but either way, what notes the proctors made that weren't lost are enough to continue the investigation into his legitimacy, and if possible, his removal from nobility." Caleb cleared his throat. "But there is more."

"More?"

"I'm leaving, George."

"What!?"

"The Alconian study referenced a place far off to the east, an island adrift in the endless ocean. It is said that there and only there is the knowledge I'll need to piece this all together." The Imperial Regent bit his thumb in thought. "Josephine will be regent in my absence."

"You can't be serious?" George challenged, "there is no mention of anything to our east, anywhere, and you're going to sail there on the basis of a single book?"

"I don't have much choice," Caleb hissed," the world is changing around us, sages are betraying the Empire, and nobles are in concert with Nachtists. Something big is coming, George, and I need to know what. I need to know how the Dweller intends to open the void."

"So that's it then, you're leaving?"

"Only for so long." Caleb put a hand on George's shoulder. "Protect the realm in my absence."

Resigning, George sighed. "You know I will, uncle."

"Good." Caleb smiled before suddenly frowning. "But one last warning."

"Yes?"

"There is a noble from Barcena named Gennisberg. The sages have been using their political pull to offer him as a husband for Josephine on the basis of strengthening our resources following the northern war, and I hate to admit it, but it has too much traction for me to stop. I don't trust it, I don't trust the sages, and I certainly don't trust Gennisberg."

George gulped. "What should I do?"

"Do what you can to delay any official marriage if you can't outright end it until I return," Caleb ordered, "and if for whatever reason you fail, keep Josephine safe."

"You know I will." George stood up straight.

"I know." Caleb put a hand on George' shoulder before looking down at the floor. "Maybe my brother can help, he may still have something left in him."

"I'll try to talk to him." George somberly looked to the floor as well.

"Good luck, George."

"And to you, uncle."

A thought crossed George's eyes and he held out a hand. "Wait, one last thing."

Caleb flashed the man a look. "What?"

"You had said that when the war was over, you'd tell me everything you knew about the Dweller."

A thought wrinkled Caleb's brow, aging him immediately. After a pause, George's Uncle nodded. "While I'm gone, use my study, use my notes, read my books, and do your work up there. All of it is yours." The regent seemed to freeze before a look of sadness hinted in the corner of his eye. "All that I know is up there. If you have any questions about anything, I'll answer them, but when I return."

A slow nod came from George, a nod of both understanding and curiosity. "Deal."

To be Continued...